Kathleen E. Woodiwiss, Johanna Lindsey, Laurie McBain, Shirlee Busbee...these are just a few of the romance superstars that Avon Books has been proud to present in the past.

Since 1982, Avon has been continuing a different sort of romance tradition—a program that has been launching new writers of exceptional promise. Called "The Avon Romance," these books are distinguished by a ribbon motif on the front cover—in fact, you readers quickly discovered them and dubbed them "the ribbon books"!

Month after month, "The Avon Romance" has continued to deliver the best in historical romance, offering sensual, exciting stories by new writers (and some favorite repeats!) *without* the predictable characters and plots of formula romances.

"The Avon Romance." Our promise of superior, unforgettable historical romance...month after dazzling month!

Other Avon Books by
Virginia Brown

DEFY THE THUNDER

Avon Books are available at special quantity discounts for bulk purchases for sales promotions, premiums, fund raising or educational use. Special books, or book excerpts, can also be created to fit specific needs.

For details write or telephone the office of the Director of Special Markets, Avon Books, Dept. FP, 1790 Broadway, New York, New York 10019, 212-399-1357.

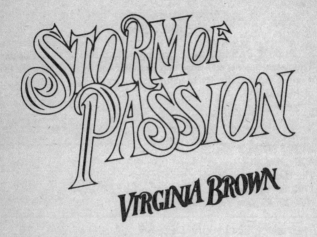

STORM OF PASSION

VIRGINIA BROWN

◆ AVON
PUBLISHERS OF BARD, CAMELOT, DISCUS AND FLARE BOOKS

AVON BOOKS
A division of
The Hearst Corporation
1790 Broadway
New York, New York 10019

First Avon Printing: September 1986

AVON TRADEMARK REG. U.S. PAT. OFF. AND IN OTHER COUNTRIES, MARCA REGISTRADA, HECHO EN U.S.A.

Printed in the U.S.A.

K-R 10 9 8 7 6 5 4 3 2 1

Dedicated to the memory of Nancy Lou McKinney

Prologue

"Are we going to drown, Papa?"

Startled, Patrick O'Connell jerked his head to stare down at the small figure who clung tightly to the hem of his drenched greatcoat to keep from falling to the heaving deck of the ship. Eyes as green as the grassy slopes of Ireland shone through thick, dark lashes as she gazed up at him.

"And what are you doing out here, Mary Kathleen O'Connell?" he asked sternly, reaching out to pull her small body close. "Don't you know that a wee bit of a girl like yourself could be swept overboard and never be missed?"

"You'd miss me." The emerald eyes stared at him confidently. "You'd miss me, Papa."

"Aye," he chuckled, "that I would! But you'd best go back below deck, Mary Kathleen. 'Tis a foul day, and I don't want to chance seeing you paddling in the ocean."

"Are you sure we're not going to drown, Papa?" Her eyes moved doubtfully to slate-gray walls of water that rose around the ship. They looked like the sea monsters in one of Grandfather's ancient books, and, for a moment, Mary Kathleen wondered if perhaps they had somehow reached the edge of the world and the *Wanderer* was going to pitch over the side and into eternity.

"Ah, Mary Kathleen, would I let you drown?" her father reproved with a smile, chucking her under the chin as he always had when she'd said something silly. Then he gently turned her in the direction of the narrow steps leading below deck.

Foamy sprays of water shot over the bow of the ship as it sliced through angrily rising waves. Frothy curls of salty sea wet the wooden decks and the passengers who huddled in anxious knots at the ship's rail. Salt crusted everything, from the lashed-down cargo and maze of rigging that stretched like giant spider webs above the deck, to the clothing and hair of those either foolish or brave enough to be outside in the elements instead of cowering in their cabins.

A woman detached herself from the rail, lurching toward them as Mary Kathleen and her father stumbled near. "Patrick," Kate O'Connell questioned her husband softly so that Mary Kathleen would not hear, but the crafty wind snatched her words and carried them to the straining ears of the listening child. "Are you sure the ship will not sink?"

"Nay, that I'm not, my love," he answered, then threw a quick smile at his slim, dark-haired wife. "Ah, Kate, we've got a good chance of weatherin' it." Yet his eyes were somber and strained with worry, and Patrick O'Connell bit back a curse. Why had he yielded to Kate's long and eloquent pleas to let his family accompany him on this voyage? They would have been much safer back in Ireland with his father in spite of the old lord's irascibility and flaming temper. Patrick had finally surrendered, letting them come with him against his better judgment, and now the storm that tossed the heavy merchant ship from white crest to white crest like a flimsy toy made him fear for their safety.

Even as he scooped up his daughter's sea- and rain-wet body to carry her below deck, Patrick wished he was certain about the prospect of surviving. The *Wanderer* was creaking alarmingly, sounding like a rusty winch as water washed over the sides in ever-increasing sheets, and the tiring crew seemed worried and grim as they scurried about the decks. The wind reminded Patrick of the desolate wail of a banshee echoing over lonely hills and loughs as it called to the dead and dying.

As he bundled Mary Kathleen into her narrow bunk, teasing her about being only a silly lass afraid of shadows and tiny waterspouts, a pervading sense of doom shivered through his body.

"I am *not* a silly lass," Mary Kathleen was insisting with a thrust-out lower lip, "and you wouldn't say that if I was a boy!"

Patrick jerked his attention back to his daughter, a distracted smile curling one end of his mouth.

"Nay, that I wouldn't. Then I'd be calling you a silly lad, my poppet."

"Grandfather says I should've been a lad instead of a lass, and then you would have stayed home more often." She had all his attention now and, folding small hands in a rebellious knot over blanket-covered legs, Mary Kathleen asked with simple and unnerving directness, "Is it true, Papa, that you wanted a boy? And since Mother cannot have any more children, you go wandering to find . . . solace?" Her tongue tripped over the unfamiliar and obviously overheard word, but the candor and trust shining from bright eyes identical to her grandfather's was unmistakable.

Damn the old lord and damn the clattering tongues of nursemaids who were more family than servants, Patrick thought wearily. "Aye, lass, I wanted a boy sure enough, but I got much more than I asked for, now didn't I? You've been both to me—you can ride your pony better than any of those clumsy-bottomed McLaughlin lads, and I've seen you outrace the blacksmith's boy several times. And if I want to hold a pretty little lass in frilly skirts on my lap, why—I can always do that too!"

"Yes, Papa, you can always do that too," she echoed, smiling now as she reached out to draw him close for a kiss.

The solid oak door crashed open with a loud bang like a pistol shot and Kate O'Connell lurched in, her fine-boned face pale and her lips tightly compressed with fear.

"Patrick! The ship . . . !" She stumbled to a halt, noting the quick jerk of her daughter's head and the smoky shadows swirling in her eyes.

"I'll go above deck, Kate, to find out if I can help," Patrick said with a slight, warning shake of his head. "You stay here with Mary Kathleen, and I'll be back for you shortly." Even as he spoke there was a loud splintering crack that sent all three occupants of the cabin to their knees on the wooden floor. The vessel listed sharply to one side before floundering aimlessly like a fish on the beach. Muttering a comment intended to be comforting, Patrick's forced smile barely masked his own strain as he left his wife and daughter in the tilting cabin to go above deck.

Kate perched on the edge of the bunk, trembling hands clenching and unclenching in the lap of her sodden skirt, fingers rising once or twice to push back annoying wisps of dark wet hair. Her face, which usually reminded Mary Kathleen of the serene portrait of the Madonna that hung on the chapel wall in Castleconnell, had tiny lines of worry etched in delicate lace on her brow, and small white teeth worried a bottom lip that was unaccountably quivering.

"Mother?" Mary Kathleen's voice was almost alien in the clamoring din of wind, rain, and shrieking wood. "Are we going to drown?"

Kate O'Connell turned to her daughter with a ready lie trembling upon half-parted lips but the words would not form. How could she tell this sometimes too-wise child a lie when their situation was so precarious?

"My love, we are in great danger, but we must trust in God to see us through—we must have faith." Kate forced a reasonable facsimile of a smile to her lips. "Shall we kneel beside the bed and offer a prayer for our safety?"

"Can God hear us over all the noise?" questioned Mary Kathleen, and Kate closed her eyes in irritated exasperation. Here was just another example of her father-in-law's blaspheming influence. Sean O'Connell would die a sinner's death, Kate had often prophesied to her husband in a tear-choked voice, and Patrick, caught in the cross fire between Kate and his father, had placated both as best he could.

Now Kate met the emerald gaze of her daughter and sighed resignedly as her right arm moved in the sign of the cross, her fingers finally coming to rest on the heavy locket that hung about her neck on a silver chain dulled by years of time and wear. It was an heirloom of the O'Connell family, passed from generation to generation, carved with the crest the first O'Connell had fashioned: a strange horned beast with wildly pawing hooves thrashing in the air in the center of four swords with jeweled hilts. A tiny emerald winked in the center of the beast's eye—Mary Kathleen had whimsically declared it to be a unicorn but Kate, shuddering, thought it more resembled one of the devil's creations—and rubies, diamonds, and sapphires adorned the hilts of the broadswords. A hideous piece of jewelry, Kate had often said, but it was precious to Patrick and so she wore it. Sean had always objected to the daughter of a bloody Englishman wearing O'Connell heirlooms, but Kate wore it in spite of him.

Now, as she cradled the locket in the palm of her hand, Kate's soft blue eyes strayed to her daughter's face. If anything should happen—God forbid—Mary Kathleen would need the jeweled piece to ensure her safe return back to Ireland. And if none of them survived, what did it matter who wore the locket?

Her hands shaking, she opened the clasp on the locket to gaze down at the tiny miniatures of herself and Patrick, painted on their wedding day. Had she always worn her love for her husband so obviously? It shone from every feature of her face. Ten years later, she still felt that all-consuming passion that left little room for anything else in her life . . . even her daughter. Ah, life was unkind at times. It had a way of giving with one hand and taking back more than it gave with the other, until sometimes the very thing that gave such happiness was the cause of heartache.

"Mary Kathleen." Did her voice sound strange, or was it just the loud keening of the wind around caulked wooden seams of the ship that seemed to make it so? "Mary Kathleen, I want you to wear this."

"The unicorn, Mother? Why?"

"It's not a unicorn, Mary Kathleen. There's no such thing. It's simply a locket—your family crest." Why did the child have to look at her with such awareness gleaming in those thick-lashed eyes? Did she sense, perhaps, the reason behind it? "I've always loved you, you know." Kate paused, feeling slightly ashamed and a little irritated, and Mary Kathleen remained silently listening. "It's just that your father . . ." Another long pause, then, in disjointed words and phrases like the random falling of raindrops, Kate blurted, "I've loved too well, child, when I should have loved more wisely perhaps. . . . Never hold on too tight or you may strangle that very thing you would give your life to hold in the palm of your hand. . . . Oh, how utterly foolish. . . . He resented me and I only made it worse . . . and then—I should have tried harder, I suppose, but I didn't."

A frown knit her childish brow, and Mary Kathleen reached out a tentative hand as if wanting to comfort her mother.

"Mother," she began, but the scream of wind and wood tore through the air with a terrifying sound. Leaping like a giant fish from the water, the ship rolled into a deep trough and floundered, shuddering, and Kate and Mary Kathleen were thrown from the bunk to the steeply listing cabin floor. Unstowed objects slid haphazardly past them, bumping and scraping, ploughing into the wall in a cluttered pile.

Mary Kathleen was too frightened to scream and Kate was too frantic with worry over Patrick. She scrambled on hands and knees toward the door, the locket dangling from her neck scratching against the wooden planks of the floor.

"Patrick!" she moaned as the door swung open in a kind of crazy motion, and then he was there, outlined against the dark corridor behind, dark auburn hair plastered to the contours of his skull.

"I'm here," he was saying, and just the resonant tone of his voice calmed Kate as she clung weeping to his legs. "We have to hurry, Kate."

Lifting Kate from her knees, Patrick soothed her with a broad hand patting her head as if she was a child. With his other arm he pulled his daughter close under the shelter of his arm and shoulder. The lanterns had blown out and the long corridor that ran the length of the passenger compartment was dark; the three felt their way along walls dark with rain and gushing seawater. The usual delicious smells of spice that had once permeated the wood of the merchant ship had been replaced by the peculiar stench of the sea, a sharp smell of fish and seaweed that was so thick it seemed as if they were already under water.

Then they were above, Patrick pulling them up the ladder and through the large square hole cut into the wooden planks of the deck and usually surrounded by a rail. It was gone, and so was the top of the mizzenmast. Instead of gracing the tip of the mast as it should have been, it was lying on the deck in a tangle of shrouded sails and whipping lines, and beneath its heavy weight lay the body of one of the crew.

Shielding his wife and daughter from the sight, Patrick edged toward the rail with them, fighting frantic passengers and crew to get close to the lifeboats swinging from davits over the angry sea. Two of the small boats had been lost in the storm and, knowing there would not be enough room, the determined sailors flashed steel in order to cut their way through to their only hope of survival. There were not many passengers aboard the *Wanderer,* which was mainly used as a merchant vessel, but several men, like Patrick, had brought their wives and children with them. The seasoned sailors mercilessly trampled all those who were in their path, slashing to the rail.

"Stay here," Patrick ordered grimly, pushing Kate and Mary Kathleen behind a lashed-down water barrel. "I'll be back."

Huddling like a half-drowned kitten, Mary Kathleen dared to peer around the oak staves of the barrel, eyes widening at the carnage. It was madness, something out of her worst nightmares, and Mary Kathleen squeezed her eyes tightly shut and put her hands over her ears. Miraculously, the wind had died, its fury spent, but the damage had been done to the lurching vessel that floated on the surface of the sea like a dying whale.

The gaping holes in the ship's side would send the *Wanderer* to the sandy bottom in only a matter of minutes, Patrick O'Connell realized as he fought his way desperately to the last remaining lifeboat. It swung temptingly just out of reach, and when he would have caught it with one hand he was yanked backward by a brawny fist.

" 'Ey, matey! Git outa th' way naow, afore ye die from eight inches o' steel instead o' drownin'.' "

"My wife and daughter . . ."

"Be damned, I say. Move!"

Flung backward by the meaty arm, Patrick lay stunned for a moment, then fury surged through him and he catapulted to his feet to grab the bos'n. Though tall and lean, Patrick was no match for a man seasoned by years of hard labor at sea. In seconds he was sprawled again on his back. He barely had time to roll out of the way as the infuriated crewman charged with drawn dagger, slicing through the hem of his wool greatcoat. They grappled like two wrestling bears at a fair, with Patrick holding tightly to the wrist of the hand that held the dagger. Finally Patrick was able to break the man's grip and the dagger dropped. He slammed a fist into the bos'n's stomach and his knee caught him full in the face, smashing his nose and laying him out on the deck.

"Hurry," Patrick panted, stumbling to Kate and Mary Kathleen, "before someone else takes a liking to the same boat."

Mary Kathleen stared at the swaying boat swung

out over the water. She was frightened, but her
father told her to be brave as he placed her in the
tiny boat so high in the air.

"Papa . . ."

Clinging to the sides with white-knuckled fingers,
Mary Kathleen tried to speak, but no words would
come from a throat suddenly dry and closed. She
saw the bos'n lurch to his feet with the dagger
clenched tightly in his fist, but she couldn't force
out a warning. Green eyes wide with horror, Mary
Kathleen watched as the glittering blade flashed up
and then down, saw the surprised expression on her
father's face and his slow turning, heard—like the
shivering wail of a banshee—Kate's scream echoing
in the wind.

Patrick fell forward with the ivory-boned handle
of a dagger protruding from his back and Kate—
gentle Kate who had never harmed a living soul—
plucked the dagger from her husband's back and
stabbed it into the bos'n's broad chest as he grabbed
for the end of the line holding the lifeboat above the
sea. Blood was everywhere, on Patrick, the dead
bos'n, and Kate.

"Patrick!" Her mother's voice, soft and pleading
as she knelt beside her husband, called him back to
the world around him and he opened his eyes to
stare up at her.

"Kate?" It was a breathy question, as if all his
life had already drained out of him with the scarlet
pool of blood he lay in. "Kate . . . see to Mary Kathleen. . . . You must go back to Ireland, back to
County Kerry. . . ."

"No." The dark head shook obstinately and she
clung to him with a fierce grip. "I will stay with
you, Patrick, and never leave you."

"But . . . Mary Kathleen . . ." He was slipping
away now, brown eyes glazing with the mist of
death. As Mary Kathleen slung one leg over the

side of the lifeboat, he raised his head slightly to
find her and cried, "No, child! Stay . . ."

"I'll keep her safe for you," Kate was saying then,
pushing to her feet to step to the rail. Her eyes were
bright with purpose as she held her daughter's gaze.
Pounding feet sounded on the deck behind her and
Kate whirled, a sense of panic filling her as she realized that if she did not release the boat at once,
others would take it from her. She had to save Mary
Kathleen and, dear God, let there be time to save
Patrick also. But then she knew that there would
be no time, that if she didn't act swiftly they would
all perish. Torn between the husband she adored
and her child, Kate O'Connell made the only decision she could.

She lifted the locket from around her neck. The
silver chain spilled from her palm to sway in the
air, crimson blood crusting the small links. "Take
it, Mary Kathleen, and use it to return to Ireland.
It's your heritage, it's County Kerry," Kate said
quickly, easing the chain over her daughter's head.
"I love you. Don't forget Kerry . . ." Blinding tears
scalded her eyes as Kate yanked the rough line
holding the boat, sending it plummeting down to
the swirling gray waves like a stone.

Whirling, the lifeboat bucked in mad, spinning
circles and Mary Kathleen huddled in the bottom
as it was tossed carelessly from wave to wave. Rain
began slashing down, pounding against her like tiny
missiles, stinging and cold. Rising up to peer over
the side, she watched the vague form of the *Wanderer* slip silently beneath tumultuous waves to dis-
appear into the dark, greedy depths of the sea.

High above, gulls screeched, sending echoes
drifting on the wind. Mary Kathleen slowly opened
salt-caked and swollen eyes. She was lying on the
sand, her clothes wet and heavy. For a moment

she couldn't think where she was or why, then the events of the past two days returned in a smothering rush. She had drifted with the whim of the sea, bobbing up and down in the ocean until she was almost crazy with thirst. Just when she thought she could not last another hour, she'd spotted this narrow strip of land jutting into a sunwashed sea.

A sob caught in her throat as she gazed around at the deserted stretch of beach. She'd never seen anything like this before. The brilliant blue of a cloudless sky and endlessly stretching powdery white sand was totally unfamiliar. Had the sky been so blue in Ireland?

Drawing in a deep breath, Mary Kathleen lurched to her feet and stumbled toward a fringe of trees not far ahead. Her long wet skirts tangled around her legs, tripping her, and she couldn't halt a sudden downward plunge onto the sand. Coughing and spitting, she pushed herself to skinned knees with the taste of sand in her already parched mouth.

Water. She had to find water. She was thirsty, so thirsty, and the sun was hot. It took all her remaining strength to force her trembling body up and toward the trees. One step . . . two . . . she was closer now. Invisible hands clutched at her bare feet and she fell. She must get up . . . must go on . . . now she was closer, the trees just ahead, promising relief from that burning sun. . . . Was it her imagination or did she hear the gentle slap of water over rocks? No, it would be too cruel if it was only the echo of the salty sea.

But it wasn't. A small pool was nestled like a jewel beneath swaying branches of unfamiliar trees, its sparkling, sun-dappled depths beckoning, and Mary Kathleen stumbled to the edge. She dropped to her knees on the hard shale, cupping her hands, lifting sweet cool water to flow in blessed rivulets over her face and into her mouth, streaming down her neck and chest. Finally easing her terrible thirst, Mary Kathleen pushed back and stretched out upon cushioning tufts of springy grass.

For long moments she sat silently in the sun-flecked shadows, the buzz of insects a pleasant serenade in her ears. It was peaceful and quiet, and she was still alive. Alive, when so many others had drowned. A pang of grief tore through Mary Kathleen then, and her eyes clouded with pain. They were dead, gone forever, and she would never see them again—never see her mother's beautiful features light up at the sight of her father and—most painful of all—she would never hear her father's booming laugh or be folded in his smothering hug again.

Her throat ached with unshed tears, yet she could not force them from dry eyes. This was a dream, another nightmare that she would wake from to find her father holding her in loving arms.

So Mary Kathleen sat there waiting to wake up, arms folded around bent legs and her small chin resting on her knees.

She didn't know how long she'd heard it before it became real, but finally a cheerful whistle penetrated her foggy mind. She turned slightly, squinting toward the sun-washed beach.

A small figure trudged toward her through burning sand, a fishing pole slung over one shoulder, feet sinking deep into glistening white sand with each step. Only when he came closer to where she sat could Mary Kathleen see that it was not another child but a small, wizened old man.

Heart pounding, she sat still and quiet, frightened but too cautious to move. Vague thoughts spun in her fevered mind as she remained frozen and watching. He would go away soon. But . . . if he did, what would happen? Was this a dream?—or was it real? And if it was real, would she be left here alone if the old man passed her by?

Her stomach rumbled, reminding her she hadn't eaten in a long time, and Mary Kathleen bit her parched bottom lip. What should she do? A soft wind blew, caressing her cheek and lifting salt-caked hair to tickle her nose, and she sneezed. It was a small sound, but loud enough to catch the old man's attention.

He stopped, peering into the shadows surrounding the pool, and he was almost in a direct line with her. Did he see her? Her vision wavered curiously, and the stooped figure seemed to shimmer in the heat. She blinked, once, twice, then rubbed her fists in her eyes.

"Quien anda allí?" the old man asked, and when there was no answer he stepped forward cautiously. Gnarled hands parted the branches of thick-leaved bushes, and Mary Kathleen instinctively caught her breath as he spotted her. The old man hesitated, his sharp eyes noting her water-stained and salt-encrusted clothing, her huge, terrified eyes and quivering mouth. *"Ah, pequeña—que es su nombré?"* he asked, and when she only stared at him without a flicker of recognition, he repeated first in French then in English, "What is your name, child?"

Still she was quiet.

"Can you not speak to me?" he asked, then said, "I will be happy to wait until you can. May I?" He gestured with a wave of his hands to a neighboring cushion of grass, folded his wiry legs, and sat down. Sticking a blade of thick grass between surprisingly white teeth, the old man lay back and crossed his hands behind his head, staring up at the brilliant sky visible through lacy branches.

"Ah," he said after a few moments of silence,

"Look up at the sky, niña! Do you see an animal in the clouds?—a horse, maybe? Or a bird?"

In spite of herself, Mary Kathleen slid a wary glance up at the fluff of puffy clouds drifting lazily across the wide expanse of blue, blue sky. The old man kept talking, as if to himself, his deep voice with its odd, melodic lilt somehow soothing, lulling her fears.

"Do you see the cat there?" he asked, pointing with a blue-veined hand to a drift of cloud.

Tilting her head, Mary Kathleen smiled as she recognized the familiar shape and, suddenly willing to play this distracting new game, she nodded.

"Bueno! That is my name. Gato, or cat," he explained when she turned a quizzical gaze to him. "And yours? Do you have the name of an animal too?"

Shaking her head, Mary Kathleen bent forward, bright strands of thick hair curtaining her face as she stared blankly at her hands twisting in the tattered lap of her dress.

The game wasn't so much fun anymore. She tried to concentrate on her fingers lacing and unlacing, anything to keep from remembering. Her name echoed again and again in her head, Patrick's dying voice haunting her. Why hadn't she been able to warn him about the man with the knife? But she had not been able to speak. . . .

Gato waited patiently, his fishing pole forgotten as he watched the girl. He'd heard of the wreck of the ship two days before, and it had been said that there were no survivors. Pieces of the lifeboats had been washed ashore, as had a few bodies. This small girl had somehow survived when the others had not. She was sunburned and obviously ill, but alive.

"I am hungry," he said at last, bending forward to wrap his arms around his knees. "Would you like to go home with me? I must know your name if you do, because I prefer eating with friends instead of strangers."

She met the old man's gaze blankly, her eyes as green as the sun-swept sea where the sandy floor fell abruptly away, fathomless and swirling with shadows. For a moment he feared he had lost her entirely. Long moments passed, and the sound of the crashing surf and cries of sea gulls were all that broke the silence before she spoke. Her voice was a whisper, dragged from deep inside the small, intense figure seated on a flat rock, and Gato had the uneasy impression he was intruding on a soul in torment.

"I wasn't brave. . . . I didn't warn him and now he's dead. . . . I can never go back, and I still hear him calling my name. . . ." She paused, the gentle Irish lilt vibrating with intensity and emotion, then Kate's last words of admonition rang in her ears like the solemn tolling of a church bell on Sunday morning. The child echoed her mother's last words without realizing she'd even spoken, and the old man thought she was saying her name. "Kerry! Kerry . . ." Her voice faded into a hoarse whisper that still seemed to quiver in the air long after the echoes had died away.

Her last word was an anguished cry and Gato reached out to draw the trembling child close, smoothing her still damp curls with a gentle hand.

"You are safe now, niña. You are safe, Kerry . . ."

Kerry? No, that wasn't her name, and Mary Kathleen opened her mouth to tell him so but the words wouldn't come. Wait . . . if she was Kerry instead of Mary Kathleen, no one would know she'd let her parents die. Mary Kathleen would have died too, and there would be only this stranger named Kerry. Yes, she would be Kerry, and Grandfather would never know she was to blame for her father's death.

Some of the shadows in her eyes faded as the child lifted her heart-shaped face to stare into the old man's steady gaze. "Yes," she repeated, "I am safe now."

Chapter 1

Blazing fires crackled and popped, brilliantly lighting the small area inside the circle of huts and creating eerie shadows beyond. Wavering patterns flickered like dark, frenzied ghosts over quietly waiting figures who sat with their legs folded beneath them, and the heavy thump of drums was echoed by the chant of male voices.

Long hair, dark as jet, whipped back and forth as young women danced into the lighted circle with sinuous writhing bodies. Thin skirts were wound around slender hips and legs, the bright floral material ending just above their knees. An abundance of native flowers crowned their heads and were cleverly woven into the waist of their skirts, blossoms which were teasingly flung at the eagerly watching young men. Bare breasts proudly thrust out, the women swayed with the movements of the dance, their coppery skin gleaming with the coconut oil that was used to enhance their natural beauty.

The drums increased tempo and wind instruments carved from slender reeds added a piercing melody as the girls danced with all the graceful movements of tree branches swaying in the soft sea breezes. It was late. The golden moon slid across the velvet sky, scattering light across the tree-studded mountain slope where the village was serenely nestled.

Still glistening with coconut oil and a pearly mist of perspiration, one of the dancers broke away from the rest, mounted a black stallion, and rode away from the celebrations. She had replaced the floral-patterned skirt with white trousers and covered her bare breasts with a loose cotton shirt with sleeves rolled up to the elbows.

Her long strands of hair gleamed red-gold instead of jet, and her smooth skin was not copper but a muted golden shade, like old Spanish doubloons. She was whistling a bawdy sea ditty first heard on the teeming docks of the bay, the melody somehow blending with the sweeter songs of the birds.

She reached down to pat the animal's sweaty neck then murmured fondly, "It's late, Diablo. We've stayed out too long." She hadn't meant to stay in the mountain village so long, but Kaliza had insisted in her frail old-woman's voice, her paper-thin hand clutching at the girl's arm as she turned to leave.

"I'll be back," she had protested at first, but Kaliza had shaken her graying head.

"You won't see me again," she'd said in her wispy voice.

Intrigued, Kerry had stayed, knowing Kaliza had what some people called the sight. The old woman's ancestors had been the Spaniards who had settled this island before the French had come, and Kerry suspected the blood of gypsies ran in Kaliza's veins. Now the English ruled St. Denis, and the natives like Kaliza had retreated even further into the thick-forested mountains.

Kerry was fascinated by the old woman's ability to stare into the flickering flames of a fire and see events far in the future. The hair on the back of her neck would prickle as she listened to Kaliza's rambling prophecies.

Peering at Kerry with her one good eye, Kaliza had motioned her closer on the straw mat before the fire. Rocking back and forth, the old woman had begun to speak in a faraway voice that gradually grew stronger. The gypsy rambled a bit, speaking in fragments of languages Kerry didn't understand, then suddenly gripped Kerry's arm with clawlike fingers and hissed, "The necklace! The necklace . . ."

Kerry jumped, startled. "Necklace?" She frowned as she touched the heavy, carved locket given to her by her mother, years before. "What . . . ?"

"It's the key to your past," Kaliza went on as if Kerry hadn't spoken. "The key to your past and your future! You will leave here soon. . . . I see a great ship with the white wings of a seabird, and it's flying so fast the hawk cannot catch it . . . and a black horse with one horn paws the sea. . . . You fight against what you really want to have . . . but you have questions, and will not know inner peace or great happiness until you pursue the answers, until your quest takes the necklace full circle. . . ."

The ancient necklace still held painted miniatures of her parents, somewhat faded with time but recognizable. It was her only link to her home, to Ireland, a shrouded land of faded memories. A land she had abandoned long before.

Not wanting to listen or remember, she'd leaped to her feet, stammered her goodbyes, then run to lose herself in the dances around the fire, surrendering her mind to the rhythmic beat of drums and wind instruments carved from wood and bamboo. For a little while, she managed to forget Kaliza's prophecies. There was something primitive yet stirring about dressing in native garb and moving to melodies which echoed times long past. It was a release, a shedding of all she wanted to forget.

But the present had finally intruded, and when the moon dipped low over the mountain peaks, spearing itself on the jagged teeth of Cielo Pico, Kerry had retrieved Diablo and begun the ride home.

Frowning, Kerry nudged the stallion forward with a bare heel. She didn't want to think about her past, didn't want to remember things too painful to dwell upon. Yet still the memory teased her, the memory of her mother's last words to her. She slowed Diablo down as they neared Gato's small thatched cottage tucked into a clearing on the fringe of the forested slope. Kate's admonition seemed so long ago; another world, another time. She hadn't forgotten County Kerry—it was a part of her, remembered whenever someone called her name. Was Kaliza telling her she was destined to go back there?

Gato tended to view Kaliza's prophecy more skeptically the next morning. "Bah, she's getting old," he commented with a grunt, settling his bent frame into the comfort of a plump-cushioned cane chair. "Kaliza should stick to simple incantations instead of filling your head with such things," he muttered as he lifted his feet to a stool in front of the low fire. "What will happen, will happen. Of course your mother's necklace holds the key to your past, niña, but you hold the key to your future." He smiled at her then, saying, "You should worry more about finding a suitable young man to marry."

Kerry bolted upright from her supine position on the woven straw rug in front of the hearth, eyes flashing indignantly. This was a familiar argument and she entered the fray with relish.

"You know I wouldn't give a snap of my fingers for any of the men on St. Denis, Gato," and her thumb and middle fingers popped loudly to punctuate her words. "Besides that, they feel the same about me."

"If that is true, then all the young men of the village are fools," Gato commented as he peered at her through the swirls of smoke from his pipe. A smile tugged at the corners of his mouth as he sucked on the carved teak stem, and the fragrant odor of fine tobacco rose lazily from the well-packed bowl of the pipe to curl through the air and tickle Kerry's nose.

"I agree that they're fools, but not for that particular reason." Kerry sniffed appreciatively, inhaling then exhaling in a slow whoosh of breath. "They simply have no motives for living other than to eat, drink, and fu—" She paused as Gato pierced her with a sharp glance, then shrugged, finishing: "Procreate." Habit and constant association with the rough, bawdy sailors on St. Denis's crowded docks had given Kerry a wide vocabulary of socially objectionable words, yet Gato hesitated to forbid her access to the exciting, teeming activities on the waterfront.

Remembering the first time he had found her on the docks after frantic hours of searching the twisting maze of streets and alleys in the small town, Gato smiled. The eight-year-old child, dressed in cast-off trousers and a shirt donated by the church, had been perched inside a stiff wicker basket sitting on the edge of a wharf, watching two sailors perform a lively jig. She had greeted Gato with a succinct phrase in Portuguese. He had immediately succumbed to a coughing fit that sent the sailors into merry gales of back-slapping laughter. His first early attempts to dissuade visits to the docks had been met with a surprisingly haughty frown and the pronouncement that since she enjoyed it and it wasn't harmful she would continue going.

"Though I would like it very much if you would not object," the disarming child had added, and Gato had only shrugged helplessly in the face of her determination. Yet now she was no longer a child but almost a woman, and he was growing old and tired. What would happen to her when he died? Gato felt an urgent need to see Kerry settled, and he wished for what must have been the ten thousandth time that he could put her on a ship bound for Ireland. She must have family there, but she still refused to talk about them.

A subtle change came over Kerry whenever he mentioned Ireland or her family, and she would behave as if she had a guilty secret to hide from him. Gato knew it had something to do with the long-ago wreck of the ship bringing her to St. Denis, but he had never been able to persuade her to talk about it. In a way, he was glad she refused to discuss her past, because then he'd feel obligated to send her back to her relatives. Life would not be the same without Kerry and he dreaded the day she would finally decide to return.

"I can't imagine," she was saying, dragging his attention back to their spirited discussion about the suitability of St. Denis's eligible males, "why those clumsy idiots think they can outrace Diablo, but they still try."

"Hmmm." A sly twinkle sparked in his mahogany-brown eyes as Gato answered, "Perhaps it is not the horse they are competing against, but the rider."

"Perhaps," Kerry agreed, "but I can outride any man on this island." It wasn't an idle boast. In the ten years she'd spent with Gato, Kerry had learned how to train most of his stable herself, and was proud of the fine reputation Gato enjoyed for owning the best stock on the island. It was a well-deserved reputation, and she had contributed her talents to earning it.

"Sí," he told her now, "you ride well, because you

know your animal better than most know theirs. It is a secret they have not learned."

She hooked her slim arms, tanned by golden rays of Caribbean sun, around her knees as she balanced herself on the floor with bare toes skimming the woven rug. "If they won't learn, it is because they don't care enough to try," she flipped back, and Gato silently agreed. Chuckling, the old man smoked and rocked, bright eyes shining with pride. Kerry possessed a resiliency that was both admirable and alarming, and a free spirit that bordered on recklessness. She was, admittedly, headstrong and impetuous, yet sometimes she astonished him with her intuitive common sense.

And he enjoyed watching her, enjoyed her careless grace and fluid movements, her unabashed love of life that sent her careening from one side of the island to another in pursuit of new and interesting things to see and do.

Restless now, Kerry rocketed to her feet, shoving the flat of her hands into deep pockets on the back of her trousers.

"I've finished feeding and watering the stock this morning, Gato. I may go for another ride shortly."

"Mucho cuidado, niña," he said softly, but she was already gone, the door shutting behind her with a bang, tiny dust motes stirring in the air and riding sunbeams that filtered through small windowpanes. Somehow the room seemed dimmer even though the sun was shining just as brightly through the windows. The spark of energy that was so uniquely Kerry's had gone with her. Ah, the vitality of the young, Gato reflected as he settled comfortably back in his cane-bottomed chair. There were times he was grateful he was an old man.

Hot dust billowed up around the pads of her bare feet as Kerry strode swiftly in her half-walk, half-

run down the path to the neatly fenced pens where
the horses were kept. It was still early, not yet noon,
and she was restless again, wanting to expend some
of her pent-up energy.

If it wasn't for the cool breezes that blew across
the tiny island it would have been hot, but the
gentle zephyrs whispered over turquoise waters and
glistening sands to tease the strands of coppery hair
that hung down Kerry's back in a silky tangle. She
breathed deeply, filling her lungs with air that was
fresh and salty, listening to the distant curl of the
surf and the chatter of brightly plumaged birds
perched in a nearby flame tree. Color assaulted her
senses, brilliant blues and radiant crimsons, irides-
cent greens that folded into a kaleidoscope on the
color spectrum—sky and foliage and tropical
blooms—everything on St. Denis was so vivid it almost hurt the eyes. Nothing was an understate-
ment, but an explosion of the senses.

Turning, Kerry laid her arms upon the rough bark
of the top fence rail laid in a zigzag pattern around
the small square of the pen, and squinted thoughtfully up into the sun. Most of the time it didn't matter when the well-bred mamas and daughters of St.
Denis stared down the length of their long noses at
her. She had plenty of friends in the mountain village who never considered her beneath them or socially unacceptable. And they weren't pretentious
like the richly dressed ladies who behaved so primly,
twitching aside their silk skirts so as not to touch
Kerry's dirty bare feet or boy's clothes. What did
she care about those haughty females who knew
how to do nothing but sew a straight seam and pour
tea correctly?

She had other interests to pursue, interests that
few girls her age shared. She could read, and write,
and do sums in her head, and she thought about
more than snaring a suitable husband. There were

things she'd read about in the tattered books Gato cherished, long poems about Greek heroes and heroines, fascinating adventures that led men and women through exotic lands—fodder for an active imagination.

The hours spent on the teeming docks had not been spent only in learning the rough art of fluent cursing in different languages, for Kerry possessed an impressive knowledge of geography and a smattering of untried navigational techniques, as well as enough mathematics to accurately gauge the successful loading of a ship's hold. She knew what spices came from various areas of the world and what plants produced the myriad of different colors of dye for rich fabrics that lay in huge bolts along the wharves.

Sailors tend to be an argumentative lot, and as many different political viewpoints as there were sailors had been vigorously crammed into Kerry's head at one time or another. French, British, and American crewmen had expounded their theories about the wars that were being fought until she had grown too weary to listen to more. It was ridiculous really, how two countries like America and Great Britain had allowed themselves to become embroiled in a silly squabble over the commerce between nations, like two children tugging at the same toy with a third child maliciously egging them on. Though St. Denis now belonged to the British, it had once been claimed by both France and Spain, and remnants of their cultures abounded on the tiny island. It was a surprisingly feverish hotbed of varied political opinions. Shrugging carelessly, Kerry smothered a yawn with a cupped hand, thinking how she much preferred ignoring the frenzied yapping of the war hounds.

A warm, velvet nose nudged her, and she turned with a smile to pat the black stallion fondly.

"You rascal," she whispered in a slightly twitching ear, "are you anxious to go for another ride?" When the animal blew softly in answer, Kerry chuckled. It didn't take her long to slip the bridle over his eager head, and even less time to mount the prancing horse. She placed one bare foot against the fence post for leverage, and then straddled his broad back.

This was one of her favorite times, when the morning tasks had been finished and the sun was high in the sky, gilding puffs of clouds and shining on the serene waters of the bay. Drumming her heels against his gleaming ebony flanks, Kerry pivoted Diablo into a wheeling arc and cantered from the stableyard.

She turned him in the direction of the deserted beach beyond the curling edge of the seaport, and they trotted down well-worn cobblestones toward the sea. Salty wind blew across her upturned face as she rode, the tang of the sea both enticing and invigorating. Surf crashed in foamy waves against glistening sand and seabirds wheeled above with lilting cries echoing on the wind.

Kerry tossed a careless but friendly wave at some fishermen repairing torn nets not far from the bustling activity of the docks. They waved back, calling salty greetings as she passed, grinning when she answered back in kind.

With the sea on one side and the sloping hills that rose into cloud-wreathed peaks on the other, Kerry felt a part of the island. All her most urgent worries would fade while she perched on a flat deserted rock high above the bay and let the sun gild her naked body a peachy color all over. Other times she would ride past the huge white houses belonging to wealthy planters, imagining the people inside. What would it be like to live in one of the houses, lying on a cushioned chaise and procuring cool drinks of mint and rum with the snap of an indolent hand? Boring, Kerry suspected, thinking of the moonlit rides she loved, the freedom she craved. She would never be content living like a spun-sugar doll in a marzipan house.

Kerry let Diablo choose his own pace as he struck out across the hot sand studded with small clumps of sea grass, and the huge stallion cantered easily at the water's edge. Finally, foam-flecked sides heaving as he dragged in deep breaths, Diablo paused beside a natural archway of trees jutting from the beach. To one side was a jagged outcropping of gray rock, to the other a steeply sloping bank that curved into a sandy crest several feet above Kerry's head. It hung over in a grassy fringe, providing shade and seclusion, a shallow spot carved by sea winds into a cozy nook suitable for daydreaming and reading.

Sliding from his back, Kerry let the rope reins of the bridle hang around his neck, and Diablo moved away to graze on the lush tufts of grass scattered along sandy fringes. It was warm and Kerry closed her eyes and tilted her face upward for the warm kiss of the sun. A lazy day, and she felt lazy and contented like a carp-fed tomcat lying in the noonday sun. She stepped into the shady alcove and sat on the warm sand, leaning back on her elbows and stretching her legs out so that bare toes crusted with sugary grains of sand were still peeking at the blazing blue of the sky. Shifting slightly, Kerry adjusted the small dagger that she wore at her waist, moving it around to the front from where her weight pressed it into the curve of her hip. Her fine-boned fingers lingered on the whalebone handle carved with scrimshaw.

The dagger had been a gift from a one-eyed man who had once sailed on a whaler. The intricate scenes on the handle depicted a long-haired girl riding a horse along a curl of beach—the knife was personalized, he'd told her with a toothless grin, and Kerry had been touched by the seaman's thoughtfulness. Gato had been less pleased, muttering that a brief course in the art of knife-wielding was not the most gentle of feminine pursuits when Kerry demonstrated a few of the knife tricks she'd been shown.

"But you must admit," she'd retorted with an impish smile, "that knowing exactly how to slice a jugular vein could be much more handy than playing a melody by Mozart on the harpsichord." Gato had not admitted anything of the sort, of course, only rolled his dark eyes and shook his graying head in resignation. She smiled now as she recalled his long-suffering expression.

It was good she knew how to use a knife, Kerry reflected. Only recently even the Lord Mayor's house had been broken into, and a servant found dead. He'd obviously surprised the thief. Even on this beautiful island, one had to be wary.

The crash of surf and pleasant buzzing of insects serenaded Kerry as she drifted into a light sleep, lowering her suddenly heavy head to the pillowing humps of sand. She dreamed strange dreams, hazy images that spun in a whirl of disembodied voices and vague impressions.

Then the voices were no longer just dreams but real, men's voices, hard and angry, their words blunt and short.

"Give me the books, Garcia. Damn it! Put your knife away, or I will use it on you."

"Por Dios! I got the books! They are mine!"

Where were these men? Kerry wondered as her eyes snapped open and struggled to focus. Her gaze darted to Diablo, who was half-hidden from the men by a tall clump of spiny palm leaves. A small spray of sand drifted down from the pouting lip of the crest over her head, and Kerry knew then that the men were directly above her.

She lay on the warm sand like an ancient marble statue, unwilling to attract their attention yet intrigued by their conversation. There was the sound of booted feet scrunching on sand and harsh breathing. It sounded like they were fighting.

"You fool! Did Sedgewick pay you enough to risk your life like this? You should have known better, Garcia."

A short pause, then a whining voice trembling with fear began to plead, "Don't kill me, señor! It is much money! And I will share. You did not think I would really have told Milford about you?" A weak laugh. "It was a joke! A bad joke!"

"I'd say a fatal joke," a grim voice replied, and Kerry could feel the disgust in that smooth, hard tone. "Give me the books. They don't mean more than your life, do they? I suppose you did what you felt you had to do, Garcia. As I will do."

Kerry could hear the jangle of metal bits on bridles and the muffled stomping of horses' hooves on small hillocks of grassy sand. Sweet Jesus, she was hearing a murder! The man Garcia was going to be killed by the other man, and here she sat helpless.

"I don't even work for Sedgewick anymore! Wait! I will tell you the truth—I wanted money, so I agreed to steal them, that is all," Garcia said with a nervous quiver in his voice, and was answered with an impatient laugh that jarred Kerry's nerves. The owner of that silky voice was not playing idle games. He was dangerous, and Kerry's breath caught in the back of her throat in a soft tangle of apprehension as the man spoke slowly and deliberately.

"Is that why you came after me with a dagger? You are a coward, and cowards can't be trusted. I don't need Milford after me as well, Garcia. Ah-ah— no sudden moves or you're dead."

There was an inflexible quality to his voice that sent a shiver down her back, and Kerry pushed further back into the shadow of the shallow cave.

Milford? The name interested her immediately. Lord Milford was the mayor of St. Denis and a thoroughly despicable man who was universally hated by most of the island. How was he involved with these obviously suspicious individuals overhead? There was a dry shuffling of feet and the creak of saddle leather, and Kerry wondered how long the men had been standing above her and how much she had missed of their conversation.

Cautiously pushing herself erect, the palms of her hands digging into shifting grains of sand, Kerry strained to hear what they were saying, shaking her head impatiently as the roar of the surf coming in drowned out their words. The one called Garcia stumbled over vague promises that went unanswered, and Kerry bit her bottom lip. She tilted her head upward, green eyes blinking to avoid trickling grains of sand from the crest. If only she could hear a little better . . .

More sand drifted down from above and Kerry vainly tried to stifle a cough, raising her hands to cover her mouth as she choked. When she regained her breath she strained to hear more sounds from the men, but the curl of surf crashing against the shore was all that she heard.

Glancing toward Diablo, she saw he was still grazing undisturbed, his sleek head lowered as he clipped succulent shoots of grass. The stallion hadn't yet scented the other horses, nor they him, and she wondered uneasily if the two men were still above her. If they were, they had probably heard her cough, which meant she was in danger too. What about Garcia? She had a dagger, maybe she could help—no, then there would be two bodies instead of one. Cursing herself for being a coward, Kerry slid to the front of the cave.

Easing cautiously along on hands and bottom, Kerry finally lurched to her feet. Running across the short distance separating her from Diablo, with full lips pursed in a long, low whistle to snare the stallion's attention, she snatched the reins and vaulted onto Diablo's back in a smooth, fluid motion.

Whipping the stallion's head around, Kerry dug her heels into his ribs and leaned over his thick neck. She was about to urge him into a gallop when a sudden thought stopped her cold. She wasn't a coward, so why was she fleeing like a seabird before the winds of a hurricane? No one would be able to catch her, not when she was mounted on Diablo. Gathering her misplaced courage, Kerry wheeled the stallion around. Maybe she couldn't save Garcia, whoever he was, but she might be able to give him a chance to save himself by distracting his killer.

The pounding of her heart drowned out the steady hum of the surf as Kerry rode back to the crest and sawed back on the reins to pull Diablo to a hoof-thrashing halt. She never knew afterward what made her choose the words she did, but her voice was strong and steady, easily reaching the ears of the two struggling men just above her.

"Garcia! Shall I ride to Milford for help?"

Whatever she expected, it wasn't the shrill answer she got, and she wondered angrily why the man was so foolish.

"Lawton has the books! From the pirate ship *Black Unicorn.* He's . . ." A fist slammed into the side of his head and Garcia swung his dagger desperately, howling curses at the man holding him. His curses ended in a gurgle, and Kerry had a brief, horrified glimpse of a swarthy face with open, gap-

ing mouth and unbelieving eyes. Her gaze flew to
the tall man standing over him, and when he jerked
around to face Kerry she didn't wait to say more,
but spun Diablo around. Her idea of helping had
certainly misfired, and she was going to be as dead
as Garcia if she didn't move fast.

Concentrating on the blur of sand that flashed beneath massive hooves as the stallion raced like the
wind over clumps of sea grass and twisted knots of
driftwood, Kerry was surprised to hear the pounding of hooves close behind, a rhythmic cadence that
spelled disaster. Damn—he must have jumped his
horse over the crest! He was gaining, coming closer
and closer, and she didn't dare turn to look back but
only urged Diablo on. How was he able to even get
close to her, she wondered furiously as she leaned
further over Diablo's neck.

And it was then that an arm snaked out to curl
around her waist like a looping coil of steel cable,
pulling her from Diablo's back and across a high-
boned saddle with a jarring thud. Muscles like iron
bands tightened around her chest when she struggled, making Kerry gasp for air, yet she still fought.
Her hair flew in stinging whips over her face and
in her eyes, and her slim legs aimed well-placed
kicks at the flanks of the bay horse as well as the
broad back of her abductor.

Wild curses in several different languages erupted
from her in panting gasps as her small white teeth
closed over the skin of his hand. A surprised snarl
of pain sounded from somewhere up above her head,
and Kerry grasped the opportunity his slightly loosened grip provided. She heaved her body outward,
bare feet finding and pushing against the horse's
sweaty sides. Kerry had a brief glimpse of the man's
blaze-faced bay before she was free, dropping to the
ground for only an instant before she was up and
running, glancing around for Diablo.

Sea wind tangled her hair as she raced along a shifting dune toward a thick stand of trees. Sweet Jesus, the man was close behind, too damned close behind, and her madly pumping heart accelerated even more. But as fleet as she was, Kerry could not outrace her pursuer. Just as she reached the small copse of trees she saw the dark shadow of horse and rider catch up with her.

A hand caught the back of her shirt like the talons of a hawk to lift her from her feet and into the air, and she dangled like a pitifully snared sparrow before being swung across his saddle once more. Lights exploded in front of her eyes as Kerry's breath erupted in a gasping wheeze from her chest and she struggled for air. She only half-listened to the man's growled comments in her ear as he reined his mount to a halt.

Then she was being ignominiously dragged from across the horse and balanced on trembling legs. A harsh hand shook her roughly as her captor demanded to know who she was.

Kerry shook loose from his grip and stood with her feet firmly planted in a challenging stance. Her coppery hair waved a defiant banner in the bright sunlight as she shared some of her choicest epithets with him.

"Well, I'll be damned if it isn't a gutter-tongued girl," announced the man in a voice tinged with surprise. Then the rich timbre of his tone altered to sardonic amusement as he added, "Of sorts."

Kerry's gaze flew from his gleaming Hessian boots up lean-muscled legs and over a broad chest to his face. The furious retort that was ready on the tip of her glib tongue died unuttered. He was a veritable Adonis! She wasn't prepared for the heart-stopping reaction she was experiencing, for the way her blood seemed to freeze in rebellious veins so that she couldn't move. One heartbeat, then two, and still she couldn't form a suitably scathing reply to his callous observation.

"Just out for a Sunday stroll, little one?" he was asking in that same cynical tone, and the biting inflection of his words did not escape her notice. Recovering from the shock of forgetting for even a moment that he was a killer, Kerry shook her head to clear the cobwebs and forced her eyes in another direction, licking suddenly dry lips.

"Then explain to me why you are here," he suggested, "and your connection with Milford and Garcia."

"None. I dislike Milford and I don't—didn't—know Garcia." She managed a careless shrug. "That's all."

"Is it? How convenient that you should . . . happen by . . . at just the right time."

"Right time?" She sounded incredulous. "For who? Garcia? I'd say the man has terrible timing myself, and mine is obviously even worse or I wouldn't be standing here now."

"No," he corrected her, "it appears that Garcia's timing was the worst."

There was no arguing with that and Kerry didn't try. With the hot sun pouring down on her head she waited for the killer with the handsome face to say something else, wondering nervously how she was going to get away. Who was he? Lawton, Garcia had said, from a pirate ship. Oh Lord, the fat was in the fire. Everyone knew that no self-respecting pirate had a shred of mercy or remorse in his entire body.

Even when she focused on the gently swaying fronds of a large flowering palm only a few feet away, Kerry could still see the man's face as if it had been etched on her mind's eye with a chisel. Strong Grecian features were coupled with eyes of a startling blue under darkly winging eyebrows, and thick hair the same hue as liquid ebony fell in wind-blown wisps over a sun-bronzed face. A cleft speared his square, clean-shaven jaw, and well-shaped lips wore a sensuous slant. Those lips were now quirking with mocking amusement.

Her narrowed eyes flashed a warning as Kerry thrust out her chin and said, "You may find the situation amusing, but I don't. Whatever your quarrel with either Milford or . . . that man . . . it doesn't involve me. I don't owe you any explanations."

"I disagree," he answered in a deceptively soft tone. Kerry's fingers trembled as she brushed at clinging swirls of sand on the sleeves of her shirt and loose trouser legs. He was making her nervous, staring at her with those glittering sapphire eyes, and she swallowed hard before taking a deep breath.

"I don't give a damn if you agree or not," she bluffed. Her shaking hand brushed against the handle of her dagger as she swept at her sand-crusted garments, and she took another deep breath. Kerry gave a searching glance around her for Diablo, and soothed her parched lips with the tip of her tongue. One hand paused to rest on her hip and the other rose to flick back annoying streamers of red-gold hair. "Now get out of my way."

"You're amusing, brat, but a little too cocky," Adonis observed with a soft laugh. His thumbs were hooked in the waist of tightly fitted buff trousers and his tanned chest looked hard as steel beneath the open front of his flowing white shirt.

Kerry's fingers coiled around the handle of her dagger as she took one step backward, and its gleaming blade flashed briefly in the sunlight as the pirate reached out for her. The razor-sharp point tore a ripping arc through the sleeve of his shirt and into the flesh stretching over the muscles of his forearm. She didn't wait to hear his curses but quickly pivoted on the hot sand and ran.

Diablo, where was Diablo? She pursed her dry,

parched lips in a whistle that should have been piercing but sounded more like a gasping trout. Her next attempt cut into the air in a shrill blast, borne of fear and determination, and Kerry's pace never slackened as she listened for hooves thundering toward her.

Head flung back, she sucked in gulps of air, her chest aching. Just ahead, only a few yards now, was the stand of trees, and just beyond that was the area where the fishermen were repairing their nets. She had to make it that far somehow, where people she knew would help her.

Then came the welcome sound of hooves scrunching on sand, and she slowed slightly and half-turned to look for her stallion. When he slowed, she could grasp a handful of thick mane and swing to his back with very little effort. His ebony hide gleamed in the hot sun and his nostrils flared like bright pink flowers. She could feel his breath on her cheek. Leaping to one side, Kerry would have vaulted to his back, but she was snared by steely coils of fingers clutching her wrist and immobilizing the dagger she still held. Damn him! He was astride her horse! He yanked Diablo to a halt with Kerry dangling like a hooked fish at one side.

Adonis slid from Diablo, and his eyes were pinpoint pools of fury as he tightened his iron grip on her wrist, removing the dagger from her hand. He towered over her, and Kerry would have been intimidated if she hadn't been so furiously angry. He stuck her dagger in his wide belt and gave her a cold, triumphant smile. Anger rendered common sense useless, and before she stopped to think about it, Kerry's fist crashed into his face. She watched with great satisfaction as a thin trickle of blood appeared at one corner of his mouth.

Retaliation was swift and unexpectedly harsh as the back of a broad hand swung in a whirring arc that left her no time to duck. The world exploded into a reeling blur of flashing light before everything faded and she descended into dark oblivion.

Catching her as she pitched slowly forward, Lawton lowered the girl he'd already decided was a thinly disguised she-wolf to the ground. Blood dripped along his injured forearm and from the tips of his fingers, spattering to the sand beside his gleaming boots. It was quickly absorbed by thousands of tiny grains and Lawton grimaced and swore softly under his breath.

Gripping her chin, he examined the large purple bruise blossoming on the gently curving sweep of her jaw. His gaze drifted over the delicate sculpture of her face. Her dark lashes fanned against dusky cheeks the color of a ripe peach, all pink and gold and luscious. She had a charmingly tilted nose perched above half-parted lips that were full and sensuously promising. Who was the little harpy? And how much did she know?

Time was limited, and he'd wasted too much already. At least Garcia had saved him some trouble by having the books already in his possession, but now the man was dead and that created more problems. Damn Garcia. Milford would immediately suspect him, so the swifter he moved the better it would be.

The girl moaned softly and he made his decision. There was nothing else for it unless he slit her throat and left her beside Garcia. Somehow that idea left a bad taste in his mouth.

He glanced down at the wickedly throbbing cut on his arm. The irritating little wench had drawn the first blood he'd shed in years, and he had to admit she was pretty good with a blade. Flicking another assessing glance at her, Lawton decided she must be just another wharf brat, some sailor's byblow who had been left to fend for herself in the streets. Survival had probably thrown her with Garcia.

Now, if he didn't get the girl and get to his ship, he might find himself facing Milford's militia. That delay would never do, and he couldn't risk losing the books.

A smile of genuine amusement lifted the corners of his mouth as Lawton visualized his business partner's reaction to the girl's presence on board the *Black Unicorn.* Wilson would be beside himself.

Chapter 2

"Have ye run mad?" Wilson demanded, trotting behind Lawton like an anxious hound as he strode across the wooden deck of the *Black Unicorn.* "Whatever possesses ye to bring a ... woman ... aboard? An' she's little more than a lass, Nick, look at her! Have ye taken to knockin' 'em silly now instead of askin' 'em proper?"

"Belay, Wilson. There's a good explanation for this one," Lawton answered as he descended the ladder below deck. "She's out cold, a fact for which you'll be grateful whenever she does come around. Bring hot water and clean rags to my cabin."

Pausing, Wilson pushed at wire-rimmed spectacles sliding to the end of his bulbous nose, then gave a helpless shrug of sloping shoulders that made his entire, rounded frame shift. He went to fetch the clean rags and water.

"A female on board the *Unicorn!*" he muttered loud enough for Nick to hear, and Lawton laughed to himself as he pushed open the heavy oak door to his cabin.

Wilson was opinionated and didn't hesitate to speak his mind, but he'd been Lawton's loyal and devoted friend since Nick Lawton had been a green lad in leading strings. In fact, the old man had been more of a father to him than his real father had ever been. Lord Lawton, eighteenth Earl of Devlin and a vastly wealthy man, had been too busy with business affairs to pay attention to his motherless son and heir. They'd been strangers who sometimes crossed paths, always polite but cool, and the young Nick had never understood why. As an adult he had ceased to care, and the old lord was dead now, so it was a moot point.

A mirthless smile flickered for a moment on his lips as Lawton lowered the girl to the soft mattress of his bunk. The earl was dead and he'd inherited estates and a fortune he wouldn't give a halfpenny for right now. He had another life now with his own fortune and estates that he had earned through ingenuity and hard work. Lawton didn't need a grand title or a country that had once rejected him.

He would never forget how he had been forced to flee in disgrace because of a false accusation. Even his own father had not believed him innocent. Nicholas Lawton had been betrayed by his commanding officer and his own cousin. Of course, Robert would inherit the title one day if Nick was dead or exiled, but it was a conspiracy Robert and Sedgewick would one day regret.

"Here's the rags and water, Cap'n," Wilson puffed behind him, jerking Nick's attention back to the present. "Where'd ye find th' lass?"

"On a rock in the woods. She was sunning herself like a lizard."

"Don't tell me then, ye scurvy water rat. Where's she hurt?" Wilson stepped to the edge of the bunk to look down at the girl. "Hmmm. Kinda young, ain't she? 'Tain't like ye to go robbin' cradles, Nick, but mebbe ye've changed. . . ."

"Instead of babbling like a brook in springtime, Wilson, tend to this cut on my arm. She's only bruised. *I'm* the one who's injured." Wilson's eyes widened as Nick pulled back his sleeve to show him the jagged cut running from his wrist almost to his elbow, and his mouth drooped as Nick informed him the cut had been inflicted by the girl's dagger.

From a crystal decanter Nick poured fine brandy into two glasses as he related the day's events. Wilson listened intently while he washed the wound, ignoring Nick's curse as he splashed a healthy portion of brandy into the gaping cut. "Damme, Wilson, that's good brandy you're wasting!" Lawton protested, but the old man's face remained serene and his composure unruffled as he wound a clean white cloth around Nick's forearm.

Flashing the older man a sour look, Lawton gave him a brief summary of the events leading to the girl's presence aboard the *Black Unicorn.* "So you see why I had to bring her with me," Lawton finished, tilting back his head and swallowing the last of his brandy. Damn, but his arm was already getting stiff.

"Aye, but I don't see what yer goin' to do with her now ye've got her. Anny idea where yer goin' to put th' lass, Nicky lad?" Wilson imitated Lawton's smooth movement with the brandy, smacked his lips, and pushed once more at errant wire spectacles.

"One or two possibilities have crossed my mind, but I'm not sure who I dislike badly enough to saddle with a foulmouthed wharf brat in a female body." Lawton peered at the amber liquid sloshing in his glass. "Who, besides Sedgewick, is my worst enemy, Wilson?"

A hesitant chuckle warbled from Wilson, and the portly little man squinted at his captain as if trying to decide the validity of the question.

"Er . . . mebbe Lord Robert?" he suggested, and was rewarded with a dark stare that made him close his eyes and shrug helplessly.

"Lord Robert is devious and a bloody fool, but even he hardly deserves such harsh punishment. No one else comes to mind? Then I guess we keep her for a few days while we ponder the problem."

"Aye, Cap'n," Wilson echoed tartly, "we keep her for a few days. That's just what's needed on the *Unicorn!*"

"Superstitious?" Lawton inquired mildly. "How archaic, Wilson."

"Not superstitious, jus' able to see past th' end of my nose. She's young an' pretty, an' there'll be trouble."

"But think how entertaining it will be," Nick answered, grinning at Wilson's exasperated snort. "Don't worry. I'll dump her at the first opportunity—when she's no longer a threat."

Moaning, Kerry clenched the sides of the mattress tightly. Rocking, rocking—jumping sailfish, why was the world still rocking?—and she wasn't lying on the ground any more but on a mattress. There was a pounding in her head like a blacksmith's hammer on his anvil, and her jaw was extremely sore. Managing to pry open her eyelids to investigate her surroundings, Kerry realized with a vague sense of surprise that she was on a ship. It didn't take a great deal of deduction to figure out that it must be the pirate's ship. She was lying in a spacious bunk at one end of a large cabin that was comfortably furnished with glass-fronted bookshelves and fine carpets. Brass lanterns gleamed on the walls and swayed from solid oak beams on the ceiling, casting small pools of light at intervals around the cabin.

How could it be night already, Kerry wondered grumpily as she swung her legs over the side of the bunk. No light showed through the wide windows at one end of the cabin, only a deep purple. She must have been asleep for hours! Sliding from the goosefeather mattress to the floor, Kerry stood swaying for a moment while she adjusted to the motion of the ship. Before she could make a move for the door, the ship rolled and Kerry lost her balance, collapsing on the carpet a few feet from it. On her hands and knees now, she began to crawl, determined to reach her goal.

"Here, here, lass! What's this?" a voice demanded, and Kerry's head snapped up to see a round little man shaped a great deal like a whisky barrel coming toward her. Or was he rolling? Maybe she was rolling? No, the ship was rolling, and the man was still chattering in a friendly sort of way, making her head reel. "Silly child, are ye tryin' to kill yerself?" he asked as she held on to the floor for dear life.

"Not today," she responded decisively as she rested upon bent arms. "Though I distinctly remember someone else trying that very thing." Her chin plopped into the cradle formed by her palm and fingers and she winced at the thrust of pain, eyeing the man's round little face. "Who are you?"

"Wilson is me name," he began, and Kerry interrupted with a murmured "and piracy is your game," before he could continue.

"Now, why would ye say that, lass? Did I bring ye aboard ship trussed up like a Christmas goose?" Wilson sounded honestly aggrieved, but he did squirm a bit when Kerry fixed him with a considering gaze.

"How do I know? I was not awake to enjoy the trip aboard."

"I gave ye my name, lass. Will ye tell me yers?" he tried. His hopeful smile wavered when she responded with an emphatic "No."

Wilson soon realized this was going to be much

more difficult than he had anticipated. Even Nick's warnings hadn't prepared him for her stubbornness. He watched her carefully, his eyes widening as he spotted the necklace peeking from beneath her blouse. It looked vaguely familiar to Wilson, and a faint memory tugged at the back of his mind. Years before, he had seen a necklace like that, a family crest belonging to someone he knew. How had the necklace come into this unlikely girl's possession?

Tiring of the silent confrontation that threatened to go on endlessly, Kerry prompted, "Don't you have any other questions you'd like to ask me? For instance, would I like to get off this ship?"

A thoughtful expression creased Wilson's broad features and he shook his head.

"Nay, lass, that's not one o' the questions I'm interested in askin' ye." He cleared his throat with a froggy sound before he plunged carefully ahead. "I've never seen a necklace like that afore, 'cept once, long ago in England."

"England?" Kerry's head jerked up with sudden interest to stare at Wilson, green eyes like glowing jewels. "And where would you have been seeing it there, sir?" she asked, unconsciously retreating into an odd mixture of Irish lilt and a softer Caribbean accent. One hand strayed to the necklace as she spoke.

"I can't quite recall," he answered, deciding without knowing why to be more evasive at this point, "but I do recollect it was a mighty fine piece of jewelry like that—and on a very lovely lady."

Kerry's throat contracted at his words, and Kate O'Connell's face swam before her eyes. There was no mistaking the poignant expression of pain or the sudden paleness of Kerry's face.

"My mother," she murmured softly, eyes distant

and hazy with memory, and Wilson realized she didn't know she'd spoken aloud.

Ah, now he remembered the young couple he'd met briefly in England, and if this girl was their daughter, she'd been a wee thing then. "It's a fine necklace, to be sure, lass. Tell me yer name, now," he tried again.

Shaken by his pricking of buried memories, she answered, somehow feeling she could trust this funny little man.

"Kerry."

"Carrie? As in Caroline?" No, no. That wasn't it. Maybe he was mistaken after all. But it had to be the same one. . . .

"No. Kerry. K-e-r-r-y. As in . . . County Kerry." Now why had she said that? Kerry asked herself crossly. One should never say too much.

"So, Kerry lass," Wilson was saying, "it's interestin' to see ye with a silver unicorn strung 'round yer neck, with th' ship bein' named th' *Black Unicorn* and all." He smiled reassuringly at her distracted expression. "Peculiar coincidence, ain't it?"

Kaliza's recent prophecy flashed through her mind, and Kerry stilled a shiver.

"How'd ye come to know Garcia, lass? Is he by way of bein' a friend of yers?"

"I never saw him before in my life and couldn't tell you what he looked like right now." She shrugged carelessly. "I just happened to be there when your pirate friend decided to kill him."

"Ah," the old man said, and Kerry read a world of meaning in that one word. Ah, so Wilson thought she was lying. Did it really matter? She had witnessed a murder whether she knew the victim or not.

"If it matters at all, I'm telling the truth. What

do I have to gain by lying now?" She gazed at him with a direct, honest expression.

Wilson was impressed. She was a cool one, she was, when any other young girl would be shaking and crying and calling for her mama.

"It's not what ye have to gain, lass, but what ye have to lose that's worryin' me." He smiled at the slight widening of her eyes. So she wasn't as fearless as she pretended to be. She clenched and unclenched white-knuckled fists as she sat quietly watching him, and Wilson gave her a comforting pat on the shoulder. "I'll see that yer kept safe."

"But who's going to keep you safe, Wilson?" an amused voice asked from the still open door, and two pairs of eyes whipped around to the tall figure lounging against the smooth doorframe. Lawton cocked a dark brow questioningly, then his rapier-sharp blue eyes rested upon Kerry with a long, considering gaze. "She's acting very much like a jellyfish, you know, all soft and quivery on the topside, but trailing stinging tentacles on the underside."

Wilson scrambled to his feet and hesitated uncertainly, while Kerry surged upward in a fluid motion. Planting feet firmly apart on the thick Persian carpet and facing the captain with a squared, though bruised, jaw, she delivered her favorite oaths.

"Are you quite through?" Lawton inquired pleasantly when Kerry paused for a deep, sucking breath, and when she would have spoken again he shook his head slightly. "I suggest that you are through, infant, or you will certainly regret the consequences of more nasty language." His smile resembled a cobra's as he added in a murmur, "It will be most unpleasant, I assure you."

"I get the picture," Kerry said. "There's no need

to beat a curious cat." Folding her arms across her chest, she gave the captain a look intended to wither him where he stood and grew silent.

"She means dead horse," Wilson corrected after a short pause. "Beat a dead horse."

The pirate captain's mouth quivered suspiciously, but he made no comment.

Kerry's surreptitious gaze flicked over Lawton in general assessment, and she decided that she was fortunate not to have a broken jaw from their earlier encounter. His broad shoulders strained the seams of the white linen shirt he wore, and she could see the smooth ripple of his muscles beneath the material. A gleam of satisfaction shone briefly in her eyes as she noted the bandage around his forearm, and when she glanced up at his face she realized he knew what she was thinking.

"I didn't expect the kitten to have such sharp claws," he said, "but I learn quickly."

Kerry shrugged and looked away. Lawton made her nervous, with those piercing blue eyes that seemed to see right inside her head, and she wondered what he planned to do with her.

"Wilson," he was saying, "I'm sure our guest is hungry, and conversation always flows so much more smoothly on a full stomach. And bring wine from my private stock, please."

His smile could charm fleas off a dog, Kerry thought irritably as Lawton turned back to present her with a blistering example. What a waste. No doubt he used it very effectively to confuse his enemies.

"I'm not hungry," she announced flatly. "Or thirsty."

"No? Maybe I can persuade you to change your mind," he answered pleasantly, once more gracing her with that potent smile. "After-dinner chitchat can be so enlightening with an excellent bottle of wine."

She'd been mistaken. That was no charming smile; it was the leer of a hungry barracuda closing in for the kill. The cabin door closed behind Wilson, and Kerry was alone with the most dangerous man she had ever encountered.

Chapter 3

Kerry looked around with feigned interest at the cabin's interior as the pirate captain seated himself with lazy posture on a plump, horsehair-stuffed loveseat. A lacquered Chinese screen, bearing beautifully gleaming pearl ibises in soaring flight on its surface, zigzagged across one end, and small tables of the same ebony shade as the screen flanked a deep-cushioned winged-back chair. To one side was a secretary with a neat stack of papers and clean pen and inkwell beside them.

Mullioned windows stretched across one entire wall of the cabin, and beneath them curved a carved rosewood couch piled with pillows. Kerry was surprised by the luxury of the ship. Thick carpet cushioned each step as Kerry wandered toward the couch. She glanced down at her toes curling in the soft green pattern of woven trees and delicately reaching vines. How unusual—unicorns peeked from behind slender swaying branches of willow trees. Kerry's hand unconsciously strayed to the locket she wore, fingering the familiar carved lines of the horned silver beast. Unicorns were supposed to bring good luck and she believed that in spite of this ship's name. Hadn't she been the one wearing the locket when the *Wanderer* sank?—and hadn't she been the only survivor?

Wheeling, Kerry walked with deliberation across

the field of unicorns to halt in front of the loveseat. Beneath the loose cotton of her shirt the unicorn nestled between her breasts on its long chain, a reminder that she had survived a much greater disaster than this.

She stared down at the captain, and her voice held a crisp edge.

"I demand you release me."

Lawton's rich laugh vibrated with pleasant sarcasm. "Of course, my lady, at once. And do you insist upon taking any valuables with you also?" One hand waved negligently toward various objects around the cabin. "There's the large vase on that table—Ming dynasty—and the gold filigreed portrait stand over there—extremely expensive, I might add—as well as those leather-bound books in the cases. And, of course, if one is in too great a hurry, I suggest just taking my box of jewelry, the diamond stickpins and solid gold quizzing glass. . . ."

"Shut up," Kerry returned in a less than pleasant tone. "I don't want your vases or your damned quizzing glass, just my freedom."

"Sorry." He slid gracefully to his feet to tower over her. "You stand a better chance of getting the quizzing glass."

Kerry's hands knotted into fists and the air throbbed with tension as she glared at Lawton's chest for a moment. Her emerald eyes rose to fasten on the harsh planes of his face. He expected her to explode; she could sense it in the coiling tenseness of his flat, lean muscles that stretched like steel bands beneath that expanse of smooth bronze skin. So she would react in a manner completely opposite to his expectations.

"Does it come with a silk cord?"

He blinked, obviously having forgotten his list of items, and Kerry smiled.

"The quizzing glass," she reminded gently. "Does it come with a gold silk cord?"

Taut muscles loosened slightly and there was a suggestion of humor in the faint crinkling of his eyes at the corners.

"So, the prickly sea anemone does have a sense of humor after all. I had thought you devoid of anything remotely resembling one."

"And I thought pirates were bogeymen invented to scare small children. Looks like we're both wrong."

"Ah, and the tongue of an asp as well," he observed with the corners of his eyes tucking even further into genuine amusement.

"I have many talents, but at least piracy and murder are not among them," she flashed without thinking. His amusement vanished, and Kerry damned her too-quick tongue.

"You have an intriguing manner of speech, little one. I find it less than amusing, however." Cold blue eyes caught her reluctant gaze and held it until Kerry's knees were weak and trembling. He was, she remembered belatedly, a pirate, a killer without apparent remorse. How could she have forgotten for even an instant?

"Sorry," she muttered at last. "I lost my head."

"Of course. Let's just keep that condition a figure of speech, shall we?"

A weak smile covered the quiver of her lips as Kerry nodded agreement. Oh yes, she was quite willing to keep her head—thick as it was—on her shoulders.

"I think," Lawton was saying in a soft murmur, "that you would be presentable if you were cleaned up a bit, brat. Your face, dirty as it is, is pretty enough, and I've never seen hair that shade before."

One hand reached out to tangle in snarled strands of red-gold hair the same color as the rays from the morning sun, cradling the weight of her head in its palm. Kerry had never felt so vulnerable, as if she were a kite caught in the branches of a tree and left hanging. What was he doing to her? And why had her normally steady legs turned to the consistency of peach marmalade?

Lawton pulled her head slowly back so that she couldn't escape the steady gaze of his deeply blue eyes that seemed to search out all her secrets and lay them bare.

She swallowed nervously. "I'm not quite sure of the rules here, but I don't allow mauling."

"No?" A square-tipped finger reached out to trace the purple pansy of a bruise on her jaw. "Did you allow this tattoo, perhaps?"

A hot, particularly nasty retort trembled on the tip of her tongue for a heartbeat while she struggled with her temper, but Kerry did not miss his veiled warning. If he chose he could do anything he wanted, of course, and no one would stop him. It was obvious her puny strength was not sufficient. Oh, his message was clear enough!

Wilson's arrival banished the need for a reply. She supposed she should be grateful.

"Here ye are, Cap'n! Cook fixed a nice meal fer the two of ye, and I had Jensen bring up a bottle of yer favorite wine." Wilson's opaque gaze finally registered the angrily flushed face of the girl standing within a breath of Lawton's embrace. His spectacles slid at an alarming pace down the bridge of his nose to the tip before popping into space. They clattered with a splash into a brimming bowl, and a tiny waterspout of turtle soup rose in a delicate arc.

"Dear me." Wilson looked up with a pained expression on his stolid face and the tray quivered in his grasp.

Somehow Kerry had never thought of a murderous pirate using such mild phrases, and the entire situation suddenly seemed ridiculous. Here she was, standing in the middle of the expensive plunder in a pirate's ship, thinking that at any moment she might be thrown over the side for a shark's breakfast, and one of the pirates dropped his eyeglasses in a bowl of turtle soup. Lord help her, it was just too much.

"You two are as sharp as sea nettles, aren't you? How droll." Kerry turned to the vacated loveseat and flung herself gracefully onto the cushions with much more aplomb than she felt. One leg hooked over the curving arm and her bare foot dangled in a slow circle while she stretched the other leg out in front of her and crossed her arms over her chest. She smiled as she looked from one man to the other; the portly Wilson with a red bandana wrapped around a bald head and fringed with wisps of gray hair peeking from the edges, and the elegantly lean captain who stood watching her with a saturnine expression on features as sharp as a hawk's.

Lawton knew she was the only witness to Garcia's death, and her life wasn't worth as much as an empty crab shell if he chose to ensure her silence. Her eyes blinked as Kerry considered her precarious position. Very few choices presented themselves to her right now. Where was her normally agile brain? Suffocating under a mountain of fear, Kerry decided.

Her wandering gaze focused on Wilson's kind face with the sagging jowls of a spaniel, and she found an odd sort of comfort in the encouraging look he gave her.

"How theatrical." Lawton's acid tones etched the still air. "While your performance is most entertaining, it is not very informative. I'm running out of patience, and the soup is getting cold." He walked to the table and pulled out a chair. "Join me, please." It was not a request but a command, and as much as Kerry would have enjoyed refusing, she didn't quite dare.

Swallowing the angry refusal, she slapped her feet to the floor and stalked to the table. When she would have ignored Lawton and pulled out her own chair, he gripped her by one shoulder and shoved her into his.

"Thank you!" Kerry snapped.

"You're welcome," was the calm answer as Lawton seated himself next to her.

Dishes rattled as Wilson removed china lids from steaming bowls and clattered silver spoons together, and Lawton sliced him a mildly inquiring glance.

"Ah, at last," he said in a pleasant tone when Wilson had finished placing the dishes on the table. "Shall we eat before we begin our enlightening discussion?"

"A last meal?" Kerry asked tartly as she pushed at her food with bored disinterest.

"If you like. It depends upon your answers," he replied smoothly, and Kerry's throat closed so that she couldn't have swallowed a bite if she'd been ravenous. Obviously a great deal depended upon correct answers. Maybe the wine would steady her shaking hands.

"More wine, lass?" Wilson asked after Kerry had drained her second glass, and she nodded.

"I hope you brought an extra bottle, Wilson," Lawton observed, and Kerry noticed that he was still drinking his first glass. Well, he wasn't the one with death or dismemberment hanging over his head, and she was.

By the time Nick Lawton had finished eating, the edges of Kerry's vision were slightly blurred and fuzzy. The room had grown warm and she felt a pleasant glow of well-being that belied the true situation. It couldn't be as bad as it seemed. Once the pirate understood that she'd only meant to help and had no connection with Milford or Garcia, he'd release her.

"Let's make ourselves more comfortable on the couch," Lawton said when he finally pushed away from the table. "It might help your thought processes."

Kerry stared at him blankly. Her thought processes were numb. Her brain was numb, and so were her feet. She hiccuped.

Lawton turned around to look at her. "Will you join me?" He held out his hand, frowning when she shook her head. "Ah, but I insist."

He insisted. Even in her numbed state, Kerry recognized the thinly veiled command and slid her chair away from the table. Where were his courtly manners when she needed help with the chair now? She stood, slightly swaying, and gripped the edge of the table for support. How intriguing. The floor of the cabin tilted as she stepped away from the table, dropping from beneath madly shuffling feet to spill her onto the thick carpet.

"Ground swell," she heard Wilson say apologetically. "Happens all the time."

Kerry's fingers parted her curtain of tangled hair as she rested full-length upon her stomach and elbows, peering up at Nick and Wilson.

"Allow me, my lady." There was a note of suppressed laughter in Nick's voice as he reached down to help her that made Kerry slap irritably at his well-manicured hand. She scowled. "Wilson," she heard Nick say then, "she's drunk."

"Aye, Cap'n, I believe yer right," Wilson answered promptly.

The room was spinning and Kerry concentrated on keeping her wobbling head upright. She was only vaguely aware of Nick's hands under her arms pulling her up so that she sat like a limp rag doll.

"Can you walk? Jesus, that's a stupid question." He lifted her and carried her back to the bunk she had vacated only a short time before. Wilson covered her with a satin blanket and she was left alone to drift into a hazy sleep while Nick returned to the table.

"There's plenty of time to talk to her tomorrow," Wilson said as he gathered up the dirty dishes and empty bottles of wine. He avoided looking at his partner. A faint smile tugged at the corners of his mouth as he heard Nick's short, disgusted reply. Ah, the lad was in a hurry, he was, but there was no need for it. Wilson had noted that spark of interest in Nick's eyes, and he didn't doubt that Kerry's stay would be a long one.

"Wilson, there are times I wonder if you are friend or enemy," Nick observed as Wilson lifted the cluttered tray. "Do you suppose you could just tell me what's on your mind instead of manipulating matters to your satisfaction?"

"Ah, that would ruin everything, Nicky lad. It's more fun this way."

"For whom?" He didn't expect an answer of course. It was obvious who was enjoying the situation. Wilson had a habit of contriving satisfactory conclusions to the most extraordinary circumstances.

"When do you meet Locke?" Wilson asked, pausing in the open doorway.

"Five weeks from today, off the coast of Spanish Florida." Nick rearranged the chair Kerry had used. "Send me a hammock, Wilson, since it appears that my bed has been snatched from under me."

Wilson's mouth curved in an innocent smile. "Aye, Cap'n, right away."

Some time during the night Kerry woke with a raging thirst and the feeling that some devious soul had stuffed wads of cotton in her mouth. The cabin was dark and she couldn't see anything but vague outlines against the dim light through the gallery windows. Slipping from the bunk, she immediately stumbled over the curling edge of the Persian carpet. Kerry muttered a foul oath as she barely managed to catch herself.

There was a pitcher of water somewhere, she remembered, stepping cautiously forward, if she could just find the right cabinet in the dark. And what did one do about natural body functions aboard a ship? The vessel rose with a wave and Kerry grabbed at what appeared to be a curve of rope to keep from falling.

The rope sagged with her weight, throwing her forward into a warm embrace. Flailing arms beat at her unknown assailant as Kerry struggled to escape, but the hold only grew tighter and she found herself lifted from the floor.

"Be still, for Chrissake!" a vaguely familiar voice growled in the general direction of her ear. "You're going to dump us both on the floor."

Nick. What was he doing suspended in midair? Ceasing her frantic resistance, Kerry demanded indignantly, "What are you doing here?"

The answer was rich with sardonic amusement. "This is my cabin, remember? And you were in my bed. Is that 'Oh' an invitation to join you? I didn't think so. Now if you will just get off me, I'll find a light for the lantern."

Backing away, Kerry stood waiting as Nick fumbled in the dark for a few moments. Then there was a hiss and the sharp smell of sulphur as the lantern was lit, the light flickering at first before growing stronger.

"How did you do that?" she asked curiously, staring at the small wood splinter Nick had used.

Replacing the globe over the flame, Nick held up

the charred splinter of wood. "With this. Wood tipped with chlorate of potash, sugar, and gum arabic. Just dip it in sulfuric acid and hey! Presto! Instant illumination."

"Fascinating." Lantern light danced across Nick in a golden pattern and Kerry's eyes widened. His chest was bare, muscles moving smoothly beneath bronze skin, and a mat of thickly curling hair tapered to a vee at his waist and below. The male body was no mystery to her, not after bathing and playing in mountain pools with the young men and women of the native village, but somehow this was different. For the first time in her life, Kerry was uncomfortable looking at a man's bare chest. "Put some clothes on!" she snapped.

"Don't look," Nick countered. "I didn't ask you to leap in the hammock with me; you came uninvited. I won't apologize for not being formally dressed."

"I didn't leap in the hammock. I was trying to find some water and it was in the way."

"Help yourself, love. I'm going back to sleep."

"What about my water?" she said to his back and he waved in the general direction of a cabinet. He was already situated in the rope hammock when Kerry asked for a chamber pot. "I assume you do have one?"

Exasperated, Nick turned to glare at her. "Look, my fine lady, I'm no damned lady's maid! I don't know where it is. Use the washbowl and throw it out the window."

"Pirates don't have calls of nature, I suppose," Kerry muttered as she banged open cabinet doors. Her brief but noisy search was at last rewarded with not only a pewter pitcher of tepid water, but a dusty chamber pot.

When she finally returned to the bunk she was wide awake. A tiny round window over the bunk gave her a glimpse of deep purple sky and pinprick stars, and Kerry lay listening to the ship's sounds. Creaks and moans, the faint flap of canvas sails, and the slap of water against the sides all melded together.

What was Gato thinking? Was he worried about her, or did he think she'd gone into the mountains again? No, if Diablo had returned without her, Gato would know some disaster had occurred. Her head ached and her stomach rolled uncomfortably. Kerry closed her eyes. This was a pirate ship and she was a prisoner. Gruesome tales returned to haunt her now, tales of horrible fates aboard ships captained by bloodthirsty cutthroats. And if she began to think of Lawton as a fairly civilized individual who had chosen an unfortunate occupation, she had only to recall Garcia and his gaping mouth and slashed throat.

Chapter 4

Pricking with golden fingers at her closed eyelids, the sunlight flooded through the panes of the gallery windows to finally wake Kerry. For a moment she was disoriented, wondering dazedly where she was and why. Then the past hours rushed back and she remembered.

She sat up abruptly. The hammock was gone and so was Nick. Good. She flung back satin covers and slid from the bunk, pausing to consider the vanity of a fierce pirate who would possess a satin quilt.

Finding a weapon was the first order of the day, but Kerry soon found to her dismay that all cabinets, drawers and cupboards were locked tightly. Only the glass-fronted bookshelves remained unlocked, and she dismally dismissed the idea of demanding her freedom by brandishing a heavy volume of Shakespeare. How dare Lawton assume she was a thief just because he was, she wondered indignantly. And how vexing that he had been so thorough.

Where was he? Did anyone remember she was here? Time passed and no one came to the cabin. Kerry's stomach growled a protest as she paced the carpet and looked out the windows, listening to all the unfamiliar sounds the ship made. Hours dragged. She even tried reading but couldn't concentrate.

By the time Nick returned to the cabin late that afternoon, Kerry had run the gamut of emotions. She'd passed anxiety and fright and hurtled into fury, so that she just sat glaring at him when he opened the door.

"Lonesome, brat?" He ducked just in time as the chamber pot sailed with deadly force and bounced off the wall, followed by a shower of smaller missiles.

Leaping forward, he managed to grab Kerry as she prepared to empty the bookshelves at him, and circled her squirming body with steely arms. "That's enough," he said in her ear, but Kerry was beyond caring.

"If you're going to kill me, do it! Either kill me or let me go, but don't try to bore or starve me to death!" She kicked furiously when he laughed, twisting and trying to rake his face with curved fingers.

Nick lifted her from the floor and hauled her to a chair. He dropped her into it, both hands holding her wrists down by her sides so that she had to look up at him.

"Enough, I said. And don't try that again," he said in a dangerously quiet tone when she pursed her lips as if to spit. "You would not like the consequences."

"I don't like being kept in a cage, no matter how gilded it is," she said in a sullen voice.

"No. I'm sure you don't." Nick stared at her downbent head thoughtfully. "Are you ready to tell me what you were doing on the beach yesterday?"

"I told you," she said patiently, "that I was just in the wrong place at the wrong time."

"Give me details, Kerry. Why were you there? Do you go to that spot often? Did you know Garcia before yesterday? Then why did you come back to help if you didn't know him? How well do you know Milford? I thought you said you didn't like him. Would you dislike a complete stranger? Have you ever heard of me or my ship before?"

Her answers, though a little rattled, bore the ring of truth, and Nick was fairly satisfied. So she hadn't been sent by anyone, and wasn't acquainted with Garcia, but she'd witnessed his murder.

He released her wrists, reaching up to let his fingers drift along the curve of her jaw to her lips, and his gentle touch completely unnerved Kerry.

"Don't!" Her slanted green eyes widened and the thick fringe of her long lashes fluttered in alarm.

"Don't you like to have a man caress you, little one?" His warm hands skimmed over her shoulders to her arms, lifting Kerry so that she was pressed close against his body. Yielding to impulse, Nick bent his dark head and touched her lips lightly with his, experimenting. She didn't protest as he'd thought she might but closed her eyes, her head falling back. The shallow pulse at the base of her throat fluttered wildly and he couldn't resist running the tip of his tongue over the throbbing hollow.

Kerry's fingers clutched at his arms and she shivered, amazed at the deliciously heady sensations he was provoking. Kissing had never held much interest for Kerry. After letting one or two clumsy village boys tease her into a stolen kiss or two, she'd refused to try it again, hating their sweaty hands and wet lips. But this was different. She forced herself to stop enjoying it quite so much—after all, Lawton was her abductor, not her suitor.

Nick sensed her retreat and let her go. She whirled away from him to stand with wide eyes and half-parted lips, a somehow appealing figure even dressed in grimy shirt and trousers like a lad's. And he knew from the sudden lifting of her chin that she was going to fling up her defenses to cover her reaction to his kiss.

"Well?" she demanded. "Did I pass the test, Captain?"

"Which one?" A mocking smile slanted his mouth at her hiss of anger. "I believe you're telling the truth, yes."

"Then you'll let me go? You'll take me back to St. Denis?"

"No. I have to be in the Florida Keys within a month to six weeks. I don't have time to go back."

Her face fell, then she brightened. Nick could almost read the thoughts skimming through her head, and was surprised at his faint feeling of sympathy for her. He held up a palm to forestall her next volley of questions.

"Sweetheart, I'm not taking you back, and I'm not getting you passage aboard another vessel. You'll sail with the *Unicorn* to the Keys."

There was a tense silence while she digested this information, and all the color seemed to drain from her face as she struggled for control. Unable to watch her distress, he gently added, "It's not forever, little one."

"Go to hell," she said tonelessly. The Florida Keys! Good God, what would she do there? And when would he let her go?—or was she to be kept a prisoner indefinitely? The future seemed grim.

Kerry sat on the couch and stared out at the glittering waves of the sea. The *Unicorn* was headed northeast, and she knew that its probable route would be around the coast of Puerto Rico, past Hispañiola, passing between Cuba and the Bahama Islands to the Strait of Florida. A long voyage with no hope for escape or rescue.

Apparently having decided she'd had enough time to ponder the future, Nick said softly, "Wilson will bring you a tray so you won't starve. Have this mess"—he indicated the various missiles she'd flung at him earlier—"cleaned up before I return."

Kerry gazed at him with casual indifference, lashes concealing the hostile glow in her emerald eyes, and Nick left, quietly shutting the door behind him. She could hear his footsteps on the stairs leading to the deck and someone stopped to talk to him, but she couldn't quite catch what they were saying. A shrill whistle blew and there was the sound of running feet across the deck, and distant shouts and raucous voices carried on the wind.

It took a few minutes for Kerry to realize the *Black Unicorn* was preparing to take another ship. She flinched when she heard the warning shot fired across the bow. The cannon on the *Black Unicorn*'s lower gundeck erupted with so loud a crack that she jumped and almost bit her tongue.

Straining, Kerry peered out the windows to watch as the flag was shimmied down the pole and the crew of the *Unicorn* gave a roar of approval. The sharp odor of gunpowder even drifted into Nick's cabin, and the gray swirls of smoke outside finally cleared. The captured ship was small, and the next two hours until dusk were spent transferring goods to the *Unicorn*.

She should have been horrified, but instead Kerry felt a thrill of excitement. Of course, she would have felt differently if men had been killed and women raped, but none of that had happened. The *Unicorn* had simply relieved the ship of its cargo and gone on its way with a flurry of white canvas sails that far outstripped any pursuer.

"How often do you attack ships?" Kerry asked Wilson when he delivered her meal on a tray just after dark. "Once a week? Twice?"

"That depends, lass, on how often we see a ship worth takin'," Wilson answered. "Eat this first." He indicated a covered bowl, beaming with pride as Kerry lifted the lid. "I fixed it myself. Cook's too busy storin' kegs and cases. Do ye like it?"

Kerry swallowed her revulsion and nodded, not wanting to hurt his feelings. Ugh. She despised fish stew even with fresh ingredients, and the suspicious blobs floating in her bowl were not easily recognizable. "Has anyone ever attacked the *Unicorn?*" she asked, swirling her spoon in the bowl. "Or is she too fast?"

"Aye, we've been fired on many a time, but never taken. But Nicky's too smart to let hisself get blown outa th' water, no matter how temptin' the prize."

"Why do you call him Nicky instead of captain?"

"We go a long way back, lass, to when he was a green lad in leading strings. 'Course, I call him Cap'n when th' sit'ation calls fer it."

"Wilson, what's he like?" Kerry surprised herself by asking abruptly. "I . . . I mean, there are times when he seems almost as if he's a gentleman, a *real* gentleman, and then he ruins it by acting like a pirate again. Who is he?"

Hesitating, Wilson let his gaze drift over Kerry's upturned face. Surely there was no harm in letting the lass know she wasn't likely to be skewered with a cutlass or set adrift in the open sea.

"I cain't tell ye exackly *who* he is, lass, but I ken tell ye that th' cap'n's no alley rat. He was brought up proper-like, wi' all th' right breedin' on his side. Ye ain't likely to come ta any harm while yer wi' him."

"Oh?" An arched brow quirked even higher as Kerry shot him a look of disbelief. "How comforting. I'll remember that the next time he threatens me with death or dismemberment."

Wilson shifted uncomfortably and cleared his throat. "Eat up, now, there's a good lass. I'll come back fer th' tray later."

Kerry heard the scrape of the key as Wilson locked her in, and immediately threw her fish stew out the small porthole over Nick's bunk. The bis-

cuits were hard as rocks but edible, and she de-
voured them greedily. She was doomed to die of
starvation if this was any indication of the menus.
Certainly Lawton didn't eat the same fare, she
thought. Fish stew and hard biscuits were not a
meal for a lord, but then—Lawton was certainly not
a lord. Lord of the pirates, maybe, but Wilson would
definitely lose his credibility with her if he expected
her to believe another fairy tale like that one.
Breeding? Bad breeding, more than likely. Kerry
snorted derisively and dusted biscuit crumbs from
her hands all over Nick's satin quilt.

She could hear the crew above deck celebrating
their prize, laughing and singing, and someone was
playing a fiddle. An ornate French clock on a table
ticked past the minutes. Finally she got up to make
another search of the cabin. Maybe Nick had over-
looked something.

Kerry crossed to the small desk with its neatly
arranged papers and pens. Ship's instruments lay
to one side and she recognized a sextant with its
smoked lenses and a chronometer mounted in a
brass case inside a gimbaled wooden box with brass
hinges. Maps curled into long tubes were pyramided
on a slanted shelf, and tucked at the back of the
desk were two black ledgers—ship's logs, perhaps?
Kerry slid them from their resting place.

The pages crackled between her fingers as Kerry
flipped open the first book and scanned the contents.
It wasn't a ship's log as she'd first thought, but some
sort of account book written in a firm hand. Perhaps
it was an accounting of the ship's manifest and ex-
penditures which should list the cargo and its value.
Lawton wrote with bold strokes of his pen in well-
formed letters with no curls, as decisively as he
spoke, Kerry thought. There was nothing of importance though, just brief descriptions of merchandise
and location, with names written beside each entry.

She opened the second book and discovered it was almost exactly like the first one. The same names and goods were listed: Lord Sedgewick, eighty thousand pounds and silver plate, three gold candelabra worth two hundred pounds each, and more until the list covered two pages. Another name, Robert Kingsley, was below Sedgewick's, with merchandise listed beneath it.

Why would he have two sets of books? Kerry wondered. Upon closer inspection, she finally noticed the dates. It was ten years ago!

Kerry snapped the books shut and shoved them both back to the same spot, arranging them carefully so no one would notice they had been moved. There was something odd about those books, and she began to wonder for the first time just why Lawton had killed Garcia. A personal vendetta? No, it had something to do with Milford, she was sure.

When Nick returned to the cabin Kerry was curled on the couch, feet tucked beneath her and head resting on a fat feather pillow. He knew immediately that she'd been snooping, and his face was dark with anger when he whirled to face Kerry.

"What were you looking for, damn it? Answer me!" He reached out to scoop up the books Kerry had replaced so carefully. "Did you enjoy reading them? Maybe you can't be believed after all, brat!"

"I don't know what you're talking about," Kerry responded coolly. Why were those books so important? she wondered as her heart thudded against her rib cage like a trapped bird. "I wasn't looking for anything. I was just bored."

Nick narrowed his eyes at her, impaling Kerry with a piercing gaze. He locked the books in a small chest which he put into a wall safe. "Don't pry, love.

It could be very dangerous if you stumbled across the wrong thing."

His chair creaked as he sat down and unlocked a drawer, pulling out a cut-crystal decanter and glass. He slowly poured the brandy and, lifting the glass to his lips, he finally looked at Kerry.

"I thought you'd be asleep."

"You mean since I have nothing else to do?"

Dark head tilting back, Nick sipped at his drink. "I'm in no mood for an argument. Spare me your self-pity until tomorrow."

"Fine." She lay still, watching him as he swirled the amber liquid in his glass, lean fingers toying with the design cut into the crystal. His white shirt was sooty with smoke, from the guns probably, and unbuttoned to the waist. A black streak smeared his forehead and his eyes were narrowed in thought, long legs crossed at the ankles and propped in the seat of another chair.

Minutes marked by the ticking of the French clock passed slowly, and Kerry's eyelids began to droop. She fought sleep, but must have drifted off without realizing it, because Nick was shaking her awake.

"Come to bed. It's late." She blinked and tried to focus on him as he added, "There's room for two."

Nick raised her up by the elbows to hold her against him. He smelled of fresh salty sea air and brandy, and she sleepily laid her head against his chest so naturally he was startled.

He slid his palms down over the slender curve of her spine and brushed his fingertips over each tiny vertebrae, pausing at her narrow waist. The top of her head fit perfectly under his chin, and he stood holding her for a long time, fighting an unfamiliar wave of tenderness.

What was there about this ridiculous girl that attracted him? She certainly wasn't very feminine in spite of sweet curves and hollows that were defi-

nitely female; she could wield a wicked knife as his
still throbbing arm could testify; contrarily, she also
possessed a delicate aura of sensuality. A wry smile
played at the corners of his mouth. Lord, what a
bundle of contradictions she was.

As his lips pressed against the top of her head, he
slid his hands up her back to the nape of her neck
and fingered the thick masses of silky hair which
tumbled over her shoulders and mingled with the
soft inky curls on his bare chest. As he drew her
head slowly back, Nick's mouth moved whisper-soft
over the curve of her throat to the gently curving
line of her jaw, tasting his way to Kerry's lips and
capturing them in a lingering kiss. How sweet she
was, like honey or spun sugar.

Kerry's hands were somehow trapped in the
heated space between their bodies, and she was diz-
zily aware of her silent surrender to the sensual play
of Nick's mouth on hers. Hot blood pounded through
her veins at the gentle exploration of his tongue,
and her lips throbbed. Her breasts were pressed
closely against his chest as his embrace tightened,
and even through the thin material of her blouse
she could feel the solid thud of his heartbeat. Where
was his shirt? And where was her resistance? This
was no village boy who was holding her, but a full-
grown man accustomed to sensual games.

With clenched hands, she pushed against his chest
and struggled to loosen his grip until Nick snared
her wrists with one hand. Laughing softly at her,
he kissed her knuckles.

"You have the hands of a scrapper, love. Do you
fight often?" he asked with tender amusement.

"When I'm forced to it." Hostile eyes stared boldly
up at him, all traces of sleep vanished in a breath.

"Ah, I see. And do you consider yourself forced
now? I rather thought you were enjoying it."

His disarming smile made her heart beat in rapid

two-step and Kerry fought the urge to melt back into his arms. "I was just curious, that's all."

"Curious?" Dark brows rose over sapphire eyes gleaming with knowing laughter, and Kerry wanted to slap his handsome face. "Curiosity can be rewarding if one pursues it, sweet."

"Curiosity killed the dead horse," Kerry retorted.

Nick blinked and hesitated a fraction as her jumbled phrase sunk into a brain swimming in excellent brandy. Kerry pulled her wrists from his loosened grip and backed away. He laughed, shrugging his broad shoulders.

"I bow to your incomprehensible repartee, madam," Nick said solemnly, matching his words with action. "My poor tongue could never be so glib."

"I'm going to bed," Kerry said irritably.

"Excellent idea. So am I." Nick crossed to his bunk and turned back the satin quilt, throwing Kerry an inviting glance. "Well? Are you coming?"

"With you?" She stood still as a stone, eyes wide and apprehensive as Nick began undressing. He flung his shirt to the back of a chair, and his hands had moved to the buckle of his wide belt before he answered her terse question.

"There's room for two in the bunk or one in the hammock. I fought the hammock last night. You can sleep with me or tame the hammock, whichever you prefer." Black pants slid down lean-muscled legs and joined his shirt on the back of the chair. Kerry made the discovery that pirates—or at least this one—did not wear anything under their pants. Refusing to be intimidated, she crossed her arms and glared at him.

"I'd rather sleep with a tiger than you!"

"Sorry," he said in a very unapologetic voice,

"we're fresh out of tigers. That leaves you with the hammock. Good night."

The hammock was coiled up in the corner, and she managed to hang it with great difficulty. It swayed innocently, white rope mesh stretched like a smile across one corner of the cabin, and Kerry snatched several pillows from the couch and approached it with determination. She'd had limited experience with hammocks, but knew there was an art to conquering them.

Spreading the mesh, Kerry arranged her pillows at one end and lay carefully across the width, swinging her legs up slowly until she was positioned properly. She closed her eyes.

"Last one in bed blows out the lantern," said a voice from the bunk. "That's you."

Her eyes snapped open. "You do it. The light doesn't bother me."

"If I get up, I'm not getting back in this bunk alone. But if you insist . . ."

"Never mind!" Muttering vile imprecations under her breath, Kerry half-fell from the hammock and her pillows tumbled to the cabin floor. As she blew out the brass lantern, Kerry rattled its glass globe as loudly as she could before returning to the now barely visible hammock.

Somehow, probably because it was dark, she missed the right angle and the hammock immediately deposited her with a singing twirl on the rich Persian carpet. A brocade and feather projectile slapped her in the face as a pillow was ejected from the still spinning mesh. Ignoring the soft laughter from the vicinity of the bunk, Kerry once again attacked the reluctant bed, this time more successfully. Lying stiffly, she contemplated several methods of disposing of Nick Lawton, none of them foolproof.

Why had she ever tried to play hero and become

involved in a situation like this? she wondered. She should have ridden for help or something instead of being so foolish as to think she could stop a murder. Now she was on a pirate ship with a man who, so far, had only assaulted her senses. There was no doubt that he would soon tire of idle play—it was going to be a very long voyage indeed.

Chapter 5

"How'd ye sleep, lass? Like a babe, I'll bet, rockin' and swayin' in that hammock like it was yer mama's cradle, heh? Sure, an' sleep 'til noon, ye did!" Wilson placed a tray on the table and pushed his trembling spectacles back to the bridge of his nose as he turned to face the tousle-haired girl standing in the middle of the cabin.

Ah, she looked like a wild creature with that tangled coppery hair over her eyes and flowing over slender shoulders almost to her waist.

"Have a bite, lass," he said cheerfully. "It won't bother Nick none if ye don't eat, but it won't be doin' ye any good."

Kerry jerked a chair from under the table and flopped into it. "I'm sick. I don't like fish stew. I don't like ships. I don't like pirates, and I particularly don't like Nick Lawton!"

"Well now, that's a list fer thinkin' on." Wilson suited word to action and gazed thoughtfully at her belligerent face. "What d'ye like then?"

"My freedom," she answered promptly. "And Gato, and riding Diablo along the beach with the wind in my hair. Decent food. And I like baths and being clean instead of smelling like a goat."

"Mebbe I ken help ye out a bit with a couple on yer list," Wilson said. "Freedom ye'll have to ask Nick about; I can't help ye there. This ain't fish stew, but I don' know if'n ye'll call it decent. Try it afore ye make up yer mind, lass," he admonished when she wrinkled her nose. "An' I've already got yer bathwater heatin' an' a tub on th' deck."

Kerry brightened, lifting a spoonful of barely warm oatmeal to her mouth. "I'll need to borrow clean pants and shirt until I can wash mine and let them dry," she said around the oatmeal. "Anyone my size on board?"

"Aye, I'll find ye somethin' to wear," Wilson promised. "Now finish eatin' yer breakfast, lass."

Kerry wasn't at all pleased with the clothes Wilson brought her. Her delicately arched eyebrows knitted into a frown as she gingerly held up flowing green muslin.

"This is a dress!"

"Aye. An' a purty one too." Wilson directed the burly sailor who'd brought the tub to Nick's cabin to pour in more hot water.

"I don't wear dresses!" Kerry's jaw thrust out obstinately and her eyes narrowed as she glared at Wilson's back. "I hate dresses."

"One more bucket of hot water oughta do it," Wilson told the sailor, and he rolled up his shirtsleeve and stuck his elbow in the water to test the temperature as he had seen women do. "Aye, Kirby, one more bucket."

"Wilson." She tapped her foot angrily. "Wilson, I don't want this dress."

"Well, it's th' best style th' *Unicorn* has to offer, lass." He sounded aggrieved, bushy gray brows lifting and spectacles slipping to the tip of his nose. "We ain't got th' latest fashions from Paris, ye know!"

"You're not paying attention. I want," she said patiently, "trousers and a shirt. Not a dress."

"Aw, give over, lass. Ye should be dressin' in

gowns and th' like instead of tryin' to romp about
like a fuzzy-faced lad."

"Why?" She stared at him with every expectation
of an answer.

"Why?" Wilson scratched at his head and
squinted one eye. "Why? Because yer female, damn
it, that's why!" He gave an exasperated sigh at her
lip-curling glance of dismissal. "Look lass, jus' give
it a try, will ye? An' I'll give ye back yer pants an'
shirt whenever ye say."

"Now? Oh, all right," she agreed when Wilson
groaned, "I'll wear the damned dress for a little
while. But only until my clothes are clean!"

Wilson smiled, his eyes crinkling into bursts of
pleasure at the corners.

"That's th' spirit, lass, but don't ferget yer wearin'
a dress and clamber up th' riggin'. Ye'll ruin yer
image. Can ye pretend yer a lady?"

"Pretend?" Kerry struck a pose that made Wilson's mouth gape open like a lobster pot. "Why dear
me, Captain Lawton!" she purred, "this sunlight is
entirely too much on my pale skin. Ladies never go
out without their parasols." Long lashes batted several times. "Would you be so kind as to fetch one
for me, Captain?"

"I'd say ye overdid it a bit," Wilson said when he
recovered from his coughing fit. "But it's plain to
see ye know what yer about."

Flinging the gown across the back of a chair,
Kerry shrugged. "Sweet Jesus, I should. I've
watched those simpering nitwits you refer to as ladies enough to know how they coo and giggle with
all the intelligence of a stewed rabbit. I refuse to go
that damned far."

"Good." Wilson paused delicately. "An' mebbe,
lass, ye could quit swearin' like ye was in His Maj-
esty's Royal Navy. Wouldn' hurt none," he added
hastily when she shot him a look of astonishment.

"I've heard ye, and ye can outswear any pirate worth his salt "

Planting her fists on her hips, Kerry demanded, "Just what are you trying to do? Change me completely?"

"Nay, lass! Just a little." He smiled innocently.

She stared at Wilson suspiciously and informed him through gritted teeth that she would wear the gown for a short time, but that was all the change he was going to get.

"And I bloody well mean it!"

When the final bucket of hot water had been brought, Wilson retreated, taking Kerry's dirty shirt and trousers with him. Lord help him, but the girl was stubborn. Ah, but she had grit, and plenty of it. And she'd need it dealing with Nick, or he'd ride roughshod over her quick enough. Wilson smiled. It should be very interesting to sit back and watch.

Once she was alone, Kerry hastily shed the velvet dressing gown she'd borrowed from Nick, throwing it over the top of the Chinese screen. Carefully she slipped the silver necklace from around her neck and laid it in a glittering heap upon the tabletop. She touched one toe to the water in a quick test, then eased in. It had a faint musky fragrance like that of sandalwood, and Kerry shook her head at Wilson's scheming. Did he think to make a lady of her? Why? So she could charm Lawton? She hadn't a prayer even if she wanted to.

Kerry lay back with her head resting upon the high sides of the tub, long legs stretched luxuriously in front of her, and thought of St. Denis. She wondered, with a stab of homesickness, if Gato was looking for her. Perhaps Nick would allow her to send a message to the old man telling him she was

alive and not drowned in a hidden cove somewhere.

Kerry frowned thoughtfully. How awful it was
for an uncaring stranger to have control over her
days. Well, she reconsidered, it hadn't *all* been
awful. She remembered Nick's arms pulling her
into his kiss, a kiss she hadn't expected and hadn't
wanted, but had responded to with astonishing
enthusiasm.

She'd never, never, had trouble controlling her
body before, but since the fateful meeting with
Nicholas Lawton, all sorts of breakdowns had occurred. Jellied knees, hands that shook as if af-
flicted with the palsy, erratic pulse, a burning
ache in a part of her stomach that she hadn't
known existed—she felt eighty instead of eigh-
teen.

Kerry sat up abruptly. She must find a way to
escape. She was resourceful and fairly intelligent
most of the time; all she had to do was wait for the
right opportunity. It would come.

It was only when the water was quite cold that
Kerry regretfully rose from the tub, wrapping her
goose-prickled flesh with one towel and the long wet
streamers of her hair with another. Catching a
glimpse of her reflection in the long mirror on its
stand in the corner, she smiled, thinking that she
resembled a Turkish prophet swathed in stifling
robes. She pirouetted in a graceful twirl of white
cotton towel and peachy-toned limbs, eyes half-
closed, pretending she was dancing on sand-swept
dunes.

The music accompanying her solitary dance was
provided by the ship's hum of hempen lines and
snapping sails, the rhythmic creaking of square-
pegged timbers in the hull and the slap of seawater against the bow. She was the wind, flowing
with erratic whim and whispering over land and

sea, then swooping with all the fine freedom of a seabird in soaring flight. Afternoon light broken into myriad patterns by glass windows played across her body as the towels slipped unnoticed to the floor. Aware of nothing more than the moment's brief freedom provided by her dance, Kerry never heard the soft click of the cabin door being opened.

Nick Lawton stood framed in the open doorway for an instant before jerking his stunned mind into action enough to quietly shut the door. A supple, slender sea nymph with wild, wet hair like coppery seaweed swayed over the Persian carpets, toes pointing first at the floor then toward the oak-beamed ceiling.

Why had he ever thought her a rough-edged wharf brat? She was grace and beauty; a painting by Gainsborough, Pygmalion's Galatea come to life.

Slender arms formed an arc over her head as Kerry whirled, presenting him with a view of small breasts like ripened apples, firm and blushing dusky rose on the pointed crests. The ridge of her ribs slid into an incredibly tiny waist easily spanned by a man's hands before flowing in a womanly swell to the curve of her hips. Beads of bathwater still glistened on long legs with sweetly rounded thighs and shapely calves.

Panting from her exertions, Kerry paused for a gulping breath of air and reached for one of the towels lying on the couch. She paused with her hand still in midair. A pink flush smeared her cheeks with color, and Kerry's eyes were big, green smudges in her face as she saw Nick leaning against the closed door.

What was he doing here? And she hadn't heard him at all. No point in trying to hide now, he'd more than likely been watching for some time.

She lifted the fluffy towel and wrapped it around her body with precise, unhurried movements, exactly as she would have done if she'd been alone. "What do you want?"

"That's a loaded question." He pushed away from the door. The brass tub filled with scented water stood on the bare floor in the center of the room, the Persian carpet having been rolled up for safety's sake. Kerry's gown was hanging limply over the chair back next to the tub, and Nick sidestepped the tub and puddles of water as he retrieved it. "I believe this must be yours?"

"Thank you." She almost snatched it from his hand as he held it out with the faintest glimmer of laughter in his eyes. She silently damned him, wishing he would be swallowed by a whale. Why hadn't she locked the door?

Moving behind the Chinese screen, Kerry stepped into the gown. The soft muslin was cool against her flushed skin, and she was quite sure her face must be the fascinating shade of ripe plums. This was ridiculous, she mused. She had never thought twice about frolicking in a mountain pool with an entire village of men, women, and children, so why should she feel so exposed now? She'd prove how unaffected she was. . . .

Head high, she marched from behind the screen with the back of her gown sagging open.

"Here," she said, turning so that her back was presented to Nick, "lace this up for me." She held her still damp hair up out of the way with both hands.

"Of course." Warm fingers brushed against her skin as Nick tied the laces, sending tingling sparks along the ridged curve of her spine.

Kerry began to think it hadn't been such a good idea to be so casual as her knees started to quiver. "And I thought you told me you were no lady's maid," she said in a desperate attempt to keep the situation on an even keel.

"You can recall that, but you can't remember to lock the door when you bathe?" Nick asked. He tied the last lace and gently turned her around to face him. "I'd be most interested to hear your mysterious logic."

There was no point in telling him she'd wondered the same thing herself. "Wilson always knocks."

"Ah," he said, which Kerry correctly interpreted to mean he considered that a foolish reason. "As you have just learned, little one, not everyone knocks."

Nick's hand gently captured her wrist and brought Kerry so close to him with his other arm that her breasts almost brushed the wide expanse of his chest. Nick paused, attention caught by the sudden rush of breath as Kerry exhaled in a soft whoosh of air. "Look at me, love. No, up here." His hooked finger lifted her chin so that she was looking up at him, and for the first time Lawton saw an emotion resembling fear spring into the smoky depths of her eyes. What was she afraid of? Certainly not him; not yet. Not that way.

But she was afraid, not so much of Nick Lawton but of the powerful effect he was having on her. Stop it! she told herself fiercely, making a concerted effort to slow her breathing to a more normal pace. This couldn't be happening to her; it was beyond her imagination. And, oh Lord, what was he doing to her now?

"Nick . . . if you don't stop, I'll scream." It was a desperate threat which neither of them took very seriously.

"Scream," Nick said against the hollow of her neck and shoulder, "if it makes you feel better, but I can assure you no one will come running to your rescue." His lips tenderly nipped satin skin. Lean, blunt fingers slid from her wrists to her elbows and up her arms, and even through the thin material of her muslin gown Kerry could feel the heat of him like a torch. He was right of course; not one man aboard the *Unicorn* would dare lift a finger to help her.

As if drawn by a magnet, her eyes rose to meet his gaze. How could he make her feel more naked now than she had felt standing before him with no clothes at all? With his piercing eyes he stripped away more than the gown she wore and reached down to her very soul to leave her vulnerable and shaking.

She couldn't let this happen. She couldn't stand like a martyr, clasped in the unfamiliar arms of the pirate who had kidnapped and threatened her, and not put up a fight!

"Let go of my arms." Even to her ears the protest lacked conviction, so she wasn't surprised when Lawton only folded her closer into his embrace. Her gown was too thin, much too thin, and her body was pressed against his like a second skin. He wasn't exactly immune to her either, Kerry discovered, but the evidence of his desire only left her shaking. She made another halfhearted attempt to resist, then her rebellious senses spun in a trembling whirl again.

Who would have ever thought that the skin behind her ears would be so sensitive to touch, that the slow massage of a man's fingers in gentle, circular movements could be so erotic? He held her head gently with both hands, his thumbs moving to trace the outline of her half-parted lips then sweeping along the curve of her jawline back to ears the same soft pink as the inside of a seashell. She would not move, Kerry decided, would not betray herself with any reaction at all. . . .

But Nick Lawton saw in the slanted green eyes—gypsy eyes—the embers of a fire he'd kindled, and his head lowered so that his mouth was a breath away from her lips. Lightly at first, then more firmly, he brushed his lips against hers. "You've got a mouth made for kissing, love. Open for me. Like that, yes. Was that so bad?" He didn't wait for an answer, bending his head a little lower to trace the delicate arch of her throat with hot searing kisses.

Liquid fire seemed to fill Kerry's veins as Nick's kisses coaxed a dozen different responses from her stunned body. How did he know how to do that?—to make her want to kiss him and kiss him, until day drifted into night and night into day?

"Nick?" He paused while he shifted slightly to bring her body closer to his, one splayed hand spreading hot, fluid magic as he caressed the hollow of her back, his hips meeting hers. Kerry caught her breath at the hard detail of him pressing against the softness of her belly, the words she wanted to say disappearing like morning mists.

Desire shuddered through her as Nick's hands skimmed over the smooth flesh of her throat to the fine etching of her collarbone, down over honey-gold skin to the very top of her low bodice. He sensed it; pausing with his mouth against the wisps of hair fluttering over her ear, he whispered a soft acknowledgment of her reaction. He gently cupped her breast, his teasing fingers making her ache inside with shattering intensity. Why should that make her shiver as if she stood in the icy spill of a mountain waterfall? But it did, and she was burning inside and freezing outside.

Although Kerry knew this shouldn't be happening, she was past any kind of coherent protest and Nick had ceased to think of anything other than his need for her. But fate intervened in the mortal form of Wilson.

A light tap rattled the cabin door before it swung open in a smooth arc. Pausing in the doorway with a startled expression, he stared at the entwined pair embracing in a patch of filtered sunlight.

"Hullo," he said with quick recovery, one finger pushing at his spectacles. "Door wasn't locked. I see yer through with the tub."

"By nightfall, the entire ship will know that this door is never locked when it should be," Nick observed acidly. "And please, by all means, take the tub. I'm sure there are men standing in line to use it." Releasing Kerry, who was grateful instead of annoyed with Wilson, Nick crossed to his desk and sat down.

Kerry grabbed at the back of the chair next to the tub, her legs quivering like a plum pudding. Lawton sprawled in a chair with no expression at all on his face, lighting a cigar as if the world had not just rocked beneath her feet. At least he didn't know just how severely he had affected her.

Indeed, both Nick and Wilson were well aware of Kerry's reaction. It was apparent in the electric glow of her eyes, the faint pink smears staining her cheeks, and the pout of lips that were still throbbing from his kiss.

Wilson knew it would happen eventually—he'd just thought it would take longer. Of course, Nick had always been a master of seduction.

A bland smile curved Wilson's mouth, giving him the serene expression of a celestial angel.

"An' how was yer bath, lass?"

"Wet," Kerry answered, surprised to find she had any voice left at all. "Thank you."

"Don't mind me. I ken tell when I'm not wanted," Wilson said cheerfully. His benign glance slid to Nick, focused, and began to sparkle merrily. "An'

Markham said to tell ye a sail was sighted off starboard, Cap'n." *An' that ought to spike any immediate plans ye might have, Nicky lad. Wonderful entertainment. In spite of incredible odds, th' girl jus' might do.*

Chapter 6

Early morning sunlight sparkled like diamonds on blue silk when the *Unicorn* dropped anchor near the pretty island. As Kerry watched from the gallery windows, one of the ship's longboats skimmed toward the harbor. Sitting in the front of the skiff was Nick. His face was tilted toward the shore where red-roofed buildings of pale yellow, pink, and ocher thrust up among bright blazes of hibiscus and bougainvillea. Steep hills rose sharply as a backdrop to the little town nestled beside white sandy beaches and aquamarine water. The tiny seaport was obviously busy.

She watched until the skiff became indistinguishable among the other small boats bobbing close to tall-masted ships. No one had bothered to tell her which island this was and she was annoyed.

Pacing back and forth, hoping crankily that she would wear holes in Lawton's treasured Persian carpet, Kerry gave another sigh of pure boredom. Three days had passed since she'd been snatched from the beach on St. Denis and dumped in Nick's cabin like a sack of flour. Since her impromptu—and unfortunate—dance, she had not seen Nick. But where had he slept last night? Certainly not in his cabin, and if Wilson knew, he wasn't telling.

Kerry moped alone in the cabin all day, pacing the lush Persian carpet as her imagination ran amok with all kinds of dire thoughts. It was late when Wilson finally unlocked the door to bring her a tray of food.

"I'm not eating." She stood with her back to him, staring out smoky glass windows at reflected light from the setting sun, orange-gold shimmers on the sea.

"Ah, are we back to that again?" Dishes rattled as the tray clunked to the table. Wiping imaginary specks from the table's gleaming oak surface, Wilson carefully arranged several bowls and plates in exact order. "Come on, lass, an' see what I've got fer ye."

"No, thanks." A wan smile flickered on her lips as Kerry half-turned, the dying light through the windows haloing her head. The green muslin gown flowed over her curves in fluid drifts as she moved restlessly across the cabin, and Wilson was reminded of a graceful doe he had once tried to keep as a pet. Without her freedom, the doe had grown listless and refused to eat, until finally he'd had to set her free or watch her die.

"Try it, lass. This ain't th' usual," he coaxed, "but somethin' special. An' after ye eat, I thought ye might enjoy a bit of air up on th' quarterdeck."

The last caught Kerry's attention, and she tossed him a considering glance. "I can leave the cabin?" Wilson's affirmative nod brought a pleased smile and, if not ravenous at least respectable, appetite.

Watching her devour slices of fresh pineapple, mangoes, banana figs, and passion fruit, Wilson spared a thought to Nick's probable reaction to Kerry's presence above deck. He would be livid. But somehow an angry Nick was better than a listless Kerry.

"I'm ready," she announced a few minutes later, pushing away a half-empty bowl of conch stew.

At anchor, the *Unicorn* rode gentle waves in a

slight, rocking motion as they stepped onto the open deck. Fresh evening breezes skipped over the furled sails and spiderweb maze of rigging, teasing wisps of hair into Kerry's eyes and making her blink. Fading sunlight glittered dully from the ship's brasswork; lanterns ready to be lit hung from the mast. Breathing deeply, she filled her lungs with the warm salty sea air. It was quiet. Just over the gunwale and a half-mile distant throbbed a town filled with action and noise, but on the *Black Unicorn* everything was peaceful.

Wooden decks were clean and scrubbed, coils of rope lay in neat stacks, and all the articles peculiar to the smooth running of a ship were stowed away. How tidy, Kerry thought as she followed Wilson to the quarterdeck.

Several men sat cross-legged on the maindeck, tossing dice against the bulwark. Their game ceased abruptly when Wilson and Kerry emerged, and she could feel their eyes boring into her as she continued walking with her back straight and head held high. She knew what they were thinking, of course; they were thinking what anyone with a fair degree of intelligence would think at seeing a young woman who had spent three days—not counting the first one which she'd spent knocked out colder than a mackerel—and three nights in Nick Lawton's cabin. Kerry was suddenly glad that she couldn't see their sly grins and knowing winks.

"Have a seat, lass," Wilson said, "and rest yer back agin th' mizzenmast. It's a fair night, and tomorrow'll be a fair day."

Smiling her thanks, Kerry sat and rested her chin on bent knees, curving her arms loosely to circle her ankles with laced fingers. Piercing calls of seabirds echoed hauntingly overhead, punctuating the rhythmic slap of sea against the *Unicorn*'s sides. With the sun's slow descent into the shimmering

line separating sea and sky, tiny stars peppering a
deep purple heaven glowed brighter. Feeble at first,
then stronger, the pinpricks of light seemed to fill
every corner of the world, dusting even the town
with bright flickers.

"Wilson," she said after a moment of comfortable
silence, "where are we?"

"That's Christiansted, lass, in St. Croix. Pretty
town, with some of the best rum I've ever tasted."

St. Croix. What were they doing here? She'd
thought pirates usually avoided populous towns that
harbored an aversion to murder and other distaste-
ful pirate trades. Nick Lawton, it seemed, had no
qualms about going where he pleased.

On the main deck someone had started to play a
hornpipe, and lively music swirled through the air
to the quarterdeck and Kerry's ears. It reminded
her of hours spent on the docks of St. Denis when
sailors would dance the hornpipe jig, pretending to
haul rope, hoist sail, and sight land in time to the
music. Often, Kerry had been pulled from her perch
on a barrel or box and into the dance, and she smiled
at the memory.

Noting the slight shuffling movements of her feet
beneath the edges of the green gown, Wilson said,
"Th' lads play a pretty tune. It'd be a shame to leave
'em without a proper audience, I'd say." When he
saw her slight hesitation, Wilson added, "An' they
won't say a word 'bout where ye sleep or why yer
here, lass. 'Tain't one of 'em dull-witted enough to
go spoutin' like a blue whale when it's th' cap'n's
bizness."

He was right. No one would dare say anything,
and it wasn't as if she'd had a choice in the matter
anyway. Why should she be concerned about opinions of men she didn't even know? For the past ten
years she had scandalized the pious population of
St. Denis by wearing trousers, cursing like a sailor,

and disappearing into the mountains for days at a time, so this shouldn't bother her in the least.

"I'm willing to bet," she said, "that I can dance a better hornpipe than any man on board." Kerry rose in a lithe movement, facing Wilson.

A bit taken back, Wilson still managed a somewhat wary nod. "Aye, no doubt, lass. No doubt." He hesitated with brows lifted questioningly, and Kerry answered his unspoken question.

"That," Kerry said, "means I plan on dancing."

The soft glow of a lantern swinging from the mainmast played over the curious faces of the crew as Wilson introduced them to Kerry.

"This be the mate, Mr. Markham, an' this scruffy-lookin' sailor is second mate, Mr. Pepper." One by one the men were introduced, each of them nodding or saying a word in greeting, until Kerry had the names of twenty-odd men crammed into her head. Pipes, Chips, Turtle, Cook—that was an easy one— Jake, Hawk—an Indian from America she was told— and other names tangled together as she tried to place name with face.

"Let's see . . . Pipes I know because he's carrying the hornpipe, right? And you have to be Cook because you still have last night's dinner on your shirtfront." Loud laughter greeted this comment, and voices invited her to identify them by name. A few names, like Hawk and Cook, were simple enough, but much laughter and teasing assaulted the still night air as the sailors challenged her memory.

"Keep a watch over her, Mr. Markham," Wilson told the tall, fair-haired young man who was chief mate, taking him aside a few steps. "I'm goin' below fer a spell. D'ye think yè ken keep her from mischief while I take care of bizness?"

"I'm sure I can," Markham replied. Then, thoughtfully he said, "She's a bit different than I thought a casual woman of the captain's would be—younger, and more innocent."

"Shrewd observation, Markham. Ye've only seen th' lass a time or two. An' yer right. She's not what she seems." Wilson slid a glance toward Kerry, who stood gaily guessing at names, her sharp wit and quick retorts a match for any of the crew.

When Wilson disappeared below decks, Markham leaned against the smooth wood of the mainmast watching as the rough crew struck up the hornpipe and fiddle. The faltering beat of the music picked up as Kerry's bare feet skipped over the *Unicorn*'s deck, her dance somewhat hampered by the hem of her muslin gown. Lanterns sprayed light over the crew and Kerry with kindly indulgence, slightly swaying as if in time to the music and thump of dancing feet.

Markham's first disapproval faded as Kerry performed the movements of the dance with agility and enthusiasm, earning surprised shouts from the crew as they formed a half-circle to watch. Her rendition was precise and perfect, even with the green muslin tangling in her legs.

"I nevah saw a sailah in skirts," one man offered with a laugh, "but I sweah that gal has sailed the coasts of the Spanish Main!"

"Aye, mon," Kerry answered with a rich West Indies accent, "an' I can outsail any man jack of you." She eyed the men expectantly watching her, mouth curving in a saucy smile and eyes sparkling with laughter.

At anchor, the *Unicorn*'s crew kept an even more cautious watch than at sea. Pirates were known to attack other pirate vessels at the favorable hours of dusk or dawn, when the fading light made approaching vessels indistinguishable from the hazy horizon of sea and sky. For this reason, in the relatively unprotected harbor just off the coast of St.

Croix, most of the *Unicorn*'s crew had remained on board.

This was why Nick Lawton was perplexed by the crew's failure to hear his approach in the longboat.

Kerry, green skirts wadded up around her knees, was concentrating on the new steps they were teaching her. When the music stopped abruptly, she glanced over her shoulder to see the reason, mouth still curved in a smile.

Her two dance partners stumbled to a halt, grins fading at the sight of their captain leaning casually against the starboard gunwale, arms crossed over his chest as he watched. For a moment nothing was said and no one seemed able to meet Nick's narrowed gaze but a chagrined Markham, who took a step forward.

He gestured to the lanternlit main deck with a sweep of one hand. "It's my fault, sir. We were enjoying the dance and I didn't post a guard."

"Are these schoolboys who have to be told every move to make?" Lawton moved away from the gunwale and into the circle of fuzzy light, eyes raking the crew with icy disdain before coming to rest on a guilty-faced Kerry. "I shouldn't have to remind you to do your duty, Mr. Markham," he said without looking at him. "It's fortunate we happen to be so close to shore, since none of you can keep a lookout for enemy action, or even hear a jollyboat approach. I'll talk with you later."

Nodding stiffly, Markham rapped out a few terse orders and the crew rapidly scattered into the shadows. "With your leave, sir," he said quietly, then retreated with stinging pride to the foredeck of the *Unicorn,* leaving Nick and Kerry alone on the main deck.

"I left," said Nick, "with you safely tucked in my cabin. Yet I come back to find you frolicking about the decks with your skirt around your knees and the crew at your heels. Do you have an explanation?"

Her first feeling of guilt evaporated and Kerry's chin lifted a notch or two so that her eyes met his. "I don't need an explanation. Prisoners aren't responsible for shipboard rules."

"No?" A cold smile slanted his mouth. "You've been sadly misinformed, infant. Shall we go below and review your responsibilities?"

"No," she said when he cupped her elbow with his palm, jerking away as if stung. "I've been shut up in that dark, dismal cabin for four days and I like it out here where I can see the sky and feel the wind. I don't want to go below, and I don't want to 'review responsibilities' with you. I'm sure that's just another method of intimidation, and it won't work anyway, so it's only a waste of time." She paused, eyes stormy beneath knit brows, and cheeks flushed with anger. It wasn't fair that he had to return and spoil everything when she'd been enjoying herself for the first time in days. And it didn't matter that he *did* intimidate her a little bit; she'd never admit it. Nor would she admit to her oddly disturbing reaction to just the sight of his handsome face with its perfect features. He was nothing more than a wolf in a sow's ear. No. Silk purse? Sheep's clothing, that was it. A wolf in sheep's clothing to deceive the unwary.

"Kerry. You misunderstood. I am not *asking* that you go below with me, I am insisting upon it." This time his hand on her elbow was firm, fingers closing like a steel trap, and Kerry had no choice. There was no doubt that Nick would not hesitate to throw her over one shoulder like a duffel bag if she refused.

"Very well," she said with as much dignity as she

could muster, "I will come with you as soon as you let go of my arm."

After a moment's hesitation he relaxed his grip and made a sweeping bow with one arm to indicate that Kerry should precede him to the steep ladder going below. What a cheeky little brat she was, and he didn't understand at all why he hadn't tossed her overboard for fish bait. He watched the gentle sway of her hips as she strode across the deck to the hatch, and wondered how such a shrimp of a girl could be so rough and ready yet still retain an air of sensuous femininity. Kerry was a puzzle, an enigma that intrigued yet irritated him.

"Do you know," he began conversationally as soon as his cabin door shut behind them, "that under the circumstances, you are behaving quite foolishly." It was more of a comment than a question, and Kerry did not dignify it by attempting an answer. Nick strolled to his desk and removed the familiar decanter of brandy from a drawer, splashing a liberal portion into a glass. His buttonless shirt was open to the waist and tucked into snug-fitting leather trousers, baring a hard, flat chest that flexed smoothly with each movement of the brandy to his mouth. He watched Kerry over the rim of his cut-crystal glass, and knew to the instant when the tension in the cabin became too much for her.

"Damnation! When are you going to let me go?" she demanded. "You said you believe me, and that I'm not of any possible use to you as a hostage, so why don't you just put me ashore here? By the time I get back to St. Denis you could be on the other side of the world."

He lazily lifted a dark brow as he stared at the amber liquid in his glass, swirling it in a thoughtful manner. "I can't afford to have you go tripping back to Milford with information which I'm sure you've realized might be profitable to you." He ignored

Kerry's furious, incoherent protests that she didn't even *know* Milford. "The time isn't yet right for what I have in mind. Garcia's untimely death in itself isn't important, but its implications could be disastrous. No, not yet, my little pigeon." His emptied glass thunked softly to the desk top as he met her arrested gaze. "I intend for you to remain here and in my bed."

Chapter 7

"Cat got your tongue?" Nick asked softly when Kerry remained still, staring at him with dark-fringed eyes like jeweled fragments. "Relax, love. You may find you enjoy it." He reached out to let his fingers drift lightly over the sculptured planes of her face.

"Never!" She struck away the velvet touch of his fingers. "And don't call me 'love.' It sounds obscene coming from you."

"Does it? I would be greatly interested in your definition of obscene, then." His blue eyes danced with wicked amusement beneath the arch of dark brows.

"Define obscene? Easy—Nicholas Lawton." Kerry tried to match his insouciant tone. Her mouth tightened angrily and her eyes grew stormy at his low laugh. Her words were forced from between clenched teeth, "I wouldn't be so quick to laugh, if I were you. It's an apt description of your sterling character."

"Is it? And I thought you liked me, little one. I was given the distinct impression that you kissed me back yesterday."

Kerry's face flamed, hot and burning with the knowledge that he was right.

"If you were any kind of gentleman at all, you

would not sink so low as to refer to my yielding to curiosity."

"Ah, but we both agree I'm no gentleman—and you, my fiery hoyden, are no lady. No, you're not," he stated firmly when her mouth opened, "and you know it. But, then, prissy ladies have never held much attraction for me. I prefer independent females who don't hesitate to speak their minds—as long as they don't speak too loudly."

"You dissipated wretch!" Kerry's temper was strained to the boiling point. Of course she was no lady, but then she'd never claimed to be—so why was she so angry at his assertion? Why did it matter what he thought or said in that mocking voice? But it did, and she damned him again, hating him for discovering a weakness. "Damn you, you bloody pirate! You've got sheep dung for brains! You . . ."

"Please. No more dissections of my character. It becomes boring after a bit, and I'm afraid I don't have the patience to give you the polite attention you wish for. Just think about it for a short time, and you will see that you have very little choice in the situation." He leaned forward to select a cigar from his case, then drew it in a smooth motion under his nose to test its fragrance before biting off the tip and lighting it.

"So you're telling me that my future 'duty' aboard your ship is to warm your bed and be glad about it?" Her hands clenched into fists as she glared at him.

"Not necessarily glad—just quiet." Nick shook out the flame from the long match he'd used, squinting at her through the curls of cigar smoke. "I expect obedience from those on the *Unicorn*, and I usually get it."

"And when you get the unusual instead?" Kerry queried sarcastically.

"Unusual occurrences are often fatal." His soft tone somehow gave his words a menacing quality.

There was a moment of stiff silence as Nick crushed his cigar into a glass dish and reached out for her. "Why are you shivering, Kerry love?" he murmured against the side of her neck where the hair fell away in shimmering curls. "Let me warm you."

"No." She felt drugged, as if she'd smoked a pipeful of opium, her reactions sluggish instead of quick. "I'd rather walk the plank."

His light laugh was muffled as his lips moved delicately against her brow. "Pirates don't force prisoners to walk the plank, love. We just toss them over the gunwale for the sharks."

"How bloody humane you are." Oh no, if he was really humane he wouldn't be doing this, wouldn't be coaxing this unwilling response from her susceptible body. There was something dreadful the matter with her, Kerry decided, some horrifying lack of strength in her character. Why else would she meekly allow this damnable pirate to hold her in his arms as if she was a Barbary Street whore?

And why did he have to look at her with those piercing eyes that seemed to see beneath her thin muslin gown to the quivering muscles beneath? Could he hear her heart pounding and see the hot blood rush through her veins? Kerry dredged up the last of her resistance.

"I don't have the muscle needed to fight you off, Lawton. Can I appeal to your better side, or don't you have one?"

Nick laughed and said she was acquainted with his best side already.

Furious as well as frustrated, Kerry struck futilely against his broad chest. "Damn you! You've taken my freedom, why not my maidenhead as well?"

"What? Are you claiming virginity?" Nick laughed. "After living on the waterfront and being on speaking terms with every common seaman between Liverpool and St. Kitts? Now that's doing it a bit strong, sweet. With your looks and impulsiveness some handsome sailor relieved you of that bit of restraint long ago."

Lawton's mocking words froze Kerry like an icy blast of wind, and for several long moments she could only stare at him with wide eyes dark and turbulent. Holding her loosely, Nick saw her agitation in her half-parted mouth and shallow breathing. The erratic pulse at the base of her throat fluttered so wildly he impulsively laid the tips of his fingers over her skin as if to still the movement. Silky strands of hair like liquid fire drifted in a whisper over her face, falling into Kerry's eyes as she began to shake her head furiously.

Nick was just able to catch her by one wrist as she struck out at him with both hands. Her free hand slammed against the side of his face with a loud crack like a pistol shot, leaving red finger-marks against his tanned cheek.

"Kerry," he murmured softly. He easily caught her other hand and now imprisoned them both in a harsh grip. "It won't do you any good to fight, and you don't really want to anyway." Nick's mouth nipped at her arched throat in tiny bites. Capturing her jaw with one hand, he held her thrashing head still. Nick's long legs wound around hers in a vise-like grip as she kicked and bucked against him, until finally she quieted. Kerry's breath rasped harshly as she glared up at him with pinpoint lights of fury in her eyes.

"Let me go." Her voice was calm enough, even though the words were forced through clenched teeth.

"I will," Nick promised. When she stared at him

in disbelief, he grinned. "When we're both well satisfied, love," he added.

Kerry had no chance to say she would be well satisfied with him on the other side of the world, because he was kissing her again. The cabin ricocheted into a spinning whirl that left her light-headed and dizzy. Nick's searing kiss scorched her mouth with an intensity that made her breathless and weak.

No, she shouldn't be letting this happen; he was a murderer and worse. Yet even when his hands moved over the slope of her shoulders to untie her back laces with deft, efficient movements, Kerry stared at him with a detached gaze. It was as though she were outside her body watching what Nick was doing. A strange, heady sensation was flooding her from head to toe, leaving her breathless and waiting.

Letting the gown fall, Nick traced the swell of her breasts with gently exploring fingers—cupping them in his broad palms as the dark blossoms of her nipples tightened to tempting buds. A flush slid from her cheeks down to her chest with a peachy glow. Any last resistance dissolved when Nick bent his head to tease one peak with a warm tongue. The burning ache that coiled deep inside flared into an explosion of her senses, and Kerry suddenly understood why lovers were so often headstrong. Shrugging away the warning voice in the back of her mind that whispered caution, she yielded to the sweet temptation of his hands and lips.

Was this what it was all about? Was this the emotion that drove people to behave like brainless idiots at times? It swept through her in a shivering, delicious quiver, and her hands somehow were tangling in Nick's hair. She did not know what to do, what to expect him to do. She floated on the sensations he had aroused, and waited.

Nick pulled back slightly, sensing her inexperience. He could feel it in the slight trembling of her slender body so close to his, and in the tentative pressure of her kiss. A speculative gleam shone in his sapphire eyes. She couldn't be the virgin she claimed to be. No woman of the streets could be for long. And because he thought she was being deceitful, he wasted little time in gentle coaxing.

Swooping Kerry from her feet, Nick tossed her onto his wide bunk where she lay motionless, staring up at him with those sea-mist eyes that had haunted his sleep for the past three nights. Her gown was twisted beneath her, half-on and half-off, baring small, firm breasts and her narrow rib cage. The pale fire of her hair hung in silken strands over her shoulders. She was a lovely, bewitching creature who had somehow managed to capture his attention in a way very few women ever had before. How did she do that to him with just a look or a sigh? He wished he knew, for then he could combat her potent magic before it consumed him.

Slowly he reached down to untangle the knot in the satin ribbon laces that still held the gown around her waist. He silently cursed the awkwardness of his usually nimble fingers. Kerry said nothing but remained uncharacteristically quiet and still, gazing at Nick like a waiting gazelle watching a hunting lion. Ah, he wouldn't hurt her. He only wanted to taste the sweetness of her and enjoy the sensuous passion she unconsciously offered with every movement of her body.

He slid the gown down the slender curve of her thighs and calves and tossed it carelessly to the floor, leaving Kerry naked on the quilted satin coverlet, wearing only the fitful light from the gently swaying lanterns. Sliding onto the bed beside her, Nick leaned over and kissed her leisurely. There was no protest, no pulling away, but no passionate response as there had been just the day before. He raised his mouth from hers.

Kerry looked up into Nick's sun-bronzed face and at his features that were etched with passion. His desire was so much more intense than hers that it left her hesitant. Part of her swelled with an urgency to finish what had just begun, and part of her mind—the rational part—urged a desperate caution.

"What are you thinking, little one?" he asked her, cradling her face in his hand, gently rubbing his thumb over her parted lips. There was no anger in his voice, only the richness of passion.

"I was thinking that I never dreamed it would happen like this," she said slowly. "Somehow, I thought it would be different."

"Did you?" He began kissing her again, lips moving in a soft whisper over her tilted nose, down the delicate curve of her cheek, to the small cleft in her rounded little chin, and then sweeping up to her eyebrows. He murmured, "Let's make it like you imagined, love."

This time his kiss took her breath away. His mouth plundered her lips with such intensity that Kerry felt giddy and strange. She lay on the feather-stuffed pillow and watched as Nick rose from the bed and slipped out of his shirt and trousers.

Her shadowed eyes followed Nick as he crossed to the cabin door and locked it. Unlike the men of St. Denis, he was tall and lean, with taut, fluid muscles that rippled smoothly beneath bronze skin instead of bulging in knots. She was fascinated by the mat of thick curling hair that covered his chest, tapering into a vee at his narrow waist and lower. There was a paler band of skin where he obviously wore some kind of a cloth around him when he worked in the sun. Her curiosity was edged with desire as she stared at him.

"Do you like what you see?" Nick stopped just in front of his bunk, throwing Kerry an amused smile. This casual disregard for his state of undress was disconcerting.

"Of course. Why not?" she answered coolly, not for a moment giving him the satisfaction of thinking her the slightest bit embarrassed. "Although you're different than most other men I've seen, I think you're just as handsome."

Nick allowed himself no reaction other than a slight lifting of his eyebrows at her statement. Not many virgins were well acquainted with a vast number of male forms as a basis for comparison. This performance should be worthy of an audience with the Royal Theater.

He was beside her in a quick, smooth motion that was startling—crushing her mouth with his and forcing her lips apart. Allowing her no reprieve from his half-angry, half-passionate attack, Nick's fingers dug into Kerry's chin to hold her head still as he ravaged her mouth. After a brief struggle, in which she silently damned Nick and her own traitorous flesh, she felt a helpless spark of desire flare then burst into a raging fire. Unable to keep from responding, Kerry found herself kissing him back. When Nick felt her wordless surrender, he released his harsh grip on her chin, and his hands slipped over the vulnerable curve of her throat and bare shoulders. He caressed her until she trembled like a new leaf in spite of all efforts to remain still.

"You're allowed to move," Nick said against her mouth after a few moments, "and you might find it more enjoyable if you do."

"Well, how am I supposed to know that? You expect me to be a mind reader, I suppose," she added in a voice that quavered slightly in spite of her best efforts.

"No. Just honest. Kiss me back. Like this, Kerry." After a pause, "That's right. Isn't that better? You can put your arms around me, too."

Everything was whirling now, just as it had the first night aboard the *Unicorn* when she'd gotten drunk and fallen on the floor. Kerry had the same sinking sensation that she was falling. "I did put my arms around you, and I don't know how you want me to kiss." Oh, this was worse than too much wine, worse than anything she had yet imagined. . . .

Warm fingers pulled her arms up to his neck so that they crossed behind his head. Kerry tingled all down the length of her body where it was pressed so close to his. Dark curling hairs whispered like silk over her bare breasts as Nick shifted slightly. "I want you to use your tongue like this," he murmured just before his mouth met hers, and after a purring silence he lifted his head. "Wasn't that better, love?"

"Much better—than hurricanes and leprosy." At least her voice still seemed to work, Kerry thought hazily. It was a good thing she was lying down, because her entire body below her neck—no, eyebrows—was not functioning properly. Her lungs were starved for air and she was breathing in short, hard gasps; why did everything from waist to knees ache? "I think I'm sick." Nick ignored this comment just as he had the last. His lips traced searing patterns over satin skin. "It's malaria. I'm cold and burning up . . . why won't you listen instead of doing that?"

A muffled laugh fanned damply curling tendrils of hair over her ear, and Nick's voice quivered with amusement. "I have a cure for your illness, love, if you'll just be patient for a few minutes."

Patience, Kerry found, brought the most exquisite shades of color: amber, rose, sun-yellow, and turquoise—all blended in a kaleidoscope of whirling rainbows in front of her tightly closed eyes. How could anyone resist the intense magic of clever hands that knew exactly where to touch and how lightly?

Kerry felt as if she was possessed by someone else, a wild, passionate creature that had entered her body and stolen her will. Her slim arms curved around Nick's broad back with life of their own, and she didn't even recall the brain impulse that must have instigated the action. But those were her fingers that were stroking and caressing his sun-bronzed skin, pausing to examine each ridge of scars that marred the smooth expanse. Her entire body filled with a vibrant ache enhanced by each touch of his mouth or hands.

Nick's mouth, no longer ravaging but still hungry and demanding, coaxed passionate responses from warm, sweet flesh. He explored the golden curves and hollows until Kerry arched blindly upward. As desire flared higher and higher Nick's iron control slipped, and he could think only of possessing this wild creature who writhed beneath him with short, panting moans. His hands coasted over her flat belly to the red-gold triangle between her legs. His fingers pushed trembling thighs apart as he sought the satin softness between her legs.

A small cry escaped her at his first intimate touch, and Kerry's entire body went rigid with shock. Memories of tangled couples glimpsed in shadowy doorways along the waterfront suddenly burned vividly in her mind. Those images sharpened, reminding her of rutting animals and the sordidness of casual coupling like stray dogs in the alleys and backstreets. She couldn't do it. Passion vanished in a heartbeat, and wrenching away, Kerry managed to roll out of Nick's surprised hold and to the cabin floor.

She knelt on the carpet, arms and chest still partly resting on the satin covers of the bunk, and pleaded into Nick's still passion-glazed eyes, "No! I shouldn't have ... I don't want to do this with you."

Frowning, Nick seemed slow to understand at first, then sucked in a deep breath and, unexpectedly gentle, said, "Ah love, it's not so bad. I'll be slow, and not hurt you." His tenderness was disarming, and Kerry slowly yielded to the subtle promise in his eyes and soft touch. He gathered her into the strong circle of his arms again, smoothing back the fiery strands of tangled hair from her forehead and eyes, and held her body close to his.

Closing her eyes, Kerry let herself be caught up again in the sensual rhythm of his hands, his gently exploring mouth, and the sweet touch of his tongue against hers, until she felt the intoxicating sweep of desire shiver through her unresisting body. When she would have halfheartedly attempted to push him away, he caught her hands with his, pulling them down to the velvet heat of him. Kerry's breath caught in a soft tangle of air.

Even as she moaned a faint protest she instinctively caressed him. It was a heady sensation to know she could affect him as he did her, and when she felt him catch his breath and tighten the muscles in his flat belly, Kerry smiled.

"No more, love, or I'll hurry what should be slow," he muttered hoarsely while moving so that he lay partially over her. Nick's hand slid up her thigh to the womanly swell between her legs and lightly caressed until she moaned softly and arched against him. All coherent thought vanished. Nothing was left but the desire to possess her, and to feel her sweet, velvet warmth wrapped around him. Nick slid over her, his mouth capturing her lips as his body pressed close.

Kerry rose to meet Nick in a hazy mist of desire and longing for an ending to the aching need inside. There was a sharp, hard pressure and she stiffened, her eyes opening wide at the discomfort, but Nick soothed her with soft murmurs and gentle caresses until she relaxed slightly. Still, Kerry wasn't quite prepared for pain that accompanied his next thrust and involuntarily cried out, immediately biting her lip to keep from doing it again.

Not pausing, Nick eased deeper inside her. He was sweating from the effort of holding back, but once inside he was still, not wanting to hurt her any more than he already had. So she hadn't lied about being a virgin, and oddly enough he wasn't surprised.

"Is it over?" came a small, disgruntled voice, and he laughed softly into the fragrant mass of her hair spread upon his fat feather pillow.

"No, love. It's just begun, but I can assure you that now it will be better."

She was stunned by the growing wave of pleasure that began a few moments later when Nick began moving inside her again. It was like a tidal wave, growing higher and higher until it threatened to engulf her in drowning waves of intensity.

Kerry's soft body and feverish passion infected Nick with an urgency he would never have believed he could feel. Driven by nameless emotions he didn't dare think about, he rocked against her until he could stand it no longer. He wanted to fill her, brand her as his possession, and take her with such passion she would belong to him forever. And she seemed to sense it as she rose to meet him, clinging to him as if she couldn't get close enough, calling his name in soft, husky cries.

Then it was over in a bright burst of the most exquisite ecstasy, and Nick was pulling away and holding Kerry in cradling arms. She was trembling, with the dark fan of her lashes lying on flushed cheeks in a thick fringe that hid her eyes from him. Nick smiled, remembering the day he'd first seen her. Who would have thought that beneath those shapeless clothes and that dirt-smudged face beat the heart of a passionately responsive woman? His arms tightened and she opened her eyes and gazed up at him through half-closed lids.

"It wasn't as bad as I'd heard," she commented drowsily, "though it wasn't very pleasant at first."

Amused and slightly disgruntled by her candid observation, Nick said, "I suppose that's as close as I'll get to a compliment."

Kerry's eyes opened wide. "Oh? Do the women you force into your bed generally thank you afterward?" A sudden sadness rose to almost choke her, and the realization that she had yielded so easily pricked sharply. "You have some very strange ideas about certain things."

"I'm not alone. By no stretch of the imagination could you say I forced you, Kerry." An unpleasant smile curled the corners of his mouth.

"You know I had very little choice!" Kerry was shaking with anger. "You practically threatened me."

" 'Practically' would not hold up in any decent court, Kerry. I'm guilty of seduction, yes, but not rape. And unfortunately for you, seduction is not a hanging offense."

"But murder and kidnapping are, you bloody pirate! And that's in the law books of every country!" she flashed, and was immediately sorry she'd said it. Sapphire eyes drained of any warmth stared at her so coldly she could feel their chill. Kerry swallowed the huge lump in her throat with difficulty. "I . . . I . . . only meant . . ."

"I understand perfectly what you meant," he cut in, flicking her with an indifferent glance as he rolled from the bunk. "It hardly bears explanation. Since we've established the deficiencies in my character, why don't we begin with yours. No? How cowardly of you, but probably very wise." Reaching into the tall armoire he pulled out his velvet robe and slipped it on, deftly tying the sash. "For someone who is usually so outspoken, you've grown very quiet, my dear."

"Are you never satisfied?" Kerry sat cross-legged in the bed clutching the satin edge of the quilt to her neck, glaring at him. "I talk too much or not enough; I refuse to share your bed or I give in."

Nick shrugged and turned his back. "None of which matters worth a damn to me. You're here, willing or not, and in spite of anything you may say about it, here you will stay until I suggest differently. And as murder and kidnapping are among my more endearing traits, I would suggest prudence to you most vigorously." Damn her, it shouldn't make a difference to him at all how she felt, or where she wanted to be, but it did. A feeling of frustration mingled with exasperation as Nick stared at the swaying brass lantern just above his head. What had happened to his normal detachment, his ability to remain indifferent to even the most winsome female? And how had *this* female, of all the many he'd encountered, managed to worm her way into his conscience? It was ridiculous, and he resented those guilty twinges that seemed to assail him at the most inopportune moments. Well, he'd learned long ago not to care too much about anything or anybody, and this would have to be the same.

Nick turned back to face her with a smile that sent a shiver rippling down the curve of her spine, and Kerry closed her eyes. Damn her too-quick tongue! Escape from the *Black Unicorn* and Nick Lawton had never seemed more impossible. Or more imperative.

Chapter 8

The *Unicorn* was three days out of St. Croix when Kerry was given her chance to escape. Late one afternoon the cry of "Sail ho!" echoed down from the crosstrees. Immediately the thud of bare feet sounded on the main deck as the crew scurried to their stations to await the verdict of friend or foe.

"She's a two-masted schooner lyin' low in the water an' flyin' no colors," Wilson observed from the gallery windows in Nick's cabin. "An' she 'pears to be ready fer action."

"Does that mean a fight?" The copper-bright head shifted to one side to see the ship, one hand resting on Wilson's shoulder as she tried to peer past him. Kerry, wearing shirt and trousers again, to Wilson's sighing dismay, climbed up onto the couch beneath the windows to see better.

"Aye. If they answer a challenge or give one, it'll mean a fight quick enough!" Excited, Wilson shifted from his position over the couch, getting up to hurry to the cabin door.

"Wilson!" Kerry caught up with him, gripping his shirtsleeve and holding him fast. "What about me?"

"Ye'll be fine, lass. Jus' fine. Won't none of us fergit yer here, so don't be worryin' 'bout that." He aimed a comforting pat at the hand on his arm before prying loose her fingers and throwing a smile in her general direction. He slipped out the cabin door and closed it behind him.

Resigned, Kerry turned toward the windows. It occurred to her as she stared with growing apprehension at the fast-approaching ship, that she had not heard the familiar grating of the key in her cabin door when Wilson left. Had he, in all the excitement and hurry, forgotten to lock it?

Her head swiveled slowly to stare at the door. In the past three days she had been left alone in Nick's cabin. She had no idea where he'd been staying. Certainly not with her. During that time, with Wilson's profound apologies for Nick's command, the door had remained securely locked.

Kerry's heart began to pound more rapidly. What good would an unlocked door do her aboard a pirate ship miles away from land? As much good as the rarely used launch swinging from davits at the *Unicorn's* side, a small voice inside her head whispered. Ah, the launch; it was a larger vessel than the jollyboat, and more seaworthy. Surely, in the confusion accompanying the preparations for a fight, she could manage to loosen the ropes and escape in the boat.

A loud explosion racked the air, tilting the cabin and sending Kerry sliding to the floor among satin and lace pillows. That was no warning shot but an entire battery of cannons, she thought dazedly, recalling the last short battle. Another explosion, followed by the watery hiss of a ball streaking the waves just past the *Unicorn's* stern had Kerry scrambling to her feet. She moved toward the door. It swung open as easily as if it had just been oiled, and Kerry gave a short nod of satisfaction.

The *Unicorn* trembled again as the carronades barked in a growling roll like thunder, and Kerry reeled into the deep-shadowed passageway. Gunpowder filled the air with acrid stench that wrinkled her nose, and a heavy haze of smoke stung her eyes as she felt her way along. This was insanity, the stuff of nightmares, but there was no time to yield to fear and she forced back the memories that threatened to undo her. The open hatch overhead framed brief, moving portraits of armed men racing over the decks wielding gleaming cutlasses, dying rays of sunlight glinting in sparks from the naked blades. Sharpshooters clung to the rigging like spider monkeys, guns primed and aimed at the decks of the other ship, and Kerry heard the scrape of iron grappling hooks being readied. They intend to board her then, she thought just before the *Unicorn* ploughed into the enemy vessel.

Shouts and curses mingled with gunfire and the clang of metal as the *Unicorn*'s hull struck, and the shuddering crash threw Kerry against the wall where she slid to the floor. Bright lights flashed in front of her eyes as her head hit the hard edge of the ladder, and sharp pain knifed with cutting precision along her hairline. Something warm and wet was trickling over her forehead and into her eyes, and Kerry put up a shaking hand. She frowned at the crimson smears staining the tips of her fingers, barely visible in the fading light.

The torn hem of her long shirttail made an excellent bandage, and she coiled it around her head. Battle sounds still raged, even louder than before though the big guns had ceased. The smoke was much thicker, burning lungs as well as eyes, and Kerry made her way determinedly up the ladder to the deck.

Her bare feet gritted against sand that had been scattered over the decks so that the men would not lose their footing in the gore of blood that so often smeared battle-thick main deck, foredeck, and quarterdeck. The maze of boarding nets strung from ship to ship cast gridlike shadows that swayed with each

roll of the *Unicorn.* Panting, cursing men fought
hand-to-hand with razor-edged swords, cutlasses,
and axes, and Kerry stared in horrified fascination.

There wasn't a single man she recognized, for they
all looked the same, with bare chests and sweat-
glistening muscles. She couldn't even tell which side
was winning.

Two men locked in fierce combat hacked their way
toward her across the slippery decks. Kerry ducked
behind a lashed-down barrel, her smokey eyes wide
as they strained and grunted within a foot of her.
One of them sunk his long knife into the other,
burying it up to the jeweled hilt in the other man's
chest. He died without a sound, eyes wide and
mouth slightly open, crumpling to the deck grating
in a peculiarly graceful motion. The victor retrieved
his weapon with a quick jerk, and without a backward glance slashed a path through a heaving knot
of men fighting near the starboard rail.

Swallowing the sudden bitter taste in the back of
her throat, Kerry gazed down at the dead man. She
didn't know him, he meant nothing to her, but a
split-second flash of another body lying on the foam-
covered decks of a sinking ship so long ago prompted
her to action. She knelt, and a trembling hand
closed the sightless eyes while some long-remem-
bered prayer was muttered yet lost in the noisy me-
lee of the battle.

As she stood, Kerry's clouded gaze skipped over
the body, riveting on a pistol stuck into the bright
blue sash he wore as a belt around his waist. A pistol. And his short sword was still gripped in lifeless
fingers.

"You won't need these anymore," she murmured
by way of an apology for stealing from the dead,
"and I probably will." She plucked the pistol from
his sash and grimaced as she wrested the blood-
stained hilt of the sword from fingers bent in a death

grip. The pistol was jammed into the waistband of her trousers and hung there, heavy and cold against the bare, shrinking flesh of her hip.

Armed now, and with mustered courage, Kerry stepped from behind the relative safety of the huge oak barrel and into the gray twilight near the capstan. The mizzenmast was behind her, the mainmast not far ahead, and the launch that would take her to freedom, was—hopefully—swung over the side amidships.

The fighting seemed heaviest near the foredeck, but Kerry could not avoid it if she wanted to get away.

Passing the capstan, which was nearly as tall as she was, Kerry saw a body draped over one of the six spokes jutting out from the hub. She blanched when she recognized the bloody face of Kirby, the man who had brought her bathwater only a few days before. Dodging a pirate who was staggering backward, she skirted the hatch leading below to the gundeck and paused in the curve of the main fife rail. Standing between the straight bar of the monkey rail and the crescent-shaped fife rail, she took a deep breath. The tall spire of the mainmast rose just in front of the monkey rail, and beyond that were the cradles that normally held the ship's small boats.

All her earlier courage wavered for an instant as she stared around her, and Kerry grabbed hold of the monkey rail for support. It was a scene from hell; reddish-orange flames spurted from pistol barrels and steel blades glittered dully in light from lanterns, while the acrid stench of gunpowder and gray clouds of smoke lay in a shifting blanket over the decks. Screams of dying and wounded men mingled with bloodcurdling shouts and hoarse curses, punctuated with the staccato shots of pistols and rifles and the harsh clang of steel ringing against steel.

Kerry's grip tightened on the sword hilt, and her other hand rested on the smooth butt of the pistol stuck in her pants as she started toward the port gunwale.

She'd taken no more than a half-dozen steps when a burly pirate appeared in the hazy gloom, blocking her path. A huge gold earring dangled from one earlobe, catching sparks of lantern light and Kerry's attention. It was all she had time to notice before he was swinging at her with a wicked downstroke of his sword.

Quickly sidestepping, Kerry instinctively made a half turn and swung her shorter sword in an upward slice that caught the man off-guard. The blade cut through the leather of his open vest and into bare skin stretched over the ribs beneath before he could recover from his forward impetus. Not giving him time to do more than emit a sharp hiss of pain and fury, Kerry pivoted on the balls of her feet to jab her sword point into his chest.

Revulsion coursed through her as the pirate clutched at his chest where the blood spurted in crimson geysers. His knees buckled, sending him toppling forward to the deck. She'd killed a man, and even the thought that he'd intended to kill her didn't assuage the sudden burden of guilt. In all her playacting on the docks of St. Denis, the mock battles with indulgent sailors as opponents, Kerry had never really thought she might one day take another life.

But now there was no time for contemplating the consequences if she wanted to live, for another pirate, with swarthy features and a brilliant red scarf wound around his head, faced her with a drawn cutlass. The jagged scar that ran from the hairline above his left eye to his chin made his grin hideous.

A blank socket stared emptily where his left eye should have been, and the left corner of his mouth was permanently pleated into a frown while his lips on the right side curled upward. He wore only a pair of white trousers that would have been dirty even without the bloodstains covering them, and a wide strip of material that matched the head scarf circled his waist.

Kerry backed away slowly, heart racing and her mouth so dry it felt as if she'd swallowed a cup of sand. She was shaking so badly the tip of her sword was trembling. The cacophony of hellish battle sounds faded as Kerry saw the merciless gleam of murder in the one dark eye that was as black and friendly as a snakepit.

The grinning pirate followed Kerry's backward flight with sure steps, cutlass swishing in a slow, unhurried motion. He was confident of victory over the lad who faced him. The coupled ships rolled with a swell and a gust of wind snatched greedily at the long hair of his foe, and the pirate frowned at the obviously feminine gesture with which the red-gold strands were pushed from narrowed eyes. This was no clumsy, youthful pirate, but a girl! And a pretty one at that, he finally noted, dismissing the bloody bandage around her head and the shapeless shirt and trousers.

"Ah, sweetheart, I've a much better sword to be pokin' ye with," he said, "an' all ye have ta do is lay down yer wee pricker fer a short space."

"Like bloody hell I will!" Kerry tightened her grip on the sword hilt and its quiver steadied. She lifted her chin and glared defiantly at the pirate. "If you want my sword," she said, "come and get it. I'll see that you get two feet of cold steel where it will do you the most good."

The man's expression altered from malicious glee to fury in the space of a heartbeat, and he advanced with expertly slashing cutlass. There was no element of surprise on her side this time, and Kerry found herself parrying blows that almost sent her to her knees with their force. She was far outclassed and she knew it, silently stumbling over the unfamiliar words of that long-forgotten prayer as she prepared to die.

Glimpsing the murderous downswing of the long blade as it rushed toward the vulnerable curve of neck and shoulder, Kerry flung herself forward and to the deck in a last desperate surge, rolling like a log to knock the pirate from his feet. He skidded on his knees and the palm of one hand, somehow managing to retain his cutlass as he struggled to keep from tumbling down the steep hatch between capstan and fife rail.

While he regained his balance, Kerry scrambled to her feet, searching frantically for the sword that had flown from her hand, but it was too far away to reach. Desperate, and seeing from the corner of her eye that the pirate was stumbling to his feet, she seized a stout belaying pin from the fife rail and stepped forward to crack it across the back of his head. Cutlass clattering to the aft deck, he pitched forward through the open hatch without a word, crashing heavily on the gundeck below.

Not wasting a moment, Kerry scooped up his weapon and bounded in the direction of the port gunwale, her breath coming in dry gasps for air. If just one more man got in her way, she would slice him to ribbons! Everywhere there was death, screams and curses, guttural shouts, and so many other frightening sounds that she couldn't think. She had to get away, even if she had to leap over the gunwale and swim for shore. Anything was better than this nightmare.

Slipping and half-sliding at times over slick decks, Kerry, spurred by fear, pushed her way forward through inky shadows that swarmed with pirates. Finally her hand touched the rail and she scanned the area for the launch. Her eyes filled with tears when she didn't see it. Crushing disappointment made her want to collapse in a heap and burst into tears, but there wasn't time enough for that.

The *Unicorn* was rolling more heavily and the waves were growing higher. She had difficulty keeping her balance. She spun around and crossed the short distance between gunwale and boat cradles. Blinking, Kerry took a moment to realize that the launch was not in its cradle. Had it been used? Or was it already lowered? she thought suddenly.

Racing back to the gunwale, she leaned over as far as possible, squinting into the dark swell of the sea, finally spotting the bobbing launch tied to the ship. A rope ladder swung over the side, beckoning limply. Kerry didn't wait for opportunity's knock before seizing her chance.

She had already hooked one leg over the rail when harsh hands jerked Kerry back and threw her to the deck. She scrambled up only to be knocked back down. Her tormentor stood with his back to the lantern; his face was in shadow, but the golden light flickered from the length of steel in his hand.

Damn it, where was her cutlass? It had fallen from her hand when she'd sprawled on the deck the second time. Scooting backward on elbows and hips, she felt cautiously on the littered deck for the weapon. She remembered the pistol still stuck in her pants, but pistols often had a tendency to misfire if the powder was the slightest bit damp.

But it was better than nothing, she decided in the next instant when the pirate looming over her like Judgment Day took a menacing step forward. She fumbled with shaking fingers for the butt of the heavy pistol and, pulling it from the waist of her trousers, she aimed it in the general direction of his chest. Her thumb tightened on the hammer just as she heard a familiar voice swear dreadfully and tell her to put it down.

It was too late. A deafening explosion ripped through the air and the recoil sent a bruising shudder through her arm as Kerry stared up in horror. Nick.

Chapter 9

No. A thin scream formed in her mind, welling in intensity and pitch until all Kerry could hear was its shrill echo reverberating inside her skull. The decks of the *Unicorn* seemed to waver and fade, leaving only the sharp smell of sulphur and the drifting curl of smoke from the pistol. The shadow that was Nick had disappeared.

Surging to her knees, pistol still clutched in one fist, Kerry stared blankly at the empty deck where he had been. Her mind could not accept the fact that she'd shot Nick or that he'd vanished. And, oh God, she hadn't meant to. As angry as she'd been with him, she hadn't really wanted to kill him. It was a mistake, and she would give anything to undo the trip of that hammer.

Hot tears prickled like grains of sand in her eyes and blurred her vision so that the scenes in front of her were viewed through a veil of gauzy mist. Puppet figures jerked in the motions of combat as if pulled by strings. It wasn't real, only absurd theatrics.

That's why when she heard the low voice behind her as the pistol was snatched from her hand she was slow to react. It was all a play, an illusion that would fade.

"Your aim is bad and you had too much powder,"

the voice was saying harshly. "Stick to swords. You do much better with those."

A hand grabbed the back of her shirt and lifted her from the deck to her feet, shaking her roughly so that snarled streamers of red-gold hair whipped across her face in stinging slaps. Before she could recover from this unexpected event, she was half-dragged across the rolling deck, right arm held in a hurting vise. The world began to slowly focus again as Kerry realized that somehow she had missed Nick with her shot, and that he was furious. It would be no use to try an explanation now, not with his temper raging as fiercely as the battle.

Nick pulled Kerry behind him, the lethal steel of his sword effectively removing any obstacle from their path, as he fought his way back to the hatch on the aft deck. Half-stumbling in his wake, she was slung forward and into the yawning black void with as much regard as a bundle of rags.

When Nick shoved wide his half-open cabin door with a booted foot and jerked Kerry in after him, the French clock on its carved cherry table was just striking the quarter hour. For a moment she stared, green eyes huge and disbelieving, then began to laugh. A quarter hour. She had been gone from this cabin only a quarter of an hour and it had seemed like a lifetime. It had been a lifetime.

Laughter turned to sobs and Kerry sank to the Persian carpet, her shoulders shaking and her palms pressed over her nose and mouth.

"Oh, for Chrissake," she heard Nick mutter, *"now* you cry!" His fingers relaxed their iron grip on her arm and he crossed the cabin to his desk, pulling out his crystal decanter of brandy and a glass. "Here," he snapped a moment later, "drink this."

He shoved the cut crystal into her shaking fingers. Amber liquid spilled over her fingers and wet her blouse, but most of it burned a path down her throat and into her stomach. Gasping and half-choking, Kerry gave him back the empty glass.

"I'll be back," he said softly. "Be here."

"Nick . . ."

"No. Not now. I don't have time for it. Just be here when I return, Kerry."

The closing door cut off any reply she might have made, which was unlikely. All her instincts urged silence.

As she sat on the carpet too tired to move, the sounds from above began to grow more faint, until finally there were no more cries or clash of swords. Forcing herself up, Kerry dragged to the couch and stared into the deep purple shadows of dusk. The stern lights of the other ship were close enough to see the tiny flames flickering inside the glass globes, and as her gaze moved from aft to fore, she saw the shimmy of enemy colors being struck from the mainmast.

The flag had a field of black emblazoned with a grinning death's-head and crossed cutlasses in stark white. Did the *Unicorn* boast a similar roger? Pirates all seemed to prefer the macabre design of skull and crossed bones or cutlasses, though some favored more distinctive ensigns. How imaginative were Nick and his crew? Maybe they flew a roger with victims impaled on the horn of a grinning unicorn.

Kerry rested her head on the smooth, cool wood of the windowsill. Her head hurt and somehow she'd burned her fingers. There was blood all over her clothes, which were torn and ripped in several places, and gunpowder soot smeared her hands. Everything hurt; muscles and joints screeched a protest at each little movement and bare feet were scraped raw by the rough boards of the deck. But in spite of all that, she fell asleep with the noise of pirates boarding a captured enemy ship as a lullaby.

"Amazin'," said Wilson, shaking his head as he stared down at Kerry's peacefully sleeping face. "I swear ye could have knocked me over with a feather when I seen her on that deck with a bloody sword in her hand, Nick. An' she fought like a blinkin' tiger, too!"

"I saw her." Nick leaned his head against the back of the loveseat and crossed his legs at the ankles, then gazed across the cabin at Kerry through half-lidded eyes. "It's a miracle she's not dead."

"Dead, is it?" Wilson chuckled and scratched his bald head. "It's a miracle she didn't kill ye with that pistol shot, that's what it is!"

Nick flashed him a sour look. "And there's always the miracle of the unlocked cabin door," he reminded softly.

"Aye. That were a bit of a miracle," Wilson agreed blandly. His pale blue eyes registered only mild interest in the subject, though he did add thoughtfully, "I wonder what would've happened if she'd managed to steal th' launch."

"A launch that was conveniently left at the *Unicorn's* side. Did you think I couldn't keep her safe?"

"Ah, Nicky. I've got all th' faith in th' world in ye, lad. There was niver a bit of doubt that ye'd win th' fight and we'd all be cozy as hermit crabs in a seashell."

"Then why the launch?" Irritation rough-edged Nick's voice and the jeweled sapphire eyes were sharp enough to pierce the old man's hide. Affection and years of loyalty bound them together, but by all the saints, there were times when Wilson's intricate machinations drove him to fury.

"Why the launch? It's always interestin' to see how plucky some people are, an' ye've got to admit,

Nicky, that it took plenty of backbone to fight her way 'cross that deck to the gunwale. She'd a' made it too, if'n ye hadn't showed up right then." An innocent smile. "Ain't ye th' least bit proud of her pluck?"

"No." He stood up in a lithe motion, well-knit muscles flowing in perfect rhythm as he crossed to the Belgian desk and the crystal decanter of brandy. A second glass followed the first, then a third, and some of his tension eased.

"That's fine liquor to be drinkin' like it was new rum, lad," Wilson observed. "Celebratin' our prize?"

Nick shrugged. "I would be if it had been Sedgewick's ship we netted. All others are insignificant."

"Ah, Sedgewick. Th' jackal of th' seven seas." Wilson joined Nick in a glass of brandy and the cabin was quiet except for the ticking of the little French clock and the muffled noises of the jubilant crew overhead. Lord Sedgewick was a powerful enemy. He had the King's ear when George was in his lucid moments, and the regent's ear when he wasn't. Sedgewick's spiderweb of intrigue fanned out over the seas to involve anything that was remotely profitable. Nick had proof that he backed several pirate ships and received a share of their plunder, but that wasn't enough. There had not been, anywhere on this globe, someone who would testify to the innocence of a young officer who had been commissioned in the Royal Navy ten years before, and who had been falsely accused of stealing and selling a ship and her cargo. The young officer had been convicted on the testimony of his commander and forced to flee his native England. No one had been inclined to listen to his claim that the high-ranking commander had engineered the theft and reaped the profit. Nicholas Lawton, next Earl of Devlin, had been that young officer, and Lord Sedgewick the commander.

The years since then, Wilson reflected, had been both hard and good. For a man with courage and ingenuity, it had been fairly simple to obtain letters of marque and sail as a privateer for the government of the United States. Their navy was small and grateful for experienced men, and willing to turn a blind eye to small indiscretions visited upon vessels from a foreign power. It had worked out well. Sailing under the protection of a strong government, Nick was still able to search for proof of Sedgewick's duplicity. But God forbid that the *Unicorn* should ever meet the *Revenge*, Wilson thought, for he didn't know if Lord Sedgewick would live through the encounter.

He examined the hard, perfect features of Nick's face. The man looked as if he had been carved from a block of fine Italian marble, and was just as cold and unfeeling. But Wilson knew better, for he could remember that young lad with the ready smile and generous heart. Somewhere inside that taut-muscled frame existed the old Nick, and Wilson intended to free him.

"Are ye goin' to wake her?" Wilson asked with a nod of his head in Kerry's direction. "Or do I?"

"Have you never heard the axiom about letting sleeping dogs lie? Snoring curs don't bark or bite." Nick flicked Wilson a sardonic glance.

"Aye, I've heard it. An' why have a dog that won't do what it's meant to, I ask ye?"

"Are you by any stretch of the imagination," Nick drawled, "suggesting that she does anything at all she's supposed to do? A novel idea, but alas, an exercise in futility to even hope for such."

"Don't come off th' highborn swell with me, Nick. I ain't in th' mood to suffer it quiet-like." In spite of his words the tone was friendly. "I'll send ye down some carron oil."

Nick's question caught him at the door. "Why do I need carron oil, may I ask?"

"Th' lass burned her fingers on that miserable excuse fer a pistol when she tried to shoot ye" was the placid answer, given just before the door shut behind him.

"Wonderful," Nick muttered. "I'm to bandage the girl who tried to shoot me. I wonder what Wilson would do if the hangman strained his arm putting a noose around my neck."

He walked to the couch and stared down at the girl sleeping with one hand curled back against her cheek like a child's, and reached down to readjust the pillow that had half-slipped from under her head. She looked like a grubby little girl who had been out all day fashioning mud pies under the spreading branches of an oak tree.

The white strip of cloth around her head was crusted with dried blood, and a smear of soot streaked her nose as well as her hands. Her copper hair was matted with blood and sweat, hanging in tangles over her shoulders. It had been that bright head of hair that had caught his attention on the aft deck, sticking out in the hazy gloom of swarming pirates like a banner. He had no idea how long she'd been on deck before he saw her, and one of his crew had noticed Kerry at almost the same time.

"Jeezus, Cap'n!" Jake had exclaimed. "Would you jus' look at th' game little beggar? She's a fighter, she is!"

If he hadn't been so damned worried that she'd be killed before he could get to her, Nick might have been more admiring of her rather clumsy skill with a sword. A rueful smile touched the corners of his mouth. What a complex, irritating, fascinating little wretch she was, and yes, he agreed with Wilson's conclusion that she had plenty of pluck.

But she also had an overlarge measure of stubborn defiance. There was only one master aboard the *Unicorn,* and until she recognized that fact there would be problems.

Chapter 10

"What're you doing?" Drowsy and irritable, Kerry pushed impatiently at the damp cloth someone was sliding over her face. "Lemme sleep."

The cloth lifted from over her eyes at the same time as Nick's voice sounded just above her left ear, and Kerry's lids snapped open. "Even if you don't mind being filthy and bloody," he said, "I mind. It offends my eyes. Be still. And be quiet," he added when her mouth opened to protest. "It would be a great pity to get soap in your mouth."

Kerry's lips pressed tightly together. He would just *love* to get soap in her mouth, so there was no point in pushing her luck. She stared up at him, with the thick fringe of her lashes slightly lowered in an effort to hide the anxiety she was sure would show. The thought that she'd almost killed him kept rolling around in her head like a child's ball in a box, aimlessly bouncing from one side to another. What if she had killed him? The *Unicorn*'s crew would have certainly taken their revenge, but that was less important than the knowledge that she didn't want him dead. She should. He'd kidnapped her, threatened her, and seduced her, and she should be satisfied to see him suffer for it, but some strange part of her was glad he was alive.

"Give me your hands, Kerry." Nick's voice jerked her attention away from his blue eyes with their

gemmed perfection, jewels in a setting of sooty
lashes. She glanced down at her hands, which, she
just noticed, had begun to throb.

"They're a funny color. Ouch! What are you
doing? And what is that smelly stuff?"

"This 'smelly stuff' is called carron oil. It's for
burns."

"Carrot oil?" Her nose wrinkled. "It doesn't smell
very much like carrots."

"Carron. As in carronade; you know, one of the
big guns on the gundeck. It's a mixture of limewa-
ter and linseed oil, used mostly by the gunners because of frequent burns from firing the ordnance."
His smile was nasty. "I'm surprised you didn't aim
one of those at me."

"It was too heavy." A brilliant smile flashed. "But
if you feel the least bit slighted, I could make the
effort."

"Ah, that sparkling wit never stops, does it?" His
finger traced a path from her left ear to the tip of
her nose. "Even," he said softly, "when you are in
a very precarious position."

Her smile wavered and she concentrated on the
raised, reddened patches on her hands where she'd
been burned by the pistol's discharge. He was always reminding her of the "precarious position" she
was in, but she was well aware of it already. If anything, her futile attempt at escape had only made
it worse.

"I know you're angry with me because I tried to
get away," she began, but was interrupted by a
murmured "How astute of you," before she could
continue. "But," she went on doggedly, "I'd think
you could understand my reasons. Wouldn't you try
to escape someone who was keeping you prisoner?
Even a velvet prison is still a prison."

"While I readily concede your point, child, you
must understand that, naturally, I am looking at it

from the captor's point of view." He continued his brisk rubbing of her hands with the carron oil, his mouth stretched in a curve that had all the menacing charm of a shark's toothy smile.

"Naturally." Purple-shadowed eyelids drooped wearily and Kerry gave a sigh of resignation. "No chance, I suppose, that you'll feel merciful any time soon?"

"None," he agreed, "but you are welcome to try suitable forms of persuasion."

The eyelids snapped open. "Oh, you'd love that, wouldn't you! No, thanks. I'd rather die first!"

"Kerry, Kerry. You're so melodramatic when a simple refusal would do." He didn't attempt to hold the hands she jerked from his grasp and looked down at the smears of carron oil on clean trousers recently purchased in London's Bond Street. "But," he added while blotting at the oily stains, "I can easily arrange your demise if you insist."

"How charitable. I wouldn't want to strain your good nature, however, so I'll refuse." Damn him for a cold-blooded bastard without a single drop of charity in his soul! "It would be easier," she added angrily, "if you would just give me your permission to leave though, because I intend to get away from you and your ship any way I can!"

He glanced up, and Kerry caught her breath at the smoldering glints in his blue eyes. Be careful, she cautioned herself silently, you're treading water eighty fathoms deep.

"I think," Nick said in that pleasant tone that made the hair on the back of her neck prickle, "that you need to learn the value of thought before action. It could save you a great deal of trouble in the future."

It was one of those statements that didn't invite an answer, and Kerry wisely refrained. A vague threat lurked somewhere in the cool delivery of

Nick's comment, leaving her apprehensive and watchful. How unnerving he could be when he stared at her with those sapphire eyes like gimlets, boring into thoughts she wanted to hide.

Turning her face to the gallery windows, Kerry stared out into the heaving dark blanket that was the sea. It was late and she was tired and hungry and her hands throbbed in spite of the oil. And she didn't want to fight with Nick anymore. He always seemed to win every verbal encounter with very little effort.

"Go away," she said tiredly, leaning her head back against the support of a pillow. "Please."

"Go away?" Amusement flecked the rich timbre of his voice. "This is my cabin, remember. Don't be rude, Kerry. It's not at all becoming."

"Oh, why don't you just go ahead and have done with it!" The bright head with its snarled curls tilted back to face him, a flush smearing rosy color along cheeks that had been pale. "You're going to have your revenge on me, and I know it, so start sawing at me! Don't try to be kind and wait 'til I feel better. Strike now, while I'm weak and helpless and can't fight back." Humiliating tears stung the back of her eyelids like grains of sand and she blinked rapidly to keep them back.

"Helpless? I can't imagine such a term being applied to you. No." He shook his head and let the back of his curved fingers slide along the slope of her cheek, over the softness that was stretched tightly across her sculptured bones in a marvelous tapestry of skin and muscle. "Somehow you bring out a feeling of kindness in me that I didn't know I possessed," he murmured softly, and the smile he gave Kerry was genuine. "Rest, little one. There's time enough tomorrow for what I have to say."

Obediently, Kerry's lashes drooped shut and hid the jade orbs that reflected soft lantern light and exhaustion in their smoky depths. Prompted by a tenderness he didn't understand, Nick blew out one of the brass lanterns and lowered the other, then scooped Kerry into his arms and deposited her in the middle of his bunk. In the deep velvet shadows of his bunk her face gleamed palely, like marble or alabaster, he thought, then corrected himself. No, those cold similes could never be applied to such a warm, vitally alive composition of exquisitely chiseled features. It wasn't that she was beautiful in the strict sense of the word; her mouth was a little too large by some standards, with the lower lip full and pouting, and her nose, though straight, might be considered too short for the European ideal. No, taken separately she wasn't perfectly formed, but the entire effect of those imperfect features, coupled with the animation that lent such vibrant life to an otherwise ordinary face, was dazzling.

And judging from the anxious inquiries of his crew as to her health, he wasn't the only man aboard the *Unicorn* who shared that opinion.

"Th' lads were jus' concerned is all, Nicky," Wilson had said after the fifth man had cornered his captain. The halting phrases had stumbled and died unfinished when the hapless sailor had finally interpreted the cold stare directed at him. "Ye know how they admire a fighter, an' by God, th' lass has grit!"

"Are you certain that what they're admiring are not the legs she was showing them off of St. Croix? I find it difficult to believe that hardened men accustomed to years of sailing the Spanish Main would concern themselves with a too-young, ill-tempered little wharf brat for any other reason. Even that cold-blooded Markham asked about her!"

"Oh?" Wilson's wide, innocent stare had sliced neatly through Nick's steely gaze. "Is that th' only reason yer concerned 'bout th' lass?"

In spite of his irritation Nick had grudgingly muttered a "Touché" at Wilson, adding that the circumstances were entirely different.

"Aye, it would seem so, Nick." Again that innocent gaze. " 'Course, it's a bit hard to see how anybody could dislike th' lass. She hadn't hurt nobody but herself, an' that by way of tryin' to escape."

True enough. She had also managed to irritate him beyond measure at times, Nick reflected. Odd that now, when he looked at Kerry sleeping peacefully in his bunk, he almost felt sorry for her. It was a nasty trick of fate to put her in the wrong place at the wrong time like that. But it had happened, and even when he felt tempted to release her he knew he couldn't. Not now. Later, when the worst of this was over and what she knew wouldn't matter, then he'd see that she got back to St. Denis.

What he had never anticipated, Nick reflected with a rueful sigh, was that now, when the situation demanded that he dispose of the girl, he would most want to keep her with him. It was not a trait he particularly cherished at this moment.

Of course, it would probably please her immeasureably to know that, and to know that there would be rumors rife in the Caribbean about the "female pirate" who was part of the *Unicorn*'s crew. Who knew? Kerry might become the next Mary Read or Anne Bonney. She certainly had the temperament for it.

What, he wondered with a grin, would Samuel Locke think when he heard the rumors of the lady pirate aboard the *Unicorn?* It would be very interesting to hear Locke's comments. The normally unflappable intelligence officer would, of course, want to know why a female was on a ship supposed to be garnering useful information for the American cause, particularly since the *Unicorn* was known as a pirate vessel to most officials. Any public or official outcry that singled out the ship and started an investigation could end Nick's usefulness as an agent.

Kerry stirred slightly and mumbled something he couldn't quite catch. Nick leaned close, one arm propped on the far wall of his bunk as he gazed at her thoughtfully. Once back in the Keys, he would leave her in the care of his housekeeper. She would be well tended and well watched in his necessarily frequent absences, and when the *Black Unicorn* did sail into home port, Kerry would be there for him. It was a situation that could be mutually satisfactory once she got over her first rush of mixed emotions about it.

Strangely, there was something rather endearing about a girl who made love with passionate abandon yet could coolly slice her way across a deck filled with battling men. How could he resist her?

Chapter 11

The galley of the *Unicorn* was fascinating, even though hot and sticky, Kerry decided as she stared with great interest at hanging pots and strings of spices and dried onions. Perched on a table, Kerry swung her legs back and forth, palms braced on her knees. Thankfully, Nick had allowed her the limited pleasure of leaving his cabin to roam the ship. After Nick delivered an ultimatum and received her solemn vow that she wouldn't attempt escape again while on board the *Unicorn*, Kerry had been given into Wilson's custody.

Somehow that had rankled, as if Nick didn't want to be bothered with her. He had not, in fact, stayed in his cabin long enough to do more than change shirts or pants. Their conversations had, for the most part, been brief. Even the day after her escape attempt, Nick had been short and to the point.

"If you try an escape again, I'll remove a fair measure of your hide with the end of a rope just as I would any of my crew who disobeyed my orders. Do you understand?" When she'd nodded, Nick had seemed surprised at her lack of argument.

There might be worse things than being held prisoner aboard the *Unicorn*, Kerry had decided, however. She wasn't sure she wanted to test the waters to that extent. It would be best to wait until she was sure of success, but why tell him that? Let him think she was sufficiently scared if it made him happy.

The large part of the past week had been spent in blissful peace during the daytime hours. Only at night, alone in the wide bunk in Nick's cabin, had Kerry entertained dark fears and ravaging doubts. They soared like black-winged bats through the twisting tunnels of her thoughts. Nick would make love to her again. Nick would not make love to her again. He was taking her to his home. He would leave her somewhere else. She would never see St. Denis again. She would be taken back to St. Denis and left without a backward glance.

Gloom. How was she expected to function normally when she couldn't even make up her mind what she wanted? And why was Nick ignoring her?

"Kerry, lass." Wilson's voice lured her attention away from dismal wanderings. "Watch yer head."

She ducked just in time. Cook's assistant, young Will, a lad from Barbados who looked to be about twelve or thirteen, stumbled into the galley with a heavy sack of meal that was almost his height and more than his weight. It balanced on his back and shoulders so that he resembled a blind turtle lurching across the galley floor, and one corner of it barely grazed Kerry as Will groped toward Cook.

"Ye dimwit!" Cook pounded on Will's padded shell with a wooden spoon. "Yer s'posed to put th' meal in th' barrel, not all over visitors!"

The sack of meal thunked to the floor. "Sorry," Will said in Kerry's general direction. "Couldn't see."

"That's all right, Will," Kerry answered politely, then laughed as Cook and Will began arguing about where the meal barrel should be located.

Due to her relationship with Nick, none of the crew treated her with less than respect. Because they liked her, they treated her as an honored guest.

Will was given a light cuff to the side of his head and sent to fetch the small wooden tubs for the crew's meal, and Cook turned his attention back to Kerry and Wilson.

"Th' boy's too damned cheeky, 'e is!" Cook said fondly. "I'm likely ta serve 'im fer supper one night."

Kerry bit into one of the few remaining apples that Cook had saved for her, saying around the juicy bite, "He seems a bit young to be on a pirate ship."

"Nah! Why, 'e's plenny big enough! I 'member when—"

"So do I," Wilson cut in, "an' I've heard this story so often I kin say it with ye!"

"But she ain' 'eard it." Cook sliced a glance at Kerry. "D'ye want a 'ear it, lass?"

Courtesy demanded she say yes, and Cook wore a triumphant expression as he launched into his tale with relish. Wilson groaned and pushed at his spectacles, interrupting to tell Kerry he would be back in a few minutes and not to leave the galley.

Cook was well into his third story about the time he had spent his fourteenth birthday sailing the Indian Ocean with Jean Lafitte and capturing the East Indiaman *Queen* when an amused voice contradicted him.

"You were fifteen, Cook. That was in 1807."

"Aye, Cap'n" came the thoughtful reply. "I reckon yer right on that. I'd fergot."

Kerry's heart began to hammer and the last bite of her apple suddenly tasted like sawdust. She could feel Nick behind her, and wondered despairingly if her reaction was evident. Why couldn't she act as if he was a sack of meal or something?

Forcing the words from a throat that had almost closed, Kerry managed to ask, "Did you sail with Lafitte, too?"

"Out of necessity." Nick leaned against the table,

his hard thigh almost touching Kerry's right leg. "I'd just lost my ship to dry dock, and had to take the next vessel out of New Orleans. It happened to be Lafitte's."

"I didn't know pirates took on passengers." Curiosity calmed her raw nerves, and the sharp impact of Nick's proximity faded to just a faint consciousness. "Why'd he let you sail with him? Or were you part of his crew?"

"Lafitte happened to be going my way and I happened to have money. I already knew him, of course."

Kerry listened with rapt attention as Nick told how he'd sailed for three months with Lafitte, preying on Spanish ships and plundering craft in the bays of the Gulf of Mexico.

"When he took me back to New Orleans to get my ship, we struck up a bargain. . . ."

"Aye, an' I wuz part of it!" Cook added gleefully, slapping a chunk of grouper into the skillet to fry.

"Lafitte had a change of heart about corrupting such a young and tender lad." Nick grinned, a dark brow lifting at Kerry's exclamation. "And I needed a cook. I'm not certain just how I got him instead, but here we are."

"Aye, an' I'm a dandy cook," the boy protested. "I may 'ave spent my time runnin' 'bout like our lazy Will, but I 'ad more of a leanin' toward cookin' than 'im."

"Keep leaning and you may fall into it eventually," Nick said to Cook, but his eyes were on Kerry. His gaze probed hers, and for the first time in days she felt totally aware of her surroundings. Everything seemed to intensify and sharpen into knifelike clarity, centered around Nick.

"I heard from a sailor out of Charleston that the Lafitte brothers had been arrested and tried for piracy," Kerry said to eyes of a deep, chilling blue.

"How'd they get out of charges the governor brought against them?" Why did she have to think about his mouth on hers, and the way Nick's hands felt holding her against him?

"Yes, but that was back in 1810. Good legal talent got them acquitted. Soon afterward, they were commissioned as privateers of the South American government of Cartagena."

"And now?" The apple core was warm and moist in her hand, and Kerry concentrated on it to keep from remembering Nick's touch.

"Now they are into other affairs I believe. Here," he said, "give me that apple core before you've made cider of it. You've squeezed it so hard the seeds popped out like bullets." Kerry dutifully released the core and wiped her hand on a kitchen rag that had seen better times.

Will returned with the containers and Cook immediately began issuing orders, most of them conflicting with the previous ones so that Will was soon in a spin and the galley noisy with argument. Taking Kerry's hand, Nick pulled her from the table and led her out of the steamy galley to the deck.

It wasn't much cooler on deck and the late afternoon shadows offered little relief from the sun beating down on the *Unicorn*. The slight breeze gently lifted copper tendrils of Kerry's hair as she leaned against the taffrail to gaze at the *Unicorn*'s wake. The same breeze ruffled Nick's hair into a romantically disheveled state that started her heart thumping erratically again. He looked every inch the pirate captain today. Tight-fitting leather pants hugged the muscular length of his long legs, and a short leather vest barely covered his naked torso. The sharp-pointed poinard tucked into a wide belt at his waist added a taste of danger to his appearance that was not at all out of character. Nick leaned, smiling, with one elbow braced against the taffrail, his bare chest alarmingly close.

She hadn't seen this much of him in a week, and Kerry wasn't sure if that was good or bad. It had the elements of both wrapped neatly in the sensual package he presented with that dazzling smile and too-perfect profile. Had she actually thought during the past days that she could remain cool and distant when with him? How childishly innocent that was. And beneath it all, lying like a treacherous coral reef in the shallow sea of her thoughts, was the agonizing conviction that he wouldn't want her once they reached Spanish Florida. Hadn't he already stayed away from her too long with no explanation?

"What are you thinking?" Nick said softly, his voice spiced with a caress that was almost physical. "You're adrift somewhere."

"Oh," she said with an airy wave of one hand, "I'm sailing without a rudder and no idea of the direction. Is that nautical enough?"

His blue eyes crinkled at the corners as he smiled. "Close. Do you need a rudder? Why not let me steer for you."

"I thought you were already. No one has suggested I take the wheel, or even wondered if I wanted to." Fragile emotions skimmed across her face like the shadow of a dove's wings, and her eyes met his gaze steadily. "You all seem so bloody busy around here."

"Ah, so that rankles, does it. Did you expect me to be at your heels every moment?" His precise, intuitive guess lashed Kerry's pride and her chin lifted slightly as she stared at him without comment. "Don't expect anything from me, love. I want you, and I admire your beauty and somewhat ill-advised courage, but that's all."

"What makes you think I want or even expect anything from a pirate captain?" She shrugged

carelessly, turning away from those piercing eyes
that saw too much. "All I want from you is my freedom."

"You'll get your wish, but not until the right time.
Why don't we make the most of the situation now."
His fingers brushed lightly over the curve of her
cheek and moved to gently cup her neck in the arch
of his palm. Tunneling through the wind-tangled
weight of her hair, one hand drew her head closer
to him in a steady motion while the other rose to
stroke the sloping line of her jaw.

Kerry's eyes widened. He meant to kiss her, and
she almost yielded before remembering Wilson's
comment about things too easily acquired.

"Nobody wants sumthin' that's too easy to git,"
he'd said when Kerry had asked why Nick was
avoiding her. "Could be Nick's th' same. Mind, I'm
not sayin' that's it a'tall, now," he'd added, but
Kerry had been struck by the observation, and
that's why she pulled away from Nick.

"No! I . . . I . . . the whole crew is watching, and I
don't want them to see. . . ."

It was a foolish thing to say, she realized almost
instantly, especially since the entire crew knew
she'd spent every night in his cabin. Why had she
said that?

Nick angrily wondered the same thing, features
darkening as he stared down at her upturned face.
"Why you little hypocrite. It's fine when we're in
my cabin where no one can see, but not here? Oh
no, you're not playing that game. . . ."

His fingers curled painfully into her arms as he
half-lifted Kerry from her feet, crushing her against
his chest with his mouth ravaging hers. The world
reeled in bright colors as she found her head forced
back and Nick's demanding lips capturing the air
from aching lungs. One hand moved down to pull
her hips tightly against him and held her there.

When Nick finally released her mouth, his breathing was still even, while Kerry's was as ragged as if she had just climbed to the main topmast.

"You ... you made your point," she managed to say weakly. Her legs had turned traitor and would not support her weight, so that she had to lean into Nick even though he'd already lowered her feet back to the deck. "It wasn't quite what I meant to say. . . . I mean . . ." She floundered for a moment before looking up into his narrowed eyes and saying, "I'm not used to this, Nick. If I made you mad, I'm sorry. I just don't know how to deal with it when it's all so new."

Well. That effectively spiked his guns. Nick's hot rush of anger faded at Kerry's explanation. It was too honest and chagrined not to be sincere. Didn't he know how basically forthright she was? Tactless, Wilson had observed with a laugh, and too guileless to know how to lie well. An endearing trait in a world filled with smiling hypocrisy, liars, and excellent cheats.

"You'll learn to cope," he said at last, "but not, I hope, at the cost of your integrity." Leaving Kerry to puzzle over the meaning of his cryptic statement, Nick kissed her again, but this time it was a mere pressing of his lips against her forehead. "Your supper should be waiting on you, love."

It was obviously a dismissal and Kerry fled with burning cheeks and hot, wet eyes, across the deck to the hatch leading below. She met Wilson in the shadowy passageway below deck and paused to steady her voice and quivering legs. "You always seem to be somewhere else at crucial times, Wilson. Why?"

Nick had asked him basically the same thing in a much sharper tone. He hadn't answered Nick either. "What happened, lass? Did someone upset ye?"

"Not someone. Nick." Her throat was tight and her eyes burned. "Why does he always make me feel like this?"

"Glands," Wilson said, and smiled as Kerry just blinked at him in confusion.

"What?" she asked. He eased his frame to a narrow step of the ladder and patted the one just below him. "I said, glands. Ye know, like spring fever, puppy love, slap and tickle, calf love, amour—all those kinds of things. Caused by glands, all of it."

"Glands. So that means I'm sick." She plopped to the ladder rung. "I knew there had to be a logical reason for all this, but I never thought to ask Dr. Wilson."

"Don't be so sarcastic, lass. It's th' truth. Chemistry. Sparks 'tween two people that ain't 'tween two others—what else could it be?"

This was crazy. He was making sense. Kerry buried her forehead in the arch of her palm. "Is there an antidote?"

"Aye." Wilson stood and started up the ladder. His voice floated back down, leaving Kerry staring after him. "Ye'll find th' antidote, lass, when ye admit th' cause."

Chapter 12

The bright morning sunlight gilded the surfaces of the sea and spattered the captain's cabin with golden beams that flowed over Kerry's strained face as she sat at the gallery windows, staring out at the island that lay before her like a beautiful, flawed jewel nesting in a bed of turquoise silk. Belle Terre. Nick's home.

Flung across the Straits of Florida between the Gulf of Mexico and the Atlantic, the Florida Keys curved in a scythe of green islands. With its uncharted tiny islands and hidden coves, bays, and limestone caves that could conceal ships, the Keys had become a base of operations for pirates and privateers.

She drummed her fingers impatiently on the smooth wood of the windowsill as she listened to the familiar sounds of the crew overhead. She was anxious to feel solid land beneath her again.

Straining forward, Kerry pressed her nose against the pane as the *Unicorn* sailed over the smooth water into a small bay. Two strips of land jutted out on each side of the bay like the legs of a crab, and at the end of both promontories stood stone towers mounted with cannon. In the harbor only two ships floated serenely at anchor, ecru sails furled and lifeless. As the *Unicorn's* bow dipped low and finally nosed into port, the long wooden docks became

crowded with laughing, waving people. Many dove
from the docks and swam toward the ship, and
Kerry heard resounding splashes as men clambered
over the rails and leaped from the decks of the *Unicorn* into the harbor.

It was a noisy, happy homecoming for the crew,
Kerry reflected, and thought suddenly of Gato. He
must be wondering about her, where she was and
what had happened, and she wished she could somehow get a message to the old man telling him she
was alive and well. It seemed like she'd been on the
Unicorn for several months instead of just weeks.
What had happened to her perception of time?

The past week had been spent in a dreamy haze
of hot, sultry days that alternated between boredom
in Nick's cabin and lazy hours on the sun-drenched
quarterdeck in Wilson's amiable custody. Sometimes she'd joined the crew in a card game; sometimes she'd climbed with them into the swaying web
of rigging above decks and delighted in the feel of
the wind in her hair and face.

Kerry had not talked with Nick since that afternoon on the stern, except in passing. It was hot, and
most of the crew had been sleeping on the decks at
night instead of in the stifling fo'c'sle. Nick, Kerry
had learned from Wilson, had joined them.

Last night in her sleep she had heard Nick's
husky whisper murmuring love words to her in
hazy, swirling dreams, and some forlorn piece of her
heart had answered. But she had awakened alone,
to the stark reality of truth. She meant no more to
him than any other woman he'd ever had, except,
maybe, that she had been a little bit more trouble.

Kerry pleated the material of her trousers with
idle fingers as she scanned the small island that
was probably no larger than St. Denis. She curled
her bare toes into the carpet and fidgeted restlessly,
wondering why Nick had not sent someone after her.

She was ready, her very few belongings wrapped in a large square of material by the cabin door.

A wry smile tilted the corners of her mouth. She had only a shirt and trousers, a comb fashioned from a pretty shell that one of the crew—blushing like a new rose and too shy to look up—had given her, and the ill-fitting gown in her bundle. She would certainly make a grand entrance at Nick's home with her few, tattered belongings.

The *Unicorn* had been moored for a half-hour when the door finally swung open and Nick was there, his dark hair wind-ruffled and blue eyes glittering like sapphire chips. Instead of the dark pants and white shirt that he usually wore ashore, he wore a fine lawn shirt and fawn-colored trousers that clung to him like a second skin. Gleaming Hessian boots with rich tassels rose to his knees, and a dark blue coat of superfine hugged his broad shoulders in a perfect fit. He took her breath away, and Kerry stilled the quick spasm of her heart as she stood up.

"It's about time, Lawton. I thought you'd forgotten me."

"Sweet-tempered as usual, I see." He arched one dark brow and crossed the floor to tilt her face up with a finger hooked under her chin. "Drag out your Sunday manners, love, and I won't beat you in front of the entire town."

"I left them at home. May I use yours?" She faked a smile and just barely dodged his grip, stepping under his arm with a quick twist. But Nick caught her, yanking Kerry back to mold her against his hard frame.

"In a hurry to leave again? And here I was thinking that you were going to be one of the crew forever. Even Mr. Markham has asked about you, and he's a cold fish if I've ever met one." A blunt finger traced the outline of her ear in idle curiosity. "I've left you alone this past week, love, but now we're here. There's more privacy on Belle Terre. You're young and more inexperienced than I first thought. Unfortunately, I'm not a man with a great deal of patience, or given to charity. You've had plenty of time to deal with your new situation." His lips nibbled at her earlobe and Kerry shivered, steeling herself against the pull of his attraction. "Remember this later, love," he murmured. His lips dragged across hers in a silky kiss that took away her breath, and Kerry's hands clung tightly to his upper arms. Broad palms smoothed over her hips in a light caress, then Nick released her so suddenly Kerry almost fell.

Glaring, she regained her balance and said, "There's a lot I'll remember later, but I'm sure you'll have managed to forget the important details."

"Such as?"

"Such as how you kidnapped me and kept me prisoner against my will." And how you called me love and whispered sweet words in my ear one night, she added silently. It was all a game anyway; why had she taken it so seriously?

"Don't become too abusive, sweet. It's unhealthy." He crossed to the door and opened it with a flourish, bending forward with one hand palm-up across his chest in a gesture that invited her to precede him. "After you, my lady."

Sunlight flooded the *Unicorn's* decks as Kerry emerged from the hatch, with Nick firmly guiding her across the aft deck to amidships and the bridge leading to land. Wilson had remained behind on the ship with a few other men and he trotted behind Nick and Kerry as they walked down the steeply pitched bridge to the dock.

"Aye, an' it's glad to be back I am, Cap'n! Even if it's jus' fer a while," Wilson said. "An' ye'll like it here, lass, even with th' velvet dragon hoverin' about ye."

"The what?" Oh no, not another formidable foe. "What is a velvet dragon, Wilson?"

As they reached the foot of the bridge to stand on the dock, they were surrounded by people offering welcoming smiles and comments, and she couldn't hear his reply. Kerry's gaze flicked over the unfamiliar but friendly faces. Men, women, and children, old and young, brown, black, and white all grouped together in a laughing knot to greet Nick. Kerry was surprised at the feeling of genuine affection he seemed to generate. Was this the man who bore such a fearsome reputation?—this amiable pirate? No one here seemed to fear or dislike him.

"I'll speak to you all later," Nick was saying to some of them, "but now I have other arrangements to make."

Kerry was pushed gently forward through the crowd, nodding and smiling back at those who spoke, feeling strangely disoriented as she was lifted into a spanking new landau pulled by a pair of matching bays. Nick settled his lean frame next to her and Wilson barely managed to squeeze his portly body into the space left as the driver snapped his whip smartly and the flashy bays pranced up the road.

The town was laid in neat squares dissected at intervals by green parks, and none of the squalor that often spoiled the fresh beauty of tropical seaports was in evidence. This was a pirate's den? It certainly bore little resemblance to what Kerry had thought it would be.

Her eyes widened when the landau turned into a curving drive topped with crushed seashells and rolled to a crunching stop in front of a huge white house. A long, low veranda swept regally across the front, and behind the slender pillars holding it up

she could see six mullioned windows stretching from
the porch floor to the second story. Three windows
flanked each side of the double doors, which bore
two ornately carved brass handles with unicorn fig-
ureheads gracing their tops. Kerry stared silently.
It didn't resemble a pirate's lair at all.

Stepping over Wilson, Nick swung down and gave
the older man a helping hand, then turned back to
her.

"Take my hand, love. Ah, don't be stubborn. This
is my den of iniquity, and no, I didn't murder the
former owners. I paid for it."

"With money earned from murder, rape, and pil-
lage," Kerry muttered, placing her small hand in
his much larger one. "A horse of a different color is
still a mule in sheep's clothing."

"Very good. Three mismatched clichés in one sen-
tence that time," Nick observed with a soft laugh.
He coiled an arm behind her back and lifted her,
protesting, from the landau and onto the front steps.
Kerry jerked away, raising a foot to give him a swift
kick, but he was already ignoring her. Nick strode
toward a short rotund woman standing in the half-
open front door.

"Happy! I swear I can smell something good in
the kitchen already!" Nick enveloped the gray-
haired woman in a wide smile, gave her a big hug,
and kissed her on one rosy cheek.

"Get on with you now." A pudgy hand slapped at
his arm but she was smiling, her small blue eyes
like sparkling half moons. "Wilson, I see you're just
as organized as ever. Take off your hat in the presence of ladies. Nicholas. Where are your manners?
I haven't been introduced." Her shrewd eyes
scanned Kerry, noting how proudly the girl bore her
scrutiny.

"Mistress Hapwell, I would like for you to meet
Miss Kerry, late of St. Denis, who has come to visit

us. We rescued her not long ago." Nick turned to include Kerry in the group. "Kerry, Mistress Hapwell manages my estate while I am gone, and me while I am here."

"For all the good it does!" Mistress Hapwell snapped, and Kerry couldn't repress a smile. "You're a lovely child, for all that you're dressed in rags, dear. Come with me."

Kerry had just time to cast a pleading glance over one shoulder before Mistress Hapwell had her through the door and into the house. So this was the velvet dragon. No other introduction was needed.

"Well damme!" Wilson gasped, catching his spectacles in midair. "Did ye see that, Nicky lad? Made off wi' her, she did, an' ye'll not be seein' th' lass agin fer a while."

Slightly disgruntled at the speed with which Happy had taken charge of Kerry, Nick nodded. Perhaps he should have kept Kerry aboard the *Unicorn* for a while. No. Sooner or later he would have to leave her, and it might be better that she get adjusted to the situation now.

"Sir? Will you be needing me further?"

Nick's attention was yanked from Kerry to the driver of his landau standing patiently by the vehicle. "No, Percy. Not tonight."

As the landau rolled away from the house Nick met Wilson's questioning gaze with a shrug, then crossed the porch and entered the house. Wilson smiled, adjusting his spectacles to the bridge of his nose, and followed. This was getting better all the time.

"But I like wearing trousers!" Kerry glared at Happy, who stared serenely back at her. Kerry was sitting in a brass tub of hot water and lavender-scented bubbles up to her neck. Coppery curls jig-gled with each movement of her head, threatening to spill from the ribbon that held them on her crown.

"They're unfeminine" was the placid reply, and without waiting for Kerry's choking retort, Happy glided away holding trousers and shirt between her thumb and forefinger as if they might explode at any moment. "And you are female," she reminded in a firm voice that floated back over her shoulder, "however much you wish to hide it."

"For all the good it does me," Kerry muttered to the mound of soap bubbles on her knee. Nick had noticed that she was female, in spite of her loose shirt and trousers and rough manners. Apparently he didn't care what she wore, so why should she? And she hated dresses.

She slapped the water in exasperation, sending up spouts of soapy water to spatter her face, hair, and the carpet on the floor. "Oh damn!"

Happy's head appeared around the Chinese screen used for privacy, her mouth set in stern lines. "Ladies don't swear," she reproved.

"I'm no lady," Kerry said between clenched teeth, and the wicked gleam in her emerald eyes gave Happy a brief warning. A volley of the finest swearing she'd ever done turned the air blue as Kerry fired off words in eight different languages, which—thankfully—Happy didn't understand. When it was over Kerry paused for breath and gave a little satisfied smile.

"Do you feel better?" Happy asked calmly.

"Much."

"Good. Now don't do it again. Ladies don't swear." The head disappeared back around the screen.

As she slid further down in the tub, Kerry's smile widened. Maybe this wouldn't be as bad as she'd first thought. But she still wasn't going to wear a dress.

* * *

"Nicholas, what have you brought home? Another stray puppy someone wanted to drown?" Happy's smile sweetened her tart words with kindness. "Where did you find her? The girl is lovely, but she hasn't the manners of a flea and can curse fluently in several languages."

"Is she back to that again?" Nick's brows drew together in a frown. "I thought I'd convinced her not to."

Laughing softly, Happy leaned over the arm of her favorite chair to lay a hand on Nick's sleeve. "You may have lessened it, but the words I heard were definitely profane." She patted his arm. "Don't say anything to her about it. I think she needed to release her frustrations and that helped. One shouldn't bottle up one's emotions."

"Release her frustrations?" Nick gazed at Happy in amazement. "She 'releases her frustrations' every time the mood hits! I hardly think she has any dangerous emotions left to bottle up." He tilted the snifter of good brandy he held, swirling the amber liquid in a slow circle before lifting it to his mouth and swallowing the last of it.

"You didn't answer me, Nicholas." Happy's eyes were trained on the neat piece of needlework she was stitching as she punched the needle through the linen with rapt concentration, but Nick wasn't fooled by her apparent inattention. "Where did you find her?"

"Is she in bed?"

"And sound asleep. I checked not more than a half-hour ago. The tisane I prepared helped, of course."

"Of course." Nick grinned. "She should sleep until morning with one of your potent tisanes working on her." He rose from his chair before the fireplace, pacing the fine Aubusson carpet like a restless tiger, rolling the empty brandy snifter between his fingers in smooth motions. "I didn't find her, she found me," he said at last, stopping to lean one arm on the marble mantelpiece. "I finally discovered who had those books, so I went to St. Denis after them. When I arrived, Sedgewick had already sent someone after them. Garcia, a former member of my crew, had stolen the books from Lord Milford. I found him, and you can probably imagine our conversation."

Happy nodded, eyes still fixed on the intricately embroidered scene of nightingales perched in a tree. "And he refused to give them up gracefully, of course."

A faint smile tilted up the corners of Nick's mouth. "Yes. I had followed him from a tavern to a spot on the beach. He had a knife. I didn't want to kill him, but I certainly didn't want Milford to know who had those books. The less Sedgewick knows, the better the surprise."

Disapproval laced the inquiring glance Happy spared from her needlework. "I do hope you didn't let him go."

"No. He forced that issue. Garcia is dead, and the girl's a witness. At first I assumed she was with Garcia."

"Ah" was the satisfied comment.

"Yes, that's how our little guttersnipe enters the scene. With misplaced bravery, she overhears our conversation and decides to save Garcia's miserable existence from being terminated. I did what seemed expedient at the time; I killed Garcia and brought the girl with me. In spite of frequent reminders that I could have killed her, she has been less than grateful."

"Silly chit." Laughter burbled suspiciously, but Happy's face was innocently composed when Nick sliced her a sharp glance. "I'm sure she'll see the light soon enough, Nicholas dear. It's just difficult for some people to be properly gracious when hauled aboard a pirate ship at pistol-point. Or was it a sword?"

"Neither." Nick's voice was tight. "She was unconscious."

"Good heavens! She didn't appear to be a girl prone to fainting spells." The needle glittered as it punched through the linen in silver darts. "See how easily I'm fooled by appearances?"

There was a moment of silence before Nick laughed. "You are not fooled by much of anything, Happy love." He draped his lean body across the chair next to Mistress Hapwell's. "What else did she tell you?"

"Kerry?" Her lips formed a curving smile as Happy deftly snipped the end of her thread with tiny gold scissors. "She told me absolutely nothing except that she would not wear a dress. No." The tapestry lifted and she bent a critical gaze upon her work, then folded it and laid it in her ample lap. "No, Nicholas, human nature provides all the answers if one knows the person involved. I know you and how you would have dealt with the situation. From the little I've seen of Kerry, I know how she would have reacted. She's no mealymouthed, simple little miss who can be easily frightened. I daresay she has done some terrorizing of her own a time or two."

"I daresay you're right." Prompted by the memory of Kerry slashing him with her dagger, Nick's lips twitched as he glanced down at the barely visible wound peeking from beneath his shirt cuff. Then he frowned as he recalled her battle against seasoned pirates. "She has courage. She just needs to learn prudence."

Happy smiled. "Perhaps she will find a competent instructor. Goodnight, Nicholas." She rose and Nick automatically rose also, giving Happy a skeptical glance.

"No plotting now. I've enough to think about without that."

"Don't worry, dear." She gave him a fond pat on the arm. "I never 'plot.' Arrangements are made and the course of life runs accordingly."

"Oh my God."

"Don't swear. No wonder the girl talks like she does when all around her men are cursing. Next she'll be shooting pistols and brandishing daggers." Another pat on the arm forestalled any immediate reply, and Happy's serene smile never wavered. "I do hope that nasty cut on your arm heals properly, Nicholas. See you in the morning."

Nick gazed after the portly figure retreating with all the stately grace of a broad-hulled man-of-war. Amazing. She was as shrewd as she was kind-hearted, and when called for, acid-tongued. Mistress Hapwell knew more about him than he did himself.

Chapter 13

"Don't you look pretty!" Happy adjusted the oval cheval glass so it reflected Kerry from head to toe, and waited expectantly for a reaction.

Framed in the mirror was a portrait by Sir Joshua Reynolds, a graceful creature attired in the latest fashion from Europe, with red-gold hair piled in delicate curls atop her head. It had to be a painting; it certainly couldn't be the same girl who had, only two days before, been wearing trousers and a rough seaman's shirt while clinging to the rigging of a ship.

Kerry took a step closer to the mirror. One hand rose to lightly touch the polished surface, tracing the reflected curve of her cheek and down to the graceful folds of her gown. Caught by a wide ribbon just under her breasts, the muslin fell in soft, full pleats to the tips of her toes. The Grecian effect was completed by a low square neckline trimmed in lace, short puffed sleeves, clocked stockings and low-heeled pumps. Though the shoes were of the softest kid, they still pinched feet unaccustomed to any sort of footwear, and Kerry tried vainly to wiggle her toes. She still thought her neck looked bare without her mother's locket but Happy said it was unsuitable for the gown and Kerry had to admit the improvement in her appearance.

"Ohhh," she sighed, "I look smart as snuff, don't I?"

"That depends," Happy replied faintly, "on the grade of tobacco used. Pay attention, child; it doesn't matter how pretty you are if you behave in a coarse manner. And don't bother telling me you grew up as a child of the streets. I don't swallow that nonsense for a moment, in spite of what Nicholas swears to be true. I can always tell quality." Happy fidgeted with the strings of a wide-brimmed bonnet that Kerry prayed fervently was not for her own head. "Well?" Happy prompted.

Kerry winced as the bonnet was tugged over her coppery curls. "It's partly true. While I didn't exactly grow up in the streets—ouch! You tied my hair in with the bonnet strings. Yes, that's better. What? Oh yes," she continued when Happy adjusted the strings, "I did have a . . . I guess you'd say . . . liberal childhood."

Surprisingly, Kerry found Happy easy to talk to, for the woman had no qualms about discussing frankly any aspect of life. Within a few minutes she knew that Kerry had been raised by Gato after being orphaned. She agreed to tell Nick a message must be sent to Gato as soon as possible for he had to be frantic with worry. She also learned that Kerry had spent most of her formative years on the teeming docks of St. Denis's seaport.

"But at least you learned a great deal of life and an astonishing amount of geography, as well as many different languages," Happy observed. "Still, it's too bad you had no opportunity for proper education, child. What of your parents? Had they left no one to see to your training?"

"No."

The short, one-syllable answer snared Happy's attention. "Do you want to talk about it?" Kerry shook her head, and Happy nodded and held up another hat. "Fine. Do you like this bonnet better than the other one?"

Bonnets were a safe—if dull—subject, and Kerry entered a conversation about them with no trepidation. Two topics were certain to gain Happy a tense silence. One of them concerned Kerry's parents, and the other concerned Nick.

Happy admitted to Wilson an hour later over a cup of tea, "She closes up like a clam whenever I mention either, Wilson. Her silence about Nicholas I can understand after what you've told me, but her parents?"

"Aye, well let me tell ye a little tale, Mistress Hapwell, that might have a bit o' bearin' on that. 'Bout ten or 'leven years ago, I was in London-town with Nicky. Locke sent us to meet someone, a gentleman from Ireland an' his family, at th' Pig and Owl tavern in a sort o' bad section o' th' city. . . ."

Upstairs, Kerry was pacing restlessly in her bedchamber. Where was Nick? She wanted him to see her in all this finery. What was the saying?—something about a pig's silk purse? Oh, whatever it was, that was a little bit how she felt. Outside she looked all brand-new and ladylike, but inside she was still Kerry in dirty trousers and a soiled blouse. Would he like her better this way? And why hadn't he come to see her yet?

She swung her bonnet in a circle by the bright blue ribbons, leaning back against the wide casement of her bedroom window as she stared out over the front lawns to the turquoise slice of the harbor.

Well, she had wanted to be free of the ship and here she was. The gleaming oak floor covered with thick carpets did not have the least tendency to buck and roll beneath her feet, and the furniture was not bolted down to keep it in place. Sheer curtains fluttered over the long windows that afforded an excellent view of tall palm trees and brightly blooming shrubs and flowers. The graceful lines of the furniture—Sheraton and Queen Anne—blended perfectly with the subdued tones of the wallpaper. All in all, it was a charming room obviously decorated with feminine comfort in mind. Whose comfort? Kerry wondered, her critical gaze returning time and again to the armoires crowded with day gowns and riding habits, light cloaks and lacy shawls. Certainly not Mistress Hapwell's comfort; she had a bedchamber down the hall.

"Oh bloody hell," Kerry said softly.

"Ah, for a moment I was worried at finding a stranger in this room. Now I know it has to be Kerry."

She knew his voice, of course, and turned slowly. Nick lounged casually in the doorway, one broad hand propped against the frame as he raked her with an appreciative stare. She stared at him hungrily, hoping the longing didn't show. Her eyes caressed the lean frame dressed in dark trousers and snowy shirt as she only half-listened to him.

"I never knew, love, that you could be so beautiful. Though I did admire your . . . ah . . . form . . . in trousers, I must admit the gown is a vast improvement."

"Is it? I am so pleased you think so," Kerry replied primly. She folded her hands in front of her, still holding the bonnet by its ribbons. She had to pretend indifference even though her heart was flying like a tern skimming over acres of sea grass. What could she say? Something, anything casual . . . "Would you care for a morning cup of tea?"

"Oh bloody hell," Nick parroted with an amused smile. "I do believe the girl is being aloof. Tea? By all means, my Galatea, by all means."

"Galatea was a statue, Nick, and I'm not," Kerry said quietly. "I'm real."

"Yes, you are, love." He was still smiling when he took her hands between his and gently eased the bonnet's twisted strings from around her fingers. "You continually surprise me, you know. I wouldn't have thought you'd know who Galatea or Pygmalion were."

"I can read. I've read Shakespeare, Chaucer, Dante, Greek classics and legends, and more. Just because I wear boy's clothes and don't speak the King's English as well as you doesn't mean I'm stupid." Well, so much for casual indifference. Would simmering resentment do? Kerry pulled her hands from his and picked up her bonnet. Unable to quite meet his considering gaze, she jerked the fluffy hat with its curling feathers over her rebelliously straying hair. "I'm not stupid," she repeated in a defensive mutter.

"No, Kerry love. You're not stupid." Nick adjusted the tip of a bobbing feather as it dipped into her eyes, then hooked a finger under her lowered chin. "I didn't mean you were," he said to her eyelids since she would not look up at him. "I just never thought your choice of reading would include Greek classics."

"What did you think I'd read?—the Civilization and Social History of the South Sea Oyster? It might be educational, but not very interesting."

"I'll wager the oysters don't feel that way. I take two sugars and no milk in mine."

"In your what—oysters?" She'd forgotten her offer of tea, but quickly remembered when Nick inclined his head in the direction of the silver teapot on its tray. What was she doing serving tea? Hadn't she once said that she would *never* sit on dainty chairs and pour out hot tea?

But that was just what she did. She handed the

fragile china cup and saucer to him with a murmured "Your tea, Captain Lawton."

"Aren't we being a bit formal?" Even his voice was warm and caressing, as his hands had been.

"Are we? I thought that was the point of all this . . ." She indicated the gown with a sweep of one hand. "To teach me proper social conduct. Don't I learn quickly enough?"

"Too quickly. Proper conduct does not necessarily mean you have to imitate an iceberg, child. Come here." The china clattered with a tinkling sound as he set his cup and saucer on the small cherry table.

Warning bells rang in her head as Nick didn't wait for Kerry to move, but came to her instead. Wasn't this what she wanted? Hadn't she waited, and wondered why he hadn't come to her again even while she fought those feelings? Yes, of course she had. And now he was here with her, holding her so close she couldn't breathe, so why was she pulling away?

"Nick . . . the tea . . . Happy will be back soon . . . it's broad daylight . . . no!"

"And on the *Unicorn* the crew was there. If we were on a desert isle the sea terns would be watching." Nick's voice was heavy with sarcasm, falling like a stone into the swiftly gathering silence. "You didn't seem to dislike it once before, Kerry. Why pretend you do now?"

"Dislike it?" Her question was a dull echo. How stupid—of course she didn't dislike it, that was the problem. Couldn't he see that? "What makes you think I'm *pretending* to dislike it?" she asked anyway because pride demanded it.

"Because," he said, "your response was so enthusiastic you left marks on my back. And you held on to me as if you were drowning and whispered my name. . . . Other than those clues, I've nothing much to go on." This time his voice was soft and rich with sensuality; the spider cajoling the fly into its silken web. "I've given you time, love, and I'm not very patient. Have I said that before? I know I have, but I want you, and I'm tired of waiting."

Any response she might have made was smothered by his lips as they met hers in a heart-wrenching kiss. The world was awash suddenly in the most brilliant colors as Kerry's head tilted back and her eyes closed. All she could feel was color; bright crimsons and shimmering blues—crimson for the flush that was stealing over her body and blue for the lingering touch of his eyes on her—and delicate shades of ebony and bronze—Nick's hair and sun-browned skin. Why hadn't she ever realized that color could actually be felt? It could. Color was everywhere, a shifting landscape of the most beautiful hues imaginable.

Her eyes opened slowly and focused on him as Nick finally lifted his head. She felt the hard muscles of his bare chest beneath her fingertips as she brushed through the tiny whorls of dark hair. The steady rhythm of Nick's heartbeat kept pace with his regular breathing, and Kerry wondered distractedly why she seemed to be the only one having trouble with madly thumping pulses and malfunctioning lungs.

It wasn't fair that she should be the one to have such a reaction when he remained cool, but there it was. Now she would have to concentrate on keeping her feet firmly earth-bound and those crazy impulses from taking wing. How could that be so damned hard?

"Nick . . . stop it . . . I don't want . . ." It was impossible to talk with him kissing her. And even more impossible to talk coherently when he began to pull down the bodice of her gown.

Kerry's determination evaporated when Nick's mouth followed the path his hands had taken, trailing fiery kisses over her throat to her breasts. The lacy edge of her bodice tickled slightly as he pulled away the soft muslin, and the cool morning air that curled in through the open windows made her shiver. It was the air, of course, not Nick's hands or his warm mouth. Damn him, he was toying with her, and seemed unaffected and amused by her reaction to his silky caresses and blistering kisses.

Galatea? Very well, perhaps she should be like that exquisitely carved statue that had won Pygmalion's heart—as cold as marble. There could be no compromise. Her emotional survival might depend upon how distant she could become.

Yet when Nick's tongue lightly explored the delicate pink swell of her breast, Kerry realized how tenuous a grip she had on the ability to become distant. It was a duel now, with Kerry struggling to remain aloof and impervious, and Nick determined to force a response from her while he showed no reaction at all.

He had no real interest in her. Why was he doing this? In that instant, Kerry almost hated him for the sensual power he possessed—the power to make her body want him when every cell in her brain was screaming denial. Even while she clung desperately to composure, there were signs that gave her away: the uncontrollable shiver that rippled from her head to her toes, the smoky jade of eyes that were dilated with passion, and the tightening of her nipples into rosebuds infused with desire.

Nick gave no sign that he was aware of her reaction, or of her resistance. Instead, his hands peeled away her gown in a single motion, letting it fall in a soft puddle of white at her feet. He curled one arm around her back to hold her close. His fingers, light and caressing, tickled over the ridged curve of her rib cage, sliding over the silk chemise that slanted off her torso.

For Kerry it was exquisite torture, and her voice was thick with longing as she muttered a husky, "I hate you, Lawton."

His answer was a soft laugh. Her head swam as she wondered if this was retribution for pulling away from him on the afterdeck of the *Unicorn.* Then all reason fled as Nick's hands dipped lower to find her, pushing aside the flimsy lace barricade with firm strokes. Shock waves from his caress whipped through her body in gathering force until Kerry was finally able to twist away.

She stood, panting like a wild creature, eyes wide and haunted as she faced Nick. In her mobile face with its unique planes and delicate curves, he could see the inner turmoil that boiled inside her. It was evident in the shallow pulse beats in the hollow of her throat.

"Kerry," he was moved to say, "come and let me love you, sweetheart."

Resistance would have been so much easier if he had not taken her in his arms again, pulling her so close she could feel the steady rhythm of his heartbeats as if they were shared by hers. As if surrounded by fog, Kerry was vaguely aware of Nick's voice and hands and searing kisses. Then somehow they were on the huge four-poster bed with its gauzy draperies of mosquito netting that provided both protection and privacy.

Then everything grew mixed up as he was naked beside her, his lean body fitting perfectly to her curves. Nick hesitated for only a moment before he thrust gently inside, and Kerry's body responded with a hunger that was startling in its intensity. She wasn't even aware when she arched upward and her legs curved around him. Someone was softly moaning, or maybe it was the tropical breezes singing through the open windows that made that sound.

Her hunger melded into an urgency that exploded finally into a shattering release that left Kerry dazed and feeling as if she had been buffeted by a tidal wave. Panting and drained, she buried her face into the hollow of Nick's neck and shoulder as she struggled for control.

His voice drifted down through the tangled strands of her hair and his breath was warm and soft against the slope of her cheek. "There, love, I knew that it would be even better than the last time."

Nick turned her gently to one side so that their faces were only inches apart and their eyes met. He smiled, and this time it was not mocking or cynical but genuine, a smile that held tenderness. Kerry was afraid to examine what might have prompted it and closed her eyes. After all, what did it matter if this time he felt tenderness? He could, like the wind, change at any moment without warning. Trying to hold on to that mercurial being that was Nick was like trying to capture the wind, and just as futile.

Chapter 14

"For a man who has often stated a refusal to play lady's maid, I find myself doing it with alarming frequency since I met you." Nick moved the china pitcher and washbowl and handed Kerry her wrinkled chemise with a grand flourish. "Why is that, I wonder?"

"Probably because you have a nasty habit of removing my clothes!" she snapped irritably. Throwing her damp washcloth into the blue and white bowl of soapy water, she snatched the chemise from Nick's hand. She was more irritated with herself than Nick. After all, he'd made it quite clear what he wanted and hadn't wavered from his purpose. Ah, she was such a fool! If she had any backbone whatsoever, she would escape Nicholas Lawton if she had to swim all the way back to St. Denis. But no. She was caught as neatly as a netted tuna.

Nick was looking at her with raised brows as he tucked his long shirttail into the waist of his trousers. "Still touchy, love? Does it rankle so badly that you enjoy it when I make love to you?"

"Is that what you're calling it now?" An angry, hot flush stained her cheeks. "Making love? That's overdoing it a bit, isn't it? I was given the idea that no more was involved than casual"—Kerry slanted him a derisive smile as she allowed the pause to

lengthen and then finished with perfect timing—
"sex."

Nick had, of course, been expecting to hear one of
her more salty terms. He didn't know why he'd
thought she would do the expected—when had she
ever?

"Kerry," he began with more patience than he
felt, "what is so bad about admitting to pure pleasure? Why do you have to complicate matters?"

"Complicate matters?" She was going to explode
with sheer rage. Damn it, why did she have to wear
these ridiculous satin and lace things that took so
long to put on when she'd already be dressed if she
was wearing a sensible shirt and trousers? "Complicate matters, did you say, Captain Lawton?" Finally the dress was on and to hell with the clocked
stockings and low-heeled kid pumps. "Do correct me
if I'm wrong, but it seems to me that *you* were the
one to screw up everything with your penchant for
kidnapping witnesses to your murders!"

"God, have we degenerated to that again? I
thought we'd done with it." He added in the same
bored tone, "You have your dress on backward."

"I hate you!"

"So you keep saying. I'm sure you'll be glad to
know that you won't have to put up with me for
long, then. That's what I came to tell you before I
was . . . ah . . . distracted."

"Are you letting me go?" she asked quickly. It
was too much to hope for, so she wasn't surprised
when he shook his head.

"No. I have business matters that demand my attention. But," he added with a cool smile, "I intend
to devote all my attention to you when I return,
love."

"That sounds like a threat."

"It isn't. I make promises, not threats." Silence
greeted this comment, and Nick shrugged as he pi-

voted on his heel and crossed to the door. He paused at the door with one hand on the brass knob, looking back at Kerry. She stood silhouetted against the light from the windows, the outline of her slim form tantalizingly visible through the thin muslin of her gown. "You're an impetuous child with manners more suited to a tavern than polite society," he said cruelly. "While I'm gone learn what you can from Mistress Hapwell. It can only be to your benefit, I assure you. I'll be back within a week, and I expect a marked improvement."

"Oh?" Kerry's head lifted proudly so that he wouldn't see he'd scored a direct hit. "My social graces have been in perfect harmony with the company I've been keeping lately. Perhaps I *have* been a bit lacking in regard to indiscriminate fornication, but I'm certain I shall improve under your tutelage. Did you understand what I just said, or shall I repeat it in pirate vernacular?"

"I understood," he cut in. "What I don't understand is how you mix two-shilling words and vulgarity with such aplomb. You've obviously been eavesdropping on the right people."

"Obviously." Did he really think she was an uneducated wharf brat who lacked scruples or morals? Well, maybe she lacked formal education, but she certainly had more scruples than he did, and she didn't go around murdering people for whatever reasons. It occurred to her to wonder once more why Nick had killed Garcia. Maybe Garcia had found out something terrible about Nick. But what? He was already well known as a pirate, she supposed. What could Garcia know that would endanger Nicholas Lawton?

Lord, she'd thought about it and thought about it in the past weeks, and still couldn't think of a valid reason for the confrontation she had witnessed. It might be worth her time and effort if she found out what Garcia had known. The information could buy her freedom if offered to the right person. That, of course, she did not say aloud. What she said aloud was, sweetly, "Bon voyage, Captain—and don't hurry back on my account."

"Does that mean you'll miss me, love?" Nick asked with a cynical twist to his mouth as he pulled open the door.

"When donkeys fly!" Damn him—what devilish instinct told Nick that as much as she protested, she would miss him the instant he left the room?

"Do comb your hair before you join us in the dining hall," he said. "And don't bother saying you won't be there. I insist."

The door closed softly behind him and Kerry stamped one foot in frustration. She felt like crying. She felt like crying and screaming and running after him, and didn't know why.

Pressing her fingertips to her temples, Kerry tried to clear her mind. She must think. She had to think about what to do before Nick returned from his trip. There would be only a week to find a way to escape.

Happy found her pacing the bedroom floor and chewing on her bottom lip. The older woman just stared at her young charge with incredulous eyes. "What," she asked in a faint voice, "happened to your hair and gown?. . ." She stopped abruptly. Nick, of course. Why had she even bothered to ask? The answer would have been easily read in Kerry's eyes even if Happy hadn't already known. What was Nick thinking of? For all that she gave an impression of careless independence, Kerry was still a vulnerable young girl.

"Here child," Happy said to cover her distress, "come sit down on the dressing stool and let me comb your hair. It's almost time for dinner. We have guests and this is our big meal of the day, so I want you to look your best."

"I'm not eating." Kerry stopped her pacing to fling Happy a challenging stare.

"Fine. That will show Nicholas you can't be pushed around. And it will also show him how easily he can upset you." She pulled out the cushioned dressing stool and waited.

After a short pause, Kerry crossed the room and flopped onto the stool. "I used to think I hated him," she said as Happy tugged a silver-backed brush through her hair, "but now I *know* it."

"Lie to Nicholas if it suits your purpose, dear, but never lie to yourself." Happy gazed critically at Kerry's reflection in the mirror and rearranged several curls and pinned them with ivory hairpins. "You hate what he does, and maybe even how he makes you react, but you don't really hate Nicholas. There." She gave Kerry's hair a satisfied pat. "Isn't that much better? Where are your shoes and stockings?"

"By the bed." Kerry's tone was defiant yet oddly grateful. Happy was so matter-of-fact when she could have embarrassed her so easily. And she was right. Kerry didn't really hate Nick as much as she resented her own emotions. "Who will be at lunch?" she asked as she smoothed on the stockings and pulled the pumps over her cramped toes. "Or am I supposed to always dress like this?"

"It's expected that you will be clean and well attired for a meal, but some of our guests are visitors to Belle Terre. That's common when Nicholas has just returned from a long voyage."

Kerry suffered Happy's finishing touches on her hair and the straightening of her gown in silence. God, she hated the thought of facing people who probably knew that she was a virtual prisoner. It was humiliating to be paraded like a prize pig on market day.

"Kerry." Happy lightly gripped her chin so that

Kerry had to look into her eyes. They were kind and comforting, and filled with reassurance. "Behave as an honored guest, because you are. Mr. Markham will be present, and Wilson. Other than Nicholas and myself, the rest know nothing of your circumstances. Remember—one can get away with anything if it is done with class and dignity."

Kerry had never known loving advice from a woman. Her mother had been too preoccupied with her husband to offer maternal advice to her young daughter and, since she was eight years old, her world had been almost entirely peopled with men. She felt a rush of warmth for this near stranger who seemed to care so much. She looked Happy in the eye and nodded.

"I'll do my best to pretend I'm a lady."

"Oh child, you *are* a lady. Don't you forget it, and don't let anyone else. I assure you that even though it may be unfamiliar at first, you will find yourself quite comfortable with it." Happy smoothed the cotton skirts of her gown and adjusted the cashmere shawl that Nick had bought her on one of his voyages. "Let us go below and beard the lions! We shall dazzle them with our beauty . . ."

" . . . And confound them with our wit," Kerry added. A smile curved her mouth and banished the pinched expression. "I'll be a lady, but I absolutely refuse to learn to sew a single stitch, so don't get any big ideas," she warned as they left the room, and Happy laughed.

A smile still played at the corners of Kerry's full mouth when they entered the small parlor off the main dining hall. With the silky tumble of curls piled on top of her head and the graceful, bare line of her throat and sun-kissed shoulders, Kerry appeared much older than her actual age. The hint of a smile that hovered mysteriously on her lips was captivating and intriguing, and the fine eyes beneath sooty lashes scanned the arrested gazes with unconscious dignity.

She recognized Mr. Markham, the mate from the *Unicorn,* and of course Wilson, who was dressed in tight-fitting trousers and a shirt and waistcoat that gave him the rounded profile of a pumpkin. Nick lounged casually with his elbow resting on the marble mantel and a small glass of brandy in one hand. He looked, as usual, as if he had just stepped out of the pages of *The Gentleman's Book of Fashion,* edited by Beau Brummell. There were several other men she had never seen before, who were staring at her as if she had just descended from heaven in a fiery chariot.

Before Kerry could decide on the proper etiquette—oh why hadn't she yielded to Gato's pleas that she attend Miss Trumbull's School for Young Girls?—Nick was striding forward and taking her arm in one hand and Happy's in the other.

"Gentlemen, I wish to present to you Mistress Hapwell and her protégée. Kerry has only arrived yesterday, and will be visiting for a short time."

Kerry marveled at how neatly he accomplished answering any awkward questions in a few words: Mistress Hapwell's visiting protégée, Kerry. A warning pressure on her arm turned her attention back to his continued flow of conversation. Nick made introductions, and she struggled to remember all the names and faces.

Mr. MacTavish who was in charge of all the storehouses and knew more about Nick's accumulated wealth and saleable merchandise than he did. The portly older man with distinguished gray hair and a kindly smile was Mr. Eldon Sanders, and though she didn't remember his occupation, Kerry did recall the twinkle in his eyes when he looked at Happy (who blushed, Kerry whispered to Wilson, like an eight-month-pregnant bride). She had met Mr.

Markham on the voyage, of course, and was well-acquainted with Nick's partner (Partner? That was a surprise), Mr. Wilson. The other two gentlemen's ship had arrived in the harbor only that morning. On a voyage from Spain to Mexico and back, they had stopped for fresh water and the repair of a crippled mizzenmast. The captain, Don Javier Lira, was young and handsome with curling ebony hair and a sleepy gaze that was as dark and hot as a steaming cup of coffee. His companion was older and dour, with a swarthy complexion, unsmiling face, and the dignified name of Bartolemé Narváez.

Kerry—to her immense relief—was greeted with respect by the men, and she felt a smothering rush of gratitude toward Nick for smoothing over what could have been very awkward. After their heated exchange a short time earlier, she hadn't been sure what he would do. Feeling a bit off-balance, she let him lead her into the dining hall, taking his arm as she'd seen the fine ladies of St. Denis do.

The dining area was airy and spacious with the customary high ceilings, and long windows looked out over the front porch. The wooden shutters had been opened halfway to let in the afternoon sunshine, and the room was filled with a hazy light. A crystal chandelier hung gracefully from the center of the ceiling, and a soft breeze played a tinkling melody on the sparkling oval globes. The carpet was thick and plush, and the long table covered in a snowy linen cloth was flanked by mahogany chairs with damask cushions.

Maids dressed in simple white cotton efficiently served platters of beef, pork, and fowl, and fresh vegetables in clever sauces steamed in covered silver dishes. Hot bread and creamy butter in tiny silver crocks were placed at intervals down the table's length. Artistic arrangements of fruit that had been adorned with leaves so shiny they looked as if they had been waxed, stood on sideboards next to towering cakes and huge bowls of pudding. Portions of soup, fragrant and hot with pepper, okra, tiny shrimp, and spices, had already been ladled into individual bowls at each place setting.

Seated between Nick at the head of the table and Wilson on her right, Kerry only half-listened to the conversations around her. None of it really interested her and she stifled a yawn. It looked like it was going to be a long evening.

The Spanish captain, Señor Lira, who was seated between his dour companion Narváez and Mr. Sanders, seemed equally bored. As she sipped her cooling soup, Kerry's gaze met his. Lira smiled immediately and, after a brief pause, she smiled back.

Directly across from her, Happy intercepted the exchange and a slight frown puckered her brow. Nick had seen those smiles as well, and he didn't like it. Nothing was said, but as he and Sanders discussed the merits of indigo and tobacco as profitable crops, Nick's voice held a slight edge.

Oblivious to Happy's concern and Nick's narrowed gaze, Kerry laughed softly as Señor Lira languidly lifted a finely etched eyebrow and shook his head. Here was someone with a gift for finding irreverent humor in dull dinner conversations. Too bad he was seated so far away that polite conversation was impossible. God, it would be so pleasant to talk to someone near her age without having to weigh every word first. And Señor Lira was charming.

Some sense of propriety returned to Kerry when the young Spaniard lifted his glass of wine in a silent salute, and she hesitated uncertainly. The gesture meant nothing, of course, but if anyone else noticed. . . .

"A toast, Don Javier?"

Kerry was startled to find Nick's cool gaze resting

on Señor Lira and his raised glass. Slits of sunshine filtered through the half-closed wooden shutters to slant across Nick's face. The harsh light of day lent no civility to otherwise perfect features, but left them cold and hard. No trace of warmth flickered in the depths of his eyes.

Taken off-guard, Señor Lira appeared surprised for a moment, but quickly recovered. "Sí, a toast would be perfect." He stood, flicking back the elegant lace of his shirt cuffs as he once more held up his glass. "To the fairest flower I have seen since leaving Cadiz—I drink to your unsurpassed beauty."

It was obvious the Spanish captain had no idea that Kerry was anything other than Happy's pupil, and Wilson leaped into the breach. "Aye," he agreed as he stood up and held out his glass, "an' may th' little blossom never wither on th' vine!"

Compliments flew thick and fast then as Mr. Markham and MacTavish added a few of their own in friendly competition, but to Kerry they were all a meaningless whirr of sounds. Her gaze was riveted on her plate, while her attention was concentrated on Nick. He was angry and she wasn't quite sure why Señor Lira's toast had irritated him. Damn. Was *everything* she did wrong?

"Kerry." Nick's caustic tone jerked her gaze from the cooling slices of roast beef on her plate to his face. "I'm sure you must have a toast of your own to make. Everyone seems to expect it."

"Do they? Then I won't disappoint them . . ." Before she paused to think about it, Kerry lifted her still-full wine glass in a mocking salute to Nick and cleared her throat. "Gentlemen and Mistress Hapwell, I propose a toast . . ." She had their full attention now. Don Javier's dark melting gaze was turned toward her, and she was aware of Happy and Wilson's apprehensive stares as she allowed the pause to develop. "To our freedom, political . . . and personal . . . from oppression and tyrants."

Perfect, Nick thought with a cynical smile. No one would know exactly what she meant if they weren't aware of the situation. He almost laughed at the expressions of relief on Happy and Wilson's faces, and at Wilson's softly muttered "Long live th' king."

Kerry drained her wineglass and glanced defiantly at Nick as she set the empty goblet back on the table.

"Freedom is not easily won, love," Nick said quietly. "Besides, adversity and trials make one much more interesting, don't you think?"

"That depends on whether you're an observer or the victim," Kerry snapped back. The red-gold curls quivered as she shook her head. "But you wouldn't know about that!"

"Wouldn't I?" The entire room narrowed to just the two of them as Nick focused on Kerry. "You're so very wrong about that, little one. Very wrong." His jaw tightened. "But I know how to cope with both freedom and adversity."

She leaned forward slightly, staring at him earnestly as she said, "Give me the same chance—let me go."

"No. Now is not the time or place to discuss this. We'll continue the conversation later."

It was an abrupt dismissal. Even though tempted to carry it further, Kerry didn't. Instead she picked up her fork and began eating food that tasted like sawdust to her, in spite of the fact that very capable and talented cooks had spent hours in its preparation. What did it matter what she wanted? He would do as he pleased without regard to her wishes.

The meal stretched endlessly, but thankfully, most of the guests seemed blissfully unaware that

Kerry sat silently picking at her food. When it was finally over and the plates had been removed and cordials served, everyone moved to the shady gardens at the west end of the house.

Graceful willows with leafy green branches arched in delicate sweeps over the lawn and beside white stone fountains. In small pools where lily pads floated with their pink and yellow flowers, huge goldfish darted like golden arrows. Garden benches cleverly fashioned from twisted limbs and knots of driftwood were scattered around the lawns, and a sundial rose from the middle of a circular bed of moss roses. Happy found a nook shaded by purple wisteria vines, while Kerry preferred the warm touch of the sun and chose a weathered gray bench far from everyone else.

She sat with her head tilted back and eyes closed as no proper lady would, pushing everything from her mind but gilded sunshine and the sleepy chatter of birds. Time dragged on drowsy feet until Kerry could hardly stay awake.

She lifted heavy lids as she felt someone near, and looked up to see Señora Lira standing in front of her.

"May I?" he asked politely, indicating the empty space beside her on the bench. When Kerry hesitated with a swift glance in Nick's direction, Don Javier smiled. "I asked permission to speak to you first. It seemed wise."

"Yes. It probably was." Kerry sat up a little straighter to look at the handsome young Spaniard, shading her eyes with a curved hand. He was older than she by about four years, but he seemed much more worldly and experienced. "Have you traveled about the world much?" she asked curiously. "How is it you're captain of a ship when you're not very much older than I am?"

White teeth flashed a grin. "My father owns the

Señora de la Merced. My older brother sails a vessel also, and is probably way ahead of me now." He shrugged. "We always compete to see who will reach Cadiz first with their cargo, and this time it will be Míguel who will win."

"Do you usually?"

"More than Míguel. But this time, I have not really lost, because I have met such a lovely lady."

"Very gallant, señor. Unbelievable, but gallant." Kerry couldn't help but smile at the spurt of flowery protests that followed. "I've met Spaniards before," she told him, "and I've heard all the charming and insincere compliments in a large repertoire, but I must admit you do it better than most."

"Do I?" Don Javier gave a rueful laugh. "I suppose I'm flattered, but that's not exactly the reaction I was anticipating."

"What were you anticipating? That I would throw myself in your arms in front of our entire audience and say thank you?" Kerry's grin took away any sting from her answer, and she laughed softly. "I am different than most, sir, and while I appreciate your charm and good looks, I would rather be a friend than a conquest."

"You sound as if you'd made this speech before. Am I that predictable?" He fiddled with the lacy cravat at his throat, dark brows raised questioningly.

"Not you. The situation." Kerry glanced at Nick and the others on the shaded veranda. "What did Captain Lawton say when you asked permission to speak to me?"

"Lawton?" Lira shook his head. "I didn't ask the captain, I asked your duenna. Was she not the proper person to ask?"

"Oh, dear me," Kerry said in a faint voice. "And she approved?"

"She said it was a lovely idea, that you probably

needed cheering up. I'm not sure of what is considered acceptable behavior here," he apologized. "At home, one must always have a duenna present, but she does not have to stay too close to the couple. Some families are very strict, and will not allow their daughters to speak to a man even with her duenna there. A woman of quality would never be seen without her duenna."

Kerry smiled as she imagined how Don Javier would react if he knew that she had grown up in trousers and a man's shirt, running unchaperoned about the docks of St. Denis. For the first time, she understood Gato's frequent frustration and his prophetic moans of doom. "A woman of quality would never be seen without her duenna." No wonder Nick valued her so little. She was like those waterfront harlots to him, with no chance of meaning anything more than a flea did.

A surge of pain accompanied that thought. But it was ridiculous, really, that she should even care what Nicholas Lawton thought of her. All she wanted was escape, to go home. So what now? Nick had made it very clear that she would not be leaving any time soon. She had to get away, Kerry thought, before he realized she would even try it again.

"Señor Lira, when does *Señora de la Merced* sail?"

Startled by her abrupt change of subject, Don Javier blinked rapidly for a moment before answering. "Two days at the most, I hope, señorita. Why do you ask?"

"You are sailing directly to Spain?" she said instead of answering his question. Her mind spun in a whirl.

"No. To England first, then Spain. The British are our allies, you understand, in the Peninsular War. They do not volunteer their services without expectation of payment, however, and I was commissioned to render a certain portion of the silver brought from our mines in Mexico." He stared at her curiously. "Why do you ask?" he repeated.

"I have a letter I would like delivered to a nearby island. Do you think you could take it for me?" Kerry flashed him a brilliant smile, deliberately flirting. She lowered long lashes and glanced up at him through the thick fringe just as she had seen Drucilla Milford, the lord mayor's daughter, do to a prospective beau several months ago. It had seemed to work quite well for Drucilla. Would it work as well for Kerry?

It did. Don Javier agreed to take the letter, and added that he would be especially certain that it reached its destination with great dispatch. And was she absolutely *certain*, he begged, that there was nothing else he could do for her?

"Perhaps. I'm not quite sure yet. Which route did you say you used?—past the Bahamas into the Atlantic?" A ship traveling to St. Denis could be found easily in Nassau. She leaned forward to gaze up at him entreatingly. "I have . . . a friend . . . on New Providence island. Would it be too much to ask. . . ?"

"I am at your disposal," the captain declared valiantly, and Kerry was amazed at her success. It was rather embarrassing to be forced to behave so badly, but there was some saying about all actions being just when it was love or war, if she remembered correctly. Both terms certainly applied to this problem.

"I don't know how to thank you," Kerry said. "Please, until I receive permission, do not mention this to the captain or Mistress Hapwell. I have not told them yet that I want to send a letter."

"Of course." Don Javier smiled and lowered his voice, leaning slightly forward to whisper conspiratorially, "I would be honored to perform such a service for so beautiful a lady. Do you write to a relative, perhaps? Or maybe"—he looked at her closely—"a suitor?"

Because it was a convenient lie, Kerry nodded and looked down at her hands twisting in her lap as if embarrassed. Señor Lira did not yet know it, but the fictional letter he was to deliver would be accompanied by its writer. . . .

Chapter 15

The late afternoon sun finally melded into a golden haze of twilight shot with purple shadows, ending another day on Belle Terre. Kerry sat on the veranda with Happy, only half-listening to the men's discussions of war between the United States and Britain, Napoleon and the Peninsular War involving Spain, and the policies of Madison versus those of George III. Normally she would have been greatly interested in the discussion, but her own personal conflict outweighed all other subjects.

An avenue of possible freedom yawned before her, yet she was consumed with an agonizing desire to remain with Nick. It had startled and dismayed her to find such an appalling weakness in her character. Nick didn't care about her, so why should she have this sudden longing to be with him? No, it wasn't sudden. Somehow in the past weeks aboard the *Unicorn* she had fallen in love. In love with a pirate! A pirate who had never mentioned love, never made a promise, never explained his past, never . . . Kerry's hands clenched around the handle of the palmetto fan she held in her lap. Dear Lord, what could she do now? It wasn't likely that he would fall in love with her and denounce the hateful trade of piracy for a more noble career, and everyone knew that pirates always ended their days hung from a yard-arm.

That cheery thought was still fresh in Kerry's mind when Nick seated himself beside her. She waited for him to speak, trying to appear unconcerned and casual, flicking her fan back and forth. Nick immediately destroyed her composure by reaching out to trace the tilting line of her nose with his finger. One of his blistering, potent smiles curved his mouth when she glanced up at him.

"Have you enjoyed the day, love?" His finger slid from her nose to her mouth, lightly caressing her lips.

"It's been . . . nice." God, did he have to do that when she was trying so hard to be cool and indifferent? The moving finger moved on, following the line of her jaw back up to her ear. Kerry shivered.

"Cold? In this heat?" Another disarming smile. "You have interesting reactions, Kerry love. Even your nasty temper has a certain allure."

"Nasty temper? I only become irritable when kidnapped by bloody pirates!" Her fan rapped sharply against the arm of the cane lawn chair. "Before then I was the very model of sweetness and light."

"I'll bet. Any other fairy tales you'd like to feed me? No, don't answer. I love surprises."

That's nice, Kerry thought, because you're in for a really big surprise soon. Not trusting herself to retort without betraying her plans, Kerry remained silent, fixing her gaze on a point beyond Nick.

"You're planning something, little one," Nick said softly, shocking her with his uncanny ability to read her mind at the most inconvenient times. "For your sake, I hope it is not what I'm thinking."

"And what are you thinking?" she couldn't help

asking. "I'd be interested in knowing what maggots are in your fiendish brain."

"Fiendish?" Nick's brows rose. "Isn't that a touch strong, love? I haven't used any of the more sophisticated tortures . . . yet."

Haven't you? Kerry thought with a pang. She forced her features into a considering pout before answering aloud, "Oh, all right, damn it. How about Machiavellian brain?"

"Better. How about watching your language. Every time you swear at me, I feel like I'm talking to a snuff-dipping tough sailing the Spanish Main."

"There's an art to dipping snuff. Anyway, I'd rather smoke a cigar if it's good tobacco."

"Somehow, I believe you," Nick said dryly. His hand moved to cover hers. "But I also believe that underneath that rough-tough exterior exists a very feminine young woman waiting to be released. Tell me," Nick said in a low, husky tone that set Kerry's heart to beating ten times more rapidly, "tell me if I'm correct, love."

"That's a ridiculous thing to say." She removed her hand from beneath his cupped palm. "I'm just me—as you see me and nothing else."

"I disagree. You're a changeling. You wear chameleon clothing to do your magic. Sorceress with hidden tricks up your sleeve, what spells are you planning to cast next?"

He was much too close; those heavy blue eyes stared into hers as if reading all the secrets of her soul, and Kerry leaned away. "I'm going to turn you into a frog," she managed to say in a weak attempt at humor, "and let you croak happily in one of your pools all day long."

"Are you?" His finger slid along her arm from elbow to wrist to slide over the heel of her hand and lightly tickle her palm. "How do you think you're going to look with warts?" Nick was willing to play

the game with her, his earlier irritation fading into
nothing as he watched her face. It was completely
irrational to become angry with the young Spaniard
for admiring Kerry, but he had. He'd been even an-
grier with Kerry for giving Señor Lira, a complete
stranger, an unreserved smile. The rare smiles she
turned toward Nick were usually reluctant and
guarded. She was like a will-o'-the wisp, elusive and
fleeting.

Nick was surprised when Kerry flashed him a
genuine smile now and laughed softly. "Warts?
Ugh! How do you think you'll like a diet of flies and
bugs?" she countered. "Is your preference natural
or boiled?"

"Boiled in honey with nutmeg and cinnamon," he
answered promptly, and was again rewarded with a
smile and laugh. "I always eat them that way."
Nick lifted Kerry's hand and fit it to his, palm to
palm, fingers to fingers, matching contours and
curves. "Where do you want your warts? Nose, chin,
forehead, or neck?"

This was a different Nick than she'd been accustomed to seeing, a teasing, whimsical Nick instead
of a steely-eyed pirate. "Knees," Kerry answered in
a murmur, fascinated by his play. "I can hide warts
better on my knees."

"Not from me." His answer reminded her of
their intimacy, and a warm flush spread over
curved cheekbones as Kerry looked from the laced
hands to Nick's face. He was staring at her intently, the humorous lights in his eyes altering to
a heated glow.

"No. Not from you." This time her answer was a
mere whisper of sound, more felt than heard. What
would it matter if she succumbed to that rush of
emotion now? She would be gone from Belle Terre
when Nick returned from his short voyage. The

handsome pirate captain would become only a memory.

"It's dark," Nick was saying, "A light buffet is served from the sideboards in the dining hall every evening. While I make the final arrangements for my trip tomorrow, you go with Happy and eat. When I return"—he raised her hand and lightly kissed the pink palm with its small, unfeminine calluses—"I will come to you. Maybe we can resolve some of our questions then."

It was a breath of hope and Kerry nodded. Maybe they could. Maybe if they were honest with one another and let the situation develop slowly, there would be a chance. A chance for . . . what? Love? Commitment? Marriage? The last thought staggered Kerry. She'd never considered marriage before, even when Gato was suggesting first one eligible young man and then another. Marriage had just always seemed so unattractive an alliance, rather like prison or being chained in a slave galley. Restriction? Connubial slavery? Oh no . . .

Nick rose and pulled Kerry up with him, calling to Happy who was only a few feet away. "Happy, your little protégée is hungry. I promised her food, but I have to go down to the docks. Please see that she has whatever she needs." He turned to Mr. Markham and Wilson, who were having a friendly disagreement with Don Javier Lira concerning British involvement in Napoleon's efforts to keep Joseph Bonaparte on the Spanish throne. "When you gentlemen have finished dissecting the inanities of politics, you are invited to join me on the *Unicorn.*" To Mr. Markham, it was a command politely disguised as an invitation, and he immediately excused himself from the group. Without Markham's debating prowess, Wilson decided further discussion would be embarrassingly weak on behalf of the British, and he followed suit.

Señor Lira, finding himself left with no one to debate, shrugged and bid the two ladies a pleasant good evening.

"It appears as if we will eat alone," Happy said with a laugh. She gathered up the needlework she had laid aside when it had become too dark to see well. The small Chinese lanterns strung just above their heads provided small pools of light that illuminated path and people well enough, but not tiny, intricate stitches in white linen. "It's just as well," Happy said, "that we have some privacy. I couldn't help but overhear your conversation with Nicholas, dear." She tucked her hand into the angle of Kerry's arm as they strolled slowly up the tiled path to the house.

"Which conversation did you overhear?" she asked Happy, even though she knew the answer. "Nick has cornered me so often that I'm beginning to feel like a treed panther."

"Are you?" Happy smiled faintly. "This way, child, through that door. The dining hall will be on our right, but I think I would prefer a tray sent up. The men will be back soon enough and I'm not sure I want to listen to any more nonsense about wars and killing. Too much like squabbling children tugging at the same toy, if you ask me."

Kerry laughed. "I feel the same way," she confided. "Why can't men settle matters peacefully, I wonder?"

Lifting long skirts in one hand so she wouldn't trip over the hem, Happy started up the wide staircase to the second floor. "It's their nature to fight," she said over her shoulder. "And it's their nature to pursue women." Happy paused at the top of the stairs with her hand on the smooth oak railing. "Don't forget that, dear. The urge to conquer is par-

amount in the male. Sometimes it's easy to confuse
it with genuine feeling, so you must guard your own
natural responses."

Should she be more blunt? Happy wondered, then
decided that no, Kerry understood what she meant.
Señor Lira was very charming, and Happy had
watched the pair earlier in the day as they sat on
the garden bench. Kerry had been animated and
laughing, a fact Nick had noted with glowering eyes,
and Happy had felt compelled to warn Kerry. The
girl was intelligent enough to listen, Happy was
certain.

Kerry did listen, but she applied the advice to the
wrong man. She was thinking of Nick, not Don Javier. It was just as well, she thought dully, that she
planned to leave soon. Had it been just a few hours
earlier that she had told Señor Lira she had no intentions of being simply another conquest? Yet she
was. She was, as Happy tried so kindly to tell her,
nothing but another conquest for Nick. That
thought reverberated in her head over and over as
she waited in her bedchamber for Nick's return. It
was foolish to think that she could mean anything
more to him than a conquest, but somehow she
couldn't help but hope.

Maybe that was why, instead of being distant and
cool as she knew she should be, Kerry graced Nick's
arrival with a bright smile. It took him aback for a
moment, but he quickly recovered.

"Glad to see me? You must be very bored, little
one. This is the first time I can recall your greeting
me with a smile that wasn't bristling with sharp
teeth."

"Is it?" God, why did he have to be so handsome?
"You just don't remember." Nick looked piratical
again. Dressed in leather pants and vest, he looked
like he should be standing on the *Unicorn's* quarterdeck instead of in a cozy bedroom with lacy cur-

tains at the windows. Kerry stepped out of the lamplight into concealing velvet shadows, wanting to observe without being observed. Nick was leaving in the morning and she would never see him again. She wanted to memorize each tiny detail about him so she'd never forget little things like the way his eyes crinkled at the corners when he smiled, or the way his dark brows winged across his forehead, or even how infuriating his slightly mocking smile could be. Oh damn—could she really force herself to leave when she knew how much she cared?

"Why are you hiding in the dark?" Nick crossed the room to a butler's table not far from where Kerry stood in the shadows beyond the tester bed. A silver tray held a cut-glass decanter of cognac and two silver-trimmed goblets that reflected the soft lamplight in shimmery sparkles. He poured cognac into the goblets and turned to face Kerry, offering her drink with a smile. "For you, love. Come drink with me."

A faint smile lifted the corners of her mouth as Kerry stepped from the gauzy shadows cast by filmy yards of mosquito netting and took the proffered cognac. No cheap rum for Nick, or any gin as so many drank. He liked brandy, cognac, and good French wines.

"Do you have another toast for us?" he was asking her. "How about something less profound than your earlier toast."

Word sprang into her head without conscious thought, long-buried and just remembered, and she quoted, " 'Drink! for you know not whence you came, nor why; Drink! For you know not why you go, nor where.' " Kerry unsmilingly noted Nick's astonishment at the quotation from the *Rubáiyát.* Why did he think her so uneducated? And why did it matter if he did? she wondered wearily.

Nick cleared his throat. "Well. Very impressive. Omar Khayyam, wasn't it?" He clinked his goblet against Kerry's and drank, watching her over the silver-trimmed rim. Always the unexpected, always a surprise. There were unexplored depths to this girl that he hadn't dreamed of, and Nick wondered how he could have been so blind. He'd been distracted by her face and body, when he should have been paying attention to Wilson's occasional observations. Now he had to rearrange his first conception of Kerry as a pretty, half-wild girl with no practical education in other than the shoddier side of life.

Soft lamplight shrouded her in amber hues and gave the silky tumble of hair cascading over her shoulders and back a golden sheen. Kerry was staring at him, waiting for something, and Nick gave himself a mental shake. Had she asked him a question or made some comment to which he should respond?

"I wasn't paying attention just now, love. Pardon me, but I was concentrating on the way the light makes a halo around your head. Are you an angel, maybe?"

"If I remember correctly, that's not the evaluation you once had. Has it changed, then?" The cognac still burned her throat and stomach, giving her warm courage. Kerry's gaze was direct and unwavering. "What's your opinion now?"

Nick's empty glass thunked to the butler's table. "Some things are remembered better if shown than told," he said. He took Kerry's glass from her and placed it beside his, then took both her hands between his warm palms. "Your hands are cold, love. Let me warm you."

Oh, but you already have, Kerry told him silently. There should be clouds of steam coming out of my ears, and I should be breathing fire like an ancient dragon.

Awakening to hot, voluptuous sensations that were all too achingly familiar, Kerry felt Nick's warmth in the heated stroke of his fingertips along her bare shoulders. His palms cupped her face in a gentle hold; his mouth brushed lightly over her half-parted lips. It was sweet, so sweet, and she cherished each moment and soft caress as Nick kissed her slowly, lingeringly.

Kerry's arms curved upward and her hands spread over his nape, touching and toying with the crisp black curls of hair straggling down. It was thick and springy, a luxurious ebony pelt that fell into his eyes and over his ears. Her finger traced the outline of his ear where it was half-hidden by too-long strands of hair.

Nick's lips seared a trail of fiery kisses from her mouth to her ear, and Kerry shuddered when he gently pushed aside the fragrant masses of hair. Pressing her face against his shoulder, she drew in a deep breath that smelled of leather, cognac, and tobacco, and closed her eyes. Delicious anticipation sent pricks along her nerve endings when Nick's tongue made a warm wet circle on the back of her neck, then caressed a liquid path to the intricate whorls of her ear. She must have sighed, a deep breathy sound made against his broad shoulder and somehow heard or felt.

"Ah, Kerry love, I like to hear your pleasure." His fingers shifted from the bumps of her spine, massaging soft skin and thin folds of muslin gown over the curve of her ribs to just below her breasts. His other hand smoothed over her slim back to the gentle swell of her hip to pull her closer against him. "I want to fill you with my love, sweetheart. No, don't pull away . . . this feels so right . . . oh

God, that's a sadly inept description of how this feels. . . ."

"Nick . . ." Her voice was a strangled gasp as he pulled away the bodice of her gown, and Kerry had the fleeting thought that the only reason he wanted her in a dress was to facilitate speedy removal of her clothes.

The room spun in a slow whirl as Nick lifted her in his arms and crossed the short distance to the high bed. She was in a cotton-wool world where everything was hazy and soft and reality was muffled. No, reality was Nick, with his caressing hands and passionate kisses that created a tight, aching knot in the pit of her stomach. Reality was the cool kiss of an ocean breeze over her bare skin, and the tickling caress of gossamer netting as it floated on the air current. Reality was here and now when nothing else mattered but Nick.

She was bold now, reaching out to tug away Nick's leather vest and unbutton his pants, her fingers exploring the taut ridges of muscle on his belly. Kerry lightly kneaded his spare flesh with gentle movements, then slid her hands along his lean hips and peeled away Nick's pants and his knee-high boots. Naked and trembling, they lay in a soft tangle on jasmine-scented sheets.

It was a revelation to realize that Nick could affect her with such earth-shattering intensity. Kerry's hands skipped lightly over him, examining old scars and the tight lines of muscles that blended in perfect rhythm over the angles and planes of his body. She was curiosity, Pandora with an unopened box of surprises. What would happen if . . . if she touched him . . . like this? Or this? Her hand brushed against him, lightly, gossamer fairy wings against heated velvet, and she felt Nick's body tense.

Encouraged by his reaction and quickly drawn

breath, Kerry leaned over to press a kiss on his chest. Hesitantly at first, then more boldly, she nipped gently at him, heavy strands of her hair drifting across his flat belly as she shifted.

Nick's touch startled her at first as he dragged his fingers deliciously slowly over the curve of her spine. Kerry softly rubbed her nose in the tiny, tickling hairs on his chest and smiled against him. He felt her smile and caught her head between his hands, tilting it slightly to stare into her eyes.

Kerry felt like a human patchwork quilt, all stitched together in different small squares that were nothing alike. Her head was a haze of fog and her hands blocks of ice; a roaring furnace constituted the area between waist and knees, and her chest was a deflated bellows. What an odd creature she must appear to him, all haphazardly connected by bone and muscle into this imperfect form.

"Sweet," he whispered, rubbing his thumb over the soft rise of her lower lip, then painting the outline of her mouth with its moisture. "You're soft, and sweet, and so warm. . . ."

Turning, pulling her body beneath him in a smooth motion, Nick lay with his elbows on each side of Kerry's head, his fingers tangling in the wealth of her hair. His grip tightened and his mouth slanted across her lips in a probing kiss that took away her breath. Kerry arched close to him with a sighing moan deep in the back of her throat.

She was aware, yet unaware, of things besides the pulsating fire that coiled deep inside her—his strong arms sliding beneath the soft swell of her hips, Nick's breathing that was as rapid as hers as he felt her sweet surrender, and the hard heat of him nestling gently between her thighs. Nick paused, not entering her at once, but exploring

Kerry with gentle caresses that gave her that first taste of ecstasy. Dimly, Kerry knew that she cried out as Nick took her to the heights with his touch, but all her emotions were whirling so fast that nothing mattered but the sweeping feeling that shivered through her. God, the feeling had to continue, and it did. Sanity had barely returned when Nick, lying on his side, plunged forward in a smooth driving movement to bury himself deep within the waiting satin softness of her, his hands pulling her tightly against him. Kerry cried out again as she felt her entire body respond to his possession, and she arched her back and curved her legs to his. Her feet burrowed into the quilted coverlet of the bed as she strained to push herself closer, panting, feeling as if the entire world hovered on the brink of a wonderful discovery. When the discovery came, somehow it was different than the last, as if every ounce of her being was caught up in a maelstrom of passion that exploded into shock waves of sensual delight.

Exhausted and drained, Kerry lay with eyes closed from the shock as awareness came slowly creeping back. It was clear now why men and women so avidly pursued such pleasure. But there was more to it than that for her. It was the emotional feeling of closeness to Nick that made her want him so badly, not just physical desire.

With a reluctance she tried not to show, Kerry rolled over to face him. Nick was lying on his back with one arm bent and behind his head, eyes narrowed and watching her. Kerry just stared for a moment, wondering how she could care so much and still plan on leaving him at the first opportunity. Perhaps it was because she knew how little she meant to him. Why stay and only make it harder when he eventually put her aside?

Nick reached out to smooth back damply curling

wisps of hair from her eyes, and Kerry determinedly smothered those weak feelings of tenderness. She would show a brave front to the very last. . . .

"A penny for your thoughts, love." His mouth crooked into a smile when she bargained for a half-crown. "You're too greedy by far, brat. What shall I do with you?"

Keep me, she said silently, but aloud: "Do you want me to remind you?"

"Ah, we're back to that again." His thumb skimmed over her love-bruised lips. "But I'm not ready to let you go yet. I'm enjoying this"—his hand slid over the full swell of her breast in a leisurely movement and his palm pressed against the pink crest—"too much to let you go right now. Maybe later."

"When you're tired of me, you mean?" Kerry shoved his arm away and sat up, whipping her hair from her eyes with an angry toss of her head. "I'm no cow to be bartered at will, Lawton! I'm a free woman with rights, and I demand to be returned to my home."

"Do you?" Nick's smile was deceptively gentle. "How do you intend to enforce those demands? What? No answer? Then that must mean you have no method in mind. You should learn now that one does not always get what they want in life, or even what's right. It could be the most valuable lesson you ever learn if you also learn patience."

"Patience? I suppose you mean I'm to wait until you kidnap some other poor soul and lose interest in me!"

"Ah, is that what worries you?" Nick laughed. "I can afford to keep more than one woman, Kerry love."

"I'm sure you can! You can keep an entire house-ful of them if you keep on taking fat prizes and murdering innocent merchants! Whoever said piracy wasn't profitable?''

She swung her legs over the side of the bed, but Nick caught her. ''I'm not in the habit of defending my actions, and I won't start now. Before you make wild accusations, little one, you need to have all the facts. There's a vast difference between piracy and privateering most of the time, though if one wanted to quibble I suppose certain allegations could be made. Piracy is illegal, privateering is not. And in case you haven't been paying the strictest attention, I have warehouses of merchandise that I buy and sell in fair markets. That's legal. As for murder, I deplore such extremes except in cases of dire necessity. And then I prefer calling it elimination of dangerous influences.''

''Oh, I'm sure you'd prefer calling murder by any other name than what it really is. What nice title do you have for kidnapping?''

Pinpoint lights of fury flared briefly in Nick's eyes. ''In your case, I'd call it masochism. It was a mistake not to have strangled you instead. It would have certainly saved me a great deal of harassment.''

Kerry felt as if she'd been slapped. She quickly masked her hurt with a rolling string of epithets that gave her time to recover, ending: '' . . . and I'll never change my mind about you!''

''No one has asked you to. Your opinion doesn't matter.'' He gave a careless shrug. ''It certainly doesn't stop me from taking what I want.''

Sensing his next action before he even moved, Kerry jerked her arm from his light clasp and scrambled from the bed, half-falling to her knees on the carpet. She scuttled backward like a crab on hot sand as Nick lunged forward. Her bare hip bumped into the butler's table and unbalanced one of the silver-trimmed goblets, sending it crashing to the floor to shatter into jagged pieces. Instinctively, Kerry snatched up a sharp, glittering shard of glass, the stem of the goblet. She held it in front of her, still on hands and knees with wild hair hanging in her face, a feral gleam in her eyes.

"If you touch me, I'll slice you from neck to navel," she promised, and Nick believed her.

"Kerry . . ."

"No! I don't want to hear anything more you have to say. Stay away from me . . ."

"Put that down. You might hurt yourself."

"In a pig's eye! It's more likely that *you'll* be the one hurt."

"Be reasonable, Kerry. You can't kill me, and even if you did, where would you go? This is my island, remember? No one here will help you. Now put down the broken glass."

He was right. She wouldn't kill him anyway, but that was nothing he needed to know. "I'll put it down when you leave this room," she said.

Nick hesitated, then shrugged agreement. He could wait, and it might do a world of good to let her think she had managed to bluff him successfully. It would certainly give her a false sense of security.

"I'll leave—for now. When I return in a week, I expect you to be much more rational. And I won't give in to your temper fits so easily, Kerry, so be forewarned." He stepped to where his clothes lay in a heap beside the bed, keeping a wary eye on Kerry and the sharp glass. Untamed little brat. Did she really think a puny splinter of glass would keep him at bay if he wanted her? And by God, he did want her. For some reason, this impudent wench had managed to touch some unfamiliar emotion inside him, but as much as he wanted her, he wanted more to gain her respect. It would not, he saw now, be gained by superior force. A week away from her would be good for both of them.

The aching void inside Kerry grew deeper as Nick silently dressed and left the room with only a half-mocking salute as farewell. He was gone and she was alone.

A sharp tinkling sound startled her as Kerry realized she'd dropped the goblet stem. She stared stupidly at the glittering pieces of glass scattered in an arc on the floor. Her life was as shattered as the silver-trimmed goblet, and in as many pieces.

It was several moments before Kerry realized that the fat, wet drops splattering on her bare thighs and the back of her hands were her own tears. Tears? She had not cried this much when she was a small child, but since meeting Nicholas Lawton, it seemed that all she did was weep.

When she left Nick and Belle Terre far behind, she would also leave her vulnerability. No man would ever again pierce her armored heart, Kerry vowed.

When the *Unicorn* sailed on the morning tide, Kerry was watching from her window. It was barely dawn and she had not slept all night. The crisp morning breeze billowed out the lace curtains over her window and filled the great white sails of Nick's ship. She stood at the window until the *Unicorn* had faded away into the blue and gold horizon.

It was three days before Don Javier was ready to sail from Belle Terre, three long, nerve-wracking days for Kerry. Señor Narváez did not like her—or anyone else, Lira apologized—and objected to Kerry accompanying them even as far as Nassau. The stuffy Spanish gentleman kept repeating that it would be unwise to make an enemy of Lawton. Don Javier swayed back and forth, wanting to please Kerry but feeling a certain obligation as captain.

"Perhaps, Señor Lira," Kerry said with the last shred of her patience wearing thin, "Señor Narváez should be the captain. At least he is able to make a decision."

Don Javier drew himself up and stared at Kerry coldly. "Your original request was to deliver a letter, I believe. Nothing was said about taking you away from Belle Terre. You are running away."

"Yes." It was said simply, and Kerry immediately appealed to the young Spaniard's chivalry as she explained that she must return home. "I am homesick, and have not seen my foster father in months. Please, Don Javier . . . take me to Nassau with you!"

He finally agreed, and Kerry slipped out of the house the next morning when it was still dark outside. Her few belongings were in the same square of material she had brought four days before from the *Unicorn*. There was an addition to the little bundle this time however, for she had stolen into Nick's office and carefully picked the lock to a small chest of inlaid ivory. Flipping back the lid, Kerry had stared at the cluster of gold coins against the dark velvet.

"No need to be too greedy," she'd muttered, and had removed only as much as she thought she might need for passage on a ship to St. Denis. She'd thought a moment longer, and taken more, leaving behind the silver unicorn necklace that had been in the O'Connell family for four hundred years. One day, she would retrieve it. The necklace was all that was left of her heritage, but she could not bear being accused of theft, even by a pirate.

The money would be little missed, she was certain, but on impulse, Kerry had brought with her two more items that she knew were far more important. They had lain in the bottom of the little chest, nestled beneath a fold of velvet. Seeing them, Kerry had recalled Nick's discussion with Garcia, and his reaction when she had flipped through the books. These meant a great deal to Lawton, and were her insurance against harm in case he should find her.

How ironic, Kerry thought to herself, that she should worry about stealing from a man known the width and breadth of the Spanish Main as a freebooter, a pirate, a buccaneer. He had stolen so much more from her. . . .

Chapter 16

Rocking, rocking, back and forth and up and down . . . Kerry moaned softly and opened her eyes to look up at the dark-beamed ceiling. It seemed like forever since she had seen land or stood on something solid. It had been almost two months since she had left Belle Terre behind and blithely set sail for Nassau. A voyage that should have taken no more than two days had—through the fickle machinations of fate—been extended to months. The Spanish ship belonging to Señor Lira had been pushed so many miles off course by a hurricane that he had refused, politely of course, to turn around for Nassau.

"Fortunately," Don Javier had explained to a greenish-pallored Kerry, "we are still riding the Gulf Stream currents and are favored by the westerlies, even though it is late summer. The *Señora de la Merced* will arrive in England close to schedule, and I can arrange passage for you from there."

Too sick to argue, Kerry had only nodded and wondered weakly if Nick had been caught in the same vicious storm that had swept over the *Señora de la Merced*.

Kerry shivered again. The cold seeped into the ship through leaky seams in the planking, chilling her to the bone. Accustomed to much warmer climates, she felt as if she would never be warm again in spite of Don Javier's best efforts to keep the cold at bay. He'd given her the most comfortable cabin, and furnished brass braziers for heat. Reddish coals glowered at her from the small braziers, but they weren't hot enough to keep her from huddling under a mound of blankets.

The thick wool blankets around her ears muffled the knock at her cabin door at first, and Kerry only realized someone was there when it slowly swung open. Don Javier's tall frame blocked the gray light from outside as he stood in the doorway.

"Are you ill, Señorita?"

"No," came a barely audible reply from the wool cocoon on the narrow bunk, "I'm just cold, that's all."

She sounded so disgruntled, the Spanish sea captain had to laugh. "You have thin blood and should be traveling to sunny Spain instead of the cold shores of Ireland, don't you think?"

"Probably. But this is something I've thought about a lot while lying in this bunk, Don Javier." Kerry peeped from the blanket folds as he perched on the edge of her bunk. "I'm not quite sure why, but I know I have to face it sometime, and I'm so close. . . ." Her voice faded to a whisper.

The past, her past, still haunted her. At times there were vague dreams of foamy seawater breaking over the splintered decks of a ship, and Patrick's voice calling to her. Was there any way to escape the past, she'd asked herself, and then remembered Kaliza. The old gypsy woman had said once that the only way to exorcise personal demons was to face them. So she'd finally decided to seek out Sean O'Connell. If her grandfather condemned her for failing Patrick, at least she would know the worst instead of fear it. There would be no more swords hanging over her head then, no more nightmares to shatter peaceful slumber.

Señor Lira reached out to touch Kerry lightly on one shoulder. "You seek peace, do you not?" he asked, and she was struck by his intuitiveness.

"Yes, Don Javier, I do. I know I can find it only in Ireland. When I leave Ireland, I will have peace of some sort." A smile lifted the corners of her mouth. "It may not be exactly what I searched for, but it will end the uncertainty of not knowing."

Shifting closer, Don Javier let his hand drift from Kerry's shoulder to thick strands of her hair peeking from the edges of the blankets. He let the silky curls slip through his fingers as he stared at her thoughtfully.

"You could have peace with me," he said softly. "I would see that you were cared for."

Startled, Kerry gazed up into his hot, dark eyes. He was staring at her intently now, his heavy-lidded eyes skimming over the angles of her face that were barely visible beneath the blankets. Don Javier was handsome, very handsome, and he was charming, but she could think of no other man—not right now. Kerry's voice was gentle as she explained this to the young Spaniard.

"But you have not tried," he pointed out. "And I can be very tender in love, querida. Sometimes it takes another man to forget the last. . . ."

Ignoring Kerry's faint cry of protest, Don Javier was lifting her in his arms and pressing her close. His mouth covered her face in kisses as he held her tightly. He kissed her cheek and brow, her closed eyelids, and the corners of her mouth.

Kerry lay quietly in his embrace until Don Javier's hand moved to cup her breast. With a swiftness that surprised them both, she twisted from his arms and onto the tilting cabin floor.

"No! Don Javier . . ."

He was kneeling beside her, lifting her up, muttering her name into the tumbled waves of coppery hair in her face, and Kerry felt a wave of panic wash over her.

"Querida, mi amor . . ."

"Don Javier! Let me go!" She twisted frantically, and her panic finally penetrated Don Javier's concentration. He loosened his hold, but still kept one hand circling her arm as he brushed at the tangled strands of her hair with the other.

"Por favor, Señorita, forgive me," he said quietly. "I thought perhaps you felt the same . . ."

"I'm sorry . . . I do not . . ." She shook her head. "I am in love with . . . with another."

"Sí, I realize that now. You are just so beautiful. I thought that because you were running away from him, that you no longer cared. I see I was mistaken."

"I find it hard to explain my reasons, Don Javier. Just try to understand that I cannot . . ." Kerry was shivering uncontrollably, and Don Javier insisted that she get underneath her blankets again. He tucked them tightly around her and stirred the coals in the brass braziers.

"We will arrive in England tomorrow," he said when he'd made her more comfortable. "I will help you find a ship sailing to Ireland and your relatives." Raking a hand through his thick, dark hair, the young Spaniard stepped close to Kerry's side again, then bent and took her hand. He pressed her cold fingers to his lips and smiled. "If ever you should need me, Señorita, you know that I will come to you. All you shall have to do is send me a message. I will be there."

After he'd gone, Kerry lay thinking for a long time. Was she really doing the right thing by reopening all her old wounds? Was the past better left untouched? No—she had to have an answer to the questions that had plagued her for so long. A thin smile curved her mouth. Gato would be pleased that she had finally decided to face her ghosts.

When the *Señora de la Merced* docked the next morning, Kerry was ready. She stood on the mercifully still decks and watched the teeming docks as she waited for Don Javier to summon the carriage that would take her to the ship he had secured for her. Ireland. It was almost November and she was arriving in Ireland in thin cotton trousers and shirt and an old, patched sweater. At least she wore shoes. They were heavy and clumsy but warm. She looked, Don Javier said ruefully, like an ill-bred street urchin.

"But if you are determined to travel alone to Ireland, I suppose that is the best disguise," he added, taking Kerry's hands in his. "I am sorry you will not come with me, but I understand. *Vaya con Dios, querida.*" He pressed a tender kiss on Kerry's brow, then placed her in a carriage that would take her to her destination. Kerry waved at him until he was out of sight.

The *Adventurer*, a heavy-bottomed sloop out of London, lurched clumsily through the waves, and Kerry felt another wave of nausea wash over her. God, she was seasick because of this wallowing old tub, and could think only of solid land.

They had sailed from London's seaport, through the English Channel, around the tip of southwest England to the Celtic Sea. Now the *Adventurer* steered through upthrustings of jagged rocks scattered carelessly along the southwest coast of Ireland. As Kerry leaned over the rail to stare at the passing coastline, a fellow passenger paused to point out a cluster of sharp stones jutting up from the blue-gray sea.

"Skellig Michael, lad," he said. "Ha' ye e'er been this way afore?" When Kerry gave a mute shake of her head, he continued, " 'Tis a sort o' monastery, it is; some say o'er a thousand years old. See th' stone markers in th' shape o' a man? They were carved wi' crosses by ancient Irish monks sae long ago, most 'ave lost count o' th' years."

"Is the monastery still used?" Kerry asked because the man seemed to expect some response.

"Only by th' starkest sort o' man. Th' rest o' us like our creature comforts," the man chuckled good-naturedly. "Where ye bound for, lad?"

Kerry hesitated. Where *was* she bound for? Instinct had brought her this far, instinct and a dim memory of names and places. Inch. Dingle Bay. Castlemaine. Ballymalis. Castleconnell. Those names had been buried so far in her subconscious that she had doubted her ability to recall them at all until faced with no choice. Castleconnell and O'Connell had struck familiar chords in her memory, and she had bargained with the *Adventurer's* captain to bring her this far. Dingle Bay should be only a few hours away, and not far beyond the bay, near the shores of Lough Caragh, should be Castleconnell, the captain had told her.

"Killarney?" the stranger suggested when Kerry remained quiet, and she quickly nodded.

"Yes. Killarney. I've . . . I've family there."

"Ah. It's goin' on ta Galway, I am. A bit farther, it is, but I don't ha' ta ride a donkey cart inta Killarney, an' that's a fact." The garrulous stranger gave Kerry a blissful smile that boded ill for the merits of a donkey cart.

He was, she decided the next day, right about the donkey cart. It was a singularly uncomfortable ride, especially for someone who had aches and pains in every joint and muscle of their body, and a fever to boot.

The cart bumped over a large white stone in the road and flung Kerry against another passenger. She murmured an apology and pulled her knit cap lower over her face to shield it from the bitter bite of the wind. A gray mist covered rocky hills and brown fields with tattered streamers that crept damply beneath layers of her clothing to chill fevered skin. The illness she had attributed to seasickness had stayed with her, and Kerry suffered racking chills as well as a lung-binding cough.

What was she doing? What if she was wrong and Castleconnell was not her birthplace? Or what would happen if all her kin were long dead? Or if they refused to recognize her? There was only a little money left, not nearly enough to carry her through a winter in Ireland and buy passage back to St. Denis in the spring. She was here, for good or bad, with no way to return.

Ireland. It looked much as it had in her dreams. White stones were everywhere, lining roads and forming low, jagged fences. The green fields were brown now, with fall's bright-colored leaves hanging from the few trees and drifting to heaps on the ground.

The land was folded into hills and valleys beneath scudding clouds that hid blue sky, and Kerry muttered a disparaging comment about the weather between dry coughs. The driver of the donkey cart heard her and turned with a jovial smile.

"It's a stranger ta Ireland ye must be, lad, else ye'd know that there's good weather just ahead. Why, there's as much blue in th' sky as would make trousers for a man!"

Tilting her head, Kerry frowned up at the heavens and discovered her error. There was, hidden in the puffs of gray cloud, a small patch of blue.

"Sorry," she apologized. "I'm not used to Irish skies or weather."

"Aye, it's plain ta see yer not from Ireland," the driver said. He bent a suspicious glance in Kerry's direction. "English?"

"English?" The proper amount of horror registered in her voice, made rough by her sore throat and nagging cough. "Ireland born, in spite of my accent! I've lived in the islands for a while, that's all. Not far from Montserrat, if you've ever heard of it."

"Can't say as I ha', lad, an' that's a fact." The driver and passengers looked at Kerry more kindly, and with a certain amount of curiosity. "What's Montserrat?"

"Montserrat was settled by the Irish about two hundred years ago, but the English"—she spat over the side of the rolling cart—"own it now. Still, it's mainly the Irish who live there."

"Is it true," a large woman wrapped in a wool shawl leaned forward to ask, "that th' skies are always blue an' th' wind always warm in those heathen lands?"

"Almost true . . ."

"An' there are birds all th' colors of a rainbow," the other passenger asked eagerly, "that talk like a human?"

"Yes. Parrots and parakeets . . ."

"An' th' cities are so rich with gold and silver that pirates attack cargo ships right in the harbors?" the driver asked. "I've heard they kill most, an' force survivors ta walk th' plank. Is that true? Ha' ye e'er met a pirate?"

Kerry's face paled and her hands shook so hard she hid them in the dirty folds of her sweater. Oh yes, she'd met a pirate. And she'd fallen in love with him. . . .

"Most towns are much like here," she answered in a remarkably steady voice, "and pirates don't make people walk the plank. They just throw them over the side."

"But ha' ye e'er met a fierce pirate, lad?" the hefty woman asked. "Do they wear earrings hanging down, and bones in their noses?"

"Some wear earrings." Kerry smiled as she recalled Cook and Chips, and an argument they'd once had about the gold earring the ship's carpenter wore in his right earlobe.

"Might as well be through yer nose," Cook had jeered, "ye look so prissy wearin' that gold heart in yer bloody ear!"

The woman's question brought back poignant memories, and Kerry realized she missed more than just Nick. She had found friends aboard the *Unicorn*.

But she was here now, and her future might well be here, too. The donkey cart swayed to a halt on the crest of a hill. In the valley below was a small town, Castleconnell, the driver told her. Across the valley on the opposite peak squatted a stone castle, a brooding sentinel overlooking the village below.

"Who lives there?" Kerry asked as she swung down from the cart with her square cloth bundle.

"In th' castle? Th' old lord, Sean O'Connell." The driver peered at her curiously. "D'ye be knowing him?"

"I know him." Kerry took a deep breath, ignoring the burning pain in her lungs. "Goodbye to you, sir, and God bless."

"God bless" chorused from a trio of throats as the cart lurched forward again. Kerry stood alone on the hilltop, shivering against the wind sweeping through her thin clothes, then picked up her bundle and started down the winding road leading through the village.

It was growing warmer now, and her forehead was beaded with sweat. Purple shadows lurked behind trees and rocks, shrouding the rolling hills that stretched to the far horizon. In the town it was quiet, with few people on the streets. No one paid much attention to the ragged youth with squared shoulders hunched against the bite of the wind whistling down alleys and over rooftops.

This was so strange, yet so familiar. Cobbled streets wound along hills lined with houses and not far ahead was a public well, and beyond that a stable.

. . . Don't lean over the well, Mary Kathleen. You might fall in . . . Mary Kathleen, are you hiding in Mr. Flannery's hay again? What will your mother say if you get all dirty? . . . Don't tell her, Papa. . . .

Kerry blinked and the hazy voices faded away. It was a long way up the hill to the castle. Where was her pretty white pony and cart?

There was the gatekeeper's house at last. Where was McCurley? He wasn't at the gate, as usual. Lazy and incompetent, Papa said. Drinking his pint o' stout, Sean would answer in his customary boom, and wouldn't be found 'til it was gone.

Kerry's hands knotted into fists and she pounded at the heavy doors. "McCurley! Open up, old man . . ." Why was her head ringing like all the church bells on Christmas Day? She closed her eyes and leaned weakly against the door for a moment. The rough wood was cool against her flushed cheek, and Kerry pressed her forehead against it. She was so hot, but she couldn't rest now. She had to get in. . . . "McCurley! Open the door for me, or I'll be tellin' Sean where you hide your pint, I will!''

"Blast ye! Stop your shoutin', I said!" A thin, querulous voice strained through the wooden doors of the gate. "An' who's bangin' at this time o' th' day, I'd like ta know?" The doors opened just wide enough to expose half a face. "Well?" the one blood-shot eye and half a nose and mouth demanded. "Who are ye?"

"Let me in, Michael McCurley" was the faint re-ply, and the door widened a bit more. Two bloodshot eyes and a gaping mouth topped a grizzled gray chin as the old man stared at her in the dim light of the lantern he lifted. The entire world was whirling now, and Kerry struggled to remain on her feet. Gray shadows flirted with black voids, and she blinked to clear her vision. "I . . . want . . . to see . . . Sean. . . ." Lord, was her grandfather even alive? Why was McCurley just staring at her like that? "I'm no bloody ghost, McCurley!" Kerry snapped with surprising strength, "so shut your mouth and open the door!"

There was the rusty scraping of metal and the protesting squeal of hinges as the door swung wide, and Kerry stumbled into a grassy courtyard. A huge stone unicorn smiled at her, and she reached out to run her hand over the cool surface of the carved statue. Trembling fingers lightly traced the whorls of the animal's horn, then Kerry turned blindly to the old man and took a faltering step forward. McCurley grabbed her elbow as she half-fell, and he lowered her gently to a stone-tiled path.

"It cannot be," he muttered, sweeping Kerry with a sharp glance. "Why, ten long years, it's been . . ."

"And it will be ten more before you get me in the house," Kerry murmured weakly. "Bless me, Mc-Curley, stir your bones and help me up."

But when the old man hastily set down his lantern and lifted her, the dark shadows that had been threatening all day shrouded the light in total darkness. Kerry pitched forward into the softly welcoming embrace of oblivion.

Chapter 17

Voices drifted in and out of Kerry's world, a hazy half-world peopled with the familiar and unfamiliar. She was hot and cold, sweating like a boiled lobster one minute, as frozen as the Arctic tundra the next. Gato spoke to her in a soft, accented voice that reminded her of the young Spanish captain who had taken her to England. No, it should be the other way around, a husky voice chided, and Kerry frowned. Nick? It had to be Nick. He was always telling her what to do, and even what to think. Faster, Diablo, go faster! Ah, the wind felt so cool and the sun was so hot, burning parched lips and skin. The sun must have gone behind the clouds now because it wasn't hot anymore. It was almost too cool, and the wind was howling like a banshee in the hills, keening for the lost souls.

"Bean sidhe. . . !"

Her Gaelic words spoken aloud brought a soft, soothing feminine voice and a cool hand against her fevered brow. "It's not for you the banshee calls," the voice assured Kerry. "Rest, child."

"She's dying." The masculine voice was gruff and loud, and even in her fitful sleep Kerry sensed pain. *"Mo muirnin* came home to die."

"Nonsense, old man! And don't be looking at me like that, you old fool, for all that you're lord here! She'll live because she's young and strong." The woman again. She was not afraid of the man, though there was a certain note of respect in her tone.

Kerry drifted away again, floating like driftwood at the mercy of the sea, buffeted by wind and waves until she was drowning in the roar of the ocean. She was cold and wet, looking over the edge of a small boat and watching as the *Wanderer* slipped into the depths of the sea. . . . Patrick! Kate . . . It was her fault. She should have warned him about the man with the knife, but she had been too scared to speak and he had died. . . . Oh, Papa! No, that wasn't Patrick, it was Nick. One image faded into another, and the *Wanderer* sported the figurehead of a unicorn on its prow. . . . The ship flew through clouds and a sun-gilt sky and the wind was fair and steady, white sails spread like angel wings as the *Unicorn* skimmed high over land and sea. Nick was at the wheel, his long legs braced for balance on decks shining with new paint and sunlight . . . oh, he was so handsome, laughing in the wind with his dark hair romantically ruffled and his eyes alight with amusement. . . . Watch, Nick was telling her, watch what would happen now. . . .

Nick rode the wind currents until he faded away and Kerry cried out with disappointment, calling to him to come back; but he was gone. She opened her eyes to a sun-bright room and a small, gray-haired woman who was busily mopping at Kerry's forehead with a damp cloth.

"Hush," the woman said. "You'll sleep easier, now that the fever's broken. Shut your eyes."

Kerry did, falling immediately into a deep, restful slumber, and when she woke again the room was dark. Lamps had been lit and threw rosy pools of light on high stone walls covered with tapestries and stone floors carpeted with thick rugs. A cheery blaze crackled and burned in a massive fireplace big enough to roast a large ox. Kerry turned her head curiously. She was in the middle of a high bed with fat pillows stuffed with a hundred thousand goose feathers cushioning her head and an embroidered satin coverlet pulled up to her neck. In spite of stone walls and incredibly high ceilings, the room had a coziness to it that was welcoming and somehow familiar. Kerry glanced at the woman seated in a large rocker nearby, her small frame dwarfed by the solid oak chair. It was the same woman who had pressed cloths to her head.

Sharp blue eyes stared back at her, and Kerry was strangely reminded of Happy. "Who are you?" she asked the woman bluntly.

"Margaret O'Connell, Sean's sister. And you are. . . ?" The gray head tilted to one side as Margaret answered her own question. "I'm thinking you're Mary Kathleen, Patrick's only child. Welcome home," she added softly, and Kerry's eyes filled with sudden tears.

"I did find it, then. I remembered after all those years. . . ." Kerry smiled through her mist of tears. "I wasn't sure, you see, that I hadn't dreamed it all."

" 'Tis no dream. You're home at last." Margaret rose and crossed to the bed, laying thin fingers on the shallow pulse in Kerry's neck. "You're still weak. Red wine and beef broth will have you up and about in no time."

"Does my grandfather know I'm here?—what does he say?"

"Sean O'Connell will be a happy man now, I'm sure." Margaret gave Kerry's folded hands a gentle pat. "He's a gruff old beastie, but means no harm. I'm thinking you're not the faint sort anyway. If you were, you could never have come all this way dressed as a lad and alone and sick."

Kerry closed her eyes again. It had been a long way and she was bone-weary and soul-sick. The journey had taken less toll than the loss of her heart, but there was no way to explain that to this patient old lady who was so glad to see her. How did one describe the death of one's hopes?

"I'll bring your broth," Margaret was saying, "and Sean will visit as soon as he hears you are awake, so be prepared for him."

"Now you're making me nervous," Kerry murmured. "Do I need to be prepared?"

"I certainly don't intend for him to be asking you too many questions, but you must realize how he has longed for answers these past ten years." Margaret pulled her light wool shawl closer around her thin shoulders. "I'll be back shortly, Mary Kathleen."

The heavy door closed behind Margaret with a solid thunk and Kerry was alone. Mary Kathleen—she'd almost forgotten her real name. It had been so long since she'd heard it, and it brought back so many echoes of the past.

Mary Kathleen, don't jump your pony over the hedges again . . . Mary Kathleen, have you been racing the McLaughlin lads down the church road again? . . . Mary Kathleen, ladies must learn to sew a straight seam and embroider altar cloths for the church. . . .

Well, she'd jumped the hedges, raced the McLaughlin lads, and never learned to sew a straight seam or embroider altar cloths for the church, and so had come to this end. Perhaps she should have listened to Kate O'Connell after all. A single tear trickled over the curve of her cheek.

"Sniveling?" a voice boomed. "Can't be an O'Connell then, because we're not a family of whiners. You must be"—a bony finger poked at Kerry from the shadows around the bed—"an imposter."

Her temper flared at the contemptuous tone. "How did you get in, old man?" Kerry demanded as a tall, silver-haired man stepped into the light. "Merchants and beggars should go to the back gate!"

"Why, you ungrateful little wench, I ought to put you right back out in the gutter where McCurley found you!" Gnarled hands tightened on the silver head of his cane as the old man met Kerry's icy glare with one of his own. The cane thumped imperatively on the floor. "Since you're my granddaughter, I suppose you shall stay for now."

"How decent of you." Kerry's gaze followed Sean as he pulled a chair close to the bed and settled his large-boned frame into it. Jade eyes peered at her from beneath bushy brows. Ten years and age had only slightly altered the craggy face of Kerry's memories. Long fingers tapped impatiently against his knee as Sean asked the question Kerry was expecting.

"What of my son, child? How did he die?"

"The *Wanderer* hit a coral reef and put a hole in her hull. Patrick died fighting for a lifeboat."

"So he never reached Montserrat, and that's why I couldn't find word of him all these years."

"Montserrat?" Kerry stared at him. "Was that our destination? Montserrat?"

"Why didn't you send word some time in these past ten years?" The cane thumped angrily on the floor. "Were you having such a grand time that you couldn't let an old man know how his only son died? I thought more of you than that, Mary Kathleen, even though you were only a child."

"Do you judge me then, without hearing a defense?" Kerry struggled against the weakness sweeping through her, facing the old man with a tired defiance. He gave a curt nod of his head and muttered that he was willing to listen since the explanation had been such a long time coming. Kerry's head fell back against the pillows as she began,

"I couldn't think about it for a long time at first, or even remember my right name . . ."

Kerry told Sean how frightened and angry she had been, and how consumed with guilt over her father's death. It had been years before she had been able to come to grips with the truth, and "By then so much time had passed it no longer seemed to matter. In truth, I didn't even know if any of you were still alive."

Some of Sean's first anger faded. "So why are you here now, child? What brought you to Ireland?"

"A series of mistakes, beginning with a murder and ending with a hurricane."

"And you'll be ending her, Sean O'Connell," Margaret interrupted, "if you don't be letting her rest! Tomorrow is soon enough to hear the tale." She set a tray down on the small table beside Kerry's bed. "Off with you, old man. Kiss your granddaughter good night and take yourself to bed. She's been here for a week, and it's likely she'll be here at least another one."

Kerry stared in disbelief. A week? No small wonder she felt so tired! She looked warily at Sean as he heaved himself up from the chair and hovered over her bed hesitantly. Then he pressed a quick kiss on her forehead and muttered a gruff "Good night and God bless" before he left.

"You two will make your peace," Margaret predicted. "You've come back from the grave, Mary Kathleen. There will be new life in the castle now." She smiled and spooned a mouthful of beef and brandy broth between Kerry's lips. "It's been too damned dull around here lately."

Life at Castleconnell had a faster pace now. Margaret had been right. Kerry's return brought an infusion of new life, new plans, celebration and laughter to the brooding pile of stones perched on a rocky crag like a scavenging bird.

Built over five hundred years before, the castle gave evidence of its Norman inheritance in the stone towers and bridges, the soaring arches and heaven-pricking spires. The first stone of Castleconnell had been laid during the reign of Henry II in England.

Kerry's favorite room was the Great Hall in the main building of the castle, and she spent more and more time visiting with Sean there as she regained her strength. Tonight rain slashed against thick glass windows and a peat fire burned in the grate. Kerry sat in a high-backed wing chair near the fire-place and smiled at Sean. The crusty old man shook his shaggy head at her, thoroughly enjoying the heated debates they exchanged during long winter evenings.

Balancing her elbow on the chair arm, Kerry propped her chin in the cup of her palm and stared steadily at the old man as she abruptly asked the one question she had not dared to voice before. "Why did Patrick flee Ireland?"

Sean coughed and bent his dark gaze on her. "Flee? Why do you think he was fleeing, child? I told you. He was going to Montserrat as a mer-chant. . . ."

"Rubbish," Kerry said rudely. "He was your only living son and heir to Castleconnell. Patrick would not have left Ireland with his family unless forced to. Why?"

Sean flapped his hand at her and tried to shrug off her question, but Kerry would not be put off. "Damn ye!" he finally boomed. "You ask too many questions that shouldn't concern you!"

"Patrick and Kate lost their lives and I spent ten years far from my own country. Shouldn't concern me? Only a bloody fool would say that!"

"You're saying I'm a bloody fool?" Sean's rasping

voice snarled into the air like the warning of a huge mastiff, but Kerry would not back down.

"If you insist—yes."

A thick silence enveloped both of them for several long moments, the old man and the girl both so much alike, chins jutting obstinately outward and eyes defiant.

"Aye, maybe you're right," Sean muttered at last, and sat back in his chair. "I must have been a bloody fool back in '98, or I would have seen how it would end." He heaved a great sigh and slanted Kerry a resigned smile. "Your father took part in the insurrection led by Wolfe Tone. The French helped, but not like we had hoped, and Cornwallis defeated us." The wan smile flickered on Sean's tired mouth. "Those not already martyred on the battlefield ended on the gallows or fled. Patrick went to England with your mother for a while, but couldn't stomach it for very long. Montserrat in the West Indies seemed a logical choice, and you were sent to London to join your parents.

"My agents who investigated your father's disappearance told me the *Wanderer* had been presumed lost in a hurricane," Sean was saying. "No survivors were reported. I thought, until you came banging on my door, that all of you had drowned." Sean's eyes were suspiciously bright. "You're the last of my line, child. All are dead now but you and your cousin, my brother's son Michael."

"Michael inherits?"

"Unless I change it in your favor, yes." Sean's sharp gaze seemed to pierce Kerry in two. "Your mother was English, but your heritage is Irish. How do you feel?"

English? Kerry was surprised. Vague memories of bitter comments between her mother and grandfather teased her, and now she understood why.

English against Irish, a centuries-old feud that had
obviously not mattered to Patrick.

"You didn't like my mother." It was not an accusation but an observation, and Sean nodded.

"No. I never thought Patrick should marry her,
but the boy had a mind of his own and would have
it no other way. She was always after him to leave
Ireland, to live in England. That's why she was so
pleased when the revolt failed and Patrick had to
leave Castleconnell. Kate had him all to herself
then. . . ." He jerked to a halt and looked at Kerry.

"I know." Kerry's mouth trembled into a curve.
"I remember feeling like an outsider at times, but
my father always loved me."

"Aye, that he did, *mo muirnin.* And Kate did too,
but Patrick was the center of her life." Sean reached
over and gave her a clumsy pat on her knee. "It's
all past. You're here now. You're home, Mary Kathleen. This is your past and your future."

Kerry glanced around the Great Hall. Ancient
tapestries hung over damp stone walls. In front of
the huge fireplace was a chess set with an inlaid
board of ivory squares and playing pieces of silver
that were carved in the shapes of Roman gladiators.
High arched windows filtered gray light into the
hall, and the wind moaned around stone gargoyles
on the outside walls. Castleconnell was no longer a
hazy dream but reality. The shadowy alcoves and
winding stairs and echoing corridors existed. Perhaps the *Unicorn,* Belle Terre, and Nick had been
only in her dreams. Maybe that was why, when she
closed her eyes at night, a handsome face mocked
her from some distant, magical sphere that could
have only existed in dreams. Oh, Nick.

Kerry never mentioned him, though Sean had
asked in his gruff way if she had married the man
whose name she'd muttered in her first, troubled
days of illness in Castleconnell.

"No," she'd answered shortly.

"But you loved him?" Sean persisted. "I ask for a reason," he'd added. "You're marriageable age, and I like to know before I go bargaining what I have to bargain with."

"Bargain?" Kerry had flared. "I'm not a horse or cow that you can barter, Sean O'Connell!"

"You sound like your grandmother," Sean had observed ruefully. "Kathleen always said I had calf brains in my bone box when it came to that subject, but the fact remains: I have to know if you're already promised, Mary Kathleen."

"No." It was said defiantly, and she added the comment that she had no intention of marrying. Sean swore softly under his breath. He'd stumped from the room and the subject had not been broached again.

Her past and her future melded into one as Sean made his plans. She would be educated as befit the daughter of his house, and would learn not only the ways of the household but the managing of the estates.

"Castleconnell is one of the few Irish-managed houses left, mavourneen, and it's taken a great deal of walking on eggs to keep it that way. Most of the landowners are English who leave agents to manage their lands and evict Irish tenants who can't pay exorbitant rents. English!" Sean snorted in disgust. "We live it and even speak it. I cannot speak my own language or practice my religion. The peasants cannot be educated or own a horse worth more than a few pounds. They resort to hedge schools and have secret Masses in caves and open fields, and end their days with 'the Protestant lease'—a grave."

"Do you expect me to change this?" Kerry settled back into her chair. "I can't change two hundred years of history, Sean. . . ."

"Change it? No, no. It's treason to even suggest we would try. Only God can change it. We just need to be ready when he does." The cane emphasized his point with a deliberate thunk on the floor. "You'll be ready." He gave her a sharp glance. "If you want to be. How do you feel about it? You're Irish born, and you're even starting to sound Irish again, but maybe you prefer living where you're more familiar with the country. There are times when you don't seem happy, Mary Kathleen. You've got a look about you like you're longing to be elsewhere."

Kerry shifted her gaze from Sean to the long windows where a cold rain pelted the glass. "I love Ireland," she said slowly, "but I spent ten years of my life in St. Denis. Sometimes the cold seeps into my bones and I feel like I'll never be warm again, and the sky seems to weep constantly. I miss hot sand and warm wind blowing gently against my face, and the sweet smell of the frangipani tree. And I miss . . ." She stopped and closed her eyes in sudden pain. She missed the invigorating company of a pirate whom she had come so dangerously close to loving too much.

"Don't stop now," Sean said testily. "I know what you're going to say anyway. You miss that man whose name you called when you were so sick, and don't be denying it! That's why you won't agree to marry." He waved aside her heated denials. "There are some things you don't know, child, even about yourself. It's lucky you are to have a grandfather who cares more about your happiness and future than you do."

"Don't fret, Sean O'Connell. I'll stay, and I'll do my best to be what you want, but I won't marry just for your sake, so don't expect it."

"Oh, you'll marry. But it'll be for your own sake, make no mistake about it."

Sean slanted her a mysterious smile and Kerry's eyes narrowed suspiciously. What was the old rascal up to now? Oh Lord—not matchmaking again, she hoped!

Chapter 18

Springtime in Ireland was, Kerry thought, the most beautiful sight she'd ever seen. It was even prettier than St. Denis, perhaps because the dull gray days of winter made soft blue skies and gentle winds more precious. Had there ever been grass so green?

The bay mare she rode eagerly tossed her head, almost snatching the reins from Kerry's hands as she pranced on the crest of a hill overlooking Castleconnell. Newly shod hooves dug into rich earth still wet from recent rains, and rare golden sunshine flooded the countryside with light. A laughing male voice called to Kerry from the edge of the new-ploughed field where she had paused to rest the mare.

"Mary Kathleen!" Hoofbeats thudded against damp ground as two horsemen caught up. "You can still outride us," Padraic and Brendan McLaughlin chorused, and they all laughed. Padraic, the elder of the brothers, jockeyed his mount in a position close to Kerry, nudging Brendan aside.

"You'll be my escort at the dance next week, Mary Kathleen," Padraic announced, and was immediately challenged by a smug Brendan.

"She already agreed to go with me, didn't you, Mary Kathleen?"

"I'm going with Sean," Kerry said with a demure

smile, then laughed at their shadowed faces. "But your names are the only two on my dance card yet . . ." She watched their faces brighten and thought how young they seemed. Both were older than she was, yet they had few thoughts other than the pursuit of pleasure and a hatred of the English.

"I shall see you at the O'Neills' dance," Kerry told the McLaughlin brothers, and whirled her mare down the hill toward the road leading to Castleconnell. "God bless!"

"God bless, Mary Kathleen," Padraic and Brendan responded.

Kerry's mare nimbly avoided rocks and hedges as she skimmed down the hill to the road still rutted and sticky with mud from the recent rains. The mare was fast and agile, purchased a fortnight before expressly for Kerry.

"I'm tired of seeing you bouncing like a sack of meal on the bony backs of carriage horses," Sean had said gruffly when he presented Kerry with the mare. "And you'll be laming one of them before long if you keep tearing about the countryside like a north wind, so don't be thanking me. I'm only doing it for myself."

Kerry had hugged him anyway and Sean had flapped his arms in mock annoyance and told McCurley not to be looking at him like he'd gone soft because he hadn't.

"Liar," McCurley had murmured to Sean's back as the old man stumped from the stableyard. "Aye, an' it's about time he acted human, I'm thinkin'. Yer good fer him, lass."

"He's good for me," Kerry had answered.

The winter had been spent poring over books with Sean and a tutor, learning formal education such as mathematics and history. The languages had been simple for Kerry, and she had progressed at such a rapid pace even Sean was impressed. The old man had—at her insistence—even hired a fencing master to teach Kerry the rudiments of light swordplay. In exchange for this instruction, Kerry had agreed to let Margaret teach her the simplest stitches of embroidery and needlepoint. Kerry could, with a great deal of effort and a lot of muttering and sighing, knit a pair of socks now.

The activities crowding her winter days had also served to keep her mind from Nick. It had been the long winter nights that had caught her dreaming of sun-swept beaches and starry nights when blue eyes had smiled at her. Where was he? Had he been angry when he'd found her gone with his books? Did he miss her just a little? Oh God, she missed him. . . . No. She couldn't think about him anymore. It was too much like a knifethrust in her heart to think of Nick.

Booted heels nudged the bay mare into a swift gallop down the winding road to the castle gates where she slid to a mud-slinging halt. Michael McCurley slanted Kerry a baleful glare from red-rimmed eyes as he swung open a gate.

"Ye should be ridin' sideways like proper ladies, an' not wearin' them fancy ridin' breeches made to look like skirts! It'll only bring trouble. . . ."

"You ride with both legs on the same side of your horse and see which way you prefer, McCurley," Kerry retorted with a laugh. She slid from the lathered mare's back. "And it's thanking you, I am, not to be meddling in my business. Go back to your interrupted pint o' stout. Do you think I don't know why you're so grouchy?"

McCurley grinned and winked. "Don' be breathin' a word to his lordship now. Fer all that he likes a nip himself now and then, he's damned hard when it comes to my pint." He patted the stone withers of the unicorn statue where his pint lay hidden among the carved granite grass and leaves at the beast's feet.

"The unicorn guards it well." Kerry's hand strayed to her bare neck where the O'Connell necklace had hung for so long. She missed it, and dreaded the day Sean remembered to ask about it. How could she tell him she'd traded it for gold to escape her pirate lover?

After cooling down her mare and giving her into the care of a stable lad, Kerry searched for Sean in the library of the castle. He was usually there these days, ensconced in a comfortable chair by a warm peat fire and poring over dusty volumes of books.

"Sit over there," he said when he saw her standing in the open doorway, "so you don't get mud everywhere." A gnarled finger pointed to a low chair in front of the wide mullioned window looking out over the hills and valleys of County Kerry. In the distance could be seen the peaks of Killarney that ringed stunning lakes. Carrantuohill in Mcgillycuddy's Reeks, the tallest peak in all Ireland, was wreathed with ever-present clouds. She pressed her forehead against the cool windowpane and idly ran a finger over the circle where her breath had frosted the glass.

Damn! Kerry swiped the heel of her hand across the pane and quickly erased the initials she'd etched in the breath-cloud: NL and KO. Impossible.

A thick volume slammed shut with a loud clap and Kerry couldn't help her startled jump.

"You did that on purpose, you old codger," she commented without malice. "I think you like to see how far people will jump when you take them by surprise."

"Heh, heh. I favor surprises, lass, that I do! It's always interesting to see how people react." Sean pushed himself up from the chair and replaced the book on a high shelf.

He reminded her, Kerry decided, of Wilson. Wilson had often made the same sort of remark, and she wondered how the two men would have gotten along.

"Have you finally decided what to wear to the O'Neills' dance?" Sean asked. "It's only a few days away."

"I know." Kerry idly swung a muddy boot. "I'm wearing my satin chemise and black lace garters."

"Is that all?"

"Isn't that enough?"

Sean cackled. "Aye, lass. I daresay that's quite enough—to get you into trouble, wed, or both!"

"You're impossible." Kerry smiled impishly and hooked her arms around bent knees to let her feet dangle above the floor. "I don't know why I put up with you."

The white oak chair creaked as Sean lowered his weight back into it and tilted a satisfied smile at his granddaughter. "I don't know why you put up with me, either. Can't be your extraordinary patience, because that's nonexistent." He hooked a finger over his chin and pursed his lips thoughtfully. "Maybe you're opting for sainthood?" he suggested.

Kerry made a face. "Too dull. I don't have a high opinion of martyrs either, so we can forget that. I know!" She sat up straight and her feet hit the floor. "It's because you're such a gracious winner at chess!"

"I never claimed to be modest, child. A winner is always the best, whether it's love or war. Indisputable fact." Sean lifted a mug of spiced brandy to his mouth.

"That," she said, "is your opinion." Kerry delivered the coup de grace with an innocent smile. "Does that mean the English are the best, Grandfather?"

Spiced brandy was sprayed on the marble hearth of the library fireplace as Sean choked. He lowered the mug and dabbed at droplets of cooling brandy spattering his trousers leg. "Damned inconvenient of you to think of that," he said finally. "But it was an excellent reply. I can't think of a thing to answer at this minute. Will you give an old man some time?"

"All you want." Kerry stood and brushed drying mud from her skirts. "Why are you insisting I attend the O'Neills' dance Saturday?"

"You need to see and be seen. Damn it, you need to find a husband, girl! Someone strong who can manage Castleconnell when I'm gone."

Kerry stared at him through narrowed eyes. "I thought you intended for me to do that."

Sean flapped an impatient hand at her. "I do, I do! Don't get yourself in a state about it. It's just that you need a man behind you. And on top of you." He waved aside her indignant protest at his crudity. "Bah! Did you think to make babies by yourself? Castleconnell needs new blood, young strong blood to fight when called upon. Good Irish blood."

"More blood to spill in the fields, you mean!" Kerry took a step closer. "If it's fighting men you want, Sean O'Connell, you'd best be calling my cousin Michael back from college. He's your choice. I won't further war."

They faced each other like two weasels with ears laid back and fur ruffled, until finally Sean relaxed. "I'm not after fighting with you about it, Mary Kathleen. You'll see the truth of it soon enough. Now what else were you planning on wearing to the dance Saturday?"

A misty rain had been falling the day of the O'Neills' dance, so that Sean and Kerry traveled the short distance in a closed carriage. Kerry kept tucking her skirts closer around her legs and rearranging her lacy shawl, and wished once more that Margaret had come with them.

"She hates these things," Sean said. He looked splendid. A starched white cravat foamed at his throat and his long coat of superfine was loosely buttoned over a frame still as lean as when he'd been thirty. He wore knee breeches and white silk hose, and heavy silver buckles adorned his shoes. Sean fixed Kerry with an appraising glance and smiled. "I'm almost wishing you'd worn the satin chemise and black lace garters."

Kerry leaned forward. "I did," she whispered, "underneath my dress!"

They were still laughing like two naughty schoolchildren when the carriage arrived in front of the O'Neills' home. It was whispered that Sean O'Connell's granddaughter had definitely sweetened the old man's disposition.

The O'Neills' home was a grand country house of sprawling wings and many windows, presiding over a green valley from its vantage point on a high crest. Like most of the houses, it was built of stone, and low stone fences crisscrossed over the grounds. The manor was gaily decorated with Chinese lanterns and curling streamers of colored paper that hung over the brick-tiled walkways in the gardens.

Sean and Kerry were ushered into the house and met with a barrage of laughing greetings. Because of the temperate weather, doors had been flung open to gardens thick with people in spite of the threat of more misting rain. Musicians played fiddles and pipes in the corner of a room swept free of cluttering furniture so there would be plenty of space for dancing.

Kerry was immediately claimed for a dance by Brendan McLaughlin, who beat his brother by three steps, and she swirled away on his arm. Sean

watched with a smile curling his mouth, then let
his eyes drift over the crowded halls. His granddaughter was the loveliest girl in the room by far,
he thought without a shred of prejudice. Light from
two thousand wax candles shimmered over the red-
gold waves of her hair, turning them to a coppery
glow that caught the eye. Her gown was expensive
and worth every shilling in spite of Margaret's faint
moans of protest. Ivory satin clung to the slender
curves of her body. The bodice was cut in a straight
line across her breasts, giving a tantalizing view of
a shadowed cleft and soft skin, and the short sleeves
puffed to her elbows. Long gloves almost met the
cuff of the sleeves, and tiny seed pearls dotted both
gown and gloves in gentle, artistic swirls. Circling
her neck was a strand of pearls that had been in the
family for generations.

Kerry whirled past Sean again, this time dancing
with Padraic McLaughlin instead of his brother, her
feet skimming over the dance floor as if she had
wings on her shoes. She was having fun. Brendan
and Padraic had made her laugh so much her sides
hurt.

She lost sight of Sean again and didn't see the old
man for over an hour. When she did see him, he
was deep in conversation with a group of men, his
gray head shaking vigorously as he stabbed a finger
in the air to make a point.

"Political, I'd say," Kerry murmured into her
partner Daniel's ear. He was a tall young man with
red hair and deep blue eyes. She gestured toward
the gathering and he laughed.

"I'd say you were right if I didn't happen to know
what they're discussing." He smiled down at her.
"A horse race."

"A horse race?" Kerry blinked. "Against whom?
I mean, who's racing and when?" She didn't hear
his answer as the music rose to a crescendo and he

whirled her in a graceful circle. A horse race . . . what fun!

"This afternoon," her partner answered when the music softened and changed tempo for the next set. "Would you care for some punch?"

"Yes, thank you. How many have entered the race and where is it to be held?" Kerry tucked her hand into the crook of Daniel's arm and walked with him to the refreshment table. She took the cup of punch Daniel offered, and a small cake.

"Only four have entered, decent horses being hard for an Irishman to come by lately, and it'll be run on the North Ennis Road." Daniel added, "Your grandfather has put up the purse for the race, and O'Neill has a third cousin who is one of the riders. Sean agreed to let the man ride a horse from his stable."

"Sean?" Kerry turned to stare at her grandsire. "He didn't breathe a word, the old sneak! I'll be knowing why before too long." She nibbled at the barley cake dripping with honey. It would be great fun to run her mare in the race. Which, she reflected, was probably why Sean hadn't told her about it. "Excuse me, Daniel Flaherty, but I'd like to speak to my grandfather."

Kerry set her cup down on the table with the remains of her barley cake and crossed to Sean with Daniel trailing behind. The old man saw her coming and took a step away from the cluster of men.

"Are you finally remembering a poor old man, granddaughter?" he boomed. "And me hungry and thirsty and wondering if I was abandoned."

Kerry tapped Sean lightly on the arm with the small purse she carried. "I should abandon you. Why didn't you tell me about the horse race? Or give me a chance to enter?"

"If I told you about it, you'd have badgered me to run that nag of yours."

"So? Don't you think I can win?"

"If I didn't, I never would have bought her for you. Aye, you could win easy, but there'd be some who'd say the race was fixed then, and that we're after keeping the purse in our own pockets." Sean shook his head and winked at Daniel. "I wouldn't want that said about the most honest man in County Kerry!"

"It won't be. The most honest man in County Kerry lives in a cottage down by the lakes of Killarney!" she retorted.

"See how she maligns me?" Sean mourned. "I'm the most miserable wretch in all Ireland, Daniel."

"Agreed," Kerry said promptly. "When does the race start?"

"In a half-hour." Sean held out his arm. "Escort an old man, child?"

Sean, Kerry and Daniel rode in a covered landau to a hill overlooking the North Ennis Road. Carriages and horsemen lined the road to watch, and fiddles and pipes filled the air with festive music as they waited.

"Who did you say is running?" Kerry asked, straining to see the four riders already lining up at the far end of the road by Mrs. McGillycuddy's thatched cottage.

"Didn't. Hey! Paddy!" Sean roared, and a thickset man hurried to the landau where Sean leaned out the window. They bargained for a moment, with both satisfied they'd chosen best as the horn pealed for the riders to get ready.

"Sean. Which of our horses is running?" Kerry asked with an edge to her voice, but the skirl of the pipes drowned out her question. A pistol's crack punctuated the soft Irish mist and four horses and their riders shot forward. Kerry leaned out of the window, half-sitting on Daniel Flaherty's lap as she strained to see.

The riders were lost in the first curve of the road now, hidden behind bushes and trees before bursting into view again. A leggy black horse was in front, its small rider leaning forward and urging more speed, then came a sorrel right behind. The last two horses were both bays, and Kerry frowned as she recognized the larger of the two.

"Sean O'Connell!" she snapped. "You're racing my mare!"

"Aye. No sense in letting good speed stand in the stable." He turned from the race for an instant and flashed her a grin. "You've kept her in fine racing form, child."

Any answer Kerry could have made would have been ignored in the heat of the race, as Sean had begun shouting encouragement again. Damn him, the sly old fox! He knew better than to ask her permission to run the mare. She would have wanted to ride her in the race and Sean knew it. Who *was* the rider? One of the stable lads, probably. Bobby? Young Ian? No, this was a big man.

A frown tugged Kerry's brows lower over her eyes. There was something vaguely familiar about that rider, and she struggled for recognition. He sat the mare with careless grace, and was coming from behind to pass into second place now. Who was that rider?

The answer hit Kerry just as the men and mounts skimmed past the landau and over the finish mark, mud flying in globs from flashing hooves. One hand rose to her throat and she found herself fumbling with her other hand at the latch to the landau door.

"Here, Mary Kathleen." Sean handed Kerry a heavy purse, putting a detaining hand on her arm.

"The winner will ride past us and I want you to give him his prize."

She stared blankly and gripped the purse with white-knuckled fingers, fighting waves of dizziness as Nick Lawton reined the bay to a halt only two feet away.

Chapter 19

Numb and struggling for composure, Kerry held the velvet purse out the window as Nick nudged the mare close to the landau. He was even more handsome than she remembered him, his face a deeper shade of bronze and his eyes a more startling blue. What was he doing here?

She half-turned to glance at Sean uncertainly, and the velvet prize sack slipped from her fingers. Kerry grabbed for it at the same time as Nick, and his hand closed over hers as she barely caught the purse.

The simple touch of his warm fingers against hers, even through the elbow-length gloves she wore, was electrifying. A small shock ran from her fingertips up the entire length of her arm.

"What . . . what are you doing here?" she asked, and her voice was just a husky breath of air only Nick could hear.

Nick gently pulled the purse from her hand and held it. "Winning a race," he said softly, then hefted the purse in the air and smiled at the crowd around him. He raised his voice so that all could hear. "My thanks to Sean O'Connell for his generosity, and to the mare for being so swift! I will exchange the purse, however, for a small token from his lordship's granddaughter—a kiss."

Kerry stared blankly. A kiss? She hadn't seen

Nicholas Lawton in nine months, and now he rode into her life again as if it had just been yesterday and demanded a public kiss? One of them was a lunatic, and it certainly wasn't she!

A hot flush stained her cheeks. Kerry's mouth opened to fling a refusal, but Sean's voice hissed in her ear, "Don't be ungracious, mavourneen. It's a nice gesture. He's O'Neill's wife's cousin, and even if he is a bit ill-mannered, I wouldn't shame a friend."

Kerry muttered a phrase that made Sean wince and Daniel Flaherty blanch, adding, "Then you should kiss him," as she leaned out the window. She gave Nick a quick peck on one cheek and tried to ignore the sudden lurch of her heart.

"Well done," Nick murmured softly. "And almost worth a heavy purse, I'd say." He handed her back the prize.

Throwing him a withering glance, Kerry sat back in the landau without another word and gave her grandfather the purse. "I'm ready to leave," she told Sean shortly. She wished Daniel wasn't there so she could ask the questions that were burning to be answered. Where had Nick Lawton come from, and how long had he been in Ireland? O'Neill's cousin? Why hadn't she seen him before now?

The landau lurched to a start and Kerry remained silent on the short trip back to the O'Neills' home, ignoring her grandfather's puzzled attempts at conversation.

"Blasted females," Sean muttered finally when the landau rolled to a halt in the curved driveway outside the stone and brick house. "I'd have a private word with my granddaughter, Mr. Flaherty," he said to the young man with them, and Daniel gratefully escaped.

The door had barely closed behind young Flaherty when Kerry spat, "Why didn't you warn me?"

"Calm yourself. The man only rode your mare in the race, and he rode her well. I know I should have told you first, but then you'd have been wanting to ride her instead of wearing a pretty dress and dancing with the lads." Sean gave her a pat on one knee and sighed when she just stared at him with a stony expression. "Ah, mavourneen . . ."

"Don't! Do you have any idea who that man is? Why did you let him . . . Do you know he's not only a pirate and murderer, but an *Englishman?*"

"What are you blathering about? The man is Brian O'Neill's wife's cousin, and even if he's an English earl we can't hold that against him." Sean shrugged at Kerry's wide eyes and audible gasp. "I know what I've said before, but at least he's got some Irish blood in him."

"An earl?" Good God, how had Nick managed to convince them of that?

"His name's Nicholas Lawton and his mother married into an English family," Sean was saying. "She was one of Margaret's closest friends at one time. I don't know why you're so full of questions, but it can wait until later." Sean beckoned to the doorman to open the carriage door. "All this fuss over someone else riding your damned mare," he muttered under his breath. "I'd never have thought you so petty, Mary Kathleen."

"Petty?" Kerry turned to Sean with an agonized expression shadowing her pale features. The tiny freckles that weren't normally visible because of her usual tan now stood out on skin pale as milk. "Petty?" she repeated. "I don't think you know all the facts, Sean."

"What's there to know? I'm not certain where you got this nonsense about him being a pirate and a murderer, but—" Sean stopped suddenly, and his eyes narrowed. Nicholas. Nick. Pirate, murderer, it all fell into place. This was the man his granddaughter had fallen in love with, the man who had treated her so callously, the man who had obviously cared enough about her to follow her to Ireland. The old man's brain spun feverishly as he considered and rejected several different reactions ranging from murder to conspiracy. This would require much thought. "We'll go into it later," he said. "This is not the time or place."

That statement settled everything as far as Sean was concerned. Kerry wordlessly followed her grandfather from the carriage up the wide brick steps to the front door and back inside the house. She automatically smiled and nodded greetings, but her gaiety was forced. The world had turned upside down in the space of a few minutes. Everywhere she looked she saw blue eyes and a sun-browned face with a familiar mocking grin.

A feeling of panic flooded Kerry. The noise had grown so loud and the walls seemed to be closing in on her. She stared blankly at the fervent young man who was offering to get her some more punch and shook her head. She had to have fresh air. . . .

When she turned and took a step away her gaze caught Nick's. He stood in a corner watching her with a slightly amused expression. A trio of young women were laughing and smiling up at him, obviously flirting, and one of them leaned close to whisper something in his ear. Nick bent his head to listen and Kerry fled from the room. She stopped so quickly in the crowded hallway that a serving maid bumped into her.

"Excuse me! Please excuse me!" Kerry blurted. She picked up her skirts with both hands so that she wouldn't trip, and ran. She heard Sean call her name but didn't slow down. It was difficult to dodge the people who stood laughing and talking, but Kerry finally managed to push her way through the throng to the double doors leading to the garden.

It had begun to rain again, and servants scurried to bring in the punch bowls and food, looking like maddened ants as they hurried this way and that with well-laden arms. Raindrops pelted Kerry until her carefully caught up hair trickled down her neck and into her eyes in drenched strands. I must look, Kerry thought, like a half-drowned puppy. She lifted a hand to push impatiently at a wet curl in her eyes, and almost tripped over the hem of her gown. Stumbling, Kerry caught herself with an outstretched hand against a stone bench. Fleeing to the garden was insanity, she supposed, but the walls had begun to close in around her like the steel jaws of an animal trap.

Nick—here in Ireland, and acting as if he had every right to be. How could he be the O'Neills' cousin? Why had she never heard that before now? She'd been in Ireland for nine long months; surely someone would have mentioned Nicholas Lawton in that time.

Another deluge of rain slashed down, scattering Kerry's unanswered questions as she ran for shelter. A summer house stood at the very end of the garden, an octagonal building that was in a state of genteel disrepair. Kerry dashed down the tiled path and into the little house built long ago for the first O'Neills. She shook her hands, staring in disgust at the rivulets of rain dripping from the tips of her gloved fingers, then pushed back cloying streamers of hair that had lost all its curl.

"Damn, damn, damn!" she said. Vague dismay that she had ruined her gown and hairdo coiled through her, then Kerry dismissed it with a shrug. That was the least worry at this moment.

A chill wind swept through the openings of the summer house and she shivered. Her arms crossed her body and both palms cupped her elbows as she hunched her shoulders against the chill.

"Cold, my lady?" The voice was slightly mocking and as cool as the air sweeping through the summer house.

Kerry whirled, searching the dim shadows to find Nick. She knew his voice as well as she knew her own. He stood close by, his lean frame casually propped against the door, and Kerry's heart leaped almost into her throat for the second time that day as she struggled for control.

"Yes," she answered calmly, "I am slightly chilled. It's cool and damp, and I'm not quite dressed for it. Why did you follow me here?"

"Why did you go running off in the rain?" he countered. Nick stepped close and Kerry shivered again. This time she didn't shiver with a chill, but in reaction to his nearness. He was much too close; so close she could have reached out and scraped her fingers through the thick ebony waves of his hair.

He took another step closer and the snowy cravat at this throat was almost brushing against her folded arms. "Why did you run off into the rain?"

His voice was a caress, warm and intimate, and Kerry wondered wildly why he'd come to Ireland. Had he searched for her? Or was this an inexplicable coincidence?

"I ran out in the rain," she said, "because I wanted to be by myself and think. Since you've barged in on my privacy, maybe you'll tell me why you're here."

He shrugged carelessly. "Haven't you heard?—I'm related to the O'Neills. I'm visiting family."

Kerry hid her trembling hands behind her. She stared at Nick coolly, masking her quivering with another question. "Why didn't you ever mention this before?"

A crooked smile curved Nick's mouth. "Why should I? You never mentioned your family. As a matter of fact, you even neglected mentioning plans to leave Belle Terre. An oversight, I'm sure . . ." His arm unexpectedly snaked out to grab Kerry around the waist, pulling her hard against him.

Nick's lips covered hers in a searing kiss that left Kerry clinging weakly to him and her head spinning. It would be so easy just to rest her head against his chest and listen to the steady beat of his heart. God, she hadn't remembered how good it felt to be in his arms.

No, she couldn't let him do this to her. If she allowed herself to love Nick, would the emotion consume her as it had her mother? At least Kate had loved a man who vowed to cherish her always. Nick would make her miserable all her life, and she had managed well enough without him these past months. Maybe he would always be in her thoughts, but at least he would not be an obsession.

Kerry jerked away, staring at Nick with wide, haunted eyes, and her mouth compressed into a tight line. "No! I don't want to be a pirate's mistress. I won't be a mistress to any man. Go back to Belle Terre, or . . . or . . . raiding ships or something! Leave me alone. Do you hear? Leave me alone!"

Wheeling, Kerry fled from the summer house and Nick. She fought scalding tears as she half-ran back to the house, stumbling over uneven stones in the path. Her satin dress was ruined beyond repair and she was soaked to the skin, but she didn't care. Nothing mattered right now but flight.

Seeing Nick again had been a shock that should have made her angry, but instead she had found herself melting into his arms like a common street whore! She should have told him what a despicable criminal he was, and how utterly detestable she found him. It was unforgivable that part of her longed to be with him even when she knew there was no future in it. Just to be able to lie in his arms one more time was so tempting.

* * *

Pacing the library floor with hands clenched behind his back, Sean stopped and glowered at the man staring at him so coolly. "You've got bloody nerve to come here, Lawton, when you're responsible for my granddaughter's kidnapping! The version I got from her was somewhat garbled, but you're also the man who . . . who. . . ." Sean paused, unable to finish.

"Seduced her?" Nick supplied helpfully. "Took advantage of her? There are times I think it was the other way around. Yes, I did kidnap her from St. Denis and hold her against her will, but I never harmed Kerry. I came to find her." Nick met the old man's narrowed gaze steadily. "I decided to marry her."

Sean snorted. "A bit tardy, aren't you? Why didn't you wed the girl before? Wasn't she good enough for you then? Is it only now, when you find out she's got family who can protect her, that you decide to do what's right? How convenient."

"It does sound that way, doesn't it," Nick replied pleasantly. "But you're wrong. I knew who she was before I ever left Belle Terre to come after her. I just wasn't sure where I'd find her." He reached into the pocket of his coat and drew out a linen handkerchief and began unfolding it. "Recognize this?" Nick lifted his hand. Dangling from his forefinger was a silver chain and locket, slowly turning in midair.

Sean reached out with a trembling hand and took it. "I never thought to see this again," he said after a moment. "It's been in the family for over four hundred years."

"I know. Wilson, who's been with me most of my life, recognized the crest the first day he saw Kerry. Mary Kathleen," he clarified at Sean's questioning glance. "Kerry's the name she used when she survived the shipwreck. I suppose it had something to do with her birthplace. Didn't she explain to you?"

"No, not much has been said about it. Whenever it was mentioned, Mary Kathleen avoided the subject. I think now that must have been because of you." Sean gave him a sharp look. "She's in love with you. How do you feel about her?"

"I traveled all over the Caribbean and across the Atlantic to Spain and then England before finding her here. That signifies more than a passing interest," Nick responded. He did not mention the theft of his books.

It had been a long nine months of searching and wondering if Kerry was unharmed. Nick had cursed her, sworn to beat her black and blue when he found her, and stayed awake at night thinking about her.

He had returned to Belle Terre early to find Happy frantically wringing her hands over Kerry's disappearance and holding the necklace that had been left as payment for the ridiculously small amount of gold she'd taken. Nick had been incredulously angry at her escape, and furious at the disappearance of his account books. He'd wanted to set sail immediately, but Wilson had persuaded him to let the weary crew rest a few days first.

Those few days had probably saved them all, because the worst hurricane of the season had ravaged the islands. The *Unicorn* was damaged in the storm, and repair was slow. It had been two weeks before they'd sailed from Belle Terre, and when they finally reached Don Javier, the Spaniard had been singularly unpleasant. It had been Wilson's suggestion that brought them to Castleconnell and Kerry.

"So you decided to marry her," Sean said at last in a thoughtful tone. "I don't think she'll have you. Oh, she's in love with you, but she's not ready to marry. She's not ready to take the chance."

"And you agree?"

"No. But she doesn't always take my advice." Motioning for Nick to take a seat, Sean lowered his frame to the comfort of his favorite chair. "I want her to wed, but I think she needs a good steady Irishman, not a roving English earl who doesn't know when to go home."

"I have business in England, but I will be returning to Belle Terre within six months. I intend to take Kerry with me when I go," Nick said softly. "I'd like to have your permission, but it's not necessary."

For a long moment Sean stared hard at Nick, then his features relaxed. "You're damned outspoken for a man guilty of kidnapping and murder. Ah, you see, she has talked a little bit. What do you have to say to that?"

Nick didn't answer for a few moments, then said, "I believe you know a man by the name of Samuel Locke. He sends his regards to you."

"Ah." Sean smiled for the first time since Nick had been announced by a servant and shown into the library. "Samuel Locke. He's doing well, I trust?"

"Very well."

"Mr. Locke is a talented man with his fingers in many different pies, Lawton. I've an idea he's living in America now, am I right?"

"You are."

The silver chain clinked softly as Sean held up the locket Nick had returned to him. "Samuel Locke once helped my son when he was in trouble. I owe him a debt. If he trusts you, then I must. You've my permission to marry my granddaughter. Just remember that she's not ready to trust you and may refuse."

"I need to be in London in a fortnight. Several matters depend upon my arrival, and I'm sure you're aware of the delicacy of Locke's machinations. I do not have time for a lengthy courtship, but I don't wish to leave without Kerry." Nick paused, then took his gamble. "Do I have your help?"

The white oak chair creaked in protest as Sean shifted positions. He stared long and hard at Nicholas Lawton. Sean had stood by Mary Kathleen's sickbed upon her arrival in Ireland, and had heard her call this man's name. She loved Lawton, he was sure, but what would happen if she was pushed into a marriage she wasn't ready for? It was an agonizing decision but Sean finally nodded.

"You'll have my help even though I know it means I'll lose her again." Sean sighed heavily. "She misses the warm weather anyway, and would have never been content in Ireland. Make her happy, Englishman, or I'll see that you regret it."

Kerry twisted the small bouquet of spring flowers between her fingers, staring out the window of her bedchamber. There had been two wedding ceremonies, the first secret one performed by a priest, and the second civil ceremony to satisfy the records. Why didn't she feel something besides this dull sense of lethargy? Perhaps it was because days of pressure from both Sean and Margaret had left her weary.

Glancing down, Kerry lifted her left hand so that the wide band on her third finger caught the sunlight streaming through the window. She'd been married to Nick for almost an hour. The reality was numbing, and she was still trying to recall how it had happened.

Shock had been her first reaction to Sean's blunt statement that he had accepted Nick's suit for her hand in marriage. She'd sat silently as her grandfather related the advantages and his reasons for accepting. Kerry had not spoken until Sean finished with the comment that she needed to marry and it might as well be the Englishman who had come all this way after her.

"Has it occurred to you to ask him why?" she'd demanded with growing anger. "And don't dare start spouting any nonsense about love and devotion at me! Nicholas Lawton came after me because I have something he wants! I'm not sure of their importance, but I brought two books with me that I stole from him. He killed a man for those books. Do you think he would quibble about marrying for them?"

"Don't be ridiculous. It's too easy to demand the books. If Lawton has had more crimes laid to his doorstep than a dog has fleas like you say, he could steal them back for that matter," Sean had argued with inescapable but flawed logic. "Be sensible. You love him, admit it. You once said you would not marry anyone else because of him. That's an excellent reason to marry him."

Nick had not presented the one argument that would have made all the difference in the world. He came to see her and she met him in the library. She stood stiffly formal and distant, listening as Nick said simply that he had decided to marry her and take her with him. Kerry remained silent and Nick misunderstood her silence for agreement. He held her loosely in his arms and said he wanted her, said that he'd spent nine months searching for her. Nick did not ask about the books and he never mentioned love.

When Nick was gone, Kerry adamantly informed Sean that she would never marry Nick Lawton. Since he had accepted the suit, he could have the pleasure of refusing it. Sean argued, ending his persuasive arguments by shouting, and Kerry shouted back. Margaret wept and said they were both being foolish, and why *wouldn't* Mary Kathleen listen?

Kerry finally refused to see Nick at all. She locked

herself in her room without eating until Sean threatened to send Nick in to make her eat. For four days the entire household walked on eggs until Kerry surrendered, irritably agreeing to marry Nick so that she could finally get some peace.

"I don't suppose it matters how big a wretch he is, if I can just stop this constant badgering," she muttered to Margaret. "I shall be a perfectly horrid, shrewish wife and Nick will regret marrying me all the rest of his days." Though she knew she loved Nick, the thought of surrendering her independence frightened her. Was this just a devious method of getting his hands on those account books? If it wasn't, what if he grew bored, and she was left wanting him and not understanding why he no longer wanted her? Would she become like Kate, holding on so tightly that she drove him even further away?

Now she waited in her own familiar bedroom for the stranger she had married. Coward, she scolded herself. Wasn't this what she had sometimes hoped for? Why had she fought so hard against it? Nick had come to her and asked for her hand in marriage, hadn't he? But a tiny voice whispered that he still hadn't mentioned love. Did he love her? Wilson claimed he did. Sean said love was just a word and actions counted, and Margaret gave a helpless shrug of her shoulders.

Kerry smoothed the pleated folds of her nightgown with trembling fingers. For better or worse, she had given her vows to love and cherish her husband.

Footsteps halted outside the bedroom door and there was the sound of laughter and shuffling of feet before it swung open. Nick slipped in and quickly shut the door behind him and locked it. He wore only a long burgundy robe tied at the waist, and Kerry's imagination supplied the details of his lean body beneath. She remembered well the smooth muscles and taut flesh, and the faint scent of brandy and tobacco mingling with the salty tang of the sea. Her breath caught in the back of her throat as she gazed at the man who had haunted her thoughts for almost a year. Nick leaned against the heavy oak door and gazed appreciatively at Kerry. His eyes crinkled at the corners when he smiled.

"Hello, wife."

"Hello, husband." She gave him a tentative smile. Her heart thudded inside her fragile rib cage until Kerry was convinced the vibrations would shake the stone floor. The satin ribbons Margaret had wound through the thick waves of her hair actually quivered nervously, and Kerry's traitorous knees were unkind enough to buckle so that she had to sit down quickly on the cushioned window seat.

"You are beautiful, love," Nick said, and Kerry flushed at the husky note of desire in his voice.

She stared at the bouquet she still held. Nick called her "love" so easily; maybe the word didn't hold the same meaning for him that it did for her. How did he equate love? With passion? Kerry carefully kept her glance from the turned-back covers of the wide bed dominating the room.

Nick pushed away from the door and crossed to Kerry, reaching down to pull her up gently. His broad palm cupped her chin and his thumb dragged across her lower lip in a light caress.

"Do you know," he began, "how many nights I spent thinking of you? I pictured you just like this, looking at me like you are now, with the light from a fire behind you and making a halo in your hair."

"How . . . how am I looking at you?" Kerry tilted her head slightly. Her heart was still popping erratically and her lungs were constricted so that her breathing was irregular and shallow. The tight coil in the pit of her stomach loosened and spread outward in a heated glow.

"You're looking at me with all the stars from the heavens shining in your eyes, love. I even see the belt of Orion sparkling like new diamonds."

"Do you see the Milky Way?" She had to say something—anything—to stop the room from whirling like a top. Nick was laughing then, telling her she was whimsical when he was trying to be romantic.

"I thought this was a marriage of convenience," she said lightly. "Romance has no place, does it?" Nick's face darkened but Kerry couldn't stop the nervous rush of words. She was in mortal danger of losing her soul to this man, and she had to know why. "I realize how flattered I should be that you came all this way for me, but I recall your once saying that you always win. This is just another game, isn't it? A play of straws that means nothing to you." She gave a brittle laugh and pulled away from Nick. She was stronger when he wasn't touching her. It was the magic of his touch that was her undoing; just a light brushing of his fingers against her cheek turned her brain to the consistency of boiled oatmeal. "You came after your books, Nicholas Lawton, not me. Right?"

Nick shrugged carelessly and reached for a cut-crystal decanter of brandy. "Is that what you think?—that I only came after you because of those books?" He poured a liberal amount of brandy into a glass and lifted it. "I'd be lying if I said I didn't want them. Maybe you're right, love."

Kerry's heart constricted. What had she expected? A denial? Yes, of course she had. She'd wanted to hear words of comfort and love, not this cold confirmation of her fears.

"I'm sure I'm right," she managed to answer. Her hands were cold as she accepted the glass of brandy

Nick held out to her. A mocking smile tilted his mouth at the corners, and he was gazing at her with that cynical expression she remembered so well. Dear God, she almost wished she had not provoked this discussion, and that she had played the game he'd begun. It would have been a charade, of course, but easier to accept than this numbing pain.

Nick filled his glass with brandy and gestured to Kerry. "Shall we drink a toast to our marriage, love?"

Kerry stared at Nick defiantly. "Why not?"

Their goblets clinked softly, and Nick's eyes held hers. "To a marriage of convenience, with short days and long nights," he said.

Kerry tilted her glass and drank. The brandy warmed a path down her throat and lent her courage. She held out the goblet for more.

"You don't need it." Nick plucked the empty glass from her fingers and set it upon the satinwood table. "This is our wedding night, Kerry, and you will remember it. There will be no wine-dreams or ghosts between us."

He didn't wait for an answer but swept Kerry into his arms and carried her to the high bed in the center of the room.

"Nick . . ."

"No. Not now, Kerry. It's been too long, and I want no more harsh words between us tonight. Forget the fact that I kidnapped you and forget the books. Tomorrow is soon enough for that. Tonight is the time for love."

Nick lowered her gently to the feather mattress and Kerry felt the cool slither of satin sheets slide over her skin when her nightdress bunched up around her hips. The bed creaked softly as Nick sat on the edge and watched for her reaction.

She reached out and untied the sash of his velvet robe with slightly trembling fingers. Nick caught her hands and raised them to his mouth, kissing her fingertips.

"Softly, love," he murmured when she shivered. "I only want to please you tonight." He pulled her close, and his bare chest pressed against the soft fullness of her breasts, the tiny hairs tickling and sensual against her skin. The low bodice of her nightdress was tugged away and gone, floating to the floor with Nick's long velvet robe. The shadowed bed was their cloistered haven from the world.

Kerry couldn't recall why she had been angry with Nick, or why he had been angry with her. The long waiting and wanting was forgotten in the rediscovery of passion. Her body responded eagerly to his touch. She wanted him too, she admitted at last, wanted that soul-searing release only Nick could give her.

Her hands wandered down the sleek muscles of his body with a childlike curiosity, tangling in the curls of dark hair on his chest and trailing over the flat ridges of his stomach. She smiled delightedly when Nick shivered.

"Sweet Jesus," he half-groaned when her inquiring fingers circled him. "you don't know what you do to me . . ."

His body strained closer and Nick hungrily pulled her next to him, his hands moving feverishly along the curve of her spine to gently caress the soft swell of her hips. He shifted positions so that he lay half across Kerry, his mouth tasting and teasing a burning trail over honeyed skin.

Nick kissed the softly throbbing pulse at the base of her throat and slid down satin flesh to the eagerly thrusting breasts pushing against his palm. His teeth lightly nibbled on rosy peaks hardened with desire. Kerry's hair was a silky fire spilling from his hand as he tangled his fingers in her waves, while the other hand lightly played across her stom-

ach, bringing gasps from her as he deliberately
avoided touching the spot that ached for him.

Twisting and moaning softly, Kerry was aflame
with desire too long denied. She was driven by an
emotion as old as time—hungering for the intimacy
that would make her complete. It was more than
physical, more than the exquisite sensations Nick
provoked. This acute longing was soul-deep. Without volition, her body betrayed the depth of her desire with sensual movements, her back arching to
meet Nick's questing hand, slim hips twisting in
abandon.

Now, at last, Nick slid his long body over hers,
and slipped easily between her thighs with his knees
nudging her legs apart. He lay for a moment without moving, not kissing her parted lips. This time
his mouth nipped gently down misted skin between
the hills of her breasts, traveling over her softly
rounded belly to leave her quivering with anticipation. When he paused briefly before sliding lower,
Kerry gave a half-moan of protest, but Nick held
her still.

"Easy love, easy . . ."

Pressing shaking fingers over her mouth, Kerry
sobbed in total abandonment as Nick pulled her to
the brink of ecstasy, then over. It was magic, a hot,
fluid magic like nothing she'd ever experienced, and
Kerry shivered in reaction, wanting to please Nick
as he had just pleased her. She lay limp and lethar-
gic, replete and depleted of energy.

Dimly, she was aware of Nick's body moving up
again, covering her, and she clung to him with all
the fierce longing of her heart. Lethargy vanished
in a heartbeat as desire flooded her again, and she
thrust eagerly upward to meet the plunge of Nick's
hard body.

Nick was oblivious to everything but the slim
form beneath him, the soft curves and sweet satin

flesh that had beckoned him across an ocean. He didn't pause to wonder why this woman above all others held him with invisible bonds, but simply reveled in the feel of her, the touch of her hands, and the soft welcome of her lips and body. She was a witch, a siren, but he didn't care. Nothing mattered now but that he was here and she was his.

Unable to hold back any longer, Nick drove himself deeper into Kerry and felt a wild burst of pleasure that tore a husky groan from his throat. Their sweat-slicked bodies were one, united in desire and the curling wash of fulfillment.

When Kerry felt Nick's sudden stiffening and the brief convulsion of his lean body against hers, she pressed as close as she could, holding him tightly. For this one moment in time he was hers alone, as close as two humans could ever be, and hot tears slipped from beneath her closed eyelids. She was helplessly, hopelessly, in love.

Chapter 20

The *Unicorn* nosed into the Thames with stately grace, riding the dirty, flowing river to a long line of wharves and warehouses. Kerry wrinkled her nose in distaste. She was accustomed to the stink of dead sea life and rotting timbers, but not the refuse and garbage that littered these quays and the winding ribbon of water.

Before them sprawled the bawdy city of pomp and wealth, home of kings and commoners, gilted palaces and gaming hells. London.

Kerry rested gloved hands on the smooth wooden rail and let her gaze travel over the decks of the *Unicorn.* Familiar faces had greeted her when she boarded the ship in Ireland. Cook, Chips, Mr. Markham, and, of course, Wilson had grinned their pleasure and pelted her with exuberant hellos. They had dulled the sharp sense of loss she'd felt on leaving Ireland. She missed Sean already, and Margaret, and wondered why Nick had insisted upon leaving Castleconnell so quickly.

Kerry felt at times as if she was teetering on the edge of a precipice. Even after the tender closeness of their wedding night, Nick had not mentioned love. Her fingers tightened on the rail as she wondered why he'd married her.

Nicholas Lawton, standing on the quarterdeck and watching the stiff river breeze tangle Kerry's skirts, was wondering the same thing. Why, of all women in the world, did he want this one? She was not the kind of woman he had ever imagined himself marrying. It had been a shock to discover that not only did he want her slim, sensual body, he wanted her—all of her. He wanted to watch Kerry when she slept with the fingers of one hand curled against her sleep-flushed cheek like a little child, and hear her soft laughter at some ridiculous comment that Wilson might make. Even when she was angry and spitting curses at him with careless fury, he wanted her. He must be, Nick decided cynically, quite mad.

At first, thinking she was only a wild, unkempt, and unruly wharf brat, he'd been amused by her. Then he had discovered that beneath her tough exterior was a warm heart and the vulnerability of a young, frightened girl. Kerry's successful bravado had caught his interest. Her quick intelligence and courage had piqued his curiosity. But until he found her in Ireland, Nick had never considered marriage. Admittedly, marriage had at first occurred to him as a means for retrieving those damning account books. The old earl had too much influence for threats to have worked, and threats had never worked well with Kerry anyway. She would have laughed at him if he'd tried it. A quick marriage and even quicker annulment had seemed the perfect solution. But now he was bewitched by her— was he trapped in the web he had woven?

Wilson's voice behind him jerked Nick back to the present. "I'd fergot how cold London could be, Nicky lad," Wilson observed. The older man stepped up beside him on the quarterdeck, pulling his long jacket more tightly around his stout frame. "Warmer by a bit on Belle Terre, I'd say."

"Yes."

Wilson stood quietly for a moment, following the

direction of Nick's gaze. "Aye, she's a fine lass. I'm glad ta see ye did th' right thing by weddin' her."

"You love it," Nick responded with a half-amused smile. "Don't think I don't know some of your tricks, old man. It just took me longer to catch on to exactly what you were planning. Did you suggest she escape with the books?"

Wilson scratched his head beneath the knit cap he wore then pushed at his spectacles with a pudgy finger. "Well now! Yer brighter than I thought. An' I'll admit, it did occur ta me that th' lass might try such a thing. But I never spoke ta her about it, no. Knowin' how hotheaded ye ken be at times, I didn' think I should tell ye everythin' I knew."

"Just a few pertinent facts might have saved me a great deal of time and trouble," Nick said dryly. "As it was, I had to chase around half the Atlantic and waste my time racking my brain for clues as to where she might be! You and Samuel Locke must have enjoyed it."

"No, no. Ye've got it wrong, Nicky," Wilson said hastily. " 'Tweren't 'til we met wi' Locke off th' coast, that I was certain of who she was. All I had was th' necklace. Then I didn't know if th' old lord was even still alive or that she'd remember. It was risky, 'tis all. I just wanted ta be sure."

"Sure that by the time I found her I'd just be glad to know she was alive and well?" Nick asked. "Maybe you know me better than I know myself, Wilson."

"Aye." Wilson grinned shamelessly. "But if I'd said ye should wed th' girl, ye'd have done opposite. I had ta let ye find out fer yerself that ye wanted her."

"I still don't know why."

"Don' ye? I've never thought ye a fool afore now, Nick. Don' prove diff'rent."

Nick shrugged. "I've never met a more maddening female in my life. One moment she's a rowdy, rough-and-tumble little wench with a dagger in her fist and cursing in ten languages, and the next moment she's a cool, haughty lady. I think I liked her better when she was just the one and not the other."

"Don' go ta lyin'. Ye were always tellin' th' lass ta mind herself, an' ye know it. An' Nick, she had ta come inta it someday, ye know. Yer jus' mad 'cause someone taught her proper manners," Wilson said with a shrewd glance at Nick. "She doesn't need ye so much now. Aye, she don' need ye at all! She ken walk and talk like she was born to do. Why settle for a disgraced earl?"

A muscle twitched in Nick's jaw. "What a marvelous opinion you have of me. Does she share it?"

"What d'ye expect?" Wilson sounded genuinely surprised. "Think on't. What would ye think of a man who bashed ye in th' head an' carried ye off on his ship fer a few months? She can't be thinkin' yer a bloody saint! Ye put th' lass through a lot, lad."

"Oh, really." Nick sliced Wilson a narrowed glance. "Did it ever occur to you, Wilson, that if I had known the little chit I thought was a street urchin was actually the granddaughter of an earl, I would have taken her to her family?"

"Of course it did!" Wilson was astounded. "Why d'ye think I didn' tell ye what I suspected?"

'Sweet Jesus! I may seem a dullard, but I can't say that I understand your rather flawed logic, Wilson."

"If ye had known she was born ta quality," he explained patiently, "ye would never have tumbled her. 'Course, I don' understand th' logic of that, but it's th' way it is. An' if ye had never tumbled her, she would've jus' been a vague mem'ry soon." He smiled. "I knew from th' start that th' two of ye should be together."

"Ah, a frustrated matchmaker. Weren't you ever

told that all marriages are made in heaven?" Nick was decidedly sarcastic now, flaying Wilson with one of those scalding smiles that had been known to peel paint off walls. "Since you obviously love meddling in my life, why don't you arrange a meeting with Lord Sedgewick? I've an idea that he will be very interested to learn that I am back in England for a time."

"Aye, ye ken count on that, Nicky lad. An' I'll do what I can about a meetin' fer th' two of ye." Wilson pushed at his spectacles and met Nick's sharpened gaze. "Ye're bound ta bump inta Sedgewick. He's livin' in town now."

A nasty smile curled the edges of Nick's mouth. "Good. I want to see Sedgewick's face when he learns I'm back with a full pardon." Nick's voice was cold and hard. "He and my dear cousin Robert will be thrilled to see me, I'm sure."

"Aye, those two snakes share th' same hole, I'm thinkin'. With ye gone from England, Robert is heir an' Sedgewick in control. They still think th' books are lost, don' they?" He laughed at Nick's nod. "It ought ta be jolly fun, Nicky lad, ta pickle their plans!"

Both men turned at a slight noise behind them.

"What are we pickling?" Kerry interrupted with a smile. "Or should I say 'whom'?" She halted beside them and balanced on her toes, hands tucked into the sleeves of her light coat for warmth. "You two gentlemen—and I use the term loosely—have been so deep in discussion, you've completely ignored me. I'm tempted to throw myself into the river in despair."

Nick glanced at the littered surface of the water through which the *Unicorn* was moving at a slow pace. "In this river, I'd say that was a particularly cruel ending. Why not the Channel?" he suggested helpfully.

"Your sympathy is overwhelming, sir." Kerry made a small face at him. In spite of her gloomy spells of doubt at times, she was deliriously happy to be with Nick. Just being near him and watching the play of light on the angles of his face was enough to keep her content. It was growing more and more difficult to keep her love on a tight leash of restraint.

"Look, love," Nick was saying. He put one arm around her shoulders and gently turned Kerry. "See in the distance there? That's the Tower of London."

The twelve-acre complex of towers and buildings stood just east of London on the Thames. Kerry was more excited than she wanted to admit at being in London. Her last stay had been short and she had been more worried about what she would find in Ireland than about seeing the sights—now she could enjoy the city.

Kerry waited with growing impatience as the *Unicorn* docked and Nick hired a carriage to take them to his home. Her earlier depression vanished as she perched on the edge of her seat and stared eagerly out the windows of the carriage. They passed the Tower and London Bridge, the Mansion House where the lord mayor of London had his residence, rolled down Cannon Street past St. Paul's Cathedral and across the intersection where Blackfriar's Road changed to Farringdon, driving west on Fleet Street. Strand, Pall Mall, St. James, and Piccadilly flashed by, and they were in the fashionable district of Mayfair at last.

"You'll see all the sights while we're in London, love," Nick drawled, and Kerry flushed. She felt like a country milkmaid up to the city for the first time.

"Of course." She sat back, aware of Nick's amused gaze resting on her, and self-consciously smoothed her wrinkled skirts. "How long did you say we'd be here? Will you be staying with me, or somewhere else?"

He shrugged. "I've business that's been long neglected. It may take some time. Why? Were you planning to flit off without warning again?" Nick's hand lightly circled Kerry's wrist, his fingers exerting the slightest pressure on the fragile bones. "I wouldn't suggest it, love. Consequences could be . . . unpleasant."

There was a definite note of warning in his soft tone, and Kerry stiffened. "Is that a threat, Nick?"

Again that careless shrug, and the potent smile that could charm the stripes from a tiger. His hand moved to trace the delicate slope of her cheekbone as he leaned close. "I told you long ago: I don't make threats, love." His fingertip explored the outline of her ear in a feathery touch. "Let's just say I would be a most distressed husband if my wife decided to leave."

It was at moments like this that he unnerved her, and Kerry was angry at her brief flutter of fear. Her chin lifted a notch as she stared him straight in the eyes.

"And why would any wife leave such a charming and solicitous husband?" she asked sweetly. "It grieves me to think you would believe me so unkind."

"I'm sure it does."

You've learned more than simple mathematics and geography lessons since leaving Belle Terre, Kerry love, he observed silently. The months in Ireland had obviously taught her the refinements of social debate. With a shade more practice, she would be able to turn a phrase quite neatly.

"Ah. Here we are," he said aloud. "Devlin House. A bit run-down and shabby, but home."

Gray light diffused the sharp angles of stone and timber, but Kerry noted the simple classic lines of

the imposing structure with appreciation. There
were none of the ornate domes that characterized
many homes, nor curious clock towers. Lofty and
majestic, it was built of stone with pilasters running
flush up to the cornice and architrave. Rectangular
windows were high and only lightly ornamented
with graceful carvings, and were the same size on
both the ground floor and the first floor. The attic
windows were smaller and square, but all the windows had architraval keystones. Only five shallow
steps led to the portico upheld by slim columns.

An impeccably dressed servant was opening the
carriage door and pulling down the step for them.
Nick ignored the step but turned and held out a
hand for Kerry as she stepped from the vehicle.

Kerry had a vague impression of marble floors
and glittering chandeliers as she was ushered inside to a line of waiting maids, valets, and butler.
She was introduced as the earl's new wife and immediately escorted up a long flight of stairs to the
bedchamber she would share with Nick. Actually,
it was adjoining chambers, connected by a small
room and two doors with no locks. A waiting room?
Kerry wondered, and almost giggled at the thought
of Nick standing outside her door waiting for an
invitation to her bed. It was highly likely that she
would be the one who waited.

Rich carpets of peach and blue lay on the floor,
and damask draperies of cream edged with the same
peach and blue hung at the windows and tapestried
bed. The fruitwood furniture bore the graceful lines
of Sheraton in the curve of the legs and turn of a
post. Italian marble framed the fireplace where a
cheery blaze beckoned, and Kerry pulled off her
gloves and held out her hands to warm chilled fingers.

"It's lovely," she murmured to Nick. He nodded

and crossed to a long window to stand with his back to the light, facing her.

"This was my mother's room. I always liked it, and I felt you would also." He gestured to the huge bed. "I had the bed replaced, as the mattress was in poor condition after all these years."

Kerry realized she had never asked Nick about his parents, and he'd never mentioned them. She remembered huge paintings that hung over the flight of stairs, and she wondered if his parents' portraits were among those she'd glimpsed.

God, she knew so little about him really that it astonished her at times. How could she be so completely enamored of a virtual stranger who was her husband? But she was. Nick was in her thoughts when she went to sleep at night, and when she woke up. At odd times during the day thoughts of him would pop into her mind even when he wasn't near, prompted by a chance word or glance, the faint smell of tobacco or brandy.

Nick glanced at the drapery-hung bed and smiled, a beguiling smile full of promise, a smile that promised and tempted. "It's customary," he said softly when the maid had left and shut the door behind her, "to christen a bed the first night."

"Oh?" Kerry pulled off her light coat and draped it over a chair. "I've never heard of that custom. Is it one peculiar to this country?"

"No. It's peculiar to my family." He came to stand beside Kerry, and small electric shocks sparked along her nerve ends. "An old family custom should not be ignored."

"I see. And what is the procedure for christening a new bed? Sprinkling it with water taken from a tree stump on Midsummer's Eve? A handful of fairy dust shaken over the mattress?" Kerry's pulses quickened as Nick began shrugging out of his coat.

"Maybe a mixture of grated horn from a unicorn and two feathers from Pegasus?"

"No. There's no magic as powerful as the flow of honey from a man to a woman." Nick's coat was gone, tossed carelessly over Kerry's, and his shirt was unbuttoned to the waist and removed to join his cravat and vest. "It transcends even the unicorn horn and two feathers from Pegasus," he said softly against Kerry's lips. "Oh, what sweet magic you possess, love. Kiss me again. Yes, like that."

Kerry's senses were finely attuned to his every touch, to the press of his mouth against hers and the light brushing of his fingertips against her skin. She closed her eyes. Nick kissed her eyelids then. He kissed the tip of her nose and the small spot behind her ear. She shivered when his mouth husked over the contours of her ear and his tongue lightly explored the curves. Kerry's head tilted and she arched away from him as Nick teased a path of tender kisses over the bend of her throat and down.

"Oh Nick . . . what . . . what about . . . ?"

"They wouldn't dare enter without being summoned," Nick said against the hollow between her breasts. "Here, love. Let's get rid of this old dress, shall we?"

Cool air whispered over her breasts and belly, while the warmth of the fire seared into Kerry's back, buttocks, and thighs. Nick lowered her gently onto the bed and held her in his arms for a moment without moving or speaking, just held her.

When he moved again, sliding his body up over hers with one bent arm on each side of her head and his legs wedged between her thighs, Kerry sighed.

"Nick? Nick, do . . . do you . . ." She caught her bottom lip between her teeth to stop the question she wanted so badly to ask. If it didn't come voluntarily without her asking, it would not mean as much.

"Do I what, love?" he murmured in her ear. He nipped gently on her earlobe, then kissed it. "Do I like frogs? Do I fly through the air on moonless nights?" His mouth drifted across her lips in a feathery kiss, light and tickling. "Or do I enjoy loving you like this . . . ?" He thrust forward and Kerry arched to meet him. Both bodies synchronized in perfect rhythm, and Kerry thought that surely there was no greater pleasure than loving a man with heart and body.

Her fingers curled into his back and her feet dug into the little mounds of satin covers formed by her heels as she met Nick's driving thrusts, until Kerry was swept on heated wings to the ultimate release. It was sweet, so sweet that tears gathered in the corners of her eyes, and she was glad that Nick couldn't see her face in the shadows of the wide bed. He had muttered her name in the seconds just before that shattering release had shuddered through him, and Kerry knew that he must love her.

Holding him, Kerry turned her head to watch the flames in the marble fireplace. Nick had married her and brought her to his home, to the room his mother had once occupied. She was married to an earl and living in a grand town house in London, a countess with all a woman could want in the way of material goods. But what mattered more than the new clothes, family jewels and courtesy title was the man in her arms.

Chapter 21

"Are you going riding again, my lady?" Constance plumped the fat goose-feather pillow on Kerry's bed and slanted her mistress a smile. Kerry was carefully adjusting a smart velvet hat with a cluster of feathers stuck in its crown over her hair. She tilted it just so, examined the effect in the polished mirror, and nodded satisfaction.

"As a matter of fact, Constance, I am. I have a new phaeton, and a pair of matching bays from Tattersall's. In a half hour, I am to call upon Lady Jane and we are going for a turn about Hyde Park."

"By yourself?" The young lady's maid stared at Kerry with rounded eyes. It was not common for a lady to drive herself through the park. She was always driven by a bewigged coachman wearing a three-corner hat and dress gloves, and usually a powdered footman dressed in full livery ran along beside the vehicle in case he was needed for an errand.

"Don't be silly. Why would I be collecting Lady Jane if I intended to go by myself?" Kerry smiled as she pulled on a pair of gloves fashioned from the softest kid. She turned and inspected her appearance in the cheval mirror once more. The turquoise velvet riding habit fit snug to her small waist, and the full skirt flared gracefully over the calf leather boots peeking from beneath the hem. She looked,

Kerry decided, very much the lady of fashion. It wasn't easy for anyone to discern that on the inside, she was still the girl with tangled hair and ragged trousers and shirt.

"I must hurry, Constance. It is a quarter past four already, and I like to be early to watch the pompous ride past. When his lordship returns from Mr. Jackson's establishment, please remind him of the dinner tonight at the home of Lord Bloomsbury."

Nick was always gone lately, Kerry thought as she left her room and descended the wide, curving staircase. He was either going off to meet someone on business—what kind he never would say—or he was going to Tattersall's to buy a new horse, or going to Brooks to sit and play cards with his acquaintances. Women, of course, were not allowed in the gentlemen's establishment—not well-bred women. And if Nick wasn't at any of those places, he was at Mr. Jackson's establishment where one could go a few rounds of boxing if he liked.

The wives of these socially active gentlemen whiled away their time shopping, visiting acquaintances, or perhaps even playing some piquet if they didn't lose too much money so that their husbands had to scold them. A vague memory teased Kerry, a memory of a copper-haired wharf brat sitting on the back of a black stallion and declaring that she would never be a spun-sugar doll in a marzipan house. And so she wouldn't. She was glad she'd met Lady Jane at Almacks, the fashionable—but deadly dull—Assembly Rooms in King Street. The young woman seemed as bored with the rituals of the London ton as she was herself, and they had become close companions.

The new phaeton had been brought to the front for her, and a footman was at the heads of the spirited matching bays. "They seem a bit fresh, my lady," he said doubtfully. It was as close as he dared come to a warning, and Kerry smiled.

"That they do, Martin. It should be a refreshing ride then, don't you think?"

She was seated in the vehicle just large enough for two people, and took the long leather reins in her gloved hands. A smart slap on their gleaming rumps sent the bays off at a brisk pace, and the footman stood watching as the young countess expertly negotiated the sharp curve in the road.

"I'll be damned," he said to no one in particular, and went back to the stables to tell any who'd listen that the earl's new wife was not only a looker, but could handle the ribbons as well as any whip in London.

The phaeton Kerry drove was high and light, so fragile-looking a vehicle that it hardly seemed able to carry any passengers, but oh, how it could fly!

"This is almost as much fun as riding my stallion bareback on the beach," Kerry told Lady Jane Parker, daughter of Lord Benton Parker, Earl of Clemson. The phaeton was at that moment careening around Hyde Park Corner, and Lady Jane managed a rather sick smile.

"Yes! Oh my dear yes, I was going to say that very thing. . . ." Jane swallowed a gasp and closed her eyes as they skimmed past a dray loaded with barrels of beer. She cleared her throat as the phaeton rolled smoothly down the road. "It has been a long time since I rode a stallion bareback down a beach, I must say. I do believe I never have." She shot her companion an inquiring glance. "I suppose it would be silly of me to ask if you have done so?"

"I did every day of my life for almost eight years," Kerry answered. They were in the park now and she slowed her pace. It was the fashionable hour of five o'clock, when anyone who was anyone drove or rode in Hyde Park. The men were mounted on su-

perb horses and the women rode in luxurious satin-
lined carriages with their coachmen and footmen.
Here were the elite of London, the dukes and duch-
esses, earls and countesses, even the Prince Regent,
all out to see and be seen.

"It reminds me of a circus," Kerry said to Lady
Jane, "and all the people are trained to do their own
special tricks. See—over there—Sir Richard Twad-
dlington? He is a trained tortoise, slow and plod-
ding, his back hunched like a shell while he nods
and smiles and says yes to everything the Duke of
Westerson suggests."

Lady Jane laughed. " 'Pon my soul, he *does* look
rather like a tortoise now that you mention it! Oh,
see how his head moves up and down and sticks out
of his high collar. . . ." She gave another gasp of
laughter behind her gloved hands. The subject of
their discussion politely touched the brim of his hat
as they passed him, and Lady Jane waved gaily.
"Oh, point out someone else," she begged Kerry
when they had gone a little farther.

"Lord Pursington. He's a trained bear. See how
big and woolly he is?—and how he snaps and snarls
at anyone who comes near? And Lord Markham—
he's a ferret, sharp-faced and cunning."

"How about that man over there?" Jane asked
slyly. She pointed to a man just riding through the
Marble Arch on a sleek gray stallion. "Is he part of
the circus?"

Kerry slowed the bays to a walk and studied the
man Jane had indicated. He was lean and tall, and
the broad shoulders beneath his tight-fitting coat
were obviously natural and not padded. Light hair
curled from under his top hat, and his snug trousers
hugged well-muscled legs. He was handsome, which
is why Jane had pointed him out, Kerry supposed,
but there was something else about him. It was a
suggestion of ruthlessness in the aristocratic stamp

of his features, perhaps. He appeared like a beautiful, dangerous lion, and Kerry said so.

"Ah, you must know him then. That, my dear, is Robert Kingsley, until recently heir presumptive to Devlin." She smiled at Kerry's surprise. "Yes. Your husband's title. Lord Robert is his cousin. I rather think he must have been disappointed when Nicholas returned to England after so long an absence."

Kerry turned to look at the man again. He was so fair where Nick was dark, but yes, there was a faint family resemblance. Maybe it was the careless way he surveyed those around him, as if he was lord and master of all he saw, that reminded her of Nick.

Lord Robert's casual, faintly sneering glance caught Kerry's as she stared in his direction. His eyebrow rose as she returned his stare without looking away.

"I believe he's coming over here," Jane said as she pushed distractedly at a strand of her dark hair. "Oh dear, and I didn't bring my dueling pistols!"

"Why do you say that? Is he so very dangerous?"

"Yes. Not as dangerous as your handsome husband, of course, but in his own way Robert Kingsley can be exceedingly dangerous. The man has no scruples, and he positively hates Nicholas Lawton."

Kerry looked again, frowning. Robert Kingsley. The name was so vaguely familiar. Where had she heard it before? Perhaps it had been casually mentioned in connection with a juicy tidbit of gossip.

"Oh Kerry, do urge the horses a bit faster. I don't really want to trade veiled insults with Lord Robert."

Kerry obligingly gave the bays more rein, holding the ribbons lightly so she wouldn't saw at their mouths. "Jane, tell me more about Lord Robert and Nick."

"Well, I know the rumors. It seems that a long time ago Nicholas was commissioned as an officer

in the Royal Navy. His commanding officer was a
Lord Sedgewick, not exactly one of the nicest men
to sail with or even speak to on a social level.
Nicholas and his father had never gotten along very
well, and the old earl was always threatening to
disown him. That, of course, suited our fair Lord
Robert perfectly. He would toady to the old earl until he positively made one nauseous, smiling and
'Yes, my lord, whatever you say, my lord; you are
right as always, my lord . . . ' Quite a dreary fellow,
you understand. Then Lord Robert, who is the same
age as your husband, suggested that since Nicholas
would one day be taking over the estate and title,
perhaps he should be familiar with command. No
one has ever understood why the old earl liked the
notion, unless it was because Nicholas had just created a minor scandal with an actress." Jane patted
Kerry's arm comfortingly. "It was just one of those
things high-strung young gentlemen do, you know.
Anyway, Nicholas was commissioned, Lord Robert
moved into residence with the earl, 'to keep him
from being lonely,' and within six months Sedgewick had charged Nicholas with the theft of a ship's
cargo. There was a great scandal and Nicholas was
to be put on trial, but he disappeared. The old earl
promptly banished him from the estates, and the
will was changed to read that unless he had received a pardon, Nicholas would not inherit."

"I see." Kerry drove blindly, wondering how Nick
had finally managed his pardon after all this time.
So now he was a free man—would Nick stay with
her? She bit her lower lip, unconsciously tightening
her hands on the reins.

Lady Jane's shrill scream and the swerve of the
bays snatched Kerry's attention back to what she
was doing. A horseman had ridden just in front of
her, and the bays reared in panic and almost bolted.
It took a great deal of skill to calm them and keep

them from running, but Kerry managed to hold the leather reins loosely enough without giving them their head, and the bays settled into a nervous prance.

"Very well done," a masculine voice approved, and Kerry turned angrily to the man who had caused the near accident.

"You bloody idiot, that's not a hobby horse you're riding! My animals almost bolted because you're not rider enough to keep your mount under control! Stay off the road if you're prone to blundering into others . . ."

"My, my, how droll!" The object of Kerry's fury was none other than Lord Robert, and he was staring at her coolly, a mocking smile twisting his thin mouth. "Why don't you just admit that a woman cannot effectively handle blooded cattle like these? You should have an old mare, child, instead of these fine animals."

"Is that right? Please recall, sir, that I was in my proper lane, while you cut directly in front of me!" She was furious and struggling for control, glaring at Lord Robert and trying to ignore those curious souls who had stopped to gawk and listen.

Lord Robert pointed to the intersection just behind them where he had cut in front of Kerry. "I have the right of way here, my dear. Perhaps you should review the proper driving procedures before taking the ribbons." He touched the brim of his hat with a mocking gesture of farewell, then paused to say, "But I must admit, you drive your cattle exceedingly well."

"Oh, my," Kerry said faintly as Lord Robert rode away and the crowd dispersed. "Did I do that?"

Lady Jane took a deep breath. "I believe so," she admitted, "but I know you had your mind elsewhere because of my story. I should have been watching."

"No. It's my fault. I suppose I owe Lord Robert an apology. . . ."

"Not at all. He deliberately rode into us when he had plenty of time to stop. I saw him," Jane said. "I should have said something, but I thought he would stop in time." She slanted Kerry a glance. "I think he wanted to create just such a scene, Kerry. I wonder why."

"If he hates Nick, maybe he wanted to embarrass me." Kerry added grimly, "He certainly succeeded! I feel an utter fool."

"Don't be ridiculous. Do you see any other woman out here with the courage to drive her own horses? Or the skill? I certainly couldn't! Lord, I shudder to think where my beasts would be if I had the ribbons. Probably in The Serpentine."

Kerry and Jane both laughed at the thought of a curicle and horses submerged in the artificial pleasure lake that extended into the Kensington Gardens.

"Nevertheless," Kerry said, "I feel an apology is in order. I shall send him a note."

Lady Jane smoothed her powder-blue skirts and fiddled with the strings of her matching purse. "I have an uneasy feeling that we've just invited trouble," she said. "I don't know why, unless it's because Lord Robert has such a reputation for hating Lord Devlin. Be careful, Kerry, for you don't have the experience to match wits with someone as diabolically clever as Kingsley, I assure you. You're too forthright and honest, and Lord knows, that has no place in his fast circle! And if I were you," she added, "I would not tell Nicholas about this. He returns Kingsley's animosity, and it would only cause trouble between you."

"I'll remember," Kerry assured her. "And I have

no intentions of doing other than sending Lord Robert a short note of apology."

But when Kerry and Nick attended a dinner at the home of Lord and Lady Brompton three nights later, Kingsley boldly confronted them.

"How delightful to see you again, my lady," he said to Kerry. "I trust your rides in the park have been without event?"

While Kerry murmured assurance they had, wishing she had mentioned the incident to Nick, Lord Robert turned to his cousin.

"I see that you have managed to capture the most beautiful girl in all London, Nicholas. You always were a fair hand with the ladies. I predict that your wife will be all the rage soon." He flashed an insincere smile at Nick's rigid face. "She is totally delightful, and has won several hearts as well as my admiration for the way she drives her cattle. You must spend many sleepless nights worrying someone will snatch her away from you."

"Not at all," Nick answered coolly. "I've always managed to keep that which is mine."

Lord Robert stiffened. "Quite so, cousin. Quite so. Let us hope that is always the case." He turned back to an appalled Kerry and kissed her hand with a Gallic gesture. "I much appreciated your short note," he whispered audibly, "and I shall cherish it for some time. Au 'voir."

"What in the bloody hell is he talking about?" Nick demanded icily when Robert was out of hearing range. "Have you written Robert Kingsley a note?"

"I . . . I . . . yes, Nick, but it's not as it sounds," Kerry began with a stammer. "I know I should have told you, but when I heard what great enemies you were, I thought . . ."

"You thought it would be better to keep it a se-

cret. Very bright of you. I certainly do not care for
the idea of my wife writing other men notes, especially when the other man is my devious cousin."

"Wait, you don't understand. There was an incident in the park. . . ."

"Now's not the time to discuss this, when everyone here is watching us. Smile, damn it!" he
ground out. "People are watching, and I won't
have them talking about this at Brooks and
White's like we were a Punch and Judy act."

Kerry spent a miserable evening, forcing smiles
and light conversation, and she noted that the curious did indeed send sly smiles and whispers in
their direction. They were barracudas, she thought
glumly, just circling and waiting for a juicy bite
of gossip. If only Lady Jane had not come down
with a head cold and was here to comfort her!

She touched her empty wineglass with one finger, and a well-trained servant immediately re-
filled it, earning Kerry a glance of disapproval
from Nick.

"Do you intend to embarrass me by falling
drunk into your dinner plate?" he asked in a low
tone. "I recall the last time you drank too much
wine."

"What a marvelous memory you have, sir. And
do you also recall that was the same night you had
kidnapped me?"

"Lower your voice!" Nick snapped. His eyes narrowed on Kerry's flushed face. "If you would like
to stand up and inform everyone here that you
spent two months with me on board my ship without the benefit of clergy, I will be happy to get
their attention for you. It would make most interesting conversation, and I am sure Lord and Lady
Brompton would be ever so grateful for the amus-

ing diversion. Dinner parties can be everlastingly dull without stimulating topics of conversation."

"Well, here's a stimulating topic for you," Kerry said sweetly. "Piracy. Murder. Kidnapping. Oops. That's more than one, isn't it? See how amusing we could be?"

Standing, Nick informed his somewhat startled hosts that as his wife had developed a crushing headache, they were forced to leave. His hand gripped her elbow with such force that Kerry did indeed have an expression of acute pain on her face, and she murmured a faint confirmation as she was half-lifted from her dinner chair.

They didn't speak until the landau door had been shut behind them and the vehicle rolled away. Nick turned to face Kerry in the dim light that flickered in the windows from the gaslights they passed.

"What do you have to say for yourself?" he demanded. "Why in God's name did you write Robert Kingsley a note?"

Kerry stared at Nick for a long moment, her eyes wide with pain and rage. "What was in that note is none of your business," she blurted out. "I refuse to tell you. Ask Robert if you wish to know."

"Robert? How familiar we are with my dear cousin!" Nick sat back abruptly. His face was tight with anger and his big hands were clenched on his knees. Violent fury shook him so that he was afraid if he even touched Kerry, he would truly harm her. Robert Kingsley! How had she even met him, when Nick had been so careful to steer her away? He had avoided mentioning his cousin at all, hoping that he would have settled the entire affair before Kerry was thrown into Robert's orbit. Now she had not only met him, she was obviously attracted to him. Damn it. Locke would have to speed up the pace of events before he behaved rashly, because if Robert so much as looked at Kerry again, Nick would kill him.

The landau stopped in front of Devlin House, and in the gloomy light shining from lanterns on the portico, Kerry saw the savage expression on Nick's face. She suppressed a shiver and thought that now he truly hated her.

Later, lying in her wide lonely bed and staring at the canopy above, Kerry stirred restlessly. She couldn't sleep. The evening's events boiled inside her head like a hot stew. Once more Robert Kingsley's name evoked a vague memory. Where had she heard it? No, she remembered suddenly, she'd seen it written.

Kerry bolted upright in the bed. The name Robert Kingsley was written in both of the account books she had taken from Nick! Throwing back the covers, Kerry slid from the bed and padded softly across the floor to an armoire that stretched to the high ceiling. Hidden in the false bottom of a chest she had brought from Ireland were the books. They were her insurance, a wedge to use against Nick if ever he should threaten her for some reason.

Bits and pieces of information cluttered her brain, all mixed together in a potpourri of confusion. Maybe if she looked at the books again, she would understand why Nick was so angry with her.

A few moments later, Kerry sat back on her heels. Angry frustration seared through her. The books were gone.

Chapter 22

"What do you think of this bonnet?" Lady Jane tied a saucy bow just under her left ear and adjusted the wide satin ribbons with a flick of her fingers. When there was no answer she sighed and turned around in her chair to look at Kerry. The slender girl draped over the curving arm of a Regency sofa was gazing gloomily out the window. "Oh, do cheer up," Jane begged softly. "I can't stand seeing you of all people in the doldrums."

A faint smile flickered briefly on Kerry's lips. "I'm as happy as a dead pig in the sunshine," she said. "It's just that my face is slow getting the message."

"I think it's your brain," Lady Jane muttered. She took off her new bonnet and tossed it carelessly on the walnut dresser. "Why don't we just think of a plan of action? First, let's outline the situation: We have here a husband who has never said those very important three words and a wife who wants to hear them. Next, we have the slight complication of a suspected lover. . . . Don't glare at me as if I were an ax murderer, I'm stating the facts as they are known. To further infuriate the irate husband, we have the undisputed fact that the questionable lover happens to be his second worst enemy, and has taken to sending you small presents. What do you do with them?"

"Send them back unopened. Unfortunately, Nick

was making one of his rare appearances in my room when the last gift was brought up." Kerry shook her head. "I still don't know why he came to my room. He'd only been there a moment or two when Constance brought in the box, and he left without a word. The door has not shut properly since. . . ."

"Rotten luck," Jane sympathized. "I suppose you've already told the servants to refuse to accept any more deliveries? Have you tried going to Nick yourself and explaining why you wrote that blasted note?"

"He's like a stone gargoyle, only colder. All he will say when I try to talk to him is that he's late for an appointment. It's damned difficult talking to a shadow. I wish that Wilson had not left London on some errand for Nick. He could get him to talk to me, I'm sure. If only I hadn't been so hurt and angry that night we argued."

Frowning, Jane rested her elbow on the chair arm and her chin in her palm. The ormolu clock on the glass lamp table struck three o'clock. "Well," Lady Jane said at last, "until you can get him to listen to you, there's not much that can be done. Didn't you tell me you wrote him a note explaining? I thought so. The bloody idiot should have read it. How stubborn men can be! I think I shall be a spinster and live in the east tower when I'm old. All the servants will think it haunted, and I can spend my declining years in glorious solitude."

"You'll starve to death. You don't have the vaguest notion where the kitchens are located," Kerry pointed out.

"Oh." Jane waved her hands airily. "I shall have meals delivered by tradesmen. I'll grow fat like the regent, stuffing myself with oysters and syllabubs. . . . You are attending the prince's grand masquerade, aren't you?"

Kerry shrugged. "Without an escort? If Nick

won't talk to me, I'm quite positive he won't be my
escort."

"Fine. You can go with me, then. We'll have such
a marvelous time everyone will be envious, and all
the men will crowd around us like flies on honey. . . .
Kerry! That's it!"

"What's it?" Kerry sat up as Jane bounded up
from the chair and began dancing about the room.
"Whatever is the matter with you?"

"I have the perfect solution! It's like a vision or
something, it came to me in a blinding flash of
light. . . . Oh, I can just see Nicholas Lawton's face
now! After the masquerade, he will most certainly
talk to you, my dear, but you will have to talk fast
because he's going to be quite angry."

"Wonderful. And what if I don't talk fast enough
and he squeezes the life from me?"

"Oh, don't worry about that. I've seen the way he
looks at you. He may want to, but Lord Devlin will
not murder you. And things can't get much worse,
can they? At the very worst, he will only refuse to
speak to you or send you to the country or something."

After a moment Kerry asked cautiously, "What
is this great plan that will work a miracle?"

"Are you certain we should do this?" Kerry asked
doubtfully. She stood in front of the long mirror in
Lady Jane's dressing room. Not daring to don her
costume at home in case Nick should by some
chance see her, she had packed it in a box and
brought it with her. Now she gazed critically at her
reflection.

"Of course we should do this. Didn't you tell me
this is how they dress?" Jane carefully adjusted the
crown of fresh flowers on Kerry's head. "How delightful that this is summer and plenty of flowers

are available. Though I don't suppose these are the
same as the ones you used to wear."

"No. They're not the same, but just as lovely. I'm
really not sure that this is the thing to do, Jane.
Nick will be livid, and I know he's attending the
masquerade. Constance told me he had ordered a
costume from Smythe and Babcock of Cockspur
Street."

"Wonderful. Then our little plan should work
splendidly, and Nick will drag you from the masquerade and escort you home. During which time,"
Jane muttered through the dressmaker's pins she
had in her mouth, "you will talk as swiftly and coherently as you possibly can." She made another
adjustment in Kerry's costume then declared herself satisfied with the results. "Perfect! We shall
both be an instant hit once we remove our cloaks.
I, for one, intend to keep my mask on, however. I
don't want a heated discussion with my father.
Ready?"

Kerry cast a last doubtful glance at her reflection
and put on her cloak. No mask would hide her identity from Nick. He would recognize her immediately, she was sure.

Carlton House was already crowded with costumed guests when Lady Jane's coach arrived. The
recent gala held by the prince at Carlton House had
not been a huge success because of the galling pop-
ularity of the Tsar of Russia. Blond and handsome,
the Muscovite with long legs and a waist as slender
as a girl's had become the absolute idol of London.
He had snubbed Lady Hertford, the regent's unpop-
ular new favorite, and was adored by all the aristocratic ladies, who vied for his attention.

Lady Jane and Kerry managed to slip in the doors
virtually unnoticed because of the tsar's presence in
the Crimson Drawing Room. They skirted the clutch

of ladies gathered around him and strolled casually through the rooms.

"Do you see Nicholas?" Lady Jane whispered. Her eyes danced with excitement behind the velvet mask she wore. "I feel as if I'm invisible with this mask on, that I can be as bold as I like and no one will know who I am!"

Kerry smiled and wished her throat was not so dry nor her heart thudding so fast. Her stomach fluttered nervously and she drew the edges of her cloak more tightly around her. The insignia of the Garter adorned velvet carpets in the Crimson Drawing Room, and ostrich plumes waved above silver helmets of the high canopy in the Throne Room. They wandered through double doors between the State Apartments on the ground floor and toward the Conservatory, a tented Gothic structure with clustered columns, a traceried ceiling encrusted with gold ornamentation, and stained glass windows looking out into a garden where nightingales sang and weeping willows swayed in the soft evening breeze.

Everywhere there were grinning devils with pitchforks in hand, a favorite costume it seemed, and bewigged magistrates, several long-robed monks and a knight in clanking armor moved through the rooms. There were milkmaids with short skirts and bare feet, a shepherdess, and several Greek goddesses.

"No one has a costume like ours," Jane observed. "I do believe we are original."

"There will be several at the next masquerade," Kerry predicted, and Jane laughed and said she had learned London society very quickly.

The regent was garbed in a Roman toga of snowy white linen, and gleefully announced to all who incorrectly guessed his identity that he was Zeus, ruler of mortal and immortal. "You must pay a penalty," he would tell the person who had dutifully given the wrong answer. Pointing his thunderbolt crafted from thinly hammered bronze, Zeus would command a song or a dance, or a passage from Shakespeare. These were performed to the great amusement of the crowd, and the result was hilarity. "By far, this is the best event of the summer," the regent was heard to declare. Even the presence of the tsar had not dampened his pleasure in the masquerade.

Darkness settled in soft purple shadows, and brilliant lights and Chinese lanterns flickered like a thousand fireflies in the night. They had arrived an hour before, and Kerry still had not seen Nick. Was he here? She had seen everyone, it seemed, but her husband. Lord Robert, disguised as a monk in a long brown robe of rough wool, had found her shortly after her arrival.

"I see that you are without your usual watchdog, my lady. Why isn't my esteemed cousin with his lovely wife?" Robert had asked. His heavy-lidded eyes had seemed to see beneath the satin of Kerry's cloak as he raked her with an assessing glance, and she'd been angered by her immediate inclination to retreat.

"Are you more concerned with where Nick isn't, or where he is?" Kerry countered coolly. "You have good reason to worry. I certainly would if I were you."

"Would you, my lady? Thank you for the warning. I shall ever watch my back. But, then, I always have with Nicholas. He has a preference for striking from behind."

"Liar!" Kerry tensed with anger, and the concealing folds of her cloak slipped slightly as she took a step closer to Robert. "You deliberately put a wedge between Nick and myself, but you shall not win. If I had known that you were despicable enough to do so, you would not have been given the ammunition to cause a rift. I regret that I was so foolish."

"Life is full of regrets." Robert's pale eyes narrowed on the tiny gap of Kerry's cloak. His mouth curved into a thin smile that was sardonic and chilling. "I am distressed that you think I would try to cause problems between a husband and wife. Lord knows, I certainly have no reason. My quarrel is with Nicholas, not you."

"But it would certainly suit your plans if Nicholas had no legitimate heirs," Lady Jane interrupted. "Then the title would revert to you once he died."

Lord Robert laughed softly. "My cousin could live to be a very old man! What good would that do me? Your logic is flawed, Lady Jane."

"No, you are flawed, Robert Kingsley! I am quite sure you'd be terribly grieved if Nicholas met with an untimely end—one that had been carefully arranged!"

"Ah, you wound me." Robert placed both hands over his heart and gave a mocking bow. "In the face of such animosity, I will withdraw. You ladies remain the victors, and I the poor loser." Before Kerry realized his intention, Lord Robert seized her hand as if to place a kiss on it. The cloak shifted, affording him a brief glimpse of her costume before she regained her composure and snatched the edges together. Laughing, he spun on his heel and left them.

"He should have come in the devil costume," Jane muttered. "It would have been more natural. I don't think anyone saw what happened just now, so our theatrical unveiling will still be a grand revelation designed to astound the masses! And most of all," she added, "a certain stubborn husband."

Kerry hoped so. Surely all this would not have been for nothing, but where was Nick?

Lady Jersey was there dressed as a celestial angel, and Countess Lieven made a charming milkmaid complete with an empty pail. Lady Cowper was a shepherdess, and the tsar's sister, the Grand Duchess Catherine of Oldenburg, was a Greek goddess.

The Duke of Argyll, Lords Alvanley, Sefton, Worcester, and Foley, "Poodle" Byng, "Ball" Hughes, and Sir Lumley Skeffington stood in a half-circle around Kerry, Lady Jane, and several beauties including Lady Cowper and Louisa Lambton.

"I say," said a masked devil with a voice suspiciously like Lord Sefton's, "why is it you two ladies are not in costume? What are you wearing beneath those cloaks, hey?" His pitchfork teased the edges of Kerry's cloak. "Don't tell me you came as Lady Godiva!"

General laughter and teasing greeted this suggestion, and the regent's attention was drawn to the noisy group.

"Ah, what is this?" he cried. "No costumes, ladies? That's not sporting of you."

"Your Royal Highness, we are in costume," Lady Jane replied with an impish twinkle in her eyes. "We've only been waiting on the right moment to unveil."

"Oh, the right moment is it? They must be very special costumes."

"They are. The countess once lived in the West Indies, and these costumes are authentic. If Your Royal Highness wishes, we will reveal them for your pleasure."

A slight frown puckered Kerry's brow as she glanced at Jane. Now? But the plan had been to wait for Nick to arrive. Her heartbeat accelerated as Jane caught her eye and gave a short nod of her head. Kerry turned slowly to gaze in the direction Jane indicated, and saw a hooded figure leaning against the wall. How did Jane know it was Nick? she just had time to wonder before the monk moved from the wall, then she knew. No one else walked quite like Nick did, with that peculiar graceful stride that kept him standing upright on the pitching decks of a ship when everyone else walked like cautious old men.

The regent was already clapping his hands to gain the attention of his guests, then announcing that as a special surprise the Earl of Devlin's lovely wife and the enchanting Lady Jane Parker had authentic costumes from the West Indies to present to them.

"So much for hiding behind a mask," Jane murmured resignedly.

"Is there any special music you would like, ladies?" the regent asked. "I will instruct the musicians to play whatever you say."

As Kerry stared past the sea of faces they became a blur. She focused on Nick, who stood watching her from the shadows of his hood, his face hidden. His shoulders were stiff and squared, and she knew he was angry.

Kerry's chin lifted slightly in that defiant challenge that Nick was more than familiar with, and she turned her attention back to the prince.

"If Your Royal Highness permits me, I would like to speak with the musicians myself. There is a special rhythm that would be appropriate. May I?"

"Of course, of course." The prince gleefully flapped his hands. "Go right ahead. And please, stand upon the dais there so that all may see your costumes. I think the potted palms make a perfect background, don't you?" He beamed at Kerry's agreement and urged them to hurry.

"What on earth are you doing?" Jane hissed in Kerry's ear as they crossed the room to the musicians. "I've begun to feel like an actress from Drury Lane!"

"I assure you that our costumes will long be remembered," Kerry said. "Can you dance?"

"What? Of course, I can dance! What . . . what kind of dance do you mean?"

"Follow my lead if you can. If you cannot, kneel on the floor and clap your hands in time to the beat of the drum. And take off your slippers before we begin."

"Dear God," Jane said faintly as she realized Kerry's intentions. "Nicholas may very well murder you!"

After a brief consultation with the rather startled musicians, Kerry was pleased to find three of them were from Spain. They were studying in England, and yes, they would be more than happy to play the countess's request.

"Ready?" Kerry asked Jane as they stood in front of the expectant guests. "We mustn't disappoint them . . ."

What had first been a desperate plan to force Nick's attention on her had now altered to a defiant challenge. She was his wife, and she loved him enough to accept him without knowing everything about him. Nick would have to do the same for her. She was who she was; she was what the years had made her, just as he was what the years had made him. Would he understand that? Kerry prayed he would.

She gave the signal and the music began. Instead of a stately waltz or a lively country dance, there was the throbbing beat of bare hands on a taut drum. Kerry was transported back to the mountain village on St. Denis. A brass horn replaced the more familiar wind instruments of carved bamboo, and a timbrel with metal jingles imitated the sound of polished wood clacking together.

Moving in unison, Kerry and Lady Jane turned
slowly, their satin cloaks billowing out like the
wings of graceful birds as they turned their backs
to the audience. Bare feet stepped lightly to the
slow, steady beat of the drum, and the cloaks slipped
from their shoulders and were spun away with a
flick of their wrists as they turned to face the regent's open-mouthed guests.

The prince's eyes bulged delightedly at the buzz
of excitement in the crowd. This was indeed a dar-
ingly different costume!

A wide swath of brightly flowered material was
wound tightly around Lady Jane's slender body,
forming a dress that reached just above her ankles.
Her shoulders were bare and a garland of fresh flowers hung around her neck, matching the crown of
flowers circling her head. Jane's dark hair barely
brushed her shoulders, swinging with each step of
the dance. She was lovely, her dark eyes gleaming
and cheeks flushed with excitement as she tried to
match her companion's dance steps.

Kerry's costume was different from Jane's. She
wore a skirt instead of a dress, and the hem reached
to just above her ankles. It was wrapped around her
so that each time she moved it exposed tanned legs
to several inches above slim ankles. A belt of flowers rode low on her hips, wrapped around the knotted waist of the skirt. In deference to Jane's horrified
protests that they would be exiled from England if
she didn't, Kerry had amended the authenticity of
the costume to include a covering for her breasts.
The material was a wide swathe circling her torso
and full breasts. It was not authentic, but much
more than the simple necklace of flowers that she
had worn on St. Denis. Even with this concession,
it was a shockingly abbreviated costume that could
have easily offended the regent and his guests.

It did not. Instead, they watched in silent awe and

admiration as Kerry lost herself in the dance. Her lithe, sinuous movements were sensual yet virginal. Provocative yet demure.

The entire dance was a contradiction. She moved like a graceful blade of grass in the wind, swaying and bending, an innocent with long coppery hair whirling in a haze of silky streamers.

Light from a thousand candles shimmered on Kerry's sweat-misted skin and she gleamed like a rare pearl. Her body undulated in imitation of an age-old rhythm and her arms lifted over her head, twining in the air, then slowly lowering as the music softened to a whisper. No one dared breathe as echoes of the melody lingered and Kerry's arms crossed in front of her face. She sank gently to the floor like the dying of the wind, her head bowed and the rich fall of her hair curtaining her face. There was no applause, only a deep hush as if a spell had been cast.

Lady Jane, kneeling to one side, finally moved in a daze to lift Kerry's cloak and drape it over her. She felt awkward and unsure, and wondered if Kerry was as drained by her dance as she had been by watching her.

The regent reacted in a spontaneous burst of quiet admiration, expressing his appreciation for the freedom of her dance.

"You were wonderful," he said simply. "I felt as if I were standing in some dark wooded forest an ocean away and watching the creation of life. I was deeply moved."

"Thank you, Your Royal Highness," she murmured. Then the moment was gone as guests crowded around Kerry and Jane to offer their praises. Even the aloof tsar approached her with words of approval, but the one man who mattered stood back.

Arms folded over his chest, Nick watched Kerry.

Her bright head was barely visible in the middle of the crowd as she fielded questions and comments. Damn her, so Robert had been right. It didn't bear conjecture to wonder how his cousin had known about Kerry's choice of costume when even her husband had not, but Nick had not given Robert the satisfaction of seeing any surprise on his face at the news.

"Your lovely wife will have more hearts at her feet than ever after this affair," Robert had murmured earlier in the evening. "I hope you appreciate the . . . daring . . . of her costume as much as the rest of us will."

"If I were you, Robert, I would be more worried about your recent activities and acquaintances than my wife's costume," Nick had countered smoothly. "It could mean your life."

"Or yours." Lord Robert had smiled frostily. "What would our gracious host have to say if he discovered that you have been passing information to those bloody Colonials? I can't think you would still be on his guest list, Cousin Nicholas."

Nick's expression had not altered. "How interesting a notion—if misguided. You would be delighted to see me hanged as a traitor, I'm sure. Then Devlin would all be yours."

Robert shrugged. "Of course, I would have to do my duty and see to the managing of the estates. But I wouldn't betray my country, either."

"Ah, now there is a surprising statement. You would betray your own mother if it proved profitable to you, Robert. Betraying blood has not bothered you in the past."

"I don't consider you close kin, Nicholas. You were always just a pampered heir to the title, far above your penniless cousin." His mouth twisted. "It was a rare treat to see you commissioned in the navy under Sedgewick. I knew it wouldn't take you long to disgrace yourself."

"You mean you knew it wouldn't take long for you to arrange it with Sedgewick." Nick matched Robert's sardonic smile. "I've almost all the proof I need, cousin. You are not as clever as you think. Did you know that I chanced upon an acquaintance of yours? I believe his name was Garcia. . . ."

Lord Robert's face subtly altered. "Yes, I heard Garcia had met with an untimely end. How convenient for you."

"And more convenient for you? Too bad, wasn't it, that your more recent burglar did not get what he was after either. I still have it, Robert."

A light shrug lifted Robert's shoulders. "I'm sure I don't know what you're talking about."

"I'm sure you don't. Now, if you'll excuse me, I think I'll look for my wife."

"Certainly," Robert had answered. "I hope you enjoy the little spectacle we planned. . . ."

Robert's mocking taunt still rang in his ears when Nick had found her a short time later talking to the regent, and then she'd stepped onto the dais with Lady Jane. He'd been first angry, then stunned by Kerry's dance. She'd done it to make him angry, of course, to gain his attention because he had avoided her. It would, Nick decided, be a pity to waste all her efforts.

Pushing away from the wall, Nick strode through the crowd, easily pushing his way to Kerry's side. She sensed rather than saw his approach, and turned slowly to face him. A shallow pulse beat rapidly in the golden hollow of her throat, and Nick was reminded of a trapped fox who had once stared at him the same way. There was frightened defiance in the smoky depths of her eyes, a faint challenge in the tilt of her head.

Nick scooped Kerry into his arms and carried her

from the room without saying a word. All of London would buzz with delicious tidbits of gossip the next day. The romantic souls had sighed with pleasure, and the practical minds immediately placed bets on the date and sex of the child. It was, the regent would say later, all in all the most successful event he had ever planned.

Chapter 23

The coach emblazoned with the gold crest of the Earl of Devlin rolled promptly to the door when Nick emerged from Carlton House with Kerry. Not a word had been said between them, and Kerry's hands were icy and her stomach knotted with apprehension. What if she said the wrong thing?—or if Nick wouldn't listen? Why had he been so distant and aloof simply because of a note written to Robert anyway? Did he think she would form a romantic alliance with his cousin?

Nick did think Kerry had formed an alliance with Lord Robert, though not necessarily a romantic one. His cousin was clever, much too clever to be drawn into affairs of the heart, so the notion that Robert would actually be enamored of Kerry had never carried any weight. It was the discovery that Robert knew far too much about his business dealings with Locke and others that had Nick concerned.

For safety's sake, Kerry's as well as his own, Nick had simply not told her anything at all. The shock of finding that she had been corresponding with Lord Robert when she hadn't mentioned knowing him had set Nick on edge. It was too great a coincidence that Robert knew the books were still in his possession, when they had been presumed lost. Why, he wondered, did Kerry tell Robert about them? Did she still resent him for kidnapping her, and for those first early weeks? Kerry would not be the first woman who played a loving part while waiting for revenge. Perhaps she'd realized her chance when she'd met his cousin in Hyde Park.

"Get in," Nick said brusquely when the footman had opened the carriage door, and Kerry held tight to her cloak as she stepped into the coach. "Isn't it a little late for modesty?" Nick observed with a caustic smile. He sat on the plush velvet seat opposite Kerry, his knees under the rough woolen robe brushing against her bare legs.

The contact was abrasive somehow, and Kerry shifted uncomfortably. Lady Jane had cautioned speed and conciseness of speech at this point, but, dear God, she was having trouble even breathing normally! She cleared her throat and smiled brightly.

"London weather is a bit cooler than that on St. Denis." Kerry took a deep breath and plunged ahead. "Nick, I have to talk to you. I feel I must explain about your cousin . . ."

"No explanations are necessary. I suppose you did what you felt you had to do. As I will do."

Something in the cold set of his face triggered a warning bell in Kerry's head, and she stared at him for a moment without speaking. This wasn't a jealous husband who gazed at her as if she was a stranger, this was the Nick she had glimpsed only briefly before. It had been a long time, and the memory was elusive, but his words were an echo of some spoken long ago.

"Nick, perhaps you don't understand. . . ."

"I must say you're right about that. I don't understand, Kerry. I would have given you anything. You're my wife, and I would have always cherished you." He smiled, a smile that wasn't really a smile. "It's a pity we must part."

Stunned, Kerry could only stare at him in the dim

light. The knot in her chest grew tighter, squeezing her like a vise. "Part?" she finally managed to echo. "What do you mean?"

"I mean, lovely wife, that I am leaving London. I don't know when or if I'll be back. You will be left the names of my solicitors, and they will take care of everything as they have in the past. You will lack for nothing."

The coach swayed as they rounded a corner and Nick's face was briefly illuminated by a bright shaft of lamplight. Lack for nothing? Kerry thought. How could he even think that for a moment? Nick would be gone, and she would no longer be able to glance across a room and catch his eyes on her, or hear his slightly husky voice whisper her name in the velvet shadows of their bed.

"Where are you going, Nick? Can't you tell me when you'll be back?" she asked. Her voice was cool and colorless, as if she didn't care at all, when inside she was churning with emotion.

"Sorry, love. I can't tell you a thing."

"Won't, you mean," Kerry said, and Nick shrugged.

"If you prefer to think of it that way. It sounds much nicer my way."

The coach stopped in front of Devlin House and Nick got out. He held out his hand to Kerry but she jerked away, feeling as if her world had come crashing down. Stepping down, she started up the steps, then realized Nick was still standing beside the coach. Apprehensive, Kerry turned to stare at him.

"I'll never forgive you," she choked out when Nick got back into the coach. "You can't leave me, Nick, you just can't!"

"Not only can I, love, but I am. You'll get over it." A tight smile curled the edges of his mouth as he shut the carriage door and leaned out the window. "You are remarkably like a cat—always landing on your feet. I have the unshakable feeling that you'll be just fine, love."

"But what if I'm not? What if something terrible happens, or . . . or . . ."

"It won't. And if it does, the names of my solicitors are written down in my study." He laughed. "I actually feel sorry for those poor gentlemen. They've no idea what a disservice I've done them. By the way, love, I didn't tell you, but your performance tonight was most effective. I don't know when I've seen members of the ton more mesmerized."

Heedless of the briefness of her costume or the fingers of wind that snatched at the edges of her satin cloak, Kerry flew down the wide, shallow steps to the coach. She clutched the window edge tightly with both hands.

"Does this have something to do with those damned books? Is that one reason you're so angry at me? I don't understand what they mean to you, but I know your cousin's name is in them." Her fingers tightened at his impatient movement. "I don't have them anymore, Nick, as I'm sure you know very well. After all, you stole them back! Didn't you?"

Nick gazed at her coldly. "I should have known you'd never hang on to them." He made a sharp gesture and the coachman lifted his whip. Whirling, Kerry demanded that the confused coachman put down his whip before turning back to face Nick.

"Don't you dare leave me, Nicholas Lawton! I won't have it, do you hear?"

Nick's gaze drifted over the sculpted curves of her face. He was tired, and there was still so much to be done before this was through. In all these months Kerry had never said she loved him, never indicated that she wanted him as more than a lover. Did she? He'd traveled for months to find her after she'd run away from him, and had been met with stubborn animosity when he'd found her. He'd thought that maybe after they were married she would realize she loved him, but it hadn't seemed to work out that way. He smiled, and his voice was gentle.

"Love, I don't think you know what you want. I'm giving you time to find out."

Nick gestured to the coachman again, and this time the carriage jerked forward, leaving Kerry standing in the curve of the road staring after him. A gusty breeze curled back the edges of her cloak and lifted bright tendrils of her hair like a banner as she watched the coach roll away. She was, Nick thought, as beautiful as a pagan goddess, and just as remote. Kerry was a chameleon, perfectly at home in the Caribbean on a pirate ship or gracing a castle in Ireland. It was a trait he did not possess, that ability to adapt so easily, and while admiring, Nick could not help a feeling of resentment.

He had not adapted easily to dispossession of his home, or the label of exiled criminal that had been thrust upon him ten years before. Clearing his name had become an obsession, and until meeting Kerry, his main purpose in life. Now that it was almost within his grasp, Nick wondered if it had been worth the price. Well, it was done now. He would see it through.

But his last glimpse of Kerry would haunt him during the following days, and Nick felt an unfamiliar tightening in his throat. She stood in front of Devlin House with the wind in her hair as it had been the first time he'd seen her. Then she'd been tearing across a hot sand beach astride a wild stallion, wearing a boy's trousers and shirt so that he'd first thought her to be a lad. There as no mistaking her femininity now. The cloak fluttered back like satin wings of a gull and revealed Kerry's slim bare legs that still retained that faint trace of Caribbean sun. He'd been fascinated by her from the beginning, but had gambled and lost.

Lights were still blazing from Carlton House when Nick returned. He walked unnoticed among the costumed revelers, one more robed monk among many. It didn't take him long to find who he was looking for, and Nick silently followed the tall, hooded figure of his cousin Robert.

Lord Robert slipped along a dark hallway and into the garden, pushing through thick bushes until he was well away from the crowd. Several times he paused and glanced over his shoulder before continuing. When he stopped beside an ornate sundial, Nick halted behind a thick yew tree and watched. It wasn't long before another hooded figure joined Robert, and the two men quickly exchanged information and a small, wrapped package.

Hoping Locke was as alert as ever, Nick waited until the second figure disappeared into the shadows before stepping from behind the yew.

"Conducting business in the shadows again, Robert?"

Kingsley whirled to find his cousin leaning casually against the thick trunk of a tree and staring at him over the barrel of a small pistol. "What are you doing here?" he demanded.

"Watching you. It shouldn't surprise you. You've been watching me. Did your accomplice have any trouble finding the book he was looking for? I instructed my valet to be sure and leave the library windows unlocked this time."

Robert's eyes narrowed. "What are you up to, Nicholas? I thought you took your lovely bride home to ravish. Is it over so quickly? Poor child, no wonder she's so unhappy with you."

"My wife has no place in this discussion, cousin. Let's concentrate on pertinent matters. . . ."

"Oh, but I disagree. Your wife is a very pertinent matter. Without her help, I wouldn't have known about the book still being in existence. It was said to have been destroyed, you know."

Nick's jaw tightened. "I heard that," he said pleasantly. "Too bad for Sedgewick it wasn't. And too bad for you that you joined forces with him. You'll go down with him, Robert. Perhaps you'll even share the same cell."

"Wrong, cousin." Lord Robert's hand whipped up in a smooth motion. "Now we both have a pistol. Shall we see who is the better shot?"

"Don't be foolish. Any shot will bring guards within seconds."

"So? Dueling may be forbidden, but it is forgivable. An unnecessary death, a short time spent abroad, then I return to throw myself on the King's mercy. It's well known there's bad blood between us, Nicholas. Who will doubt me when I say you attacked me? Especially when I can produce witnesses?"

"Well-paid witnesses, of course."

"Of course." Lord Robert smiled. He slowly raised the pistol to point directly at Nick. "I always was a better shot, cousin. . . ."

Two shots fired almost simultaneously, both thudding into flesh and muscle. Like mirror images, two brown robed monks swayed, then one arced gracefully forward to stretch lifelessly on the regent's well-manicured garden floor.

Holding his left arm, Nick tried to staunch the flow of blood. The ball had passed through the fleshy part of his upper arm. He didn't have time to do more than wrap his linen handkerchief around the wound. There was too much to do yet, and he hadn't counted on Robert's forcing him to shoot. Nick spared only a brief glance at his cousin's body before stumbling through dense bushes to his waiting coach.

"This is the spot," Nick told the coachman, and the easily recognizable coach rolled to a stop in another part of the city. Pulling the hood of his monk's habit over his head, Nick got out and gave the coachman his directions, then ducked into a dark alley.

This was the seedier side of London, the streets and dark, blind alleys of St. Giles's Rookery, Clare Market, Cloth Fair, Clerkenwell, and the slums of the East End. Entire families lived like rats in the East End, with a bundle of rags for a bed with no hope of honest work, and with cheap gin their only comfort.

Nick walked the refuse-strewn alleys deeper and deeper into the heart, past taverns offering to make a man drunk for a penny and dead drunk for twopence. Free straw was also offered so that the drunk could sleep off the effects. Here small children were sold as chimney sweeps for only a few pounds, and the money spent on gin. Pawnbrokers were everywhere, ferret-faced men ready to advance a few shillings for a stolen coat or watch. More desperate men would perform almost any task for a few shillings more.

Stepping over a drunkard snoring with his head in the gutter and red-eyed rats nibbling on his feet, Nick rapped sharply on a shadowed door. A shutter was quickly opened and one eye appeared to inspect the visitor, then disappeared. Behind him the rats squealed and growled over the drunkard, and somewhere in the evil-smelling gloom of the alley someone cried out. A weak, thin wail of a baby wavered in the air for a moment, but was drowned out by a burst of raucous laughter, then the door swung open with a creak of rusty hinges.

"Be ye th' monk?" the huge, bulky shadow just beyond the open door asked.

"I am your salvation," Nick answered. The shadow beckoned and he stepped inside.

"D'ye 'ave th' Bible wi' ye?" the shadow asked as the door swung slowly shut. He barred the way to go farther.

"I have the book."

There was a satisfied grunt and the shadow held out a hand. "Gi' 'em ta me."

"No. I will deliver it personally." Nick's eyes slowly adjusted to the light and he could see the faint flicker of a candle in a room just beyond this small entrance. Another hooded figure could barely be seen seated at a table, and he heard a soft, imperious voice give a curt order.

"Let him enter."

Moving across a floor littered with things he didn't like to contemplate, Nick stepped into the adjoining room and stopped just inside the doorway. The hooded figure was sitting in concealing shadows, hands folded in front of him. A great gold ring caught splinters of light from the one candle, and Nick's eyes narrowed. Here was his quarry, the man who had eluded him for ten years, the man who had been responsible for his disgrace.

"Give me the book," Lord Sedgewick said to Nick. He pointed to the table. "Lay it there."

"What about my payment?" Nick hedged. "I was promised a hundred pounds."

"Greedy bastard. Kingsley is far too generous with my funds." Sedgewick motioned to the shadow. "Pay him, Grundley. Don't short our wily thief."

A chuckle preceded the shadow's movement forward, and Nick was ready. Grundley reached out with hands as big as a bear's, thick fingers ready to curl around Nick's throat while his knee lifted to slam into his back, so that with one easy movement,

he would be broken in two as carelessly as a twig.
But Grundley depended upon his immense size and
strength coupled with the element of surprise, and
was not prepared for the sudden thrust of a knife
between his ribs. He never uttered a sound beyond
a soft, shocked sigh. Tottering for a moment, Grundley slipped silently to the floor at Nick's feet and
was still.

"Well done," Sedgewick said calmly when Nick
turned back to face him. "I'd say you've earned your
hundred pounds, plus a bonus."

"I'd say you're right." Nick moved into the shallow light of the cheap tallow candle. "I'll name the
bonus. Ah, you agree too easily, sir. I haven't named
my price yet."

"I haven't seen the book yet. We may both be
disappointed." Sedgewick's hands disappeared into
the folds of his monk's robe. "Where is it?"

"Oh, I have it, your lordship. What is it worth to
you?" Still standing in the guttering candlelight,
Nick reached inside his robe and pulled out a small,
black book. He held it up. "What am I bid for this?"

Sedgewick half-stood, and his voice was impatient. "Put it on the table, man! First I'll see it, then
I'll pay!"

"Certainly, your lordship. I know you will be generous." Nick leaned forward and placed the book in
the center of the scarred wooden table, then let his
hands rest on each side of it. He was weak from his
loss of blood but determined not to show it. "It must
be worth a great deal to you. You've gone to a lot
of trouble to get it. I was told that you had followed
the owner for some time. How is it that you were
never able to get this before now?"

"I'm quite sure you would not be interested in
such boring details. Just leave the book, take your
money, and go."

"Oh, but I am interested. I risked a lot for this

little book, your lordship. Humor me." A razor-sharp dagger flashed in one hand, its point menacing Sedgewick.

With an impatient shrug, Sedgewick shifted in his chair and snapped out, "I don't know where Kingsley manages to find you impertinent thieves! Wait!" The knife point slid coldly over his throat like a deadly whisper, leaving a thin red line. "Don't—since you insist, damn you, I'll tell you. This book has been in the possession of a former . . . business partner . . . of mine. He was sent to some god-forsaken island in the Caribbean as a puppet mayor, and according to him, kept the book as a form of insurance against reprisal. It took much persuasion to redeem it. Unfortunately, it was stolen soon after recovering it. The man you took it from would have tried to use it against me." Sedgewick was in a cold sweat, and he swallowed convulsively as the dagger point moved slightly.

"Then it's worth a great deal?"

His mouth twisted bitterly. "I had a feeling you intended to up your price, you bastard. Yes, it's worth a great deal." Sedgewick edged up carefully to stand in the light. He reached out for the book lying just out of his reach on the table. As he lifted it Nick shook back the hood of his robe with a quick tilt of his head, and Sedgewick leaped back as if stung. "You!" he rasped, and Nick nodded.

"Yes, Sedgewick. Surprised? Don't be." Swift reflexes in spite of his wound shot Nick's right hand forward to grab Sedgewick's wrist as a pistol flashed from beneath his robe. "Ah, ah. That's not very nice." He twisted his fingers and the pistol dropped to the floor. He kicked it with one foot, then held his dagger up in the light to examine its wicked point. "Let's discuss this like civilized gentlemen, my lord. I have in my possession a book that will clear my name of a theft that *you* engineered. Of course, it will also condemn you for that same crime. I'm sure you now realize what a mistake it was to keep records of the ship's transfer and cargo, though it was very tidy. But then, you'd never been caught before, so duplicate records seemed a very satisfactory method of keeping up with how much you'd stolen." Nick smiled at Sedgewick's inarticulate mutter of rage. "You were doing very well until a too-honest young officer newly commissioned in the navy came along and accidentally discovered that the ship reported to have been seized by pirates had actually been sold. Lord Milford grew very wealthy from those business transactions also, I believe. I think it was very wise of him to squirrel away proof. It did manage to keep him alive and unaccused of the crime—as I was."

"You should have accepted my offer, Lord Devlin! You would have been wealthier than you could ever imagine!" The robed figure sank back into his chair and stared at Nick from the shadows of his hood. "You could still be. Destroy the book. Join us. With the war between Britain and America, we've managed to amass a fortune of immense proportions. It's so easy to claim a ship was sunk by those Colonials, then repaint and refit her, sell the cargo and the vessel in a remote Caribbean port . . . and I've learned not to keep records. There's no way to be caught."

"It does sound tempting." Nick draped one leg over the corner of the table. "But what if I prefer clearing my name, Sedgewick? That means more than what you're offering."

Sedgewick made a light, fluttering movement of his hands. "It will be unfortunate to report the disappearance of such a well-known young earl who only recently regained his title and estates. A pity. It will be said that your disgruntled cousin did away with you, of course. Kingsley was becoming tiresome anyway. Devlin will revert to the Crown and be put up for auction. I've always fancied your town house, Nicholas." Sedgewick's hands slapped together with a loud noise and two burly figures armed with pistols appeared in the shadows of the doorway. "It's too bad you refused my offer. I'm left with no choice now."

The hood of his cloak slipped back as Lord Sedgewick stood up, and Nick's hard gaze riveted on the face of the man who had haunted his nightmares. He was a bit grayer perhaps, but the same ruthlessness was still stamped on sharp features like a hawk's. Lines of dissipation grooved each side of his mouth, and the thin lips were twisting with a sneer as Sedgewick ordered the two silent men in the doorway to escort their visitor to the bottom of the Thames. He was smiling as the men stepped forward, and he reached out to lift the book from the table.

It was not the original account book, but the fake one filled with false entries, of course. Sedgewick had suspected the trick immediately upon discovering Nick's identity.

"It doesn't really matter once you're dead," he told Nick. "I believe that Milford and I can effectively refute any accusations from a bitter voice already beyond the grave. These things are so easily forged. Besides, with you gone, I'm sure I can find the genuine article." He tossed the book to the table. "Get him out of here," Sedgewick told the two robed men standing beside Nick.

But the men stepped forward to accost Sedgewick, and beneath the concealing robes they wore the uniform of the King's Guard. "You're under arrest, my lord," one of the officers said politely.

A slight figure neatly attired in frockcoat and trousers emerged from the shadows to confront Sedgewick. "I find you very disagreeable, Lord

Sedgewick. I am sure England will be much better off without you, and I am certain America will. Lord Castlereagh gave me the distinct pleasure of assisting Lord Devlin in your removal." Samuel Locke gave a nod and Lord Sedgewick found himself surrounded.

Sedgewick coolly inclined his head in defeat, but his glittering eyes focused on Nick.

"Don't become too complacent, Devlin. You may be rid of me for a while, but there are others who would see you ruined. England is too small a country for you."

"Sedgewick is right," Nick told Samuel Locke as their coach rumbled down dark streets. "I'd already decided that. I'd forgotten how much I disliked cold, damp weather, and endless rounds of masquerades and evenings spent in Brooks or White's." He gave a wry smile at Locke's surprise. "I enjoy spending time in Belle Terre where the sun shines and the wind blows soft and fair. No questions are asked there, no answers expected. I'm going back to stay, Locke."

"What about your bride?" Samuel Locke gave Nick a shrewd glance. "Does she feel the same?"

Nick shrugged and stared out the window at the blur of light and shadow. "She'll be well provided for. I don't think it matters to her where she is as long as there are amusements."

"Ah," was all that Locke replied. After a solicitous inquiry about Nick's wound, he remained silent until they reached the dock where the *Black Unicorn* waited. "Lawton," he said when Nick stepped from the carriage, "please take these papers back for me. See that they get to a General Andrew Jackson, who is now, I believe, near Baltimore, Maryland."

Nick's eyes narrowed on the wrapped sheaf of papers in Locke's hand. "You know I won't deliver information that will endanger England, Locke. I appreciate your help with Sedgewick, but his removal was as much a service to you as it was vengeance to me."

"Of course. I would not think it would even need to be discussed. With Sedgewick gone, it will greatly reduce the information getting past British forces as well as American. Castlereagh was relieved to have proof of duplicity. We have been wanting his removal for a long time. He has done great harm to both governments." Locke stared at Nick coolly. "These are not highly classified documents. You have my word on that."

Nodding, Nick took the parcel from Locke. A misting rain had begun to fall, and he shook Locke's hand goodbye and walked to his ship. It was late, and he wanted to leave England as soon as possible.

Chapter 24

Amused by his companion, Nick raked a hand through his thick hair and stared at the man sitting directly across from him in a New Orleans hotel room. Nick ruefully shook his head, thoughts wandering from the general conversation and his glass of brandy to the past few months.

He had been caught in the middle of England and America's war after all, it seemed, thanks to Samuel Locke. Those damnable papers had been carried to Baltimore, Maryland, only to find General Jackson gone to the Gulf Coast. The American general had reached Mobile at the end of October, and marched on Pensacola in Florida in November. After driving out the British there, he'd left part of his forces with Mobile and departed for New Orleans.

Nick had finally tracked him down at his headquarters at 106 Royal Street in New Orleans. In spite of illness, General Jackson dictated orders for a day and a night after the British victory at Lake Borgne on December 14. The British now had control of the lakes and water approaches to New Orleans, and martial law existed in the city. Jackson had issued a call to duty of every ablebodied man, British subjects excepted.

Times were desperate, and General Jackson had

finally agreed to accept the help of Nick's long-time acquaintance, pirate Jean Lafitte and his men.

"They're hellish banditti," Jackson had grumbled to Nick, "but I can't afford to refuse any help right now. I've formed artillery detachments under Dominique You and Renato Beluche, God help me." The general passed a hand over his eyes. "Pirates as patriots! What manner of war is this?"

Nick had grinned. "You're speaking to a man who's been called pirate for the past ten years, General. I'm the wrong man to ask."

Startled at first, Jackson had finally thrown back his head and laughed, saying if Lawton had been sent by Samuel Locke, he couldn't be too black a criminal. During the following days Nick had been impressed with the Tennessean's commanding presence. Though he was sick, Jackson's determination drove him to great lengths.

Even Wilson's admiration had been stirred. "I think we should git while we ken, Nicky lad," Wilson said, "but I have ta admit Locke's general is a hell of an officer." He'd looked at Nick for a long moment. "Yer thinkin' about stayin', ain't ye."

"Yes. Belle Terre is off the Florida coat, Wilson, and I plan on living there. I won't fight against my own countrymen, but I'd like to stick around for the outcome."

"There's a battle jus' waitin' now, Nicky. What'll ye do?"

"Wait."

And that's what he was doing. He'd renewed his acquaintance with several New Orleaneans, and they often shared a good bottle of brandy and reminiscences.

"What did you say, Jean?" Nick asked his companion, his attention returning to the idle conversation. Nick shifted in the comfortable chair, propping his booted feet on the small table that held a bottle of brandy.

Jean Lafitte gave an eloquent shrug. Dark eyes gleamed like sharp pieces of jet. "I said troubles, *mon ami.* Women are the cause of all troubles. Me, I say if we were to investigate, we would find that a woman is the cause of this little war, heh?"

"I agree that women are the cause of most troubles, Jean. So a woman is the reason I am here, you say." Nick laughed and tilted the brandy down his throat. "I am married now, did you know?"

"Aha! Did I not tell you? And because you are married, you leave home! *Voilà!* Simple. Is it not so?"

Nick gave a noncommittal grunt. No, it wasn't simple. He'd had a lot of time to think, and every time he shut his eyes he saw Kerry standing in front of Devlin House. Why couldn't he shut her out of his mind? But he couldn't.

Rain beat against the windows with a light patter, and the fire in the small grate popped. It was a gloomy afternoon near Christmas, and New Orleans was preparing for a British invasion. Why was he still here? Louisiana weather was miserable this time of year, when Belle Terre would be sunny and warm. Nick felt strangely at odds. He was straddling a fence between countries.

On one hand he was an Englishman, with estates and a title. But on the other hand he'd adopted a home across the ocean from England. So far, he'd successfully managed to juggle his loyalty and preference, but the time was near when he'd have to make some kind of a choice.

Leaning forward, Nick poured more brandy into his glass. Any choice he made pivoted around Kerry. He'd been gone for over five months. Would she have missed him in that time? Nick held his glass up to the light and frowned at the amber liquid. He doubted it. If Kerry thought of him at all, it was because she was angry. Perhaps after this confounded war was over he'd go back to England and give her a divorce. She'd have her freedom then.

A loud knock sounded on his door and Nick called an indifferent "Come in" over one shoulder without turning in his chair. It was Wilson, as he had thought it might be.

"You weren't gone very long, Wilson. I was hoping to have finished the bottle by the time you returned."

Wilson coughed politely. "I've brought someone wi' me, Nicky. I hope ye don't mind."

Though he groaned inwardly at the thought of entertaining a guest, Nick courteously stood up and turned. He stiffened, his gaze flicking from the rotund, grinning seaman to the girl with him.

"See what the men fished from the Gulf?" Wilson asked innocently. "She's a present from Samuel Locke, given ta my custody. I nivver made so fine a catch before."

The hood to her satin pelisse was pulled back, and Nick met the green eyes that had haunted him for so long.

"Hello, Nick," Kerry said softly. She smiled at his shock as she moved gracefully toward the fireplace, a vision in a green satin pelisse. Turning, Kerry regarded Nick calmly, peeling off her gloves.

He'd forgotten how beautiful she was, but he knew he could never have forgotten that air of regal composure. Little Kerry had certainly grown up, and he wasn't sure he liked it.

"What the hell is she doing here?" Nick asked Wilson, but his gaze remained on Kerry.

Wilson's gray brows rose. "Ah, that ye'll hafta ask the lady, lad. I jus' read th' letter she brought from Locke. It says fer me ta deliver her safely to

Nicholas Lawton, an' that I did. An' now, I think I hear a bottle callin' me."

Neither Nick nor Kerry moved for a few moments after the door shut quietly behind Wilson and the very discreet Jean Lafitte. Finally, Nick slammed his glass of brandy to the table.

"I want you on the first ship out of here," he said coldly, ignoring the sudden hurt in Kerry's eyes. Damn it, didn't she know there was a war going on? What was Locke thinking about when he gave her that letter? It took all his willpower not to pull Kerry into his arms and soothe away the pain showing in her eyes. "Don't unpack, don't even sit down," he said. "I'll get you a carriage, and you're going right back . . ."

"Damn you!" She flung her words in his face at the same time she swung her heavy reticule against his chest. Her quick reaction took him by surprise and Nick staggered back a step before recovering. Using her advantage, Kerry advanced, shoving the heels of her hands hard against his chest. "How dare you talk to me that way! I traveled two thousand miles to find you, and you throw me out as if I'm nothing more than an unwanted spaniel! I'm your wife, damn it!"

Grabbing both her wrists, Nick held her away from him. "It's about time you remembered that little fact, love. If I recall, you had trouble deciding whether to be loyal to me or my cousin. An interesting situation, but not one I'd care to repeat."

"You idiot! Let go of me!" She struggled vainly for a moment, but Nick's fingers were steel coils that could not be budged. Her eyes flashed a warning so that Nick was ready when Kerry's foot lifted to kick him.

His heel quickly hooked behind her other leg, so that without support Kerry plummeted to the floor with a thud. A gasp of pain was forced from her

lungs and tears stung her eyelids. Bending
slightly, Nick still held her wrists imprisoned in
his hands.

"Still violent, love?" His fingers tightened when
Kerry kicked out at him in a rustle of green satin.
This Kerry he understood. This was the girl he had
first met, the hot-tempered little termagant instead
of the cool, unapproachable lady in stylish clothes.
"Be quiet, and I will release you," he said.

After a moment Kerry nodded. Her face was
flushed with anger and her eyes bright with unshed
tears, but she kept her composure when Nick let go
of her wrists. Rubbing them, Kerry threw him a
sullen glare and muttered, "I think you broke my
arms."

Nick's lips twitched. "Really? I don't think so.
You can still move your fingers, can't you?"

Kerry frowned at her waggling fingers. "Yes. No
thanks to you," she added. Her head tilted back to
stare up at him. She felt at a definite disadvantage
with Nick towering over her like a giant bear, and
said so.

"Get up from the floor, then." Leaning back
against the table, it dawned on Nick why he now
felt a lifting of the ennui that had haunted him for
the past five months—no one else could irritate him
like Kerry. No one else could provide that spark of
life that she brought into a room with just her presence. Whether she was laughing or crying, angry or
happy, Kerry radiated vitality like the sun radiated
light. Nick fought the urge to laugh at the sight of
the dignified woman of a few moments earlier now
sitting in a crumpled puddle of green satin pelisse
and straggling waves of hair.

"You're sitting on your dignity, love," he said.
The remark earned him a haughty glare and irritated sniff.

"I don't know why I let you make me so mad,

Nicholas Lawton." Kerry took his offered hand to stand up, then brushed at the wrinkles creasing her skirt and the enveloping pelisse.

"Practice self-control," he suggested helpfully. He lifted his brandy, watching Kerry over the rim of the glass.

Kerry snatched irritably at the neck strings binding her pelisse, then slung it over the nearest chair. "That thing's stifling at times," she said.

Nick eyed the offending garment. The long cloak was lined with rich fur that looked to be ermine, and was fashioned from an expensive glossy satin. "How much did that set me back?" he asked. "Never mind. I'm not at all sure I want to know."

Slowly recovering her aplomb, Kerry patted at flying strands of her hair before deciding her coiffure was ruined. She removed ivory hairpins and placed them in a neat pile on the table. A silky ripple of hair cascaded around her shoulders and down her back as Kerry shook her head to loosen crimped waves, then raked her fingers through it. When she looked up, Nick was watching her with narrowed eyes.

It was almost as if he had reached out and touched her. The sensation was jarring, physical, a jolt that scattered her thoughts in a thousand different directions at once. Drawing in a shaky breath, Kerry said, "I am not leaving New Orleans without you."

Nick tilted his head and swallowed the rest of his brandy in a single motion, then set down the glass. "You are doomed to disappointment, love. I am not ready to leave, but you are."

"No, I want . . ."

"It does not matter to me in the least what you want! Can't you understand that a battle is imminent? Those shells won't stop to politely inquire if you are British or American before they'll hit, and you will not be here!" Nick took three steps toward

Kerry. "Just this morning Jackson received a message from Colonel Pierre Denis de La Ronde telling him that the British fleet is in a position that suggests landing. Do you know what that means? Or are you more concerned with the lint on your skirt?" Angry now, Nick snatched Kerry's skirt from between her fingers where she had been picking at imaginary specks of lint. "Listen to me, you hardheaded female!"

"No, you listen to me," Kerry countered. "I have listened to you. I listened in London when you announced your departure in such a grand manner, and I listened to all those people who were so anxious to tell me how you shot your cousin and ran away, and I even listened to your fat Prince Regent's extravagant compliments and sly innuendos! I'm tired of listening, Nick. I'm tired of people saying one thing when they mean another, and I'm tired of being tired. I want to go home." Kerry felt her nose and eyes filling with tears. "I want to go back to St. Denis or even Belle Terre. I don't like London, and I don't like Ireland either. I like sunshine and warm winds and blue skies. I like riding a horse across a hot beach, and I like listening to seabirds." She was choking on tears now, and fumbled for a clean handkerchief in the reticule that matched her pelisse.

Nick produced one from his coat pocket with a flourish. "Thank you," Kerry said between sniffs. She dabbed at her nose with the linen square that smelled faintly of tobacco. "I can never find one when I need it."

"How often do you need one?" Nick repressed the urge to fold her into his embrace, but he had to cross his arms tightly over his chest to keep from it.

"Since you left, embarrassingly too often," she admitted candidly. "I can't seem to help it. I cried so much Jane was positive I was breeding, but I'm not."

"Breeding?" Nick smiled faintly. "Do you possibly mean pregnant?"

"Breeding, pregnant, with child, enciente—whatever you want to call it. I'm not. I think I'm barren." Kerry paced the floor around the satinwood table in front of the fireplace. "You can probably use that as grounds for an annulment. Men want fertile wives, I understand."

"Farmers want fertile cows. Men want loving wives."

"What do you want, Nick?"

"Do I look like a farmer?"

She gazed at him with a serious expression, and Nick almost laughed aloud. "No," she said at last. "You look more like a London swell."

"Good Lord, spare me that appraisal, please. I'm not sure if my vanity will survive it."

"Your vanity would survive a carronade at close range," Kerry observed acidly. She sighed, pulling distractedly at long strands of her hair as she moved to stand in front of the fire. The crumpled square of linen handkerchief was kneaded between her fingers as Kerry turned to face the remote stranger who was her husband. "Nick, I don't want to argue with you anymore. I just want peace."

"You came from England to tell me that? And how did you know where to find me?" Nick answered his own question in the same breath. "Locke, of course. I have a feeling he's behind this." He sat in a straight-backed chair with his long legs stretched in front of him and crossed at the ankle, gazing steadily at Kerry.

Firelight shimmered behind her in dancing patterns of orange and gold, light and shadows hiding in the soft muslin folds of her gown and silhouetting her slim form. The long-sleeved spencer she wore hid Kerry's bodice, but Nick's memory supplied the vision of her soft breasts beneath the material. Most of her tan had faded, but a subtle golden tint like that of a newly ripened peach gave her enough color so that she didn't appear washed out. Of course, with eyes that glowed like precious jewels, there wasn't much chance of being considered colorless. She was still pacing, walking back and forth between the table and the fire, glancing at Nick now and then.

"Are you angry that I came here?" she finally asked.

"Not angry. Just curious." Nick pulled a cigar from his coat pocket. Leaning forward, he lit it from the small lantern on the table then sat back. A thin plume of smoke curled into the air above his head.

She watched the gray trail until it dissolved into nothing, then her gaze dropped to meet Nick's narrowed eyes.

He was squinting at her through his cigar smoke, studying her, and Kerry asked, "What are you curious about, Nick? If you're not angry, why do you want me to leave?"

"I told you. It's dangerous here. If the British take New Orleans, you may be all right provided you don't get killed in the shelling. If the Americans keep New Orleans, you may be safe provided you produce that letter from Locke—if you don't get killed in the shelling. Did you think this would be a garden party or an afternoon ride in Hyde Park? Think again, love. This is war, where men shoot guns and cannon at each other. Samuel Locke must be out of his mind to have given you that letter." Nick shook his dark head disgustedly.

"Mr. Locke was very kind. He understood that I was upset, and he offered me safe escort when I insisted upon finding you."

"How convenient."

She stamped one foot on the floor in annoyance. "Oh, do you have to always be so cynical? Can't you ever believe anything I say?"

"I believe you. I also believe that Locke had other, not so kind, motives. Did you by any chance deliver any papers for him?"

"Why . . . yes. How did you know? They were just general dispatches and correspondence. . . ." Kerry stopped. "Why, that absolute fiend! Do you mean . . . ?"

"Exactly. Samuel Locke has high scruples in certain matters, but not when it concerns war. I can't blame him. A young English countess would hardly be suspected of carrying messages to American forces. You were too perfect a temptation for him to pass by."

Kerry sank to the cushioned settee by a walnut lamp table. "What a fool he made of me! How did you ever meet him, Nick?"

"I met Locke when I applied for letters of marque from the United States government. As a privateer, I sailed all over the seas, and he thought I might be useful. Unfortunately for Locke, I refused his offer."

"But . . . but he helped you in London, and he's the man you met several times to exchange information . . ." Confused, she stopped.

"Information about Lord Sedgewick, love. Nothing else. I do have my principles, you know. The disposal of Sedgewick suited both of us, that's all."

Kerry leaned against the back of the settee. Staring thoughtfully into the flickering flames, she asked, "Is Mr. Locke the man who told you where to find me in Ireland?"

"No. Wilson remembered your necklace. He'd met your parents a long time ago in London. Locke helped your father leave Ireland, by the way. Did you know that? At any rate, Wilson suspected your identity a long time before I knew who you were. I certainly never expected to find the daughter of an earl when I arrived in Ireland." Nick shifted in his chair, watching the play of emotions skim across Kerry's face. Her face was an ever-shifting canvas for an entire range of reactions.

Caution was etched into the faint lines of her brow now as she asked the question she'd not dared ask before. "Why did you follow me to Ireland, Nick?"

"Truth?" he asked, and Kerry was reminded of the old game where the players were given consequences if they were caught in a lie.

"Truth," she said solemnly. "You forfeit if you lie, Lawton."

"Then truth it is. I had two reasons: One, I wanted to see you, and probably shake you until your teeth rattled from your head for running away. Two, I needed those books you took from me."

"And three?" Ouch. Number two had been fairly sharp a truth.

"No number three. Those are the reasons."

"Only two? How distressing. I was certain you could invent more than that."

"Oh, Kerry. I don't know why you appeal to me so much, but you do." Before she could grow accustomed to the heady pleasure of hearing that she appealed to him, Nick ruined it with the murmured observation that he'd always been drawn to the dangerous and ludicrous.

"Into which category do I fall?" she snapped.

"Both. You're so ludicrously gullible that it's dangerous."

"Is that so? I must be gullible, or I would never have fallen in love with you!"

"Did you?" Nick crushed his cigar in a glass dish and turned back to stare at Kerry. "Did you fall in love with me?"

"Well, I didn't come two thousand miles to bring you a pair of dry socks! Of course I love you, Nick

Lawton! That's what I came to tell you." She laced and unlaced her fingers, staring into the fire and not quite able to look at Nick. There. She'd said it. She'd taken a chance and said it when he hadn't said it first. Somehow it didn't matter so much that Nick had never mentioned love. She wanted to be with him.

"It wouldn't have sounded the same if I'd put it in a letter," she said, still not looking at him. "I can't write letters very well. It's easier to say it."

"It's easier to come two thousand miles?" Nick's dark brows arched high. "I will agree that it's more personal."

He'd not said he loved her too, Kerry noted. Her bottom lip quivered and she closed her eyes. Not now. She could not cry now and shame herself any more than she already had.

A gentle hand on her cheek made Kerry's eyes snap open. Nick was kneeling in front of her on the floor, his eyes level with hers, his mouth curved in a smile.

"You realize, I suppose, that it's just not at all the fashion to be in love with your husband? What would members of the ton say?" he asked.

"To hell," Kerry said clearly, "with members of the ton! How do Americans feel about wives loving husbands?"

"A little more lenient. I believe that it's actually permissible in some states, but I'm not positive." Nick's fingers strayed from Kerry's cheek to her lips, dragging across the moist surface in a sweet caress. His face was a breath away from hers, his lips so close she could reach out with the tip of her tongue and taste him. Kerry did.

"What are the laws concerning a husband's loving his wife?" Kerry murmured boldly against Nick's mouth. "Punishable by death?"

Nick's laugh tangled in the softly curling waves

of Kerry's hair. "In some cases. If the wife happens to be a black widow spider, for instance. Oh yes, love. Kiss me like that again." Both of his hands cradled her face as Nick's lips slanted across Kerry's in a kiss that was as fiery as it was sweet.

"Nick . . . ?"

"Hmmm," he answered, his mouth moving from Kerry's mouth to tickle her ear with soft, erotic kisses.

"I'm not a spider."

"I'm not an alligator. What's that supposed to mean . . . ? Oh. I won't die from loving you, right?" Now he moved to sit beside Kerry on the settee, his arms curling around her and pulling her close. "Ah, sweetheart. You have to know how I feel about you."

Patience was not Kerry's foremost virtue. In fact, she'd never remained within shouting distance of it for very long. She pulled away from Nick. When he blinked in surprise and reached out for her, she shook her head.

"No! I don't know how you feel about me, Nicholas Lawton. I don't know anything because you won't tell me! I can't read minds. I wish I could, but I can't. All I know is what you tell me, and that's not very damned much." She paused for breath. "You have to trust somebody sometime, Nick, even if it's a risk. I know you were betrayed by your cousin, and in a way, your father. I can't help that. I won't suffer the rest of my life because two people you trusted disappointed you."

Kerry pulled away from him with an effort. She pushed herself up and stood looking at Nick. One hand lifted in a slight gesture, then dropped to her side.

"Nick, I won't stay in New Orleans. I'll leave right now if you tell me you don't love me. Or if you don't tell me that you do. I have to hear it."

She waited while the round clock on the mantel

slowly ticked and the rain pattered on the window-panes. A branch popped in the fireplace and sent a shower of sparks up the chimney.

Frozen, Nick couldn't speak for a moment. Kerry was demanding that he tell her he loved her. If he didn't, she would leave New Orleans and he'd probably never find her again. The coldly logical part of his brain told him that she was issuing an ultimatum that wasn't just and fair. Love could not be conjured at the snap of his fingers. But he did love her. All he had to do was say it, the more sensitive part of his brain argued.

When Kerry turned to pick up her pelisse, Nick stood. He held out his hand to her and she took it.

"I love you," he said simply.

Chapter 25

Disappointment turned to joy at Nick's words, and Kerry suddenly realized how crushing a blow it would have been if he hadn't said them. A tremulous smile touched her lips. She stood on tiptoe and pressed a kiss on Nick's mouth, a light kiss that was passionless yet loving.

Nick's arms circled her waist, and Kerry's head tilted forward to rest on his broad chest. Slim fingers toyed with the lapels of his coat. The soft material folded beneath the press of her cheek and made a slight crease in her face, but she didn't care. Nick loved her.

"It's not yet noon," Nick said, and Kerry understood what he meant.

"The time or place no longer matters, Nick. Only the man matters." She smiled into his coat. "I don't care if we're in the middle of Canal Street!"

"It might be a bit damp now, love. We'll save Canal Street for a day less wet." His hands caressed her back, bumping along the spiny ridge to the spot where it flared into the swell of her hips. "I know this sounds mundane, but would a bed do as well?"

"For now. I expect more imaginative bowers for love in the near future," Kerry answered.

Nick lifted her in a tight embrace and crossed the small sitting room to another door. He shoved it open with his foot, and Kerry saw the dim outline of a bed against one wall. "Would the velvet seat of your new landau be imaginative enough, love? Or maybe beneath the Marble Arch in Hyde Park?"

"They're too far away. And I can't wait. . . ."

Gray light filtered through curtains over the windows as Nick gently lowered Kerry to the bed, dusty streamers of winter light sliding over them. The day was soft and quiet and the bed wide and comfortable.

"Here, love. Like this," Nick muttered against the curving hollow of Kerry's neck and shoulder. He guided her hands as they undid the buttons of his shirt. Each article of clothing they removed was added to the growing pile in a red velvet-covered chair close to the bed. It was cooler in this room because no fire burned in the grate, and Kerry shivered at the chill.

"Cold?" Nick pulled the coverlet down and back up over Kerry, then joined her to cuddle under a blanket decorated with flowers woven in happy abandon along the hem. They were enclosed in a warm little world of moist breath and heated whispers, wrapped around each other like vines. Kerry snuggled close beneath his chin, her cheek on Nick's chest.

She could feel his heartbeat as well as hear it, a steady, rhythmic thud. The hair on his chest tickled her nose and she laughed, rubbing her face against him playfully.

Nick caught her jaw in one hand, holding her head still as he traced a path along the curve of her cheek with his mouth. His lips moved down the arch of Kerry's throat to the rapid pulse fluttering in the shallow hollow.

Soft moans floated above the bed as Nick teased Kerry's breasts with lips and tongue, cradling their weight in cupped palms. He lavished kisses over the ridged arc of her ribs and the taut skin of her belly, over jutting hipbones and rounded thighs to the sharp angle of her knees and slim calves. Then he turned her over. Strong hands massaged the delicate bones of her feet and ankles, the pads of his fingers making tiny circles along the tensed muscles of her calves. While his hands moved slowly along the muscles of her thighs and buttocks, Kerry could feel her body relax. She lay on her stomach with her head buried in a pillow, enjoying these new pleasures that were somehow stimulating without being erotic. Nick's hands slid up her back to her shoulders, dug in with short, strong strokes then tested her arms all the way down to Kerry's fingertips. He massaged each finger until her hand felt boneless and weak.

Never had Kerry felt so totally relaxed. She drifted in a hazy half-world of dreams and reality, unable to move.

Nick turned her over. He was straddling her, his hands cradling her head, and he began to kiss her again. His splayed fingers massaged her scalp as his mouth teased her ear, her eyebrows, her eyes and nose, even the stubborn tilt of her chin, everywhere except her mouth. This he saved for last.

Warm and moist, his tongue flicked out in quick imitation of a serpent, tracing the outline of Kerry's mouth in light, delicate touches. Her lips parted and she put out her tongue to touch his, shyly at first, then boldly. "Yes, love," he whispered. "Oh yes."

For Kerry this was the most exquisite pleasure she had known. It was total sensuality, a melding of the senses of sight, smell, and touch with sound and taste. She could see Nick in the gloomy light, smell the rich aroma of tobacco from his cigar, and feel the mesmerizing caress of his hands on her. His soft words were whispered against her mouth, and she could taste the mellow brandy still on his tongue. One without the other was pleasurable. Combined, the effect was ecstasy.

Hearts beat faster and their breath rasped as Nick and Kerry surged toward that soaring crest. It was a sweet, wild mating, a meeting of hearts and bodies.

Outside the rain had stopped, and inside the storm had passed, leaving Nick and Kerry floating tranquilly.

That tranquillity was shattered by a pounding on the door of their room an hour later. Nick got up, pulling on his trousers as he answered the urgent knocking.

"Monsieur Lawton," Henri, Jackson's errand boy began, "please to come at once! The British are only nine miles away from New Orleans!"

"What?"

"It is true! Even now someone takes the news to Royal Street."

Nick was dressed in less than three minutes. He woke Kerry to tell her to stay in his rooms, and she clutched at him with her eyes growing wide.

"You're not going to fight, Nick!"

"I don't know. I am going to Jackson's headquarters." He kissed her quickly on the tip of her nose. "For God's sake, stay here. I'll be back as soon as I can."

For a long time after the door closed behind him, Kerry remained staring at the empty air where Nick had been.

Chapter 26

General Jackson was lying on his sofa in Royal Street when Nick arrived. Augustin Rousseau delivered astounding news, barely finishing when others, including young Major Villeré, upon whose plantation the British had landed, arrived muddy and out of breath.

Still not well, the general leaped from his sofa and pounded on the table with renewed energy. "They shall not sleep on our soil!" he said. Quickly becoming more calm, Jackson called his aides and told them, "Gentlemen, the British are below. We must fight them tonight."

New Orleans was vulnerable so attack was imperative. No major forces or defensive works stood between the British and the city. Also, Jackson had the advantage of darkness and surprise.

Troops assembled rapidly, and the schooner *Carolina* took position opposite the British encampment. The little army divided after nightfall, when there was only the light from a dim moon. Nick had accompanied Jackson, and stood in the darkness with the Seventh Infantry.

At 7:30 the *Carolina* opened fire, her broadside hitting the unsuspecting British with lethal fire. The British recovered quickly, but their muskets and rockets had no effect on the schooner. Even their three-pounders didn't help. Jackson let the ship fight alone for ten minutes, then ordered his division to advance. The company of the Seventh Infantry was the first to clash with the enemy.

Its advance was met with a discharge of musketry. Hot balls of lead sped past Nick's face and shoulders, and he heard the man beside him scream and fall. He raised his rifle and fired without thinking. Horses screamed in panic and everywhere there were the cries of the wounded and dying. Smoke was punctuated with red-orange bursts of flame from guns and the belching fire of the cannon.

In the darkness, troops from both armies became separated from each other, and the battle broke into many small fights. The Americans drove the invaders back; the British were reinforced and both forces continued to shoot at each other. Combat was briefly illuminated by flashes of gunfire, flickering images that were quickly gone.

The *Carolina* ceased firing as fog made all further action impossible. The Tennesseans had turned their horses loose, adding to the confusion, because the cane fields where they fought were cut by ditches. The Americans under General Coffee were frontiersmen experienced in Indian warfare and accustomed to night battles. They advanced and drove the British back. Finally, both wings of the American army withdrew to a place near the de La Ronde mansion to wait for daylight.

In the city of New Orleans, Kerry had listened throughout the night to the battle. It was easily heard in the town, and she cringed at the thought of Nick wounded or dead in a bloody cane field. Had she come all this way only to lose him now?

No! She paced the floor, chewing her bottom lip and trembling on the brink of mutiny. She couldn't stand waiting and not knowing what was happening. She had fought in a battle before, hadn't she? True, it had been a ship battle, and she had been

thoroughly frightened, but it was better than cowering in a closet to wait for bad news.

Kerry was sitting in a chair staring blankly into
the fire when Nick returned. He was muddy and
weary, and blood stained his coat.

"My God! You're wounded!" Kerry half-moaned,
running to him.

"No. It's someone else's blood." Nick curled one
arm around her. "I have to go back as soon as possible. It's not over, though we seem to have won this
round." He collapsed wearily into the chair Kerry
had just left.

Kneeling, she began pulling off his muddy boots.
"Nick, who are you fighting for?" Kerry's gaze met
his rather startled glance. "I mean . . . you haven't
really said, and I don't know. . . ."

A faint smile touched the tired line of his mouth.
"I suppose that's a normal question. I'm fighting
with Jackson, love. Somehow I feel more a part of
America than I do England. I have to admit to mixed
feelings, but I suppose I've made my choice." Nick
let his hand rest on the dark fire of her hair. "Where
does your loyalty lie?"

"With you." She didn't hesitate. "If you decided
to go and fight for the Turks, I'd go with you."

Nick didn't answer. He stared into the fire and
let its warmth seep into him. There was a lot to be
done, but he'd had to come back to Kerry first. The
immensity of his decision was almost overwhelming. Not only had he finally admitted aloud how he
felt about her, he had thought of her welfare above
everything else. Events were moving so swiftly now,
when time had dragged its heels for so long. Nick's
glance fell on a calendar. It was Christmas Eve,
1814.

Once more Kerry was pacing the floor of the little
sitting room where she stayed with Nick. It had

been almost a fortnight since she had arrived in New Orleans. During those two weeks, Nick had spent most of his time with the American army.

On the 27th the *Carolina* had been blown up by the British, removing the schooner that had so effectively kept the flanks of General Pakenham's army peppered with shot. The Americans had dug in on the Rodriguez Canal, the best defensive position in the vicinity. The canal formed the boundary between two plantations, Macarty and Chalmette. Mud walls were built and fortified. Lines were built and armed.

New Orleans was under martial law. Jackson ordered the mayor to have houses searched for more guns for his troops, and cannons were mounted behind mud ramparts at Chalmette. Night after night, Tennesseeans slipped through the woods and underbrush to kill British sentinels. Between battles, the Americans harassed the enemy by day and night.

New Year's Day morning was foggy. Soldiers in back of Jackson's line were in their best uniforms, preparing for a parade, and a band was playing. The civilian visitors included women who were gathered for the celebration of recent American successes.

Kerry joined Nick, holding on to his arm and trying to keep her skirts from dragging in the mud.

"I knew I should have worn trousers and a coat," she muttered, and he laughed.

"Think how scandalized people would be. Or you might have been drafted to fight, love." Nick's eyes searched the wispy streamers of fog, and he felt uneasy. Throughout the long night before, the sound of hammering had come from the camp of the British. He hadn't wanted Kerry to come, but she'd pleaded until he'd given in.

Nick's fears were realized when there was a tremendous explosion, followed by shells and rockets. Women screamed and men shouted orders as spectators ran in all different directions at once. American troops quickly manned mud ramparts, and briskly returned British fire.

Having been under fire before, Kerry didn't scream and hide like the other women, but stayed as close as possible to Nick until he forced her to safety.

"Damn it, woman! Have enough sense to duck when a shell lands close!" he growled at her once, shoving her roughly behind a wooden rampart.

"All the ducking in the world won't help if it lands on my head," she replied calmly. Tucking her shaking hands into the muddied folds of her skirts, Kerry hoped he couldn't see how frightened she actually was, and cursed herself for a coward. Shells continued to burst around them, until the area was so thick with smoke it reminded Kerry of fog in London.

The cannonading continued all morning, but fortunately no one was hurt. Once back at their hotel in New Orleans, Nick flatly refused to consider allowing Kerry close to Chalmette battlegrounds again.

So now, for the first time in ages, she found herself at loose ends while Nick was gone. It reminded her of the hours spent in Nick's cabin aboard the *Unicorn,* when she'd cooled her heels and waited. Some of Kerry's time was spent helping to clothe the ragged Kentucky Militia, who had arrived January 4th. A subscription was taken in New Orleans and the surrounding country to raise money to buy woolens. The women of New Orleans kept their minds and hands busy making clothes for the Kentucky soldiers.

There was going to be another battle, Kerry worried fretfully, a big one. She bit a thread in two and folded the finished woolen garment. Too many preparations had been made despite the shortage of supplies. Nick would be at Chalmette, and she would be in New Orleans, too far away to see what was happening.

A log in the fireplace cracked and popped, and a spray of sparks shot up the chimney. It sounded like gunfire, Kerry thought. She glanced at the clock for at least the tenth time that evening. Nick had left that morning to rejoin his division.

God, his stays with her had been so brief, and so sweet. It made his leaving that much harder. Accustomed to action instead of waiting, Kerry rebelled against her enforced inactivity, and had demanded that Nick take her with him.

"To fight?" He'd stared at her incredulously. "Now I know that boredom has deranged you, love." Nick had adamantly refused, and so she waited.

Kerry looked at the clock again. It was two minutes later than the last time she'd looked. Frustrated, she snatched up the little gilt clock and threw it against the wall where it shattered into pieces. Tiny springs and wheels flew all over the floor, but she felt better.

"It's the damned waiting that's getting to me," she muttered. "The waiting and not knowing."

Again she paced, feeling like a caged tiger prowling the perimeters of its confinement.

The cypress swamp was to Nick's left, the river to his right. He stared into the murky light for his company's position, cursing the damp cold. "New Orleans Rifle Company is at the river end," he muttered, trudging through mud and stubble. "Next . . . the Seventh Infantry . . ." The Seventh. It was about damned time. Nick turned to the right and moved cautiously along the faint path worn by hooves and boots.

After the initial challenge by a sentry, no one paid much attention to another mud-spattered soldier

stepping around the lines. Nick's gaze narrowed as
a faint blur of light took the edge of darkness from
the field so that he could see the troops. Four thousand men stretched along the breastworks from the
river to the swamp. He moved silently behind the
ramparts where men waited three and four deep,
past men he knew and men he didn't know.

There were times Nick wondered why he'd chosen
to fight for the Americans, and times he wondered
why he doubted his reasons. It was a foolish war,
especially when he had no real stake in it, but somehow it appealed to his sense of justice that he was
judged not on who he was, but on his character and
accomplishments. In England, he would automatically be given rank because of his title. In this young
nation, his superior officer might have been born in
a drafty log cabin in Kentucky, but he would be a
man of wit and spirit. Nick was impressed in spite
of himself by the warmth and camaraderie found
between the fighting men and the men who led
them. They were bound together in a common cause,
and he was one of them by choice.

Nick reached his lines just as a rocket shot up
from the British forces near the woods, followed by
another from their ranks near the river. This was
the signal to attack. It was answered instantly by a
shot from American artillery. Sir Samuel Gibbs's
British column gave three cheers and started forward in close order. American batteries six, seven,
and eight began to pour round shot and grape into
the column.

The noise was deafening. There was a constant
rolling fire like the rumbling of thunder. Fire spat
and cracked from rifles and cannon, and the acrid
stench of gunpowder filled the air.

Nick could barely hear orders over the noise of
battle, the shrieks and screams of the wounded and
dying mingling with the boom of cannon and spit of

rifles. A ball slammed into the mud bank only inches from his cheek, and he ducked instinctively. A green lad not more than fourteen years old was beside him, and the youth stared blankly at the muddy furrow ploughed into the trench by the ball. Nick gave him a brisk shake.

"Load the rifles!" he snapped. Powder and balls were slapped into the boy's hands. "Hurry up . . ."

Another ball whined past, this time slicing through the loose material of Nick's coat sleeve. He ducked behind the log and mud wall, pulling the boy with him. Trembling, he lay beside Nick with his head buried against the ground, his back curled like a cat's. Nick felt a twinge of sympathy for the boy, and gruffly reassured him.

"What's your name, lad?" he asked. Nick's fingers moved deftly as he reloaded his rifle.

"Martin." The boy peered at Nick over one sleeve. "Ain't you scared, sir?" His voice quivered slightly.

"I'd be a fool if I wasn't, but there's no time to think about that now. We'll have plenty of time later, and one day we can both tell our grandchildren how we watched Andy Jackson chase the British back home with their tails dragging. Now sit up and shoot, lad."

Martin grinned. Then he was sitting up, aiming his rifle again and squeezing the trigger. As the battle raged, he began to automatically reload the rifles, pouring powder and stuffing balls and wadding until his fingers were sore. His hands were burned and black, and blisters began to form on tender fingertips.

"They'll pop," Nick said briefly. "Keep loading." He stood behind the breastwork and fired, then stepped back to let another take his place. A continuous round of men rotated, and the hail of hot lead slashed through the advancing troops as if they were made of butter. Vast numbers of the British rank and file lay down on the field to escape the murderous slaughter.

Even sea battles had not prepared Nick for this carnage. Everywhere men lay dead or dying, sprawled on the ground in oddly disjointed poses. Only a very few Americans lay dead, but the British were suffering overwhelming losses.

When the fighting slowed, Nick climbed from the trench and pulled Martin with him.

"You did well, lad. General Jackson would be proud to know he has fine soldiers like you in his army." Nick ruffled the boy's wheat-colored hair. "I need you to take a message to the city for me. Can you do that?"

Nodding, Martin glanced around him as Nick led him a short distance away. The boy didn't know where to look. Moans and shrieks filled the smoke-thick air, and even Nick was reminded of Dante's vision of hell.

They were standing away from the battlefield now, but sporadic shots still sounded in the distance. The air was clearer, and they could draw in a deep breath without inhaling the stench of death and sharp bits of acrid smoke.

"The message is to my wife," Nick said, "and she's staying at the small hotel on the corner of Canal and St. Charles. . . ."

Kerry had finally fallen into a fitful slumber, draped across the arm of the decidedly uncomfortable settee in the little sitting room. When the light tap sounded on her door, she jerked awake immediately. Nick!

Her smile drooped when she pulled open the door to see only a ragged-looking youth. Tears of disappointment stung her eyes as Kerry managed a polite answer to the boy's inquiry.

"Yes. I am Mistress Lawton—" How strange that still sounded, even after a year!

"Your husband sent me with a message, ma'am . . ."

"He's well? Is he hurt? Where is he?" Kerry's words tumbled over one another, then she broke off abruptly. "Please excuse me. Won't you come in and have some hot tea? You look cold and tired."

Soon Martin was perched gingerly on the edge of a chair and sipping at a cup of hot tea, staring appreciatively at Kerry. He'd never seen a woman quite so lovely, he decided, and thought that she was very suited to the tall dark man who had helped him in the trenches.

Kerry scanned the note Nick had sent her, pressing out the wrinkled paper against her lap as she read. He was safe, and he would return to New Orleans as soon as possible. She smiled. He'd known that she would worry, and had probably sent her this message to forestall any precipitate action of hers—such as following him to the battlefield as she had actually contemplated.

"Are you going back?" she asked Martin, folding the crumpled paper. "Tell him . . . tell him I send my love and prayers," she said when the youth nodded. "And tell him I'll wait for him for as long as it takes."

Nick would understand what she meant.

It was early afternoon when Nick returned to New Orleans, and though she had waited by the window for what seemed an eternity, Kerry wasn't prepared. She had wrapped a scarf around her hair and begun to attack the cobwebs strung in lacy abandon from the high ceilings of their room. It was a duty that should have been performed by the maids, but they were busy celebrating the American victory. Unable to join them—and unwilling to just sit—Kerry did the first thing that came to mind.

Balancing herself on the back of a chair while batting with a feather duster at scurrying spiders, Kerry never heard the door open. When a strong arm coiled around her middle and lifted her from the chair she gave a startled squeal that quickly turned to delight.

"Nick!" She gave him a bat over the head with the feather duster. "I didn't hear you come in ..." The rest of her words were smothered by his mouth over hers. All her questions faded as she concentrated on Nick, on his arms around her and the sweet warmth of his lips as he kissed her again and again. He was back, and he was safe, and that was all that mattered.

Much later, when they finally left their room to stroll down Canal Street, Kerry asked a question that had occurred to her many times in the past weeks.

"Nick, have you decided to go back to England? Or do you intend to stay here?" And what about me? she wondered silently. Do you want me to go with you?

He didn't answer for a moment and her heart plummeted to her toes. He still didn't want her. ...

"That's a question that has haunted me too, love," he finally answered. His arm curled around her waist as Kerry tried to match his longer stride. Afternoon sunshine filtered through the latticework of wrought-iron balconies and gates lining the street, spraying softly across Kerry's upturned face. "I love Belle Terre. It's where I think of when I think of home." Kerry didn't mention Belle Terre anymore—did she still like it there? Damn, he'd never thought to ask her. "I feel more at ease there, and it's comfortable." He paused when she didn't comment, and his arm dropped from around her slender waist. His island home might hold unpleasant memories for her. Did it? "Are you going with me?" he asked abruptly. "Or do you go back to England?"

"Who will inherit Devlin House and estates now, Nick?" she asked instead of answering. "Do they go back to the Crown if you abandon them?"

"Good God, do you think I would just throw away land that my ancestors fought for?" Nick slanted her a glance of surprise. "It is perfectly legal to be an owner in absentia. I shall appoint Wilson as trustee to care for the estates. When we have a son, he will inherit, title and all. I intend to stay on Belle Terre."

"And if our son is a daughter."

"Then she inherits," Nick stopped and caught Kerry around the waist. "Answer me, love. Do you go to Belle Terre with me?"

"I thought I already answered that. Didn't I say I would even go to fight for the Turks with you?"

"Yes, but you didn't say you'd live with them." He smiled against coppery hair tangled by the wind. "Be specific. Pay attention to details."

"Fine. I will live on Belle Terre with you. I will live on the *Unicorn* with you. I will live in a grass hut on the slopes of Cielo Pico, if you like. I just want to be with you, Nick."

"Does that mean you missed me?"

"Missed you?" Kerry thought of the past months of longing for him, of wanting him and loving him and not being able to tell him. "Yes, I missed you, Nick."

"Ah," he said in satisfaction. "I recall your once telling me that you'd miss me when donkeys fly. Should I watch my head?"

A smile tugged at the corners of her mouth as they started walking again. "It might be wise," she said. "You remember such trivial things, Nicholas Lawton. I shudder to think what else in my past will return to haunt me."

" 'Curiosity killed the dead horse,' " Nick quoted. " 'A penny saved is pound foolish.' " He shook his head. "You have the most fascinating clichés of anyone I know."

"Thank you."

"You're welcome." He stopped beneath the spreading branches of a live oak hung with Spanish moss, and pulled Kerry beneath nature's lacy curtain. Nick leaned against the rough bark and cupped Kerry's chin in his palm as he had so many times before. This time there was a difference. It wasn't because he wanted to kiss her, though he did intend to; it was because he just wanted to look at this girl who had made such a big difference in his life.

If he dissected and analyzed each feature, she would be only ordinarily pretty. It was something else that had attracted him, some indefinable part of her that was so uniquely Kerry. She was a marvelous blend of bone and muscle held together with more heart than he'd dreamed could exist. She was tender, funny, provocative and daring. Irritating and unfuriating were traits best forgotten.

"I love you," he said, and watched her eyes widen and catch the afternoon light in their depths.

"Oh, Nick . . . I love you too!" Stretching to her tiptoes, Kerry kissed him on his beard-stubbled jaw. Life might not be perfect, but surely it would compare favorably with perfection if she had Nick by her side.

Epilogue

Lacy curls of surf formed a scalloped fringe on hot sand as turquoise waves washed ashore. It was hot, but a refreshing sea breeze cooled the air. Stretched on a quilt, Kerry shifted lazily on the cushions of sand. One hand cupped to shade her eyes as she scanned the beach.

A smile curved her mouth. Nicholas Sean Patrick Lawton, future Earl of Devlin and already master of Belle Terre at the age of one year, played happily beneath the shade of a canopy under Happy's watchful eye. The toddler ruled his island home with cheerful tyranny, capturing the attention of his doting parents and the entire household. Nick frequently threatened to discipline his young son's entourage of admirers for spoiling him shamelessly.

"He won't be worth a brass farthing," Nick would grumble, making Kerry laugh.

"You're worse than even Gato or Wilson," she told him once. "And Lord knows, they think Sean does no wrong!"

Kerry stretched like a tawny cat, closing her eyes and letting the golden rays of warm sun wash over her. This was contentment and Belle Terre was heaven. Her life was complete. She had Nick and little Sean, and enough love to fill her days with happiness and her nights with ecstasy.

In the almost two years since returning to Belle

Terre with Nick, Kerry had developed into the full bloom of womanhood. She was mistress of Belle Terre instead of unwilling occupant, sharing with Happy the care of the household. It was a large responsibility to run the plantation now since Nick had settled into a business. He was a successful planter as well as dealing with the trade from ship to market.

Wilson had returned to England and Nick's estates there, but frequently visited Belle Terre. On one of his visits, he had brought Gato with him. The old man had finally consented to join his foster daughter after much urging, and had brought his most prized horses with him. It was a delight to see Gato after so long, and Kerry had cried when Diablo had pranced down the bridge from the *Unicorn* to the dock.

All it would take to make her world complete, she thought, closing her eyes against the glare of the sun, would be Sean O'Connell. The old man had obstinately refused to visit, saying he preferred solid land beneath his feet in his old age. Kerry had sent him a painted miniature of the great-grandson who bore his name.

Perhaps, she reflected, they could visit Ireland before the old lord died. It would be so wonderful to see him again, and introduce him to tiny Sean. Her cousin Michael had returned from college, Sean wrote, and had brought new life into Castleconnell with his young wife. Another child was soon to be born into the family.

The pounding of hooves on sand caught Kerry's attention and she raised her head, squinting at the tree-fringed slope behind her. A dark shape rode toward her, and she recognized Nick on Diablo.

"Hello, love," he said, reining the stallion to a halt in a shimmering spray of sand. Nick grinned

as Kerry threw him a reproachful glance and brushed away grains of sand from her bare legs.

"Hello yourself. If you insist upon riding my horse, I wish you would be more tidy about it."

"Shrew." Nick plopped onto the sand beside her, pulling Kerry into his arms. "You need taming again, I see." He nibbled at her earlobe with his teeth. "Mmm. You smell good. And you taste good. Why are you pulling away? I'm not through tasting . . ."

"Nick! Stop that . . . and don't be pulling my skirt higher either! Have you no shame? Anyone could come along, and Happy is looking this way . . ."

"I love it when you're so breathless with passion." He pressed his mouth into the hollow of her neck and shoulder. "If I didn't know how easily excitable you are, I might become discouraged, love."

"Oh Nick." Kerry's voice was a soft sigh. Her arms lifted to coil around his neck, and she smiled. "Don't ever get discouraged. I'd have to go to great lengths to encourage you again."

"Oh? That possibility sounds interesting. Let's see what I can do to get you to encourage me . . ."

Kerry squealed as Nick lifted her into his arms and strode over grass-studded sand toward a line of swaying palms. Over his broad shoulder she could see Happy shaking her head and smiling as she watched. Kerry grinned. Little Sean waved a chubby hand at his parents, his sky-blue eyes crinkling in delight at their play. What would Nick say when she told him Sean would soon have a brother or sister?

She'd tell him, Kerry decided as Nick lowered her gently to a palm-shaded bower of thick fragran grasses, later . . . much later.